THE BLACK HORIZON

I found a glass in my hand. I tossed some cubes of ice into it, listened to the chinking rattle. And poured a little amber liquid from a decanter. And then more than a little.

"Why do you keep asking about Shangri-La?" I asked. "*Why?*"

Her smile was sad, as if she knew what I was doing. But she played the game.

"Why not Shangri-La?" Blake said. "Why not Atlantis? Why not Mars or Alpha Centauri?"

"I don't know," I admitted.

"You keep saying that," she said. Forceful. "But you *should*. You can do all these things, you have all this power. You look in all these realities, find all these universes where anything can exist and happen, and still... you stay *here*."

I fought a shrug. "There are the rules."

"The rules, the rules, *the rules*," she said. Really angry now. Her eyes flashing. She threw her book down, it hit the floor with a slapping kind of thump. "You have these rules, have you ever asked yourself *why*?"

THE BLACK HORIZON

THE FIRST BOOK OF THE REALITY THIEF

CHRIS J. CRANFORD

FORGED IRON PRESS

First Paperback Edition May 2023

Cover Design by Sadia Shahid

Published by Forged Iron Press
www.forgedironpress.com

www.chrisjcranford.com

Acknowledgements:

When I first started looking at getting my books published, I reached out to Dean Wesley Smith, who encouraged me to believe in my work and publish independently. That path has led me here, it continues to lead me to shores unknown, and I'll always be thankful for his advice.

A second thank you needs to go to Kristine Kathryn Rusch, who without her video on researching for novels, this book wouldn't exist. While watching the video (from a stair climber on a gym), I heard the words "you need to steal a piece of reality".

Those words struck that imagination chord in my brain, and resonated in the way certain things will. I went home and started writing in that moment. Couldn't stop writing until the book was finished. And, maybe my favorite book to date came from those words.

Thank you both for everything you do for us independents. Maybe most of all, for helping me understand I need to write the stories I believe in.

Now, onto eating that next elephant...

CHAPTER ONE

THE BEACH WAS SUNNY TODAY.

It was one of those mornings where the waves crashed along the shore in those big, frothy curls that tumbled over the beach. Where the water ran like fingers, racing up the tan, shell-covered sands before it hung there for a long moment. Where, hanging there, the wet fingers looked like the watery hand of a god, dragging each wave back into the swirling depths <u>of</u> the ocean.

The sun was perfect—a yellow orb staring from the bluest of skies, its golden rays breaking through a puffy white cloud or two, high-lighting tourists tanning on long, striped towels. Surfers ran into the ocean, laughing, legs splashing through the waves; they tossed tall, waxed boards in the water, jumping on them and paddling further and further from shore. A few people sat back in webbed chairs, hidden from the sun under large blue and white umbrellas, reading a book, having a cocktail, or both.

The breeze flopped and fluttered. It would die off just enough for a person to feel the perfect sun, feel the heat soak into their skin, hear the whispering rush of the water, before the wind picked up again. Cooling you off. The air brought a taste of salt, the perfect hint of the sea, the wide expanse of the ocean, the inescapable wonder of what it might be like to jump on a sailboat, its canvas billowing full of wind, and wander away to shores unknown.

It was perfect.

And I wasn't in the mood.

So I changed it. Like a person might change a channel. On one of those old television sets, the ones with the knobs.

My fingers twisted, made a little motion, and in that moment the blue sky, the white puffy clouds, the golden sun and the white sands, and the beautifully clear water all disappeared.

Dark gray clouds, so dark they were almost black. A hurricane-like wind, pushing the water high up on the beach. The sun was gone, hidden behind a storm, thundering overhead. Booming and crackling along the sky, loud enough my skin felt the vibrations of the sound across it. Lightning flickered down in forks, struck the ocean, stabbed it in the distance, over and over.

The people were gone. The tourists, the relaxed cocktail drinkers, the tanners, the surfers... all gone. One person struggled up from the beach, a red towel held over their head. A towel soaked in rain, thick cold drops that blew sideways in the gale. The man struggled under the towel, the fluffy red cloth whipped around him, and he fell a couple of times under the wind. The towel blew away in a streak of crimson, the man fell again, and later I think I realized I had never seen him get back up.

The rain was hard. The wind unrelenting. The warmth of the sun gone.

Perfect.

I took a sip of my drink. Not a celebratory cocktail. Not something to relax with, not a fruity concoction with lots of syrup and ice and —*maybe*—a little alcohol tucked in. It was straight bourbon. And not the good stuff. The cheap stuff, that they have right by the register in all the ABC stores. The stuff that's more black than golden brown, held in a plastic bottle that easily could be dropped a thousand times by a stumbling drunk (trust me, that's been tested), stuff that's rough and sears your tongue, burns the back of your throat, and leaves a fire in your stomach that all the anti-acids in the world couldn't soothe.

I drank. I didn't grimace at the taste, or the burn. I stood on the patio overlooking the beach, my feet braced on the smooth concrete floor, one hand holding the cool, copper metal rail. I drank, let the rain chill me, let my drink burn me, wondered how I had gotten here.

The drops stung my skin, icy pellets reminding me of the mistakes I made. One, two, a thousand. Millions. All tapping me, saying *remember this? Remember that? Man, did you ever fuck this up...*

You might be wondering who I am. I'll get into that, though I've told you before. You just don't remember, see. The fuck of it is, you won't remember after this, either. You'll listen and nod and pat me on the shoulder, you'll tell me there's nothing more I could have done, nothing I could have learned, nothing more I could have figured out. You'll say I missed no detail, and you'd be right.

So, you'll get it, you'll kick back and understand it all, in one beautiful moment.

And then that moment will be gone.

Why?

Well, me of course.

Gavin Ambrose.

The one-and-only, a living, change-the-world-in-front-of-your-eyes Reality Thief.

I needed to charge tickets for this show.

CHAPTER TWO

Like with anything, there are rules. I had to learn them the hard way. Trial and error. A lot of times, those errors resulted in deaths (not mine).

Speaking of which, that's Rule Number One. I can't bring anyone back to life. Dead is dead.

That, oddly enough, leads to Rule Number Two. I can live forever, in this world. As I am.

To explain, somewhere out there a reality exists where people live forever. There actually is an infinite number of those places. One where people live forever and still age (I tried stealing some of that one, and the wrinkles *really* get wrinkly). One where people age and their skin becomes all kinds of different shades and hues (if you thought the eighties were vibrantly... colored, then this is your jam). And one where people live forever by getting to a certain age and kind of just, hold there (my go-to reality in the realm of universes where we all live forever). All kinds of varieties on that theme, and more to boot.

Still, dead is dead. I've said it. That's Rule Numero Uno. And, to be fair, I *can* die. I can be killed in a freak accident, or more ominously, I can be murdered. I wasn't sure what would happen to the world I lived in if that happened. If all the realities I've stolen and switched will suddenly revert, if the Jenga tower of realities I've pulled my block from will suddenly pile itself back up, after it had toppled.

Maybe it all will go away. Maybe I'm not just a Reality Thief, but the one-and-only Reality Creator. It's a thought that comes along, after enough drinks.

The sober me always says *nah*. Someone exists who created me. Or that created me, let's not limit the benevolent power to just people. That created the rules that bound me. That keeps me tipping back rough bourbon alone, instead of a margarita or two among friends.

What do they say? God has a funny sense of humor?

He must, if he existed. I wanted to believe I had a purpose, and if that purpose was some creator laughing at me, then at least that was *something*. But, more and more lately, I've begun to believe that some things are just random. That the great joke was that there was no purpose.

At least, not one that I've found, yet.

Not that I haven't looked. I have been alive for a long time.

Anyway, back to the rules.

#1 – I can't bring anyone back to life

#2 – I can live forever (but I can also definitely die)

And, there's Rule Number Three. We *all* can change reality. Most of us in small ways. At some point you've done it and not realized it. Maybe you've walked along singing a song in your head, and then turned on the radio only to find it playing. Likely at the exact place you were singing.

Maybe you needed a card at poker. Or a heads or tails in a flip of a quarter. You needed it, and you got it. And you did it stealing reality.

This one might be the toughest for you to get, but trust me, it's as real as the first two. Where you notice it most often are the feelings of déjà vu; if someone steals a piece of reality, your mind notices it. Your subconscious *knows* it. But it also can't explain what happened.

All you can feel, or understand, is that you've missed something in your life. Something has changed, and you just can't remember what that something was. It happens all the time, even if something occurs where a flip of the coin changes, where a heads becomes a tails, someone else will walk by and pause. They'll look around in a puzzled manner, feeling something different, and wondering what's changed. What they've missed.

That's what happens when other people steal reality around you. That's what happens to them when you steal a tiny piece of reality. Someone gets that puzzled feel of a world that has changed around them, without knowing what that something is. Remember that, the next time you walk around humming a song and find it on the radio. Look for those around you, with a suddenly puzzled air. Remember these things as you wonder, *Did I just make that happen?*

Yeah. You did.

We all have a little bit of the thief in us. A varying amount of the power. Most of you have the ability to change our reality in small, unimportant ways. The change of a song. The pull of a card. The flip of a coin.

So, remember your déjà vu moments. The quick moment where you swear you've forgotten something. Where you look around and wonder what that something missing is, but the moment is gone, and you just shrug and go along your way.

Trust me here. You *have* forgotten something. And you'll never, ever, remember it. Not clearly, maybe in little moments, where you pause and look a little up into the sky, wondering *what is that* tickling the back of your brain.

Now back to me. Who, for some reason, can do more than the little moments. More than the flip of a coin, or the pull of a different card. If something exists in another universe. I can steal it. I can bring it here. Whatever that something was.

And when I first found that out, I had a lot of fun.

Now, I wouldn't wish this on anyone.

What's the problem, you ask? Especially if I can just be whoever I want, whenever I want? If I can have whatever I need, whenever I need it?

You're right. You just saw the example. If I want it sunny, it's sunny. If I want it stormy, I get it stormy.

Well, let me answer your question with a couple of answers. The first part of is, I'm not really switching realities. I'm a thief, actually. I steal something from another universe, and in its place I put something from ours. Kind of swapping things around.

It took me a long time to realize that, unfortunately.

The worst part, the greater understanding I had come to—much later than the first part—was that swapping realities wasn't like pulling out one block and putting in another. All realities are inherently different. They never match. Changing them out was always like putting a square peg in a round hole. No matter how much you pounded the peg, it always splintered along the sides. And parts of the peg always came off, pieces drifted away, fell to odd places.

Over the centuries weird things started happening in my world. Missing civilizations. Disappearing cities. The Loch Ness Monster. I assume the same thing is happening in others (though I have no way to really check).

And here I am. Thousands of years later. With splinters of pegs everywhere. Bringing Unintended Consequences. And now the world has changed so much now that I'm not sure I'd recognize the one I was born in.

And one thing about change, it accelerates. Change brings change. All the realities I've stolen and brought here, all the splinters that have fallen off, well, that's a lot of change. And it's brought about a lot of advances. Maybe too much.

People talk about how much technology has grown. There are all these graphs showing the recent rates of technological, social, and economic change. The world people were born in always ended up to be much different through the years. People used to have to find a pay phone if they wanted to call someone while out and about. Now we're surfing the internet on a hand-held device while driving a car that can drive itself.

Here, I want to be clear that cell phones have nothing to do with me. I mean, maybe I wondered, after watching someone with a beeper jot down something and race to find a payphone, *wouldn't it be easier to just call someone back from that same device?* But I couldn't have imagined what they would end up being, with the smart screens and the constant texting and messaging and all the social media. I mean, all I wanted was an easy way to call someone. I never imagined what they could end up being, some kind of soul-sucking time-wasting digital handcuff.

Of course, I might be lying. It's hard to tell sometimes. Lies seem to be my default, but when you steal for a living, when you steal for thousands of livings, your memory starts to blend it all together. So, *honestly,* sometimes I just can't remember what's real. What I did and didn't do. After a few millennia, my memory has gotten to be a little cloudy.

At least, in the little details.

In the big ones, I remember all too clearly.

So maybe blame me for cell phones, but I had no idea what they'd end up being. No idea that people would walk around with them in their hands, staring at the screens, taking video of everything, the loud talkers in the grocery stores, and the incessant, never-ending fucking *beeps.*

Beeps for messages. Beeps from notifications from apps. Beeps from apps that tell you about changes in other apps.

Good night people, just turn them off once in awhile. There's a world out there. Be a part of it.

(Says the guy drinking alone at the beach.)

So, I wasn't a part of cell phones. I didn't think. At least I didn't want to be. Can you blame a person for the start of something? When he didn't know what they would ultimately end up being? Yes? No?

Anyway, in the communal spirit of honesty, DVR'ing shows might have been me. For some reason I never wanted to sit down during prime time and watch television. I always preferred drinking around that time. A lot of things people take for granted, some of the things that make their lives easier, might have come around because I was looking for things to improve the kind of life I wanted.

Mostly.

Maybe. I'm sure other people wanted to be lazy too. Plenty of people like kicking back and doing nothing, nowadays.

Maybe I started that. The slow fall of the workforce into the subtle sink of couch potatoes. Hell, I don't know. It's definitely likely. I guess.

You see, I've kind of lived my life spur of the moment. Drifted from place to place. Did things on a whim.

You may have read stories, maybe about elves that live forever. I think Tolkien wrote something like that. These long-lived people that look far into the future and plan, that take measured, thoughtful responses, because they know they'll be around to see the results of their choices.

I did some of that in the beginning, but I'll tell you, that kind of stuff gets boring quick. There's only so long one person can wait, when everything and everyone passes away. And lately, looking at stock reports, real estate values, stuff like that, building an empire, it's cool for the first twenty or thirty years.

After that, you kind of realize it's all meaningless. It all changes. One way then the other.

Especially if you're me. If I wanted something, I'd just kind of *take* it. I just had to have the idea.

Like with television, I mean, I was busy with life, but I had my favorite shows. There were times I wanted to go back and watch things from time to time. It was pretty easy to find a world where a person had created the device I was looking for, and appropriate said device. Like a VCR.

And later, maybe, TiVo.

What would you do, if you could steal anything you wanted, and make it yours?

I'm guessing the same thing. Because at first the power is kind of a wonder. Like a *holy-moly-I-can-do-this* kind of wonder. It's intoxicating, when you realize there really are no limits to it.

Then you see no one else really understands it or can do what you do. So, you're alone, and you press your limits. You see what you can do. You see how far you can take it. Because—in your mind—there are no consequences. No rules.

Maybe you realize, without realizing, you were taking something that didn't belong to you. Some signal in the back of your brain was telling you it was wrong. But stealing is a habit, and it was strong then. Almost like breathing. I'm making excuses here, but honestly, it was hard to stop.

I was living my life, too. Trying to find my way. Like the rest of us. Looking for that reason I existed. Not just humanity, but *me*.

I'll pause for the laugh.

I'm sorry, not *your* laugh. You may have forgotten already. The chuckle from the person who made me. Who forgot to tell me why.

And, back to the truth. I'm sorry about all the mistakes. Like Betamax. Like *The Bachelorette* (honest mistake there), and for the love of heaven, I am really, really sorry about that new *Star Wars* trilogy. The first three were perfect all on their own.

In my defense, I had been drinking a lot that day.

I had been drinking a lot, recently.

I set my drink down. Took a breath. Looked out at the storm, the pounding rain driving into the sand, rippling the water of the ocean like bullets. The black clouds and whipping winds. The tempest of tempests.

And I swapped the realities back.

Well, not quite back. The storm wouldn't quite go. Maybe telling me I had one too many. So, I pushed it into another reality, a different reality. But one close enough to where I was that only minor differences remained. Surfers still surfing. People still drinking. The webbed chairs weren't quite webbed, they were more of a plastic ribbon, weaved in a crosshatch pattern, instead. The beach towels weren't striped, now they were mostly print animals. The one closest to me was dotted with little sea creatures, little somethings that looked like a cross between a horse's head and a curled, mermaid-like tail.

Hmmm. I had never seen that thing before. It was kind of horridly ugly.

Still, the reality was mostly the same. Mostly.

Hopefully no one would notice. Especially the seahorsey creature. Some kind of seahorse like monster, small enough to hide under the frothy water, maybe even in bubble baths, with a spiny tail and thorned plate-like scales, could scare the hell out of kids.

Have you guys seen that before? If so, you're in the same reality as me. Or some similar universe. At least for right now.

But I'm drifting. Something else that happens when I drink. Back to where I was. The truth.

I had learned that I could do the mostly thing. Change the moment and change it back. So the world was close enough to what it was before the switch. Sometimes so close you would never know the difference.

Occasionally, (like now) I wondered if the other world suffered. If there were a million worlds that used to have a bright sunny day, and each of those worlds now have a storm of their own traveling through them, pounding its fury on each separate beach. Or did each world have their own version of me, and those versions of me kept swapping those storms out with their own sunny days, in some infinite loop? Maybe there was just one monster storm, and all of us together kept swapping it out, over and over, so that this reality-ending storm traveled, not just across the oceans, not just across the shores of my world, but the shores of *all* worlds.

I... may have drank too much. I could usually tell, when I got into these kinds of thoughts.

You may think now, what's your problem? I mean, I live forever. It's fairly hard to die, as long as I pay attention to the world around me. As long as I make sure I don't get murdered. And I can make the world pretty much the same after the change, as before. So really, what I'm living should be a great life, right?

Well, pretty much the same isn't the same. I learned this the hard way. And when you take a perfect reality, and patch in a bunch of *pretty much the sames*, it starts to look funny. Act funny. Things happen, where one reality didn't merge quite the same as the one before. The splinters fall off of the square peg. They start to accumulate. And long, long after you've stolen your first reality, not just centuries later, but dozens of centuries later, you start to see the changes.

I've been on this Earth a fuckload of a long time. I've stolen a lot of realities. And lately I've begun to realize my mistakes, thousands of years too late to fix any of them. And, thinking I couldn't do anything about them, I will say I've tried to find other things to take my attention.

You might see why I want to record shows. And drink. Though I'm still sorry about the new *Star Wars*. Mostly.

You do have to crack a few eggs, you know.

CHAPTER THREE

I TOOK A LAST, DEEP BREATH OF THE SUNNY MORNING. Listened to the screams and shouts of kids running across the sand. Watching the surfers, the tourists, the people relaxing with a book in their chairs. Closed my eyes and felt the breeze whisper over my face one more time and steal some of the sun's warmth, leaving a chill across my skin, like a faint touch of an old ghost.

Or maybe a new one.

I walked inside. Slid the glass door closed with a hard push. Set the drink on a nice wooden bar the hotel had placed against the wall for just an occasion. The glass clinked on a nice little round mirror that seemed to be on all little bar carts everywhere.

Then I got ready. Took a shower. The water hot, the streams hard. The shampoo smelled like the old Coppertone suntan lotion, heavy on the coconut. The conditioner somehow more so. I scrubbed my hair, thick dark wavy curls, then I lathered up my skin and let the water rinse it all off, and then for long moments just leaned my forehead against the tile and let the water pound into the base of my neck.

The tile was cold, the air in the shower was hot, humid, the steam thick enough that it was hard to breathe. But I remained in that position a while, until my skin started to itch from the heat.

I was a big believer a hot shower could cure the worst hangover. The worse the hangover, the hotter the shower. There wasn't any science to back that up, but I hadn't seen science to explain anything else I did, so maybe all of that was par for the course.

After all that I toweled off. There were even animal prints on my towels inside. Before, they had been big fluffy, white Egyptian cotton things. They were the same here, just with those seahorse things on them now. Swimming among little coral reefs, with squids and clownfish.

I shuddered at the picture. I thought the squids and the clownfish should fear those things. Hell, I feared them, and they were just on a towel.

I ran some product through my hair, let the dark waves lay where they would. Dark circles ran under my pale blue eyes. I preferred the stubble look, so didn't shave, though I probably should have. Threw some deodorant on, a spray of cologne, and lightly ran some lotion over my skin.

I liked to look good. Sue me.

Besides, you try not keeping skin soft after a few thousand years. Not as easy as it looks.

The lotion was smooth, not that greasy. I rubbed it in, trying to compensate for the hot shower. As if I could replenish all the oils I had burned out. My skin tanned well, it carried a healthy bronze, as well as a number of white lines. Newer lines crisscrossed older ones. All kinds of scars that accumulate naturally over time. Especially if you've been alive as long as I have.

A few of the scars maybe happened more, well, *naturally* than others. A few I remembered. This one, along my leg, from playing at swords back in Athens. This, near the knuckle on my third finger, from trying to learn how to sashimi something. This one was from some kind of vicious man-sized blender attack. Yeah, I'm not sure how it got there, either. What happens in Margaritaville should stay in Margaritaville.

But this scar is the one you probably want to know about. The one by the ribs, the thing I was careful around in the shower. The skin looks angry, right? All puckered up and pressed together? The scar tissue swollen, stitch-marks still all dark and crisscrossed over each other. It kind of looks two lips of a mouth sewn together, the whole wound curved, mad. The wound still ached, a sharp pain kind of ache, and I could almost feel the beat of my heart there, if I laid my fingers lightly along the scarlet skin. The scar felt hot, like it wanted to open up and scream at me.

That was quick knifework. The guy was good. Fast. And the worst part maybe, unmemorable. I hadn't even seen him, until I had felt the blade go in. A hot piercing pain. A quick moment of *unrealization*, of shock, as if I stood outside myself, feeling an immediate burning in my ribs, and yet not believing that pain really existed.

Have you ever been like that? In a moment where you could feel everything, and yet nothing? Kind of hard to describe, isn't it?

The fear wasn't, though. It hit me hard, hammered my body in the heavy, thumping beats of my heart. After that moment of consciousness/unconsciousness, I understood I was being murdered. The guy's hot breath on my neck, as he leaned into me, one hand holding my shoulder, the other on the hilt of the knife. He was about to angle the blade deeper into my chest, and in that moment I panicked.

I robbed reality. Switched the thin blade out with something... shorter. I hadn't had a lot of time, so the knife itself was more jagged. But still, short enough to keep the blade from working its way up and lancing my heart.

The man felt the change. I saw that now. He pulled the knife out and looked at it in wonder, as if he had heard of a thing, but never really believed in it. I remember him in a wash of gray color, a gray suit, gray hair, and a burst of bright yellow on his breast. Some kind of flower.

That moment of the gray man had saved my life.

I pushed him away, back into the alley. I needed to run, and I needed to make sure this man couldn't chase me. Blood already swelled out of the cut. I robbed some reality to help. Put a wall between me and the would-be killer. I had been walking down a city street, one block after the next, just one person among a faceless crowd. I had just passed the entry to an alley when I had all of a sudden undergone a murdering.

Instincts kicked in. I blocked off the alley with a wall, keeping something between me and the killer. A second thought had me put a store with the rest of the wall, some kind of new café with a black cup of coffee steaming on its sign. I grabbed it all from wherever it was and pulled it and hammered it where it would be from now on. Right where the alley had been.

For a moment, there had been me, the guy, and the knife, standing there where the alley had met the street.

Then there was a café.

A bunch of tables, people leaning back against dark, diamond-metal chairs. Sipping lattes. A store, all walled in, with the assassin somewhere inside it. The crowd around me changed subtly, people who were *here* went *there*, and some of the people who were *there*, came *here*.

Maybe you're one of those people. It's hard to tell. You ever pause and look around and wonder where you're at? What you were doing?

None of the switched people would know what had happened. They might have a brief headache. A flash in the eyes. A slight feeling of missing something, forgetting something, like had they locked the door, or did they bring their wallet. A slight patting of a pocket, a slight reassurance that all was well in their world.

That would be it, for them.

I had run after that, pushing my way through the crowd. Holding my side with one hand, feeling a wetness and a warmth push into my palm, leak through my fingers. Wondering who the man was, and how he had gotten that near me.

Even now, I shook my head at the memory. It had been too recent, and too close. The wound still ached, still looked at me, mad and angry, though it was healing well enough (there's a reason for that).

I went to the closet. I had only been here a couple of days, and I had packed light. I wasn't a big fan of South Carolina anymore, the heat had gotten too hot in the last century, the air too humid, the sun too bright. The mild winters couldn't overcome that combination, so the bug population had exploded. Mosquitoes, fleas, gnats (who the hell ever heard of a silent *g*?), cockroaches, all over the place.

Of course, people knew that about me now. People who wanted to kill me. They knew the places I liked to frequent, the homes I had cultivated in certain areas. They seemed to find me better, faster. So, now I was more... *transitionary*. I went from place to place, never staying in a town long. Moving to another place with the silent-*g* gnats, the cockroaches, and mosquitoes. Right now, Charleston was as good a place to hide as any. At least for a few days.

I pulled out a nice pair of gray slacks. Clothes make the man, right? I matched it with a light linen shirt, buttoned it and left the collar up. Then, even though it was a humid summer day, I grabbed a matching gray jacket and shouldered it on. The suit was light, I'd compromised with the heat by not wearing a tie, and that was as far as I was willing to go.

I had seen a few movies that I really liked. The John Wick ones, where the main character had a suit that somehow could stop bullets. Thin, sharp-looking clothes, but made of a fabric tough enough to stop a 9mm bullet.

Yeah. You guessed right. I may have found that reality. I may have stolen bits of it. I might be wearing a similar jacket now. I hoped that some other guy hadn't put on my regular coat, the non-bullet-stopping one, in his universe, and walked out to take two to the chest.

That would be unfortunate, but between that guy and me, I kind of preferred me having the jacket. I mean, I didn't even know that guy.

And things had been escalating lately, in ways I couldn't predict. A bulletproof suit seemed like a necessary precaution. I kind of wished I could find a knife-proof t-shirt I could pair with it.

Maybe someday I'd get back to my home. My real home. Where I was born. If I could remember where I began. It had been a long time, and since I'm being honest, it was hard for me to even recall my mother's face. Much less where I had once lived with her.

For now, though, it was living day by day. *Transitionary*. Kind of funny for a guy who had lived for thousands of years. Months used to go by without me noticing. Now I was living—for the most part—on the run. Taking it a day at a time.

Well, you may not see the humor in it, but trust me, I find it funny.

I put on my shoes. It had taken awhile to find a nice pair of dress shoes I could run in. Something with a nice shine on the leather, but that could handle a couple of miles, in case of *inadvertent emergencies*. I had used to be a big fan of all the Stacy Adams collections, but the soles on them wore quick, got slippery, and well, it only takes a few uncontrolled tumbles across a sidewalk before you end up making a change.

Why did I run? It's a good question. Honestly, it wasn't like I feared a fight. It's just that lately, I never *had* to. Especially with guns around now. It was easier for me to just steal another reality. It was so much simpler to do. Quicker. Faster. And I was a big fan of all of that.

My skills in the more modern ways to kill someone lacked a bit, sadly. Firearms for the most part. I'm fairly good with a blade. But there's something scary about a bullet, for a guy who can live forever.

So I've been practicing, as much as a guy on the run can. I'm not someone who's afraid to learn new things.

Especially when the time calls for it.

CHAPTER FOUR

WHAT I DIDN'T REALIZE IN THE BEGINNING WAS RULE Number Three. That other people could change reality too. I think maybe it was just me at the beginning, but I'm not sure. Maybe as all the splinters of the broken square pegs added up, maybe then more people could kind of... kind of *drift* into a time and place where they could use the power, in a quick moment.

Maybe you've encountered it. Ever flip over a card you needed in poker, or cribbage, or canasta, and have it be the card you desperately needed? The card you wished for, secretly, in the depths of your mind?

Ever watch a football game, maybe watch a kicker line up for a last second field goal, and right before they kick it, you just *knew* it was going to be good?

Ever scratch off a lottery ticket knowing, *without a doubt*, that you were a winner? Or maybe scratch a card knowing that there was no way you would win anything? (Pro-tip, both are true).

Well—you've changed reality.

And then again, it's not really changing it. You've actually stolen a piece of reality from another universe. Let some other poor sod lose his card game, or have a football donk off a post, or scratch a losing ticket.

Or maybe you had some other person win a ticket. Not many seem to win scratch-offs in this world. I think there's something wrong with us, some part of our brain that secretly wants us to lose. This whole scratch-off thing seems to be a madness to me, people rubbing the edge of a quarter on a card worth a penny, hoping to see three pink piggybanks underneath, but knowing that, at best, they might get a buck or two back.

In my mind, there's quite possibly a billion people scratching off tickets now, winning millions of dollars, in a million other realities. Maybe they've won so much in their universes that it causes inflation, and the dollar there loses its value. Causes a destabilization of the economy, and world wars, all because people never seem to win anything here.

It's all about balance, I guess. The good with the bad. The world seems to find a way to even these things out. Some call it karma. To me it's just life.

Man, I can really drift off topic.

Back to the point. There's a lot of us that can steal little pieces of reality. Though most of those people can't control it. I just happened to be able to steal a lot more than a piece. More than just a moment. I could pick and choose what I stole. And while I did so, over the years, as I pounded the square pegs into round holes, as all the splinters fell and accumulated, little crazy things started to happen.

Things I didn't notice at first, because, well, it's hard to notice something going on in Romania, when you are living in Japan. Especially in the fifteenth century. There was no internet back then, or telegraphs, or anything back then. No way for me to understand the consequences to one part of the world, if I switched out a little reality in a completely different hemisphere.

So, maybe it was all my bad, then, everything that happened then.

That's happened since. I know it all is now, at least. But you can see, there was really no way for me to actually see, actually verify, *know* Dracula was real. That he existed. Not at the time.

Though, after the fact, the reality seemed to say he did.

How about that island that sank under the sea, with an advanced people living on it? A far-fetched tale, maybe? The Bermuda Triangle? Bigfoot? Maybe you think those are things you find in the tabloids, articles about all those people who build pyramids in their back yards. That none of these things are real.

Not in the world I'm living in.

Throughout this universe there are cities, places, times, that *should* have existed, but no longer do. Alexandria, gone. Roanoke, lost. The Hanging Gardens of Babylon. The Minotaur of Crete. Could I say that none of these things were really... real? That they had never happened in this reality? In this world?

Like I said, it's hard to know. My reality has become... blurry. For lack of a better term. It feels like, sometimes, I don't have to pound a peg in so hard anymore. That all the square pegs fit a little easier in the holes, I don't have to hammer them so hard. That my universe has become soft enough that almost anything will fit. Sometimes I even see invisible threads, like the universes all were tied together. It was my imagination, I was sure, but I could almost see all the little strings still hanging onto everything I've stolen, like one day all the pieces will be yanked back.

Maybe that's the drink talking.

What's worse for me is the people. For thousands of years, I've been on my own. Like I said, you won't remember what I'm telling you now. Most people don't. But there's a small group of people growing, of people who, for some reason, maybe the splinter theory, *stay.*

These people remember what the world was like before I stole a reality, before I switched things up.

They keep remembering, every time I do it.

I don't know the first person this happened to. Maybe that person died in a fit, trying to explain to everyone what had happened. Maybe other people thought that person was crazy, the one guy who saw Atlantis sink under the ocean. Or the first person who saw Dracula. Maybe in the beginning, those people got sent to the mental hospitals, or worse.

But the group that remembered grew over time. People remembering husbands they used to be married to. Other families. Friends they had, who all of a sudden disappeared. Small things like that. Or larger things, like driving on the wrong side of the road. Wars. A day at the park with someone they were hot for, or a space shuttle exploding on takeoff.

Those people remembered. And their numbers grew. Though I had no idea they existed, the whole time I had been alive. Not until now.

Still, that group was real. And once real language had come along, once people could write things down, they passed down their knowledge. Of things they thought had been forgotten. Of things they had seen and felt.

Hell, some of them even published books about what they remembered. I can't really blame these people that remember, why not make a buck while trying to keep something you think important around? We've talked about Dracula, but there were plenty of others that may or may not have been in this reality once upon a time. Creatures like Grendel. Medusa. Winged horses. (You might think those are crazy, but if a seahorsey thing can exist, why not a horse that can fly?)

Anyway, these people that remembered, that stayed when I switched out realities, they grew in number. They copied more information down. They tried to figure out how to stop what was going on, and when they couldn't they tried to figure out who was causing it, and why. They did this for centuries, passing on a certain hate, confusion, and a rail-against-the-gods kind of rage.

Of course, I didn't know about them (see the whole no internet thing above) until it was too late.

Boy, are they pissed. One of them in particular.

CHAPTER FIVE

I LEFT THE HOTEL ROOM, LOCKING THE DOOR BEHIND ME.

I probably should have packed everything up, but I was running later than I wanted. Later than I needed. The anxiety ran through me, it churned in my stomach, and the bourbon really hadn't quite helped that nauseous feeling go away. The rough liquor had just burned it down some.

The hallway seemed too bright, the fluorescent lights hummed above a shiny blue carpet and did their best to mimic the sunny day outside. A nice air circulated, like the breeze. The blue carpet was full of little red diamonds patterned themselves across the blue, interlacing through each other. It seemed garish and a little eighties to me, but sometimes everything felt that way. Especially after cheap bourbon.

I had a home I could go to, it's hard to live as long as I have and not have a few places here and there, but I was running now. So I was booking a place for a week or two, always at a random location. And I always left before the checkout day, a day or two before, always random as well. I went by feel, and I made sure my comings and goings weren't predictable. Just to keep those who are tracking me a little more lost.

Whenever I did a thing twice, it seemed like the Remainers found me.

It's what I had taken to calling them. Those who stayed after a switch. Those who remembered the reality I had stolen from them.

Maybe you think the word a little bland. I found it fascinating. Having lived through a few language... transitions, there was a feeling with certain words that was hard to describe. It was like, their meanings changed over time, but pieces of them found a way to hang around. Sometimes the core of what a word meant stayed with the word, sometimes it evolved, branched out. Sometimes the word even became something brand new.

More rarely, I would stumble on a word that had somehow kept itself intact, had weathered the storm of Latin dying away, of the splintering off of French and Spanish and Italian, and Portuguese and, strangely enough, Romanian.

Funny that English isn't a part of that group, right?

So the words that hung around, that evolved and changed but still somehow kept a part of themselves intact, those words felt much like me. Weathered. Standing the test of time. Slightly rough around the edges, sometimes meaning many things, but also at its core the same word it had been a thousand years before.

Shit. I'm late. How do I get into these thoughts?

I took a breath. The air smelled like maraschino cherries, like the ones in all the cocktails the tourists were drinking on the beach. I strode down the hallway, to the stairs (I never took elevators—those aren't something I did, I couldn't trust them), and down to the lobby. There, I walked past a long desk along a long wall where people checked in and out. People with half-open shirts and bathing suits that may have needed to be a couple sizes larger. There was a young girl behind the desk, different from the day before, and she waved at me with a smile, as if she recognized me, and told me to have a nice day.

I guess it could be, if I wanted it to.

I left, pushing on the hard glass revolving door that separated the lobby from the outside. Fingerprints of the person before me sat on the glass, wide fat prints of four fingers and a fatter thumb. Greasy, as if the person was covered in suntan lotion, or maybe just they were naturally oily.

The door took some force to rotate. An older lady had gotten in from the outside, wearing a lavender coat, pulling a lavender suitcase behind her. She seemed to be trapped. She couldn't push the door enough to get into the lobby, so I had to do it for the two of us. Making sure that I didn't push too hard because the lady moved in very small steps. Little staggered things.

It took some waiting, and some wrestling, but we both got through.

Outside was bright. But we knew that already. The sun was brilliant, the sky blue, the clouds white puffy pieces of torn cotton strewn about the sky, as if Mother Nature had pulled them out of a bag and rolled them, like dice. It was hot, but there was a cool breeze fluttering steadily in from the ocean, carrying a promise of cool moisture and a hint of salt. Maybe a bit colder than earlier, as if hints of the storm I had brought in and disappeared, still remained.

I headed down the street, inland. I was close enough to the beach that the sidewalk always had sand on it, making that scritching sound as I walked over it. Each shoe felt like it slid, just a hair, with each step.

I moved against the crowd, all of them headed to the beach, the tourists and surfers and other beach-goers. Locals, doing their last-days-of-summer thing. Most of the men in shorts, wearing flip-flops, no shirts, their skin burnished bronze, walking around with an eye to the girls. Or women, in bikinis, some scantily so, laughing together groups.

I got to the bar. Bubba's. One of those beach bars with tables sat up outside, umbrella poles in the middle of each, and a wide-open door between the outside of the bar and inside. Ceiling fans all spinning, a dark bar with plenty of taps behind it, and a ring of televisions above the bar and scattered throughout the room. The outside tables were empty, this early in the day, with their yellow umbrellas still closed.

Inside it was a little less hot, at least in the shade. The tables were dark wood, old, scratched with hundreds or thousands of little knife and fork marks, over the years. The chairs, the stools, the bar, all the same.

Though the bar was more polished. A young man behind it, wiping it down. Black hair, black hat, black shirt with the word STAFF on the back in bold white letters and the man's name, Cohen, on the front. His face had some stubble, as if he had woken up late and rushed in, though his eyes were friendly underneath an old, torn, green-and silver Philadelphia Eagle's ballcap.

I walked in, taking a quick survey around. Not a lot of games were on now, there were some soccer games from Europe playing, ones that no one ever seemed to watch. A rugby game on, in a television in a corner, with a few men sitting underneath it. Three full pints of amber-colored beer in them with an empty pitcher in the middle of the pints. One of the men yelled something like *ruck that mother over*, and kept kind of yelling it, over and over in a weird rhythm, as I walked in. *Ruck, ruck ruck ruck*. All three men wore some kind of polo jersey, something with thick horizontal stripes on them, black-and-white lines.

They looked a little like criminals. But maybe that's just rugby.

I walked over to the far end of the bar and pulled out a stool. It made the same scritching sound on the floor that my shoes had, outside. Made sure my back was to the empty back of the room, so I could watch the rugby fans, the open door, and try as best I could to keep another knife from finding my ribs.

The bartender came over. The young man was a little tired around the eyes, as if he had a late night. Beach people generally do. He stood next to that area all bars have, the stand with all the cherries and olives and straws and things they put together for drinks. One of those stands that held black plastic cups of all those things, with a drawer underneath.

"What'll you have?" he asked. He had a little white towel in his hands, and he made a little washing motion with it, as if drying his hands off.

"Tequila," I said.

"Margarita?" he asked.

I shook my head. "Give me a repo, if you have one. With a nice bit of ice." This early in the day I always liked the flavor of most of the reposados. Then I paused. Something citrusy might make my stomach feel a little less nauseated. And it was fruit, so I could maybe call it breakfast. "Actually, make it a Blanco. And a wedge of lime in it, if you will."

"Man, we're all out of limes," he said. "We got more coming in later today."

I paused. The lime had sounded good to me. My stomach kind of uneasily rumbled. "You sure?"

He pulled out the drawer to check again. A single lime rolled forward and touched the front. Skin a nice, bright, fresh green.

"Well, damn," he said. "Your lucky day."

I smiled back, an empty smile. Maybe it was. Likely it wasn't. It could be either, if I wanted it to be.

It made me wonder what the day would be, if I just left it all alone and let it happen. Naturally. On its own.

What a scary thought.

The bartender, maybe because of my suit, pulled a tequila off the top shelf. A ceramic bottle, white, tall, with blue lines painted in flowering circles around it. The bottle looked like a thin vase, something for flowers, maybe.

Tequilas were like that, though. Bottled up in crazier and crazier things. Ceramic skulls, Day of the Dead jars, skeletons and butterflies painted across the glass.

The bartender opened it and poured a hefty amount of clear tequila in a glass, something about a hand high with straight sides. Plopped a big square ice cube in the middle of the glass and then cut a nice wedge from the lime and plopped it in.

Then he grabbed a nice coaster, something square and made of cork, and placed it in front of me. Placed the glass on it. I tasted it and took a sniff, the lime was sharp and rich, the agave, the alcohol, hidden by the citrus.

I sipped it. The tequila was much smoother than those I was used to, almost like water, with the lime being the predominant taste. The glass was cool in my hand, the drink was cool, and the citrus made its way down to my stomach and tried to ease the ball of nervousness there.

Maybe the bartender sensed that. He had the towel over his shoulder now. "You want something to snack on? We've got peanuts."

I thought about the salt, and the flavor, and shook my head. Wouldn't go with the drink. Still, I hadn't eaten anything recently. That I could recall. "You got any pretzels?"

"Sure," he went back, got a wooden bowl out, poured something from a bag that clattered against the bowl. Brought it back and sat before me. There were pretzels there. At least, I thought they were pretzels. They were bent in a funny shape I hadn't seen before. Like a heart, with two looping sides, but some kind of twisted knot in the middle.

I tasted one, carefully. It had a good crunch to it, and it tasted like a pretzel. Like a hard piece of bread. Not a lot of salt, which was good.

Sometimes, when I had robbed enough realities, the tastes of things changed. I remember taking a bite of something someone had called a chocolate chip cookie. It had looked like the ones I remembered. Felt like one, the cookie round and crispy feeling in my fingers. When I had taken a bite though...

I shuddered with the memory. The black things in the cookie were definitely not chocolate chips. I had changed that reality fairly quickly.

The bartender mistook my shake. "Pretzels not good?"

I shook my head again. "Perfect." I said.

He looked at me oddly. "You okay, man?"

I shrugged. Was I?

I sipped my drink. It went down smoothly again, although this time I could feel the slight burn of the tequila in the aftertaste. It warmed my throat, just a little. The lime hung on my tongue and mixed with the bread taste of the pretzel well enough.

I nodded back at him.

He hung a bit longer, one hand rubbing at his eyes a bit. Like he was tired. Nice enough kid, Cohen, to be that concerned with a customer this early in the morning, even if he looked like he might have partied a bit too hard the night before.

One of the rugby guys shouted. There was a clash and a clutter. I looked over, one of the pints of beer lay on its side, and the guy in front of the pint standing, his shirt soaked. I thought it was the rucker.

The bartender took a breath, maybe he knew that group, and headed over.

I sipped some of the drink. Ate some more pretzel. I was late, but the person I was meeting was even later. Maybe they were having second thoughts. Maybe I should be having them, too. Maybe I shouldn't have had all that bourbon already, this early in the day. A straighter mind wouldn't be here now.

I pulled out my wallet. Pulled a photo out. One of me and a girl. The photo was fairly recent. A few months old. I never carried a phone (like I said, don't blame me for those things), so it was one of the cheap pictures that came from a photo booth. Like they had in malls, or on a stand near a beach.

I was careful with it. The photo was folded in half, so it would fit in my wallet. I didn't know where else to keep it, but I didn't want to lose it. I had pulled a lot of things from other realities. Stolen a bit of things I missed. But this photo to me was a one-and-only. It would never feel the same if I had to steal another. It would be someone else's photo, from someone else's reality.

So this photo was mine, in a way I didn't know I had before. It was the original. If I had to replace it, I would lose its meaning. It would become blurry. And that would lead to me forgetting it. Forgetting *her*.

I couldn't let that happen. And maybe that was odd, since I'd lived a thousand lives, and couldn't remember everything in ever one. But it was also natural. Blake and I had a meant-to-be type of feeling, which was rare, in any of my lives. Rare to *me*. To a person who can have whatever they want, whenever they want it.

I had committed to serious relationships before. Many times. Other women, who had meant a great deal to me. They ran all across the scale, from a princess to a variety of them, from a princess in Paris during the French Revolution (*that* was a story) to a young flower-child type of girl back in the sixties who just liked to sail over the blustery New England waters.

Somehow, with each of them, with *all* of these women, I had known there would be another. So some relationships had been casual flings, many had been one-night stands, and a few had been longer, intensely serious relationships. But still, a common thread had run through all of them. As much as any of those women had meant to me at the time, each of them had been replaceable. A word that came easy to me, with what I did.

She had been different though. From the very start. I had known it, inside, at a level that almost convinced me I had finally found the reason I existed. It had been that kind of feeling.

And it had been brief. Brief for anyone's life, but especially for mine.

The picture didn't have the feel of a Polaroid. It wasn't thick, it didn't feel durable. It was more like the page of a magazine. Or even a newspaper. My thumb and forefinger held it, lightly along one edge. The photo waved a bit, from the slight stirring of air of the ceiling fans.

It remained bent at the crease in the middle, and flapped enough that I could see the back, white, with a cursive scrawl diagonally across it.

Miss me yet? xoxo...

Blake

Maybe the bartender had a reason to ask if I was okay. I was thinner now, than in this picture. If the bartender's eyes were blurry, mine were bloodshot, with almost-permanent dark circles underneath them. My cheekbones too prominent, my face too haggard. What I pretended was stubble was more... rough than stubble should be. A little long, for the look I tried to cultivate.

I was nothing like I had been in the picture. My smile there, too wide, mouth too open. In the middle of a laugh. Blake, snuck up along my shoulder, green eyes like emeralds, blonde hair lying back over my arm, face turned up in the photo and whispering something into my ear, heart-shaped lips so close to my lobe.

With my eyes closed, I could still feel her breath on my neck. Could almost still hear the words...

The tequila lay forgotten. My head bent a little, my hand moved, until I felt the coolness of the glass against my forehead. A cold, wet spot, like a bullet hole maybe. Something that opened my head, drilled into my brain, and spilled out thoughts of Blake.

In my mind now, that was all. It never occurred to me to eat another of the weird heart-shaped, knotted pretzels. The rugby fans no longer existed for me. The bartender. The bar. This beach. This place.

In this moment, right now, eyes closed, all that existed was the moment in the picture.

So, back to the rules. As I know them. Or, I guess, as I've learned them.

    #1 – I can't bring anyone back to life
    #2 – I can live forever (but I can also definitely die)

#3 – We all can change reality, in some way

And Rule Number Four – Dead is Dead.
Yeah, it's in there twice. Because I needed the reminder.

CHAPTER SIX

I WAS USED TO PEOPLE DYING ON ME. AFTER ALL, I WAS THE only guy on Earth that couldn't. At least, not from natural causes.

Her fingers trailed across my chest. Light. Warm. Electric.

The memory of Blake would fade, I was sure. The memories of other women had, with time. I got over the loss, I always did.

Still, something about Blake had been different. She had understood me better than anyone before. I had even told her about me, and it was like she hadn't even been surprised. She had loved it, in fact.

"There's a storm coming." Her voice was soft, but not quite a whisper. More of that guttural low timbre that hinted at need. Her breath was hot against my neck. Her head laying in the crook of my shoulder, her body laying against mine, long and lean, one foot tucked between mine.

We lay on my couch, in my condo in Chicago. I was on the bottom, my shirt was off, my jeans unbuttoned and loose around my hips. Blake was tucked in between me and the back of the couch, a little on me, a little on the couch.

A fireplace crackled in front of us. It wasn't a real fire, it was something simulating red and yellow flames, but it still crackled and threw out enough warmth we didn't need a blanket. Blake wore one of my shirts, a blue t-shirt that lay flat across her lean body, and she had a book precariously propped up on the back of the couch, opened and faced down. *Lost Horizon*, I think.

I had interrupted her reading. Which I did from time to time. But she read a lot. This book was one of a few odd selections. *Number of the Beast, Hitchhiker's Guide, The Garden of Rama*. Blake loved her fiction and read any number of books when she came back from one of her trips.

Neither of us had on much else. Me just the pants. Her just the shirt. My hand was trapped behind her back, but it held her close, so I didn't mind. Her free hand slid up and down the skin of her legs, dropped under the shirt to slide along her belly. She did that some-times, almost-absentmindedly, and I wondered if she liked the feel of her body, or if she was still, in a way, getting used to it, or I guess I meant us.

It was raining outside. Not quite a storm, not yet. Just a humid Chicago evening in the summer. The rain was a thick drizzle, tiny drops that splatted in waves against the windows, gusts of wind rhythmically beating against the glass.

The Chicago place was something we both liked, out of all my places around the world. Well, it was a place Blake seemed to like a lot, and hell, I was easy-going enough to stay there a bit. In the middle of summer it was warm, but windy, with rain occasionally coming in off Lake Michigan. There was a ton to do for a young couple in this city. Or a young woman with a much older man.

"It's not really a storm," I said. "Just a little rain." Enough, I happily thought, to keep us both inside.

Blake nuzzled the side of my neck, tucked her head under my jaw. Her breath came out warm across the nape of my neck. The night hung around us outside, dark behind the rain. The spatters of drops trickled down the windows, the city lights bright enough behind the wet haze they appeared in tiny illuminated globes. Like stars, but bigger.

"Right now," she said. Which was a funny thing to say, with the rain outside. As if echoing her words, the wind slammed into the glass. A big-fisted splatter and pounding of water that echoed in the condo.

Windy city, right?

"What would you do?" she whispered.

"Now?" I mistook her question, and kissed the top of her head, strands of her hair sticking to my lips.

"No, silly," she said. "If a real storm came."

"What I'm doing now, I guess," I said. We were going to go out, but the storm had come on, and I had looked over at Blake reading and … well here we were. I smiled. "What *we're* doing now."

I could feel her body pull back a bit. Not literally, just the sense of another person thinking. Forming a thought inside, before speaking it.

"Not something like this," she said. "Something... otherworldly. Something really powerful."

"Powerful?" I raised my head, looking at the rain outside.

"Yeah. Nothing like this one. A storm like this world hasn't seen before."

Something about her words struck me. And I recognized they came from the book she was reading. So I smiled (but didn't roll my eyes, because I knew from experience Blake took these things seriously) and pretended to think about her question.

"Like a hurricane?"

She frowned, as if recognizing my game. "A hurricane that spreads out and covers the world, maybe. Such a storm that rages, until all human things are leveled in some vast chaos."

It *was* from the book, but it was also a deep thought. Blake did this to me occasionally. Like she was testing me. Testing the limits of what I could do. Or maybe would do.

"Are you asking me if I'd send the storm away?" I asked. If I'd reach out and steal a nice sunny day from some other reality, and swap this storm out for that.

"Would you? *Could* you?"

I was sure I could. I didn't know if I would. So I gave her a little mistruth, instead. "I don't know."

She liked to talk about what I did, but the truth was, I tried to do it as little as possible now. Nothing grand, anymore. I kept it to smaller things now. But I had done great things before, great swaps of large pieces of reality. At the time I had felt those thefts justified. I would probably do it again, if the circumstances were right.

I didn't know the answer to her question. Blake still seemed to see what I was thinking. She had that ability. I wanted to shrug, but my arm was still trapped, so my free arm did a little motion on its own. "I've done it before."

Blake looked unhappy with my answer. Maybe she wanted something else from me. Maybe her thoughts were elsewhere. "You have?"

"Yes," I admitted. "I guess, honestly, I don't know. But maybe." I mean, it would depend on the storm, right? If a tornado was headed my way, I'd probably steal a sunny day to replace it. Especially if it was me or it.

But Blake stayed quiet then. Stayed withdrawn. I could tell my answer didn't make her happy. I wondered what answer she wanted. Maybe I was just reading too much into this, and she had just wanted to go out tonight, and the storm had derailed our plans.

I mean, she was around less and less lately. Always on some trip to some place. She joked she was an archeologist, like Indiana Jones. Trying to save what she could.

"Do you want me to send it away?" I asked.

I could feel her frown, the tightening of her brow, against my neck. "You don't get it, do you?"

I never did. I thought I knew where she was going, but I was never quite sure. Part of her allure. I know she wondered why I had this power. Why I could do what I could do. She wondered now, like I had for a long time, what my purpose really was.

I hadn't found an answer. And concluded there was no real purpose. Thousands of years hadn't told me different.

I smiled, a partly empty smile, thinking about it. "Not right now."

Her hand pushed against my chest, hard enough that I could feel my muscles bunch up against her palm. "Really?"

"You know I don't. What would the purpose be?"

It's hard for others to understand. When you can have anything, *everything* loses its luster. You lose interest. Because if there's no reason for it, then there's no point.

(I've told you this before. You may recall it. If there's no point, we should all enjoy the little things. The smaller moments. Because one small moment gets you to the next, and the next after that. And the next after that.)

Remember this, if you remember anything I've told you. If the big things have no purpose, then enjoy the hell out of the smaller moments, the Blakes of the world, and do what you have to do to get by. Because they are what get you through it. Through life.

Her eyes flashed, even though her smile stayed. Testing me again. Or playing a game. Like I said, I was never sure which. "Why do you need a purpose?"

I let out a breath. I know it sounded frustrated. This was a discussion we had a lot, lately. I tried to distract her by sliding my hand underneath her shirt, and smiling to take the edge off of what I was saying. We had talked about this a lot, and I knew the word came out harsh. "Again?"

Blake loved to bring this up, to talk about what I could do, and why I didn't do it more. Exactly what my limits were. (I didn't know if I had any.)

I needed to change the subject. I waggled my eyebrows suggestively.

Blake pushed my hand away and pouted. Her lips made a great pout. And then the lips spread into a sly smile. Something devilish.

"Again?" she said, echoing my question in a sing-songy exhalation. Her hand moved to where my jeans lay unbuttoned, slid the tips of her fingers just under the waistband of my briefs.

Then paused there.

She waited. I turned my face so that we could lock gazes. I could feel the force of it there, the intensity that Blake had inside her. Her eyes had a power, almost a hidden knowledge that captivated me.

"All these worlds that could exist," she said. "Places that could have existed once. Civilizations like Atlantis, cities like Shangri-La, all this history out there..."

Places of knowledge. Places of power. Places of old wisdom and hidden secrets. I knew, being in the field Blake was in, that would hold a certain attraction to her. Which I didn't mind, not really, in times like these.

"Don't you want to *know*?" she asked. Her voice intense.

I had once. Thousands of years ago. I had tried to *know*. And I had found no answer.

And honestly, had those places ever existed? Maybe. Maybe Plato or James Hilton had seen the places they had written about. Maybe they had heard a rumor from a traveler somewhere. Maybe all those places had existed, and had disappeared, because I had put a square peg into a round hole one time too many.

If I had only not done as much of that, in the beginning. Then the world today might feel a little less fuzzy, a little less... *soft*. Maybe everything would be different.

Though it was more likely that all those places were just dreams of a creative mind. Just like everything else Blake brought up. Rama. Spaceships. Other worlds and historical peoples.

If I could only tell the difference between the world today and the world as it should be. Maybe that's what the strings were for, but there were too many now. And maybe that was what Blake was getting at, but it didn't feel like that. It felt like she wanted a specific answer from me. One big test I kept failing.

I couldn't tell you what that answer needed to be. Only that it had nothing to do with a storm.

"Blake, what do you really want from me?"

She sighed, a big warm breath against my chest. Her finger traced little circles there. "Gavin, it's what you want. It's always going to be about what you want..."

I snorted. "Atlantis. Alexandria. Shangri-La... What would you do with a lost city of knowledge? Of old monks and old books?"

She raised her head. Her tongue flicked out and licked the bottom of my earlobe. That and her breath had goosebumps rippling across her skin. And her fingers slid just an inch lower.

"What wouldn't I do?" she asked. "If I could do what you could? All of this knowledge lost. Everything that could be saved..."

It was her job. History. Archeology. I thought that's why she read a lot of science fiction, to get away from what she did.

And I knew what she was talking about. Or I thought I did. I hadn't been the reader Blake was, but you got to find something to do when you live forever. For me though it was more of a wistful thought, a wondering, if what I read about, even though it was fiction, might once have been real.

For Blake it wasn't wistful. She loved knowledge for knowledge's sake. She'd want to find a world where Shangri-La really existed, where she could find the Library of Alexandria or even the lost city of Atlantis and read what was written from the very beginning.

Blake would want to look for a lost civilization on Mars, with its empty canals where water might have once flowed, and figure out why people had gone there. She wouldn't be curious about starships, or spacecraft, and where people took those ships too. She would want to know the *why* of it.

Part of me had once held the same curiosity. A long time ago. When I had first found out what I could do. Now it felt more like a party trick than anything else. And all party tricks get tiring the longer you perform them. Which is maybe why I kept avoiding Blake's question.

Something in that moment scared me. She did that sometimes. She paired some search for wisdom with a frolicking passion on the couch, the moment confused me. Her intensity, the flashing of her eyes, there was something there that drove her far beyond other mortals. It both frightened and thrilled me, which were feelings I hadn't had in a long time, and I loved it.

I grabbed her hand and pushed it down further. Let out a breath when her fingers touched me.

Light. Warm. Electric...

Her voice was a whisper. I almost couldn't hear her words.

"You should figure this out," she said. Pushing my pants down. Sliding her leg over the pair of mine. The t-shirt loose around her lean frame, her hair hanging down over her face, hiding her eyes. All I could see were Blake's lips. Thick. Curved, deliciously so. "Someday, you're going to need to know."

Some day. Long after Blake had gone from my life. Hundreds of years later, thousands. Maybe then I'd need to know. But I pushed the thought away. I always pushed it away. Even if her words stuck with me a bit.

A part of me still wondered. Still wanted a reason for why I was born. Maybe the last remaining part of me that felt really human.

Someday, you're going to need to know...

Honestly, in memory, it was kind of an odd thing to say. You'll understand though that at the time I had become a little distracted. There was Blake over me. Deliciously curved lips. The crackling of a fire. The drumming of the rain against the windows.

And then I had forgotten. Until it was too late.

CHAPTER SEVEN

I WASN'T SURE HOW LONG I SAT THERE, MY EYES CLOSED. Long enough to hear the bartender set a new pitcher on the rugby table. Long enough to be able to pick up the whispering turn of the ceiling fan above me, the slight rub of the bearing inside the fan, the jingle of the chain dangling from it, as the fan rocked slightly in its cradle.

Long enough to hear someone pull out the stool next to me. Someone who smelled like lavender, with a hint of citrus. Or maybe that was just the big wedge of lime in my drink.

"Jesus," a voice said. Full of contempt. "You look like shit."

I opened my eyes.

A woman sat beside me. Not like the girl in my picture. That girl was lean, tall, graceful. Blonde hair, green eyes.

This girl was thin enough, but short. Not really lean, but compact. More athletic, though she hid the curves of her breasts under a tight white shirt and a blue jacket. Her nose was hawklike, perched between flashing blue eyes. A strong chin. High, sharp cheekbones that somehow looked elegant on Blake, but always made this woman look angry instead.

Which this woman was, usually.

Or maybe it was just usually around me.

I took a sip of the tequila. The drink was thin now, the cube of ice had melted, and it tasted like I was drinking one of those lime-flavored bottled waters. The all-natural ones that really don't taste like anything. "Good to see you too, Cassie."

She sat there, small black purse in her lap, arms folded over it. Curly black hair, much curlier than my waves, cut short, tied up in a little bob on the back of her head.

We both waited. She arched an eyebrow, which made her look both angry and impatient. I noticed she had a light dusting of freckles on each check and her nose, and that her skin was a little red, maybe from being at the beach recently.

I took another sip, set the glass down on the coaster. Smiled, not at Cassie, just at the situation. Took the photo and carefully folded it back along its crease, tucked the picture back in my wallet.

We could both play this game, and I could play it longer. For centuries at a time, if needed. And if this woman wanted me to believe she had a more important place to be, well we both knew that to be a lie. Nowhere right now, in any of my realities, was more important than here.

Still. Maybe there was something to be said for being the first to offer an olive branch. What was the saying? Politics made for strange bedfellows?

The same could be said for revenge.

I corrected myself, offering the branch. "Cass."

One corner of her lip turned up, just slightly. As if it she was measuring points between us. And now that she had counted that coup, she could move on. "You going to tell me what happened?"

What wasn't happening, lately? After losing Blake everything had tumbled into a tailspin, I rarely knew which was up, which was down, and how close I was to hitting the ground. The Remainers were always close by, I could never shake them, it seemed like every time I found a place to stay, I had to leave that place faster.

Right now I was just holding on to a tiny thread of hope, something to keep me going, the slim whisper of revenge.

I guess we both were. Cass and me. She just handled it better.

"What's been happening a lot lately," I ended up saying. I unbuttoned my jacket with one hand, motioned to my side. "Someone tried to kill me."

Silently I wondered if Cassie (I paused here in my thoughts, because Cassie was looking at me, and her eyebrow looked like it was going to thunder back down again, so I—again, in my mind—mentally changed the name) *Cass* had anything to do with that.

I probably shouldn't think that about Blake's sister. But I had lived a long time alone, even in relationships, I was kind of a solitary person. Blake had been the one for me, the one in a lifetime. She had also been Cass's older sister, and though they fought sometimes, like sisters always do, they had always had a bond not many others shared.

The two of them were Remainers. When I say that, I mean that the two of them stayed around after I stole large pieces of reality. If I swapped out this bar, Cass would remain. If I swapped out something Cass was drinking, she'd remember the difference.

That was what happened with Remainers. As the world changed, as they went to sleep one night and woke up the next, they would remember things different from the rest of the world. One day the Twin Towers were gone, the next they stood again. Things like that. For Cass and Blake, it had been the day the space shuttle had exploded. The next day they had woken and found out it had made it to orbit. And only the sisters, from everyone around them, remembered it differently. Remembered it *correctly*.

Events like that had piled up through their lives. It had started with their father, who one day had forgotten both of them and walked off. That had bonded them tighter than normal sisters, and the more things they saw and found, the tighter their bond had grown. For a long time they had believed themselves the only real people, until they had found the group of people that could remember the world, before shifts.

For them, it was like one of those fill-in-the-blank-anonymous meetings. Drugs, alcohol. Being heavy. It was a place people could go to feel better. And through that, I thought they had learned about me. At least, that was my guess. And Blake had also learned about the other cells, the angry Remainers, the ones trying to kill me.

Blake never really talked much about the Remainers. What I learned about them, I learned more from Cass. Who I had met much later than Blake.

I thought the Remainers a loosely organized group. People that through the centuries had written down shifts. Keeping track of changes. It was only lately, the past six months, that they had grown more organized. They had figured out what was happening, and more importantly, who was doing the happening to them, and their new leader had decided killing me would stop it all and return their world to some semblance of non-shifting normalcy.

Which wasn't wrong. I thought that was fair. I even understood where they were coming from, could cheer them on a bit, except I objected to the whole killing me thing. I didn't have anything against the Remainers, except for that little detail.

The bartender walked up. Cassie ordered a beer. He motioned to the taps and she shook her head, instead pointing to a clear-paneled fridge behind him. He told her the same beer was on tap, and she asked him if he had a problem with his hearing.

Cassie had that way with people, from the time I've been around her. From the word go, it was always a fight with her. Ordering a beer, a dinner, any and all conversations. Even coming up with a plan of revenge.

Maybe that's why she missed Blake. Blake had seemed to be the one person that always got along with Cassie. Even when they fought, it was more of an intense sisterly kind of debate, than real contention. Blake always seemed to be able to bridge the gap between Cassie and the rest of the world.

I noticed the glance. Wondered if she could read minds. Reminded myself to use Cass. And ignored her sly smile.

The bartender pulled out a bottle of Modella from the standing fridge. It was a dark Mexican beer. He popped the top with a practiced motion and handed it to her.

She took a swig and looked at me. Really looked at me. "How close was it?"

"Close," I admitted.

"Was this a week back?" she asked.

"Yeah." Ten days, to be precise. Long enough for the wound to close some, but still look mad at me. As if *I* had been the one to actually put the knife there...

"You stole then," she said.

"I had to."

She shook her head, as if I were a few years old, and not a few thousand. "You know what that does."

"I know," I said. "Turns out, I don't really think of those things when there's a knife pushed in my side."

She frowned, looked like she wanted to say something, then looked away. Like she knew where that whole conversation would go.

I knew it too. She wasn't talking about the damage I did when I pieced another world's reality with this one. Cassie was talking about how the Remainers found me.

It was obvious, once I had thought about it.

They had people everywhere now. I wasn't sure how many had accumulated, over the years, but it stands to reason as the population of the world grew from two, to eight billion, the number of Remainers would grow as well. Just if the number grew in proportion.

However, if by stealing reality, if by trying to fit square pegs into round holes, I was creating more Remainers, then maybe the number was more of a skyrocketing line, than any kind of proportional figure. But they had a network, they had cellphones (not my fault), and any Remainer in any city could easily contact others if they sensed a shift.

Like tiny dots appearing on a radar, they could map out where I had been. Where I was going. And they could narrow down where I was.

Hard work. Slow, and they would get an approximation of where I could be. But the Remainers were dedicated.

And lately, they were getting too close. It was as if they had found something that got them a lot closer to where I was. They found me faster, even if I hadn't stolen reality recently.

I worried about that.

But what could I do, against a group of people I couldn't shift anywhere else, and who would never forget?

I waved the bartender back over with a refilling the glass motion. He gave me a rueful grin, feeling the way my conversation was going, and gave me a slightly larger pour. A smaller cube of ice. And another big wedge from the same lime.

"Lucky man," he said. "You got a few more drinks out of this."

Cass's face paled at the man's words. She looked at the lime, then glanced outside. "You didn't?"

Well, I did, but now I didn't want to admit it.

Her words were low and soft, with a hint of panic. "This morning, too?"

I took the tequila and just looked at her. A little guiltily, which I shouldn't feel at all. Some days didn't deserve to be sunny. Then I knocked the drink back. It had been a good-sized pour. The tequila was still smooth, but a small burn still worked its way from the back of my throat, all the way to my stomach. Joining an uneasy fire there, that I thought the lime had taken care of.

"Yeah," I said.

Cass's glances were quicker. Her glances outside seemed more of a practiced, scoping motion. As if she could feel an enemy closing in on her.

I wish I had that kind of instinct. I seemed to only know something after the fact.

"So, the storm and the lime," she asked. Scoping the bar. "Anything else?"

I looked at her and shrugged. If she knew something, she should tell me. Then I tilted my head back to take another large drink.

That's when a bee buzzed my face. It had to be a large bee, the size of maybe a hummingbird, the way it felt. I felt the light touch of it across my skin, along one cheekbone, down the side of my head, right above my ear. It hummed like it had wings beating a thousand miles an hour.

Cass tackled me. We both fell behind the bar. More bees buzzed around, followed by thwacks of high-velocity objects hitting wood, concrete, softer thumps of the same objects hitting people. The tinkling of glass and the beginnings of screams, coming from outside.

Not bees then. Metal insects instead. Hard casings blurring through the air.

Bullets.

Tearing up the bar around us.

CHAPTER EIGHT

I'm not sure if you've ever been in a random gunfight. I know I've been in a few, and I can tell you, it takes a minute to figure out what's going on. Even for the most experienced of gunslingers, there's a split-second pause. A wondering, if you actually heard what you think you just heard. A pause, trying to figure why the nice young man serving you just fell forward. And a disconnect, as the hot splash of blood sprays over your face.

I mean, your body gets ramped up quickly. It's why the best stay around. They practice. They get their body to respond before their mind gets them killed.

And while I had stayed around, I hadn't practiced. Apparently, Cassie had. *Cass.* She had leapt off her stool and tackled me with the all-pro form of a linebacker. Somewhere I heard my glass of tequila shatter on the floor. Behind that were the screams, plenty of screams of people from outside, screams of the rugby fans, screams everywhere. It all added to the confusion in the place, along with the thuds and thwacks and zings and pings.

Back to a random gunfight. It's always hard to tell where the bullets are first coming from. It's hard to see who's shooting, in the beginning. The confusion masks them. You're still looking around, wondering what the hell is going on. It's hard to tell how many, and from where. Both of which are vitally important pieces of information.

The key is staying alive long enough to figure those things out.

Cassie dragged me back to the side of the bar, one hand on my jacket. She was strong, for a slight girl. I tried to help, or at least my body —ramping itself up—tried to help, my feet pushing against the floor, my pants dragging along the wood.

Maybe I wasn't practiced in a gunfight, but at least my feet knew how to respond quickly. They were used to running. The idea seemed funny to me. I bit back a laugh as we sat back against the short side of the bar.

My mind was still spinning. It was still in the motion of drinking the tequila. Still in the fog of not wanting to be around Blake's sister, because Cassie (I was really having trouble with this) was just a reminder of what I had lost.

At least I had picked where I was sitting correctly: the far end of the bar, deep inside the restaurant, with the long runway of the wood between us and whoever was shooting outside. The poor bartender hung over the lip of the bar, his sightless eyes glancing down at us (want another, sir?), his hand loosely flopping to the side.

I felt bad for the guy, when I had come in he looked hung over, he looked like I had felt, but he still put in a yeoman's effort at what he had been doing. Like he had cared. He had paid attention to the customers, kept chatting, cleaning up the broken mugs, cleaning up the bar. Poured a little extra when I had needed it.

Hell, he had taken a bullet for me. Maybe accidentally, maybe by stepping between me and the shooter at just the wrong time, but still, it probably counted.

Cassie hunkered down next to me. Lined up at the corner of the bar, as if she was thinking about peeking around outside. Her purse had fallen during the dive, and she snagged it with a quick motion, smoothly pulling a Beretta 9mm out.

Like someone who practiced those kinds of motions a lot.

Bottles broke behind us, as bullets traced the back of the bar. More screams, from outside. The crunching wreck of one car hitting another, and all kinds of horns.

"Idiot," Cassie whispered, glancing at me.

I looked around blankly. "The bartender?"

"No, dolt," she said. "You. For using your power today. *Twice.*"

I wanted to say something, but didn't. It was hard to argue with her logic, with random gunfire punctuating the point. Well, it was something I *could* argue with, being the type of person I was, but for now I was going to err on the side of caution.

Besides, Cassie had a gun.

We huddled together. High-powered whines zipped through the air, became the hard thwacks of bullets against wood, sharp pings of bullets hitting metal, and the soft thumps as they found the occasional body.

On the other side of the room, one of the rugby guys was huddled underneath their booth. I wasn't sure which of the three he was, but the other two were motionless where they had been sitting. Which couldn't have been a good sign for them.

"They're spraying," Cassie said. She knelt on one knee, Beretta in one hand, back against the bar.

"Is that a good thing?" I asked.

"It might be," she said. "It might mean they don't know what you look like."

That was an interesting fact. I thought all the Remainers knew me by sight. I would have thought, in a world where reality could shift at any moment, they would have committed my face to memory.

Cassie shrugged, then. Maybe thinking the same thoughts. "Or maybe they're just trigger happy."

She glanced at me. Rolled her eyes for some reason. The bartender's hand dangled above us. Cassie reached up and grabbed the towel he had been using to clean the surface.

"Here," she said. "You're bleeding."

"It's the bartender," I said. Nodding at the sightless eyes. The blood dripping over the edge of the bar.

She arched an eyebrow in response and waited. So I probed my cheek, right where I thought a bee had flown by. Realized a nice line had been sliced there, not quite a furrow, arcing back from my cheekbone and along the side of my head. It wasn't deep, but it was open enough to bleed a good bit.

Dammit. I took the towel and pressed it to my face.

Cassie's voice was disgusted. "I can't believe you used your power, the day I was going to meet you."

"I know."

"Twice."

"I know."

"You know that's how they find you."

"I *know*," I said, trying to put emphasis on the word. As if I hadn't been on the run the past week. As if I wasn't a ten-year-old getting scolded.

She kept going, right over my objection. "Knowing *we* were meeting today."

I was going to keep objecting, but I felt like once Cassie got going it might be best to allow her to let it all out. She seemed like the type of person that needed to release the steam, once it built up.

Instead, I just gave her the "I know" expression. You know, where you hold both hands open, and kind of open your eyes a bit larger than normal, a little upset. Like, hey, *I know*.

Not that she acknowledged it.

Of course, she didn't have to. She was definitely right. I should have known better.

It was weird to me, being in this kind of funk. It wasn't something I was used to. I was the kind of guy who moved on. Who found a kind of fun and joy in the little things. I mean, when you grow up being able to do anything you want, after a period of time you can either get bored or take pleasure in the little things.

I usually was the second type of guy.

The flood of gunfire slowed down to a trickle. The screams outside had dwindled away, as people had run away from the scene. The silence felt odd, to me. Like I was on the other side of an echo, in that space of waiting, knowing there was a shout far up the mountainside thundering back down to me like an avalanche.

Cassie's chest rose and fell in quick breaths. She took a quick peek. "The street's empty."

"They're waiting," I said.

"I know," she said. In much the same tone I had given her, saying those same words, if you can believe that.

"You have a gun?" she asked.

I didn't. Thinking about it now, I wasn't sure why. Maybe I had thought the suit enough. Weird that I would get something to protect me from getting shot, but not the thing that does the shooting.

Maybe running was more of a practiced thing than I wanted to admit. Maybe it had become a habit. Not that I was someone to run away from a fight, but when you can live forever, you tend not to want to risk being in random firefights. One bullet kind of ends the dream, you know?

Cassie shook her head, looking at me. "You should always have a gun."

I could fix that. I was sure there was a reality where Bubba's had a bar underneath the counter. One within a quick, easy reach.

Cassie saw the look on my face. And guessed where I was going. "Are you really going to use your power again?"

I looked at her, and I don't think my look was sheepish, but it felt that way. "They already know I'm here."

"Yeah," she said. "But maybe they think they got you. Maybe they think you're dead. If you use your power now, then they don't know that anymore."

I wanted to argue, but it was a good point, so I just clenched my jaw shut.

Like I had said, at first I believed the Remainers knew I was somewhere because they remembered what the world was like before I stole a reality and changed it out with the one around me. They could figure out that general area, through word of mouth. They might know I was around New Orleans, if some of them remembered a hurricane closing in on their shore, but the weather stations were reporting the hurricane wandering back out to sea.

(Not everything I do is selfish. Though some of it happens to benefit me, too.)

So they knew the general area, but finding me was a lot harder for them. I'm sure they had been trying for centuries. It was only lately that they found me faster. A lot faster. Within a day. And lately, hours.

It was like they had some kind of radar that pinged each time I used my power. I didn't understand it, but it certainly made living my life a lot more difficult. There'd been a lot of running this past week.

Just then, someone screamed from inside the bar. The last rugby player. Maybe the silence got to him, or maybe he was screwing up his courage. Either way, he screamed and scrambled out from under the booth. Took off running outside the bar.

There was a shot a moment later. Followed by an *oomph*-like sound, and a thumping of a body hitting the floor.

Cassie took a peek. As if she was trying to figure out where the shooter was, by where the rugby fan had been shot. Then she turned back to me. Eyebrow arched.

"I'm not using it," I told her. And said the next words quietly, to myself: *Not yet*.

She kept her eyebrow arched.

But if it came down to it, I'd use my power. Because I was going to live. That was for damn sure. I hadn't ever had a need for revenge before, felt the burning need inside requiring a sense of personal... justice. But I felt it now. It was a hot emotion, fiery, and consumed most of my thoughts, lately. It was what kept me going.

That and drinking.

Cassie gave me a face, a little roll of the eyes, a little shake of her head. As if she could follow my thoughts. And to be honest, I knew she understood them.

Then a voice called to another. There were steps outside. The crinkling of a boot stepping on broken glass. And heavy breathing, of someone jacked up. Excited. Of a person who maybe didn't know they had a certain blood lust, and now that they found out they had it, was into it. They had come into this pumped up to kill me, but now they were just pumped.

This cell had enjoyed their killing. Even indiscriminate killing.

I understood where the Remainers were coming from. Why they were after me? I had fucked up their world. Their worlds. That didn't make them nice people, though. Or necessarily even good. It just made them angry. Especially after the new guy arrived.

The Remainers didn't particularly believe laws applied to them. Because, in their mind, the world they lived in wasn't the world they had been born into. Not exactly. So they didn't think they had to—exactly—follow that world's rules.

Kind of fucked up reasoning, if you asked me. It wasn't like I had known I was doing something that affected their lives. Especially things like the space shuttle. I was trying to fix something. Something I thought I could fix. Should fix. Things that felt like the right thing to do then. I didn't intend for others to be hurt when I used my powers. Although sometimes hurting others did happen, and maybe I wasn't sorry enough when it did.

So maybe I am fucked up a bit. You try living my life and seeing how you feel, after a few thousand years. Maybe you feel like you'd be different, but I'm guessing you would be a little jaded. Time has a way of doing that to all of us. You just don't know it yet.

"It's going to be more than just one," she said.

"Three," I said. A typical Remainers cell. "I know."

"Likely," she said. "Could be more."

She was worried. People in the Remainers had known Blake. They could know Cassie, too. And if they did, and saw that she was here, meeting me, well, her life would be about to change.

Or, more likely, end.

Cassie deserved revenge just as much as me. Blake had been her sister. So as much as we didn't get along, I was going to make sure Cassie survived. Just like I was going to make sure I survived. It was what I thought Blake would have wanted.

And—just perhaps—I didn't want to try this revenge thing alone.

Though I wasn't going to tell Cassie that.

The footsteps crunched more glass. The person was walking into the bar. He, at least it sounded like a he, whistled a bit as he came in. The whistling was off-key and broke a lot. I wasn't sure of the tune, but it sounded suspiciously like the guy was hunting wabbits.

I went through a Saturday morning cartoon phase for a bit. An hour show where people regularly bent reality and survived dropping anvils on each other? You might see the attraction.

"Joe," a voice called from outside. Not far off. It sounded nervous.

The whistler turned back.

"Clear?"

"What?" the whistler called, maybe sounding impatient.

"We get him?"

The whistler let out a deep breath. "Just stepped in, Reid," the whistler called back, his voice a little rough. Like his throat had a problem breathing.

Cassie held up two fingers at me. I knew she was waiting to hear from the third. If that person was good, they would be the sniper. Working from across the street. With some kind of assault or hunting rifle, their scope trained in the bar. Maybe even at where Cassie and I were hiding.

Still, the bootsteps of the guy hunting wabbits resumed their crunching of glass. They were coming closer. With Reid outside, in the street somewhere. And likely a sniper further out.

No place to go. At some point, whether Cassie liked it or not, I was going to steal some reality. Maybe see if there was a world where this bar was an apartment complex. Preferably one where there was a locked door or two between us and the wabbit hunter.

Because if not, things were going to get messy quick.

We were running out of time.

CHAPTER NINE

———

The boots crunched their way into Bubba's. There was a heavy slap, of a man's palm hitting the top of the bar. The slap echoed through the quiet room.

I tried not to take a deep breath. My body seemed to want it, want *air*, suddenly it felt like there wasn't enough oxygen in the room. All I could smell was the alcohol, all the whiskeys and bourbons and tequilas mixing together, from all the shattered bottles behind me.

I wondered where the police were. If they were even coming. If maybe a Remainer worked in dispatch, slowing everything down.

Worse, maybe I had picked a randomly wrong town, and the Remainer was the police chief.

Or commissioner.

Maybe the mayor.

I knew I didn't like Charleston.

Cassie sat next to me, back to the bar, legs drawn up so that her knees were close to her chest. She held her Beretta in both hands and breathed in and out in quick breaths. As if she was pulling in as much oxygen as she could. Pumping herself up.

She was getting ready to do something.

I hoped it wasn't going to get us killed. Although there didn't seem to be a lot of options.

I peeked around the other edge of the bar. The place where the bartender would lift the flat top of the bar and step in behind it. Where a waitress would stand, waiting to take drinks back to the table.

The dead bartender kind of blocked a lot of my vision. His body leaned across the top of the bar, and his legs lay limply behind it, in front of me.

All I saw of the whistler was a lot of hair and a ball cap. The ball cap was colored in camouflage, with some kind of marlin on its front, the fish twisting in the air, with a curved hook next to it. The hair was black and gray, more gray than black, and long and stringy. The face, what I could see of it, was tanned, with blotches of red near a bulbous nose. The red of drinking, or exertion. Blotchy red. Over his far side, the tip of a rifle poked up in front of his chest, like he was holding it with one hand, the butt of the gun resting on his hip.

This close, we could hear his breathing. Maybe that was why the man whistled, to cover that sound. Each breath sounded like he had to work the air past some obstruction.

The whistler's arm rest on the bar. It raised itself again and pounded down. Then it reached over the bar and pulled out a bottle. One of the cheap scotches there, with the little nozzle-thing on the top of the bottle for easy pouring.

He took a sip. Coughed a bit, and then did that phlegmy-thing where you're trying to swallow whatever it is that rests in your throat after that kind of cough. I got a clear shot of the side of his face, he had a short beard, mostly gray, and his eyes glittered a bit.

The bottle slammed back on the bar. The whistling resumed.

I pulled back. It might have been my imagination, but the breathing sounded a little easier.

I tapped Cassie's shoulder. She jumped just a little. I made a little finger motion, like wizards did in the movies.

She shook her head.

I made it again. Waggling the fingers.

Her jawline sharpened, as if she was gritting her teeth. She shook her head again, then held up one finger. Asking me to give her a second.

This time, it was me that rolled my eyes. But I nodded.

The crunching of the glass resumed. Less crunching now, this far in the bar. More of a twinkling sound, as little bits of window got kicked across the floor.

The man was heading down the bar. The hunting wabbits whistle grew in volume, as he neared. He wasn't walking into the middle of the room but staying near the long run of the bar. Taking one slow step after another.

Cassie lay one hand on me, as if holding me back from using my power.

The tip of the man's rifle showed at the corner of the bar. Right in front of Cassie's head. The barrel was dark, black. A round cylinder of metal, with an empty hole in its center. The gun showing no signs of all the killing it had just done.

At just that moment there was crunching at the front of the bar, too. As if the second guy, Reid, had just entered.

My heart raced. I normally didn't time things this close. It was why I had my bulletproof suit now. Usually by this time I was already running, with some kind of building or storm between me and whatever was hunting me. Those were my "*go-tos*". And one of them, maybe both of them, were right now my "*about-tos*".

Whatever Cassie thought, I was getting us out of here.

The whistler took one more step.

And Cassie sprang into action.

She slapped the barrel of the gun aside with one hand. Slid around the corner of the bar, somehow pivoting to one knee. Used her other hand, pointed her gun up at the Remainer and pulled the trigger, twice.

The whistler grunted. The grunt somehow still came out whistly. The wabbit hunter fell to both knees. Cassie still held the barrel of his rifle. I caught his eyes and they looked surprised, confused. This time the wabbit got him. Then the man coughed once more, then again, and blood started rolling out of his mouth, running over his lips and beard.

Then he tipped over.

Cassie was up even before the man had finished falling. I heard Reid shout, but even as he did Cass fired, and the shout ended in a gurgled *galloomp* kind of sound. Then Cassie spun, her feet dancing over the dead wabbit hunter, placing each foot in such a way that she was angled towards the street, presenting just her side, giving the smallest profile she could, her arm straight as an arrow, pointed to a building there, the gun steady in her hand.

She fired, once. As she did, she leaned just a little back.

At the same time something kicked a tuft of thread up from her jacket. Right above her shoulder. Where the meat of her shoulder would have been had Cassie not leaned a little.

The sniper's bullet thwacked into the wall behind us.

Cassie waited, still standing in her profile mode.

There wasn't a second bullet.

Slowly, she lowered her gun. Looked at me, as if checking to see if I was using my power. Her chest rose up then down one time, releasing one large, held in breath. The only sign she had been worried.

Like I said, some people practiced certain things until they were second nature. Almost a muscle memory. For me, those things were using my power, stealing some reality, and then taking off, if I had to.

For some people that second nature was almost like a cloak, they could throw it on and become something else at will. Become a predator. A creature that hunted without peer.

It appeared Cassie was one of those. A badass.

It wasn't going to be hard to stop saying Cassie anymore. In fact, I made a mental note to strike it from my thoughts. To really start calling her Cass. When I spoke to her, spoke to others. Even when I just thought about Cass in my mind.

I had a sense now of what it would be like, if I made a real enemy of her.

CHAPTER TEN

————————

There was a sense of stillness in the bar. The air, stirred by the ceiling fans above, moved quietly. Furtively. As if the currents themselves slunk around the place, circling, touching upon me only occasionally, as if the air was hiding too.

It felt like I was in the eye of a massive storm, a protective circle, and though it was quiet now, there were shrieking winds in the distance. Blowing icy, pelting rain drops that dented roofs, cars, people. The gusts whipped around wildly, they circled and searched and hunted. The eye was safe, but outside the storm stalked me, tossing aside buildings and bodies, growing ever closer.

I got up, breaking the hold the invisible tempest had on me. Moved across Bubba's, stepping around one of the dead rugby fans. His black-and-white polo shirt was spotted with a couple large, red, dots.

Cassie checked out Whistler and Reid. Our shoes made the same crunching sounds on the floor theirs had. There was glass everywhere, from the bottles behind the bar, to the shattered front windows, the large panes that had separated the bar from the street.

Cassie pulled out a couple of wallets from the dead Remainers and put them in her purse. Added their phones. Reid ended up being a smaller kid, maybe eighteen or so, with fuzz on his cheeks and surfer's blonde hair.

There'd be no more surfing for the kid now. They breed them to hate young, in the Remainers. I felt neither good nor bad about it. I wasn't the type of guy who liked killing, but I also wasn't the type of guy to avoid it. Life and death held a weird kind of meaning for me, I had seen so much of each, throughout my own life, that I could easily have been overwhelmed by the sheer amount of it.

I didn't think about death any more than I thought about life. There's a reason I didn't go around holding a newborn baby in my arms anymore. A reason I actively avoided doing that very thing. A tiny babe in your arms evoked too much, the smell of talcum powder, the gurgling laugh, the smile of innocence. Bright eyes, new to the world, staring at you, bringing everything into a tiny mind.

Those kinds of feelings are best left undisturbed.

Instead, I looked across the street. There was a row of shops there, one or two stories high. The second story of one had a window up. If I focused, I could see the slant of a rifle poking up out of the dark room behind it. Where a person had suddenly released it upon death.

Cassie—*Cass*, was a little scary.

I stared at the window, calculated the distance. Kept pressing the bartender's rag against my cheek, occasionally glancing at it to see if there was new blood. I'd have another scar to add to the collection.

At least it would look cool.

Cass tapped me on shoulder, nodded outside.

We hurried out of the bar.

The street was empty. The cars on the street were empty. Everyone had fled. A few bodies lay in the street, not moving, that I could tell. Back towards my hotel, at the corner of the block, one car had T-boned another. The blue fender crumpled up on the first car, the red side-panels of the second car all dented in. Both cars lay across the intersection, there were other cars stopped around them, but all the car doors were open, and drivers long gone.

Here and there a face appeared. Someone hiding, behind a closed door, a shut window, poking out their head, or holding their cellphones up from where they hid, camera lenses pointed outward.

Far to the north called the faint sound of a siren, warbling in the distance. The police, finally coming. Maybe help, maybe more Remainers. The sound had me move faster, but Cass actually stopped me. Asked me to wait, while she rushed into the building with the sniper. I saw her outline briefly in the window, as she flipped something over. Then a few more items went into her purse.

She'd have to get a larger bag in the future, if she kept shooting the way she had.

The thought made me laugh. The laugh was almost a giggle, or a snicker, or some mixture of both, maybe a gicker. Or a sniggle. I realized I was a little manic. I guessed most people got that way, after a shootout.

Cass came back down, hurrying out the door and into the street. We walked south, away from the alarms. The sun had risen, it was noon, and the humidity and the heavy salt smell of the ocean air was all I could feel and breathe. The thick scent clogged my nose, the heat beat down on my skin, and instantly a sweat broke on my temples.

There's a reason I hated this town.

I want to blame Charleston for the sweat, the heat and humidity, but likely it was a post-stress type of reaction. My body's response after being wound up, now finally relaxing in a shuddering kind of sigh. After all, I hadn't sweated on my way to Bubba's, and it had been almost as hot and humid then. The only difference seemed to be I just hadn't been getting shot at then.

We kept walking, turning here and there, heading down the blocks in a zig-zag pattern, each zig bringing us closer to the beach. There was a breeze on the zigs, coming in from the ocean from the east, bringing the salty smell of the sea. The breeze chilled the sweat on my skin and helped me to feel even more clammy.

It wasn't far before we started seeing people again, most of them looking back the way we had come, standing in the sidewalk, talking to each other. The first few groups tried to talk with us, but Cass kept saying things like "they've got guns" in a pretend-panicked voice, and that phrase got people to cut out their chit-chat.

Though everywhere we went, people had their phones out. I was sure the two of us were in a number of pictures and videos. Man I hated those things (saying don't blame me just sounds like a broken record, but *really*... don't).

I wanted to go back to my hotel, but Cass turned that down, saying the Remainers could have someone there. And she was probably right, but I still wanted to go there. Even though there wasn't anything there I really needed.

There wasn't anything in my room I had to have. Just a sense of leaving things behind, that feeling got to me. Normally it never did, and I didn't like it.

I did have a few more of the bulletproof suits there. It would be nice to have a few of those to change into. Maybe one or two other things I had stolen reality for. Things I liked to have around, so I'd have to steal some reality again, at some point. After Cass left, likely. I could already see *that* argument happening.

"We're going to have to get that looked at," Cass said, looking at me.

I realized I was leaning on her a little. And I was still pressing the rag against my face as we walked. The wound stung a bit, but it wasn't deep. "It'll heal," I said.

"Not that one," she said, and pointedly glanced down at my ribs.

I looked down. Some of the stitches around the wound in my ribs must have broken. The light shirt now had a red blotch spreading out under my chest, so the angry mouth was open now.

I hadn't felt any pain. Maybe that was because I was still in some kind of shock from the gunfight. Once I saw the blood, though, the pain kicked in. A sharp hot stinging, accompanied by a warmish wetness on my skin.

"Dammit," I said, shrugging out of my jacket. Keeping it away from the blood soaking through the shirt.

"We'll get a doc," she said.

I shook my head. "I'm not letting anyone near me. It's too easy for someone to stab me if I'm shot up with painkillers."

Cass looked at me, with that arched eyebrow of hers. Not saying anything, but conveying.

"Yes," I said. "I understand the irony."

Still, I'd have to do something. Sew the wound shut again. At least that was something I was practiced at. Though the clamminess had me worried. My fingers shook a little. Maybe I was lower on blood than I thought.

"You haven't magicked something up that keeps you healed?" Cass asked. "I thought that was your thing."

I shook my head. I wish it was that easy. I mean, I talked about all the ways I had tried to live forever. The wrinkly me and the multi-colored one. Those were just a few of the realities I had stolen from. I mean, there are an infinite number of universes out there. At some point, you lose the patience to try them all. You just want something that works.

So I made it easy. Found the reality where the Fountain of Youth existed. Stole the fountain and jumped in it. One call, that's all. Easy-peasy.

Now I could live forever. But healing took time, even for me. The universe is a big place all on its own. It's hard for the human mind to really grasp, how big infinity is. You really stretch the bounds of under-standing, if you say there's actually an infinite number of infinitely large universes. The mind just can't grasp infinity on its own. Infinity times infinity? That's something children tease each other with.

I'm rubber and you're glue, whatever you say bounces off me and sticks to you... times infinity.

We say it, but we don't understand it. Not as a kid. Not as an adult. Not ever.

Looking for a particular universe was like digging through a moving box for a specific picture you wanted to hang. Or the screwdriver to hang it with. Or a can opener, because you're starving and the can of Beanee Weenees is mocking you. Or maybe you need that automatic thing that opens wine bottles, because it's midnight and you just want to celebrate for a moment.

Maybe you're looking for the wine.

So you're looking for the right box in the truck, looking for that thing you knew you had packed somewhere but couldn't find. Except, in my case, the truck was infinitely big. It held countless boxes. So even though I had the wine bottle thingy I still needed to find the right box holding the bottle of freaking wine. (Stick with me here, I know people don't pack wine bottles in moving boxes, but I have been drinking, so the allusion works, at least for me.)

Always, always, to find what I needed I had to open every box until I found it. In the infinitely large moving truck. I had to take a peek and search through all the old clothes, all the good dinner bowls, turning each box away before moving on to the next. And on and on, looking for that one box I needed. That held the one item I was looking for.

I might get lucky sometimes, because I knew that area over there was all stuff for the garage, and that area in the truck was where I had packed the office supplies, but otherwise, the search was all.

Think about doing that yourself. How many boxes would you open, looking for that one painting? That can of Beanee Weenees? That bottle of wine? Maybe you're hungry, or really want a drink, so you think you're dedicated. Maybe you open twenty boxes. Thirty. Fifty.

What about ten thousand? Would you open that many before quitting? Be honest here, because I'm telling you, I'd have given up nine thousand and nine hundred boxes ago. Probably.

And ten thousand was on the short side of infinity. The universe was a big place. With an infinite number of universes. Something hard to picture, and the only thing that even gets you close is however big you think it is, it's bigger than that.

And bigger than that.

And bigger than that.

So, digging through one box didn't quite capture what I did when I looked for other realities. Digging through a truck of boxes didn't either. Not even one infinitely large moving truck.

I liked the moving box analogy though. I thought I'd keep it. Maybe it was like a box of files, and that box was infinite number of boxes. Maybe the box was put together and filled in some factory, maybe each box rolled down some assembly line, one behind the other, an endless conveyor of boxes, robotic arms cramming all of them with handfuls of universes.

A better description. Imagine walking into a factory, something with a huge warehouse floor, concrete and dark. The floor stretching far into the distance, the area bigger than any football field, with bright fluorescent lights hung high overhead, row after row of lights, repeating so many times all you could see was each assembly line, one after the next, repeating so many times, for so long, you couldn't see the opposite wall.

All of the lines held countless boxes. They run by you, from left to right, each belt carrying boxes past you. The conveyor belts only stopping for each robotic arm to cram more realities into the box underneath the arm.

Each of those lines was infinitely long, so long you couldn't see the beginning or end of any of them. You just stood in the middle of them somewhere, watching an army of robotic arms move in synchronous motion, stuffing every box full of more realities, the box moving to the next arm, that arm pushing more realities in, and the next arm pushing more realities in, and the next arm pushing even more realities in, until the cardboard of the box almost split.

And still, the belts kept running. The boxes kept coming. Kept moving past you. Kept heading into the distance.

So looking for something specific in all of that? When every reality I could access, was one of an infinite number of realities? When the universes were all stuck together in unlabeled boxes, packed in some factory somewhere, with an infinite number of assembly lines cramming reality after reality into box after box across a never-ending warehouse floor?

I sniggled again. Or gickered.

I had drank too much. Or lost more blood than I thought. Or a combination of both.

I took a breath, tried to make sure that breath didn't turn into some kind of gicker-sniggle. Took a few more. The air seemed to even me out. I returned to the present. I was still walking, and my feet still felt loose, walking, so I focused on them a bit. Cass was looking at me funny, her hand was on my arm, and I wondered how much time had passed.

You can lose time, thinking about infinity. It's just bigger than anything you can grasp, and when you have the ability to look in every single box that's ever been built, every reality in every box in every factory, you can lose a lot of time.

Still, the eye-opening thing about all the boxes and assembly lines in the factory, all the arms stuffing all the realities into them, the thing that will really blow your mind as you look for that one reality in that one box, as you look over an infinite number of boxes scrolling by you on an infinite number of assembly lines, is when you realized there was *also* an infinite number of factories.

Try finding one wine bottle in all of that.

"It's tougher than you think," I said. "Finding realities."

"I thought you just did *this*." She made the little motion with the fingers of her free hand, the one I usually did before I stole something.

"I wish," I said. I focused on my feet. They kept getting loose. Like the sidewalk moved right before the sole of my shoe touched down on it. I had to place each foot carefully.

I had been in shock before. More times than I could count. Enough that I was practiced at functioning through it. I was worried, because I knew I had lost more blood than I thought. I pressed the bloody hand towel against my side, feeling the warmth of the blood spread across my belly, the sharp warm pain becoming a piercingly hot kind of pain.

"It's tougher than you think," I said. Or repeated. I wasn't sure.

"Explain it," she said. I didn't think she was listening. I thought she was talking to me, just to keep me awake. Her arm had snaked around me a little, helping keep me steady. Maybe she was trying to distract me from the pain.

I tried. I gave her the moving box analogy. I didn't think she got it, and I didn't know if it was because of how I explained it, or because I was in a deeper state of shock than I realized, or if infinity really couldn't be grasped, unless you stood in the middle of it.

Cass's arm tightened around mine. Maybe I was having trouble with more than just explaining infinity. She looked at me, multiple times, with a puzzled, or maybe a worried expression.

I ended up giving up on the factory analogy halfway through. Maybe using the boxes was a bad way to go about it. Maybe it sounded crazy.

I was leaning more on Cass now. That was quick. We kind of walked together down the street. The sidewalk kept moving underneath my shoes.

Tricky, tricky sidewalk.

"We've got to get away from these people," she muttered. I didn't think she was talking to me.

An alley opened up, leading away from the beach. Cass directed me in there and leaned me back against a wall. It felt sturdy, against my back. Each of the buildings on either side was a tall enough that the alley was shadowed, though it smelled a little musty, a little wet and moldy. An ammonia-like scent, light though. Maybe people used this place as a bathroom, after a night at the bars.

"You okay?"

I nodded. My head felt a little loose, a little light on my neck. My temple still beaded in sweat. "Probably."

Cass unbuttoned my shirt, swore when she saw the wound. She didn't like the way the mouth stared at her, either. Maybe it was just angry at everyone. (I did not sniggle-gicker here, I promise.)

"Did you stitch this shut?" she asked.

I gave her a loopy kind of grin and nodded. I had a lot of practice, stitching myself up. Thousands of years of it. I felt like I could handle a needle and thread alright.

Cass shook her head though. Everyone's a critic. Then she gave me the fisheye. "Can you hang out right here?"

I nodded.

"Promise me," she said.

"Promise," I said, solemnly. The kind of promise a drunk guy might make. The kind of promise that the person you were promising knew you might not keep. But I figured I'd stay. Nothing better to do. Me and angry mouth would strike up a conversation, maybe. He might even tell me why he kept throwing up red on my shirt.

Cass frowned. Or maybe that was her natural state. Honestly, I hadn't seen anything to tell me otherwise.

"I'll be right back." She pressed my hand with the towel against my side, hard. It didn't hurt so much now, and I tried to hold it there. Then she disappeared, quickly. Turned left down the street, back the way we had come.

Which was smart, the universe was a big place. If you didn't go down the ways you knew, you could get off-course quick.

CHAPTER ELEVEN

Getting lost was easy to do, if you were searching for a certain reality. When I first had learned about what I could do, it had been a parlor trick of sorts. I could make something appear in my hand. I could magic up a new bottle of wine. A snake, where no snake had been before. An apple, in my hand. Snakes became horses. Chairs became boats.

It took a long time before I figured out I wasn't creating things, but stealing them. That had been a countless number of thefts later, I was sure. At least thousands. After all those times of stealing random things from random universes, I had found out how big the world I lived in really was. How many other worlds existed, almost just like mine, all packed together into a universe that was packed next to an infinite amount of other universes. With all of those stuffed into just one box, with countless boxes before and after them, on countless conveyor belts, until it all seemed to go on forever...

You could get lost, searching for something, among all that.

Sometimes, like when I found the bulletproof jacket, it all lined up just right. I'd watch a movie, see a guy with a bulletproof jacket, *want* that same jacket, and that reality would appear in my mind. In the moving box analogy, I just happened to be in the right factory, next to the right conveyor belt, with the exact box I needed on the belt in front of me, open. The reality I needed being the first one, right on top of the box.

It was rare, but those times happened. It was all easy, crystal clear. It was as simple as reaching directly into that reality and pulling out what I wanted.

Pulling, stealing, exchanging, whatever you wanted to call it.

Other times, like the storm this morning, were just as easy. Just in a different way. The reality with the storm was loud, it out-shouted the other worlds and universes. The box that storm reality was packed in was larger than all the other boxes, that box stood tall and loomed over every box around it. The storm-universe reality was like a magnet, it could pull your thoughts directly to it, if you didn't consciously will yourself away from that reality.

It was why I thought it moved, from world to world. This destructive storm, eating away at the world it existed in, until it was pulled into another world. Where it could begin its meal anew. Consuming everything, like a black hole, and only getting larger. Until the storm was the only thing left, a string of empty realities behind it.

Hell, I was always a romantic.

The lime was easy too, just in a different way. The way I used the most. There were an infinite number of Bubba's in an infinite number of universes. Most of those realities had limes, because it was a natural thing for bars to be stocked with. Common things stayed common across the realities. And because most bars always had limes, lemons, cherries, well-stocked liquor shelves, those universes were easy to find because there were an infinite number of them.

So, you can see how the lime was easy. Because it was common. And the closer the other reality to mine, the easier to steal, because they were so close to being the same, it was just like reaching my hand in and pulling out a piece of fruit.

Abracadabra.

Here, you could easily take my argument and present the counter. Trust me, I have done the same to myself, many times. You'd say something like, *sure, there are an infinite number of bars, all well-stocked with limes, but aren't there also an infinite number of bars that also have run out of limes, too?*

Exactly. You're one hundred percent correct.

There's the same amount of bars with limes as there are without. An infinite amount. You're just going to have to trust me, when there are that many, it's easy to pick the ones that are *with*. It's like a feeling, or an intuition, maybe. I knew, if I looked on the conveyor belt of boxes of universes to the right, none of those would have limes. I could almost see the stamps on the boxes, like something the post office would place on the outside of each box, in bold red letters, *No Perishable Foods Allowed*.

But all these belts to the left, they all have plenty of limes. The boxes almost burst with them. I could *feel* it.

Finding something specific, something maybe more unique to that world, something other than a common green citrus fruit, that was the hard thing to what I did. Incredibly hard. It took discipline, to keep searching through the infinite number of universes without getting overwhelmed by the number. Without getting lost in the search.

Sometimes I could get lucky, pick the right line, pick the right box in that line. Like when I had found the world with a real Fountain of Youth. There aren't an infinite number of those, and it took some time to find, and–if I'm being honest–I kind of just stumbled into that reality on a bit of luck.

I've told you about all the easy times. Most of the time though, finding something really specific was impossibly hard. So hard that some universe that I had found before, I never found again. That fountain reality was long gone, it appeared it wasn't one in a million realities, or one in a billon, but just one out of an *infinite* number of realities. However I had stumbled on it before, I wasn't going to stumble on it again.

Hard to grasp, I know.

The universe is just that big.

Blake had understood, though. She had gotten my box analogy. Even had one of her own. It had reminded her of her father, taking her out to the fields on their farm, late at night. With all the stars brilliantly lit overhead. Her father had challenged her to count them all, and every time she came back with a number, he would just shake his head and tell her there were more than that.

She had understood the boxes. I liked her stars thing though. I'd have switched to it if I could, but I kind of understood things the way I understood them, and that was hard to change.

I mean, we all stand out and look at the stars. Wonder what's out there. Wonder what more there could be. And for all of us, there's a slight twinge of uneasiness in the back of our minds, because we know what we're looking at is really just a small part of everything that's really out there, and we can never fully grasp that the universe extends far beyond the constellations in our skies.

Man I can really drift sometimes. I guess that's what infinity does to you. You ever do it? Think about what's out there, all the different combinations and worlds and galaxies and what the word infinite really means?

Just me?

A pain twinged along my side. Faint, but enough to have me open my eyes. I hadn't realized I had closed them. I felt cold, and the beads of sweat on my forehead had evaporated, without being replaced by more.

I didn't think that was a good sign.

Cass was back. The twinge was her moving my hand from my side. I wondered if she was proud of me for not going anywhere. I seemed to have kept one promise.

She was kneeling in front of me. My nice shirt was unbuttoned and the side that was soaked in blood tucked up under my arm, the bundle of linen there warm and wet and sticky. I was leaning back against the alley wall, the plaster side of the wall a little cool against my lower back. She poured rubbing alcohol on a towel and wiped my wound with it. There was some slight stinging. I thought it should hurt more.

I still wanted her to understand. Maybe Blake's analogy was better.

"Imagine the biggest universe you can."

She paused what she was doing and looked up at me. "What?"

"Just imagine it," I said. "You're out in a field somewhere, looking up at the night sky. Counting stars. Realizing there are more stars than you can count. But still, you keep counting, right?"

Maybe Cass had other conversations, in the store she had gone to. Other thoughts than mine. Maybe she was having trouble getting back to the infinity thing. The explanation of the factory, why it was hard to look for certain realities. With why what I did wasn't the easiest thing to figure out.

She shook her head, and kept working on the wound, but I thought she was listening. I told her what Blake had told me. About the stars, and their father taking Blake out to the fields to look at them.

That story seemed to make Cass angry. Her forehead was scrunched up, and I could tell she had stopped listening. Maybe I just couldn't explain it right.

Though now that I thought about it, they had different mothers. That was something Blake had mentioned to me, once upon a time. I hadn't talked with Cass a lot before, because well, it was pretty apparent she didn't like me.

Had they left the farm by the time Cass had been born? Had their reality changed, and their father changed into some daily trader, instead of working a farm? Or something else, or me?

"So you're counting these stars," I said. "But you also know those stars are just the ones you can see. That there are millions more, just in our galaxy. Billions, maybe."

"Okay," Cass said, the word coming slow. *O-kaayyyy*. Like she was humoring me without really listening. She was focused on what she was doing. There was a white plastic bag next to her, on the ground, and she pulled out a box of the non-stick pads, as large as they came. She liberally laid those over the wound, layered them over each other, and then had me hold those there while she grabbed a roll of duct tape.

"So you're counting these stars," I said. "Each time one appears. But you also know these stars are the smallest number of stars in this galaxy. That more will appear. So you keep counting, and the sky keeps getting a little brighter, with every star you count."

"Sure," she said.

I didn't think she was doing it. She was winding the duct tape around my stomach and pulling it tight. But maybe she was listening. I kept trying to explain.

"So you're counting. And stars keep showing up," I said. "There are billions. You realize you're never going to stop counting. The stars keep appearing, the night sky keeps getting brighter, and then there's many that it's bright as day."

Cass paused and looked at me. Maybe she had been listening. Maybe I had explained something correctly. And then I realized she was hiding a smile. "That many?"

"That many," I said. "And how hard is it to find something, to find one star, when the whole night sky is that bright? When you realize that there are still more stars out there. More galaxies. There are millions more. Trillions..."

You could do the same thing with galaxies as you did with the stars. Think of as many as you can, spiral-shaped creatures, stars flung out along their arms, radiation bursting from their centers, where the sheer number of suns created large beams of light that shouted out across the vast emptiness of space. Pack all those galaxies into your mind.

Then keep packing.

I could see I lost her. Again. It had to be me. I just couldn't explain it.

"As big as the universe is," I muttered, my voice low, repeating something Blake had told me. "It's always bigger than that."

Cass tore the duct tape from the roll. It ripped with a quick zipper-like sound. Then she wound the last bit of tape around me. It was going to pull the shit out of the hair on my chest when we finally took it off. Unless I just always kept the duct tape on me. Like a second skin.

Cass stood up. She had a sports drink bottle in her hand. The kind they give athletes to replenish performance. A big bottle filled with something blue, like Artic Mountain Blast or some shit like that. It tasted pale, and wasn't sweet enough, the flavor was a lot like overripe blueberries.

She made me drink all of it.

"You're saying there's no place to go to magic up a new body," Cass said. She actually had been listening. "Or there isn't a place where nanobots exist, where you could put those into your body, have them repair your wound."

I shook my head. "That's not what I'm saying," I said. "Those places exist. Those *realities* exist. But finding that one universe, among all the universes with all the limes and all the universes without the limes, it's impossible, most of the time."

I was mixing my analogies. Maybe you understand. But Cass's frown grew. She placed the back of her hand on my forehead. Like my mom used to do, long, long, long ago. "Limes?"

I pushed her hand away. I felt a little better. Maybe not as out of it. My head didn't wobble so much on my neck.

I tried explaining why what I did was difficult in a different way.

Maybe in a more concrete way, that Cass would understand. One last try for the Gipper.

"How you shoot," I said. "How'd you get to be that good with a gun?"

The arched eyebrow came back. "Practice," she said.

"But there was more than that, too, right?"

"Practice," she said again. Then a moment later. "Desire. Drive. Maybe some natural talent, I guess."

She said the last as if she was a little embarrassed about it, oddly enough.

I pressed. "Still, there was something else. Or *someone* else, right? Someone had to show you how, train you how to hold a gun. A person with a lot of experience with a gun who could help you get better. Point out little tips and tricks."

"Oh," she said, her eyes opening a little wider. As if she finally got it. "Of course. Someone showed me the ropes."

People may have talent, may not, but it would be hard to just pick a gun up and be as good as Cass was, even if they were the most naturally gifted shooter on the plant. It was always easier if someone helped show you the way.

Something I had never had, with what I did. For all I knew, there was no one else like me. You would think I would have found that someone.

The universe was a big place.

I think I told you, it would have been nice to have a purpose. I used to believe I had one, but that had been long ago, in the beginning. Now, after thousands of years of falling for the prank, I thought I was more of a cosmic joke. A random act. There was no one else like me. Just me, stuffed in a box, crammed between countless other realities, those worlds all the better because in them I didn't exist.

Which is why there wasn't a person to train me. Show me the ropes. Help me understand what I can do, and *why*.

"Exactly," I told Cass. My voice less shaky, more firm. "Must be nice."

CHAPTER TWELVE

Somehow we got moving again. Cass had more sports drinks in her bag, and I finished another. Still the same taste of overripe blueberries. I swigged it a couple of times, wiped my mouth with the back of my hand, and leaned forward, off the alley wall.

When had that become the thing holding me up?

My knees loosened a bit, so I forced my legs straight. Walked a few steps like I was walking on stilts, Cass keeping one hand on my arm.

"You good?"

Was I? Sure.

She had a shirt in the bag. A white cotton t-shirt, the cheap kind you get at a convenience store, or local pharmacy. This one had a surfboard across the back, right in front of a crashing blue wave, and little sand creatures like crabs and fish dotting the front of the shirt. And not just those.

I peered closer at one of the patterns and rolled my eyes.

"What?" She took a closer look.

Those little monsters, the sea horse thingies. That's what. "Nothing."

Cass looked closer though, bringing the front of it right to her eyes. Then she let out a little gasp. "Those aren't dolphins."

"Nope," I said. *Those are something to frighten little kids, if they don't finish their dinner.* "They are not."

The shirt rolled around in her fingers, as she went from one colored sea horse to another. "What the hell are they?"

"Something that shouldn't exist," I said. "At least not in this world."

Cass shook her head. "This was part of the morning, then?"

I nodded. The storm switch. Took a final swig of the second sports drink, pushing my tongue out of my mouth a few times, like I was pushing out the taste.

"Dolt." She made me take off my nice dress shirt, with the big red splotch on the side. Cass took the dress shirt, balled it up and put it into the grocery bag, and handed me the t-shirt.

I tugged the seahorsey shirt on. My side twinged a bit. The bluish sea horse monsters went well with my granite slacks. Maybe I'd start a new fashion. They could call it seahorsey-slate. All the models from the under the sea would love it.

Cass was looking at me funny. Her hand and went back to my arm, and her fingers felt overly tight. "You sure you're good?"

"Yeah," I said. My side throbbed like someone had hit it with a fifty-pound hammer. A Fifty-pound hammer covered in sharp needles of ice. "Let's get off the street. I'll sew this up again, be right as rain."

Maybe I could even be as right as the rain that morning. The storm, that kind of vengeful fury. Unabated. Unrelenting. Something even the Remainers might pause at. Give me a break from being chased.

We staggered out of the alley, me leaning on Cass more than I thought I would need to. After a few steps we started getting a good rhythm, we walked like we were in one of those three-legged races that all the work picnics have. Where they put two people together that don't really like one another and watch them stumble to the finish line together.

I smiled to myself, looking at Cass.

Her face was still all kinds of frowny. And when she caught me smiling, her brows came down even harder. "What?"

My grin got wider. "I don't think I can explain it."

Or that I should.

"If it's like the moving stars or unpacking boxes or whatever else." Cass paused a second, shifting her shoulder under mine. She held the grocery bag in one hand, her other hand wrapped around my back and got a little too close to my wound. But it was enough to keep me up. "Then please don't."

"You got it, chief," I said.

The brief time in the alley had given me a rest. It helped that the alley was cooler than the bright sunlight of day. Which I discovered again, as soon as we hit the street. Torn black clouds drifted overhead, just a few here and there, strange with the brilliant yellow sun burning in the blue sky. It was almost like this world was a blend of the two realities of the morning, the sunny day I had woke to, and the remnants of the storm I had brought into this world.

Bright sun, black clouds, a breeze that kept up its morning flutter, sometimes there, sometimes not, and definitely not enough to keep me cool. The skin on my face felt like it wanted to sweat, but couldn't. I focused on putting one foot in front of the other and allowed Cass to direct where we headed. Luckily, we didn't have to work our way through the crowd of people on either sidewalk. Apparently they saw us way in advance and steered clear.

We were definitely recognizable. It wouldn't take long for any kind of detective to track us here, after Bubba's. Whatever time we were trying to get for ourselves, it wasn't going to be much.

One foot, then the other. That was the rhythm. The first, then the second. I just focused on that. A two-step kind of thing. As long as I stayed focused, no matter how long it took, we'd get to where we needed to go. Even in the three-legged race from hell. So, one foot, then the next. First the first, then the second. Now the third.

Wait, was that three feet?

That was apparently one too many.

Shit.

Cass caught me with a grunt, before we all went down.

"That's it," she said. "We got to get off the streets."

"Not far enough," I said, my teeth clenched, basically to keep me from screaming. We were still too close to where the Remainers had found us.

Cass's hand made a nice counterpoint though. Her fingers had dug into my side, right next to the wound, and that area felt like someone held a blowtorch right under my ribcage. The pain was... exquisitely unique. I couldn't pinpoint the pain, it was too large, too hot. Too burny. "They're going to find us."

Cass was looking towards the beach. Like all beaches, with tourism, there was the ocean, a long strip of sand, crowded with tourists and people taking their one week of vacation a year. Between the beach and the block we were on was a long row of hotels, block after block of them, all set up to take advantage of the season. I had stayed at one of them, a few streets more north of where we were.

"We've got to get you patched up," she said. "Then we can move on."

"Not far enough," I said again. I knew it, it was the same type of feel I had when I found the exact reality I was looking for. An intuition, born of long use. Born of running for a long time and knowing when the predator was close. Like a fox, chased by hounds, their panting breaths, the padded steps hitting the ground as the pack ran, their sharp teeth scraping the back of my neck... I could almost hear the braying.

"We're going to have to risk it," Cass said. Looking at me funny for maybe the fifteenth time. "Maybe they were the only Remainers in the area."

I laughed, but it was more of a snort of a laugh, then anything from the belly. Not a sniggle, thankfully.

"Look," she said. "You think we're going to be able to get on a plane, or a bus, or anything else, with you in that condition?"

She had a point.

"Why not split up?" I asked.

"What?"

"Split up," I said. "Look, we both know why we're here. What we want to do. But there's no reason for you to go down with me."

I pulled in a shuddering breath. That seemed a lot for me to say, with the blowtorch someone had wedged into my side. But Cass splitting up from me made sense. We both wanted revenge for her sister. Not only to kill the person who had killed Blake, but whatever secret they were protecting, we were going to take that too. One of us should do it, even if the other fell.

She looked at me a long time. "You're not thinking straight."

I gave out a gicker. *Dammit*.

"Of course I'm not," I said, trying to explain, but having a hard time with the pain digging into my side. "There's an effing blowtorch in my ribs."

Cass cursed, as if she realized what was happening. Her hand relaxed where it was holding me, slid up to my armpit. And the blowtorch feeling went away a bit. It was a large enough relief that my legs relaxed a little, and I almost sunk to the ground, and would have, had Cass not caught me, her hand tugging up under my arm.

I struggled to stay standing. I struggled to take a breath. Then another. Breathing seemed easier, now that the blowtorch wasn't burning my side.

"Look," I said. Cass had been meeting me this morning, she had gotten some information about what Blake had found. But the three guys who had found me were dead, no one else had seen us, so she should be safe going back. Being just another Remainer cell, out there.

"Just help me find a place. Leave me there. Then get back, so at least one of us make it out."

She sighed, a *you're not getting it* type of breath. "There's going to be pictures, videos out there."

"Video?" I still wasn't getting it.

"Yeah," she said. "All the cell phones, you think some of those aren't going to have you and me on them? Together?"

I got it then. I did really hate those things. "Dammit."

"Yeah," Cass said. "Dammit."

She was stuck with me. She had realized it, even if I hadn't. We had been a loose team to begin with, coming together because of Blake. Figuring out why she had been killed. Who had killed her. And what Blake had found that had triggered both of those events.

"They'll recognize you?" I asked. I knew Cass was a Remainer. I didn't know how deep she was in with them.

She didn't quite answer. "They'll know I was with you."

Which she had only been because we had figured out who had killed her. And we were going to plan out revenge, at Bubbas. It was more of an initial meeting, really, we hadn't quite got to the details.

"What about..." Cass made the motion with her fingers.

"You *want* me to?" I asked.

"If it's a last resort type of thing," she said. "Then yes."

"You know they'll find us anyway," I said. However they were doing it, they could tell when I changed reality. And they found me faster.

"Yeah," she said. "But if you can give us some time, we can patch you up, and then figure out the next step."

I looked out over the crowd. The people, all headed to the beach. From the beach. In and out of the little dive bars and restaurants over the place, sipping on margaritas and fruity rum concoctions, laughing and joking, the scratching thwacks of flip-flops hitting the sidewalk.

And me, styling the seahorsey-granite fall lineup.

Maybe I could do two things at once.

"I can," I told her. "But you're not going to like it."

Her mouth became a thin line. "I'm not going to like it anyway."

Well, that was fair enough.

"Get us to that hotel," I said, picking the closest one out at the beach. Not one of the thirty or forty story hotels, the tall palaces of glittering glass windows and white stone edges. This hotel was five or six stories high, painted with the same tan stucco plaster a lot of the generic places had. A red roof-shape sign hung on a tall poll at its front, with a letter board below the sign. The board had white and black words on it, arranged to spell out *Free Beach Chair with Your Stay! Only $250 a night!*

Not a place I would normally stay. I usually liked a few more amenities than a free beach chair.

Cass pulled me through the crowd. I could hear the crashing of the surf over the sand, as we got closer to the hotel. The calling of waves as they wore down the shore.

The press of people got thicker, even just the block or so we were from the beach, as if everyone was funneling down the blocks and heading to the dunes. People bumped us all the time, most of them not paying attention. A lot of them face down on their cell phones.

It was funny, no matter how many realities I switched, cell phones were a constant. Like every universe was plagued with them. I might have brought the first ones over, but I think they were going to make it here anyway. So honestly, let's not blame me for them. They're like cockroaches. They're everywhere.

A young man walked right into us, almost knocking me down. He was one of the heads-down crowd, wearing a pair of white seahorsey shorts that he probably didn't remember buying, and no shirt, flashing his pecs and abs to everyone.

Cass almost dropped me, swore, then kicked the man in his shin. Hard enough he almost dropped his phone.

He cursed and looked at us, his eyes flashing, his free hand balling up into a fist. His eyes caught Cass's eyes though, and he paused. The three of us stood there, gumming up the funnel, the crowd pressing in around us. I felt Cass shift beside me, and wondered if she was going into terminator mode.

Maybe the young man felt the same thing, had even seen the same move, because he quickly muttered an apology and walked around.

I had no idea how a woman all of a hundred pounds could do that.

We got to the door of the hotel. A thick glass door, the kind made for the occasional heavy winds. Cass was able to prop that open long enough to work me into the entryway, a little square area, maybe ten feet wide. The two of us were in a little glass box, with a second glass door separating us from the hotel lobby. There were tiny smudges of handprints on the glass there. Fudgy smudges. As if some kid had been eating ice cream with his hands, before trying to push open the door.

I let out a sigh. It was cooler in here. Though for some reason I was sweating now.

"Okay," she said. Watching expectantly. Like someone in the crowd right before David Copperfield disappeared the Statue of Liberty.

I know you want to know if I helped with that. I can't say, one way or the other. Though I will say I met David Copperfield and liked the cut of his jib.

I'm wandering again. It might be hard for you to follow. The usually happens when I drink. I guess it also seems to happen when I lose a lot of blood.

Cass's eyebrows were raised. As if I had been standing there too long. I took a long breath and let it out, felt the pain radiating from my side, leaned back against the wall in the little cubicle-like entryway. Turned my head from the fudgy handprints on the inside glass door, and back outside.

Watched all the people walking back and forth. The kids screaming and running around. The cocktail drinkers, the book carriers, the young girls with the tight bikinis and the beach guys following them, everyone with those effing towels with that fucking seahorsey thing.

They all passed the hotel, walked into the dune area separating the blocks of the city with the beach. The tall thin reeds, the scrub of brush that always lay right behind the shore. The reeds fluttered a bit, and their shadows fluttered with it. Dark shadows, on a bright sand. Dark clouds, under a bright sun.

Cass wanted time. She didn't care how much, something to give us a breather. She was right, I wasn't going to make it out of here without getting fixed up a bit. And I needed to make it out of here, because I needed to make what happened with Blake right. For a guy who could live forever, Blake's memory was going to stick with me a long time, because it had been one of those once-in-a-lifetime type feelings.

Maybe those just did hit you once. Whether you lived fifty years or five thousand. Maybe there was just one soulmate for us all, one true love, and when you lose them, everyone else is just a poor imitation of that person.

"Gavin," Cass said. I expected her voice to sound rough, but for some reason it was gentle.

She was right. If we were going to get revenge, we needed to patch me up. Then get out of us here. I knew a way we could get us that time.

I closed my eyes. Made a little finger-waggling motion. I didn't have to do that, but I usually did. Maybe because it was how Cass thought of it, though I wouldn't swear to that.

Anyway, I did it, like I was turning a knob, changing a channel. Finding a sure way to get us some time.

And I brought back the storm.

CHAPTER THIRTEEN

ONE MOMENT, THERE WAS THAT PRESS OF PEOPLE. COCKTAIL drinkers, with tall plastic see-through glasses, holding red or yellow or blue colored slushy drinks, something fruity with rum. People carrying coolers and chairs and towels. Other people carrying chairs and a book.

Some of those people had earbuds in, white ones with the white plastic ends tucked by their earlobes. Bobbing their head to some music. There were the young girls laughing, with tight bikinis showing way too much. Young men, smiling and flexing around those same young girls. All of them enjoying the bright sun and the blue sky.

The next moment they were gone. The sky was thunderously gray, so gray it was almost black. The outside glass instantly splattered with heavy, thick rain drops, drops so cold I knew they felt icy, stinging the skin. The change in the moment was instantaneous, so that the spattering of the rain sounded like the quick trigger pull of an Uzi. A brutal splat of icy bullets that struck the window, the door, the world.

Cass jumped.

And that was just the beginning. The storm raged, as if angry I had called it before and dared to put it away. A moment ago the sky had been sunny, and the next, the dark tempest.

The Uzi-pull of rain drops got louder. More insistent. The glass started to flex, under the weight of the water hitting it. The battering of the wind driving the water. It was hard to see past over the millions of drops hitting the window, but occasionally the wind blew so hard it would clear everything, the glass door, the glass window to either side, like a windshield wiper on a car.

In those moments we saw chaos.

Large blue umbrellas tumbled past us. Chairs, towels, plastic coolers battered the door and then were carried away. All of that was mixed with the rain, so that it was hard to see anything, every image happened in a sudden, mixed moment and then was gone. Occasionally there was a flash of pink skin, barely clothed, as a person ran by. Or was blown by. It was all too quick and too violent to really make anything out.

The blue sky was gone. It was nothing but black clouds. Not gray-black, but black-black. There was some light from the sun, enough so we could see, but I couldn't tell you how or why. Maybe the light came from the storm itself, something inside it, a burning fire, full of rage, a glow that radiated just enough to see the world burn underneath it.

Thunder started. Not the low rumble or roar rolling under clouds, but huge booms of cannons. Loud, like we stood right next to the cannons making the sound. The thunder went on and on, the barrels fired so fast no man could be reloading them. Not cannons though, the explosions sounded like the guns on a battleship. Those artillery cannons that fired sixteen-inch hunks of metal.

I had seen those guns fire in concert. Battleships, when they had fired all their guns broadside, the force of those explosions pushed the ship sideways in the water. It was an incredible display of power.

These explosions were like that. Every rattling boom of thunder seemed to push against the hotel. I could feel the foundation shift, maybe even start to give, as if the storm was going to push the hotel across the Earth. The building *leaned* away from the shrieking winds.

I shivered. The thunder kept booming. Lightning flashed behind it, but not little strikes. There were large, forked bolts of fiery blue electricity flaring down from the sky, sizzling through the atmosphere, striking the ground hard enough I expected to see dirt, or buildings, or people thrown up from the blow.

The lights in the hotel started to flicker, then they went out. The building shook and shivered, as if the wind and the thunder and the lightning were loosening its foundation. As if the storm battering the hotel had worked the building loose, like a child might work a loose tooth in their mouth. Back and forth, the wind toggled the building, the rain spattered the glass, and all the while the vibration of thunder rumbled and rolled along the walls, as if a low bass note rhythmically pumped underneath me.

The storm was unrelenting fury. Anger incarnate. An unabated vengeance, from an elemental monster that ate worlds.

Something slapped my cheek. Cass. She screamed something at me. I couldn't hear what it was. I was lost in the storm. The large strikes of glowing blue forks, stabbing into the ground, over and over. The wind battering the glass. The feeling of the rumbling bass, traveling the air, the ground, the walls behind me.

She slapped me again. Her mouth formed the words, *Stop, Stop, Stop,* over and over.

I got it. I understood. And I shook my head. I was tired. It was easy to get lost in this world, to the storm, to succumb. To face this kind of fury and release myself to its judgment.

Maybe that's why I had first called it, this morning. To feel the violence all around me, the test my desire to keep going under the storm's fury, and be washed away in the blink of an eye if it judged me false.

It would be easy to let go, and just let it happen.

Too easy.

I struggled to make the little finger motion. And nothing happened. Which was something that had never happened before.

I frowned and made it again. Worked hard to turn the knob. Worked hard to push this storm back into another place. Really shoved the storm into another reality, as if I was trying to push one more universe into the box of realities I had opened, cram one more shirt into a suitcase.

Normally doing this was easy. It took no energy, it didn't even need the finger-waggling motion. I just did it sometimes, just to do something. Maybe to make what I did feel more significant.

This time it was different. The walls shuddered behind me. The floor bounced under me. The tempest from another reality seemed to be eating the world. At least, that's how it felt, to a guy with a good amount of blood loss.

Maybe it was the amount of blood I had lost. Maybe I was more tired than I thought. Or maybe the storm itself fought me. Maybe the storm, having tasted this reality twice now, found it delicious, and wanted it. Wanted it all.

I closed my eyes, dug deep and *pushed*. Not literally, I wasn't in the factory trying to force one reality into a box that was overloaded with them. But metaphorically, I pushed. I found the world from this morning, where I had placed it, and I worked hard to push the storm back into that world, and trade back for the morning's reality. The striped towel world, that the seahorsey monster towel reality had replaced.

As I've said, sometimes it was more like hammering a square peg into a round hole. The edges of the block curled back, were trimmed off. Splinters split away, fell away. Bits and pieces of both realities shaved off and mixed, as I hammered at the peg harder and with greater urgency.

The storm reality started to give. To move. And like a heavy block of stone hitting a patch of ice, it went. Suddenly and completely, leaving just small pieces of itself behind, little shavings.

The trade was complete. The exchange. The theft.

Whatever you wanted to call it.

Outside, it immediately went quiet. Or I had gone deaf. I wasn't sure which. When I finally opened my eyes it was to bright beams of sunlight again. A clear blue sky. White clouds.

And I was sitting on the floor of the entry-cubicle thing. My legs flat against the floor, still leaning back against the wall. The lights of the hotel were still off, though the vibration in the foundation had stopped.

A towel lay against the outside glass, wet. A striped towel thick with sand and water and dirt. The glass of the door itself ran with raindrops, even though there was no more storm, like a thousand condensation drops racing each other down the door.

Through the glass and the raindrops, we could see an umbrella laying crooked in the dunes, the fabric torn from its spines, hanging loosely in fluttering air. Other things, chairs and coolers and more towels, lay strewn among the tall weeds. I could see the sign of the hotel, out at the corner of the lot, just the lower part. It was a blue square with the number six on it.

Cass was still standing, the plastic bag of stuff loose in one hand. I thought she actually shivered once, as if she had been goosed. She opened the door to the beach and listened for a moment. People called out to one another, shouts and questions. There was the sound of a siren, an ambulance, far in the distance. Getting closer as it made its way down the street. Echoing funny. I listened closely. Multiple sirens. Multiple ambulances.

Cass shut the door, cutting off the sounds from the outside. It was just the two of us, inside the glass cubicle. Her breathing too loud in the tiny space.

Check that, the breathing was mine. Loud and almost... whistly. I didn't think breathing should sound like that.

She was actually pale. The paleness that came from being too close to something terrifying. Something that would give you nightmares.

"My god," she said.

I sighed. It came out whistly. And then I frowned, pressing my hand to my side. Where the wound was. "You wanted time."

My voice came out hard. I had to work and push it out. The sound coming from my throat sounded, well, rocky.

Cass stared at me. The lights flickered back on. A hum came from underneath it, like the comforting rumble of a large air unit, pushing air. A light cool breeze washed across my face, from the register in the ceiling above.

It felt nice. Like I had been staring into some abyss, some fiery hell, and the air conditioning a faint reprieve. A reminder, maybe.

Cass got herself together quickly. Pulled me up, ignoring my protest. I felt the duct tape on my side, it was warm and wet and slick.

She walked us into the hotel. There was a young man at the desk, a beach kid with long hair, tan, dressed in black-striped, white shirt and a pair of dark slacks. He took a look at me and then went to say something to Cass.

"The storm," she said.

"The storm?" he asked.

"You didn't see it?" she asked him.

He just looked at her.

Cass was experiencing something I experienced all the time, stealing realities. The people inside them never remembered. The only people who did was me, and Remainers. Like Cass was, and like Blake had been.

But the more I switched a world out, the fuzzier it got around the edges. The more stuff got trimmed away. The square block, the round hole, they were never the same size. Not that they ever really matched, but sometimes were easier than others.

That fuzziness, those splinters, resulted in things like now. The aftermath of the storm left outside. The ambulances, heading down a street. The drivers likely not remembering where they were going.

Whole crowds of people outside would be the same. They would be standing on the beach, looking around at the destruction, and wondering what had happened. There could be people injured, people from the other world, people that remembered differently colored towels with seahorsey monsters on them. Some of those people might be Remainers, some might just remember these things like a faint dream.

There would be dead people too. Like the guy with a red towel, struggling under the storm. There was no telling which world the splinters came from. The edge of the round hole, the square peg, maybe even a splinter from another theft. They all just mixed together, whenever I stole—*switched*—realities.

The guy here working the lobby was a lucky one. He wouldn't remember anything, because he hadn't experienced anything.

"Go look outside," Cass said.

He looked at her, a little leery. Maybe he caught something over her shoulder, through the entry glass cubicle. He did something at his computer, maybe locked it, and walked that way. Opened the door to the glass foyer, then the one outside. Paused there for a long, long time.

I waited, hanging around. Literally, from Cass's shoulder. She was pretty strong, for a slight woman. And she didn't complain. Which I could appreciate, in the moment.

The young man rushed back. He was pale now.

"Jesus," he said. "We never felt anything in here."

"Some storms are like that," I said. My voice hoarse. "Sudden, right?"

He nodded at me. "Yeah man, yeah."

Cass's voice sounded curt. "Can we get a room?"

"Sure lady. Sure," he said. He seemed to like to repeat himself.

We traded cash for a key. Cass put us under some made up name.

The young man wasn't paying us much attention, he was on his cell phone, maybe calling emergency services, maybe calling his friends. Cass half-carried me to a room that thankfully was on the first floor.

The key wasn't a literal key. It was one of those cards all universes seemed to have now. The ones you slid into an electronic lock on the door, the lock would maybe beep, maybe not, and *not* unlock. It always seemed to take a few tries to get the sliding of the card and the twisting of the doorknob done in the correct order so that the door would open.

Cass got it the first try, though. So maybe the issue with the cards was me.

The room was small. Dark. Musty. A little warm, as if the air conditioner was set on a high temperature, so it wouldn't run as much, and save the hotel some money. The walls were a light tan and covered in little floral prints. There was a small bed, more than a full, less than a queen. Probably cost us like a king.

A door to the bathroom was right next to the entry door. A dresser lay in front of the bed, a flat-screen television on top of it. Way across the small room, past the bed and in front of the window were two hard chairs, covered in a white cloth, a small round table between them.

Cass laid me on the bed. The mattress was lumpy. The pillows the same. Then she flicked on the lights.

I'm not going to tell you I shut my eyes, but the lids seemed to close. All on their own.

"You're going to have to stay awake," she said.

"Sure," I said. My voice still a little rocky. A little slow.

"I'm serious," she said. "You've lost a lot of blood. And something isn't right in your wound."

"You're telling me," I said, and gickered. Then coughed.

"Dammit." Cass pulled me up on the bed.

The motion pulled the angry mouth of a wound back open. Pain flared up again from my side, as if someone had fired up the blowtorch again. Enough that I swore and opened my eyes.

She had another bottle of the sports drink in her hand. The old blueberry flavored one. "Drink."

"Fine," I said. I took it and drank. Just as good as before. Just as old and squishy and overripe as blueberries shouldn't taste.

"I'm going to have to run back out," she said. "I need needle and thread."

I raised my eyebrows. "You're going to stitch it back together?"

She nodded.

I laughed. Or gickered. Whatever. "Funny."

"What?"

"You saving my life," I said. "Twice, in one day."

She frowned at me. I wasn't sure what that frown meant. Cass had never liked me, had never liked me with Blake. Maybe she was regretting the first save, earlier today.

There was a culture that believed once you saved someone's life, you were responsible for that life forever. Maybe she was just realizing that and wishing she had made a better choice.

"Well, the second one is still up for debate," she said. "So stay awake. I'll be back as soon as I can."

"Sure," I said.

"Really," she said, her voice insistent.

"Really," I agreed. This time I raised my eyebrows. I was an adult, after all. Thousands of years old, in fact. I could certainly stay awake if I needed to.

She sighed. It was a loud breath. Then left.

I took another sip. And another. I should have asked her for a different flavored drink. Maybe asked her to turn on the air conditioning. It was too warm in here. Too sweaty.

Though as lumpy as the mattress felt, it was still comfortable. The pillows too. The lumps were like puffy little hands, pushing against me here and there. If the lumps would move around a bit, they might even feel like a massage.

It really was warm in here.

I seemed to slide down the bed. From sitting back against the pillow to lying back down. It didn't make the lumps feel any better. And the relative motion was not really a massage. I had had high hopes for it.

But still, the mattress felt a little better, this way.

Not a bad place to close my eyes, really.

Cass would be pretty angry, when she came back and found me dead.

I gickered at the thought.

CHAPTER FOURTEEN

"Have you ever been to Tibet?" Blake asked. She folded up *Lost Horizon*, it was next to her on the nightstand, and now had another book in her hand. Something with a guy who had something put in his eyes so he could see in the blackness. *The Chronicles of Riddick*, by Alan Dean Foster.

I had read his Pip and Flinx series. Didn't know Foster had written a book about Riddick. Thought it had just been a movie. Liked it enough. If I remembered right, it was about a guy who had to take on some lord of an evil empire, think they called him the Lord Marshal. He liked destroying worlds.

Movie plots, right? Not always the most believable things. They're more about special effects and big-name actors. At least in this reality. Which is probably yours. Since you're still reading this and all.

I muffled a sigh into the pillow. The softness there held a faint scent of Blake, something ... *jasminy?* It was rich and sweet and overpowering on her, but all I caught in the pillow was a floral scent, and then it was gone.

I moved next to her, in the bed. Our legs touched briefly, warm bare skin against warm bare skin. The sheets were smooth, the mattress cool and hard enough. I lay on my belly and had my arms wrapped around my pillow, my cheek pressed against the satin cover. Turned to Blake, so I could watch her, without letting my thoughts show.

This again.

Blake lay next to me, her back propped up against a few pillows, a book in her hand. It was early morning and the blinds in my condo were pulled, but the sun was bright behind them, lending the room a quiet, contemplative light. Just bright enough that she didn't have the lamp on the nightstand on.

She was always reading something. I would wake and she would always have a book, and it could be anything. The archeologist in her loved history, so she read stories about Atlantis, the Bermuda Triangle, Nostradamus, tales about mythological creatures and forgotten cities. Lately she had moved into science fiction: *Chronicles of Riddick, Hitchhiker's Guide, The Number of the Beast.*

And of course, because we had talked about it before, *Lost Horizon.*

I could never figure her taste out. Not with me. With books. Sometimes it felt like she was reading as kind of a personal research project. As if trying to figure out what might be real, what might have been forgotten, lost cities and fantastic creatures I maybe caused or uncaused unknowingly.

Other times it was sci-fi, stories about the future, cylindrical ships with unpopulated cities inside, and I didn't see how I could have created that. Those and other stories. She loved the John Carter stories, and Mars, too. *Ringworld,* by Niven. Maybe that was a pleasure thing for her, something to relax with.

Though I didn't seem to get the same relaxing. She would read a story, then ask me questions. What did I think of the Garden of Rama? Did I think Mars once held water? An alien species that seemed human? Or like today, would I stand up to some lord, some marshal, bent on destroying the world?

She loved asking questions though. Next she would be asking if I would destroy a world. Or maybe save one. Excuse me, if I *could* save one. Which I liked better than the whole world-destroying question. I mean, why in the world would I do that?

"What's this? Twenty questions?"

Blake flipped a page. She was somewhere in the middle of the book. Her eyes flicked over to me. "Just curious."

I grunted. Blake was never just curious about anything. She was a creature of relentless passion, and chased whatever and whoever she wanted. And maybe, just maybe, what she thought I wanted.

"Why?" I asked.

"Why what?"

"Why are you asking?"

She shrugged. "Some things you don't know until you get there."

"It's just a book." Although I may have known better, in a case or two.

"So you never wonder if they were real?" she asked. "If any of the stories are real? Of what they might point to, what might be lost?"

That was the archeologist in Blake. The learning. The wanting to know what had happened. And what could be saved. If I was honest, who knew what was real anymore?

I certainly didn't. I had stolen enough realities to make our world questionable, at best. Fuzzy. I couldn't tell you if there had been a lost city of gold somewhere in South America. I couldn't tell you if a writer heard some story from a traveler, and turned that story into a mythical Shangri-La. Or if that place was real.

Though I knew exactly where and why and when the Fountain of Youth story had begun. I was still living that mistake. Even though I had tried putting it in a place no other person existed at the time, the whisper of it still had gotten out.

"You know I don't." And I didn't. Not anymore. Wondering what was real and what was fiction, what had really existed in this reality, on this Earth, and who could have made it, that was a recipe for madness. I could never really know, because I had lived too long. Done too much. Stole too much.

Had the space shuttle really exploded, back in the eighties? The Chicago Fire? The attack on the Pentagon? In your reality, were two cities bombed in Japan at the end of WWII, or three? If I went to New York now, in this world, would I see the Twin Towers or a large pit in the ground?

I didn't know, and I didn't want to know. I just took things as they came. If the time came I ever went back to New York, I'd see then.

What do you remember? What do you think has changed? Had some big earthquakes happened in California lately? Was Polio a thing in your world?

I mean, how could I keep track of what I had stolen and what had disappeared? It wasn't like I had jotted everything done. And even if I had somehow kept track, and remembered each and every detail, how could I tell the difference between what was happening in the world around me *normally*, and what might be happening because of me hammering square pegs into round holes a hundred years ago?

There was always going to be that. The unintended consequences of me stealing other realities. The unknown effects from something I had done, centuries before I realized what I was doing was affecting others.

Maybe Blake had a theory. Maybe the Remainers had kept track of everything. Maybe this new guy that led them could tell me something. It'd be nice to know what to blame myself for.

"Just because someone wrote some story about a lost monastery in Tibet doesn't mean I caused it to be there," I said. Going back to answering her question. "Or not be there."

"But you *were* there?" Blake asked. Her gaze suddenly intense. Focused.

I so didn't want to get into this. Not again. Not another question and answer that led to another question and answer. "Maybe I just read the book."

Her jaw set. She folded the Riddick book up. I think she wondered if I was playing with her. And that annoyed her. I couldn't help but grin.

It was nice to have the shoe on the other foot sometimes.

"Seems to me," she said, "you'd want to meet someone else who might be long-lived."

I snorted. Right. Because one long-living person hasn't fucked up this world enough. Why not add more?

Blake looked disappointed. Which she often did when we had these kinds of talks. I just couldn't convince her that disappointment was an emotion for those with shorter lives. Because people like Blake never lived long enough to really see.

She liked the fantasies. I dealt in reality. (The play on words here wasn't intended, but it's also kind of little... true.) Blake chased old histories and tall tales; I lived in the present. She tried to save things, she loved it, and I realized that's why we had these kinds of talks. Deep inside, Blake wanted to save these things. Save history. And I knew, in a hundred years, whatever Blake would have saved would likely be lost again. That the only person who would remember her would be me.

So I understood her need. Her desire. And why she wanted to ask me these questions. But honestly, and this spoke to me as a person, I just wanted to live a life with Blake, while I had it.

I knew it would be more fleeting than I wanted.

"I thought I got it," I said.

"Got what?"

"Why you read these things," I said, adjusting my pillow. It was starting to feel hard under my cheek, and I kept trying to fluff it to get it soft. "The tall tales, the cities of gold, a sword in stone, lost libraries, sunken islands."

She smiled. Waved her book at me. Because Riddick was none of that.

I smiled back. Rested my hand on her arm. Her skin warm.

Blake always pushed for things, like Mars, like other worlds, other systems. She wanted me to try more with my power, during a time when I was trying to do less.

I mean, she wanted me to save the world from "a storm." (Yeah, I made the air-quotes.) Saving things, saving the world, saving the city from a storm, all of these things she was interested in. But it was in her blood, she was an archeologist. And I liked that about her. But I had enough on my plate, from consequences of things I did in the past. I was just trying to live my life peacefully. All the things Blake was looking to save, wanting to save, well I had already lived through those lives.

The Remainers were a new thing to me. At least, relatively. I had only really discovered what had happened to the world I lived in when I stole reality. I was trying to keep my thefts small, when Blake seemed to keep asking me about the big.

There was a difference in our worldviews. I was okay with it. But more and more, I sensed Blake getting frustrated.

"What'd you come up with?" she asked. Genuinely curious. As if wondering what I knew about her, down deep.

"Huh?" I had forgotten what we had been talking about.

"Why you think I read these things?"

Oh.

"Honestly?" I gave up on the pillow. I couldn't find a comfortable spot. Or make it comfortable. So much for saving the world, right? "I've got no idea, now."

And I didn't. Not about what she was looking for, and maybe not even about her. I liked her because she seemed to get me, but maybe I was interested in her because I didn't know why. Could've been her just wanting to see aliens on Mars, could've been her wanting a city of gold, could have been a million things.

"Just tell me if you were in Tibet," she said, *Lost Horizon* still on her lap. As if it was something she wanted to check off in her search, and I was keeping her from moving on.

I wanted to know what she knew. But she was holding her cards tight. Whatever she was looking for, she wasn't telling me.

So I didn't give her an answer. Maybe it was spiteful. And she knew it. And she knew I was holding back as well.

"Sometimes they are just stories," I said. "Tall tales. There's a reason these books are on the fiction shelf."

Blake went back to the book. "*Quia impossibile est.*"

"Really?" I held back a smile. I knew Latin better than most, and the specific argument she was alluding to. "It's true because it's impossible?"

She blew out a breath. Closed the book. "Doesn't mean it isn't true."

"Of course not." I waited.

She waited.

I waited some more. Patience was one of the few things I was better at than Blake. I had more practice at it. Although she would describe it more as lethargy. And maybe there were a few commonalities in the two words. Or maybe the only thing that they each had in common was me.

"You're going to tell me that it doesn't mean that it *is* true," she said.

This was something we had talked about many times. So we both knew the argument.

"I might say something like that." The grin I had been holding finally broke out. Just a little. Just enough for Blake to see it.

"I hate it when you do that."

"Do what?"

She slapped my arm with the book. Not hard, but not soft either. "Grin like an idiot."

My grin just got wider. Blake shook her head. But she smiled some, too.

"But what if it is?" she asked. "What if it is true?"

"What if what was?" I argued. "There's some alien ship with empty cities inside? Lost cities of gold. A forgotten Shangri-La? What if Captain John Carter was real and there are parallel universes we could all travel back and forth to?"

Why would I want to be a part of all of that? I let the silence hang a bit. Let Blake think about it. Because to me, the next revelation was the big one.

"If all of that was real, if it *all* existed," I said, "then what does this world really matter? This world *here*, that both of us live in. If all of that other stuff exists, then what makes this one special?"

I could see her think about it. Her eyes became... not unfocused, but inward-looking. And then I saw her reject it.

"You're wrong," she said.

"Am I?"

She nodded. Refocusing on me, with her intense gaze. "This world has you."

Ah, she appealed to my ego. Never a bad move. Even if this part of the conversation always made me a bit uncomfortable. I squirmed a bit, under the look in her eyes.

Still, I knew I was right. And there was no pleasure in gloating over it. After all, I had lived the realization of my life for a long time. And that knowledge was something that only came with experience, and time, and I had plenty of both.

There was no purpose to what I did. As much as Blake looked for it, *wanted* it. I was a random accident of nature, and this reality, this Earth, these people, the rumors of young people looking prematurely old or old people remarkably well preserved, the lost cities of gold, knights at a round table, the missing monasteries in Tibet all were consequences to things I had done long ago.

There was no purpose.

It was all random.

And I just happened to be the guy who could see it all.

CHAPTER FIFTEEN

To my surprise, I opened my eyes again. In a different bed than the memory of Blake, one lumpier and less soft in places. With pillows that smelled musty, and sheets that felt more scratchy and starchy than silky smooth. A darker room.

The motel room.

Maybe you aren't surprised though. After all, the world still exists. The sun is still up. Air is still getting inhaled and exhaled. Drinks are being drank, videos are being watched on cellphones, and some people like you are still reading a book.

I wasn't sure if all that would be the case, if I died.

I was never sure if what I did was bound to me, in some way. If there was something tying me to all the worlds I had stolen, if there were actually thousands of ties between all the realities I had stolen, so that all the lines together looked like broken rigging on a ship, or maybe a giant, twisted cat's cradle, with hundreds of thousands of strings, all of them taut with the strain of holding square pegs into all the round holes they shouldn't be in.

If I died, what would happen to all those ties? Those bindings?

What would happen with all that latent energy of all those realities forced into places they shouldn't be?

I guessed the rigging could all just break, and leave all the square pegs shoved and splintered into their round homes. Maybe all that latent energy would explode in the breaking, and tear all the worlds down around them. Or maybe everything would snap back, suddenly and in the same instant, crashing all the worlds back to where they had been, after the switch.

Would the Bermuda Triangle never be a real thing here? Would the Titanic have made it to New York? Would World War III come a few years after World War II?

Maybe one of those. Maybe two. Maybe all of the above and maybe at the same time none of them.

A part of me, maybe a narcissistic part, believed everything would snap back. Maybe you feel the same way, that we're all the center of our own universes, and that once we are gone, it all leaves with us. For me, if I left, the lynchpin holding all these realities together, I thought it would mean the universe would collapse. All the realities I had stolen would snap back together, and a lot of those worlds would break in that snapping.

(I admitted it was a narcissistic thought.)

But there was really no way to test that theory. Unless I died. And then *you* might know, but I definitely wouldn't.

Most people asked themselves the *Big Question*. They may not admit it to others, but everyone wondered what would happen to them after they died. Where they might go. If there was an actual place *to* go.

My Big Question was different. I never thought about what might happen to me, after I died. Maybe I just stopped thinking about it, after the first thousand years of living. I was more curious in the knowing of what might happen to the world around me, if what I did would survive my death.

That was the problem with narcissists, we wanted everything to be about us.

So I didn't know the answer to my Big Question. *Couldn't* know the answer. Maybe we could work something out, between us. You could tell me, when my number is finally called. I'd just have to figure out how you could get the information to me.

You believe in seances?

Yeah. Me neither.

Still, I think about it all. I'd say just occasionally, but it's been more often lately. Usually in times like these. Times that are happening more and more frequent. Me, barely surviving. Escaping. Waking up, sore, scared, wondering how many more of these I had left in me. After all, I had made it much longer than anyone had a right to.

Much longer than Blake.

Dammit. Those thoughts keep happening too.

I let out a breath. Moved a bit, weakly. Found that I was tucked underneath the lumpy blanket of the lumpy mattress. Naked. My side was heavily bandaged, and ached something fierce, a hot aching, but at least the sharp piercing blowtorch pain was gone.

The hotel room was dark, it must have been night outside. Something was on, a sound carried low in the air. Little muted mutters. The television, turned on the dresser and pointed to the window, the light of its screen outlining the chair before it. The chair was empty.

My mouth was dry. I was thirsty. My tongue was dry, and I smacked my lips open and closed. I wanted to get up and get some water, but the air outside of the blanket felt chilly, and the air under the blanket warm.

There was a flushing sound from the bathroom. The sound of water running from a sink. Then the bathroom door opened, briefly illuminating the hotel room before Cass turned off the light and walked lightly back towards the bed.

She saw my eyes open and paused.

"I guess I'm still alive," I croaked. Man was I parched.

There was a long moment of Cass just standing there. She looked tired. As exhausted as I felt. But she just shook her head. "Dork."

Cass walked over to the dresser. There was a little mini fridge there, placed behind the television, which I hadn't seen before. Maybe she had gotten it from the front desk while I was out. There were more sports drinks in there, a different color. She pulled one out, opened it like she would for a kid, and gave it to me.

I pulled myself up in the lumpy bed. Cass helped readjust the lumpy pillows behind me, to keep me propped up. I was careful of my side while I worked myself into position, kind of scrunching up a little at a time, and the wound didn't rebel against me.

My mouth salivated at the thought of something to drink. The plastic bottle was heavier in my hand than I remembered. I took a few large sips, coughed on them, feeling my wound sharply ping at each cough. My stomach burned with a sharp pain, after the large sips.

But the drink was good. *Felt* good. Felt like it was restoring something in me. So I took a few smaller sips. The drink wasn't quite cold, no mini fridge actually made things cold, but the liquid was cool and had a nice rich cherry flavor.

I closed my eyes and sipped it again, enjoying the sweetness of the fruit on my tongue. Until the bottle was empty. Which happened fairly quickly.

I opened my eyes. Cass still stood there, beside the bed. She held another bottle in her hand and switched it out with my empty one.

I started on that one. The same flavor. Delicious.

"Close," Cass said. Speaking not about our escape, but how close I had been to death.

Unfortunately, when you live as long as I had, these things happen far more frequently than they don't. I tried speaking again. My voice felt a little less rough, a little less froggy. "Yeah."

"Maybe still close."

Another sip of the cherry drink, a healthy swallow of the sweet drink. Maybe this one had real sugar in it, and the other one, the Artic blueberry blast had been the fake kind. Or maybe it was the other way around. Either way, I liked this one.

I took a breath. A drawing of air into my lungs, large enough my chest swelled with it. My side burned at the peak of the breath, as if I was stretching it a little. I thought I was out of whatever danger zone I had been in. Maybe barely out, but out. "I'll make it."

Cass didn't say anything. I'm sure her mind was going through what had happened. She had seen the wound, stitched it up, and I'm sure she felt like she knew better than me what kind of shape I was in.

I was hardheaded, though. And I knew my limits. They were more than a regular person, walking around the street. The Fountain of Youth kept me young, kept me alive, and kept me going in times like this. I just needed a bit of time to get right.

She finally spoke. "If you say so."

Cass spoke like I had a choice. Like we had a choice. I would heal, or I wouldn't. I felt like, knowing my past, I would. And knowing I would, I knew that we needed to move on.

Blake was dead. And we were looking for the man who had killed her. The recent new leader of the Remainers, the guy who had come on the scene less than a year ago. We were looking for him, we were going to find him, and once we put all that together, we were going to extract our vengeance.

Cass still stared at me. I didn't know why, I couldn't read her eyes in the dark of the room. So I kept drinking out of the bottle, staying in the moment, feeling the sweet cherry on my tongue, feeling the goose-bumpy delight ripple on my skin, the kind of delight you get drinking something sugary and cool when you've been long parched.

She finally left the side of the bed, sitting back in the chair in front of the television. The light from the screen illuminated her brightly in the chair, revealing dark circles under her eyes, and a haggard expression. I wonder how long she had been up. How close it had been, for me.

Cass turned off the television and returned to the darkness. I finished the second bottle. My mouth still felt dry, I still was thirsty. I wanted to ask Cass for another, but maybe my stomach wouldn't handle one right yet. It felt full, but also a little nauseous.

Besides, Cass looked tired.

"You do the stitching?" I asked.

Cass nodded. Her head moving up and down, in the dark.

"That another thing you get practice at?" I asked.

She shrugged. "I'm good at some things."

I thought that was an understatement. There were some things she was fantastic at. Like shooting a gun. Like killing.

"Well," I said. "Thanks."

Her head nodded. It was hard to see her face, even with the light from the television. "It doesn't look the best, but it'll hold."

There was a pause. Her tone implied that the previous stitches were somehow at fault, for the wound opening up again. I wanted to ask how good she could have stitched herself up, with no anesthesia, with hands cramping from dehydration, but I was afraid of her answer.

"And we have some time, I think," she said. "They're still recovering from that storm. It's brutal, out there."

That's one of the reasons I had stolen it, again. Pulling the same reality over, multiple times, always seemed to fuzz the edges of both worlds. Shaved more of the pieces off, from each, leaving bits and pieces of both realities to mix, in both universes.

Things from the seahorsey reality remained, when they should have left. Things from the storm side of reality also remained, the fury and the destruction and maybe even some of the deaths, when all of that should have left when I had put the storm back where I had originally stolen it from. Even bits of the storm itself remained. All of those things would mix together, here in Charleston, and leave the city befuddled for days.

That confusion, not to mention the wrath of the storm, coming out of nowhere, the sheer power appearing and devastating Charleston would hide us. Whatever trail we had left after the shootout, that trail was forever gone, now. The Remainers might find us, but it wouldn't be tonight. It would likely not even be tomorrow, or this week. Not by following us from Bubba's, at least.

I hadn't realized how quiet it had gotten, in the room. The television must have masked how sober the world was, outside. Normally, in any hotel at the beach, you would hear people stomping outside your door, up and down the hallway. Screaming and yelling and maybe a little drunk.

"You have a lot of scars," Cass said, into the quietness.

She had undressed me. The thought made me uncomfortable for some reason. Like my clothes, my suit, they had been a kind of armor. Something I presented to the world. Now I was naked, literally.

You would think that I would have gotten used to people seeing me with my clothes off, with having a few thousand years of practice, but apparently it worked differently than I supposed. The older we get, the less we want people to see us naked. Without any armor. Just our skin, and our scars. Because the older you get, the more we have to hide.

Me, more than most.

I had a lot of scars. I cover them up with jokes. Angry mouths of wounds. Or blender attacks. Because remembering what caused them, remembering the cause of each scar over the thousands of years I had been alive, that was too much. I'd rather build thick tissue over them all, thick tissue of jokes and irreverent grins, because thinking too much about them took me to dark places.

"You live as long as I do..." I said, then left it at there, shrugging. It was a weak motion, a slight up and down of both shoulders, from maybe a weak man.

She just nodded. The quiet was about to return when the air conditioning kicked on. A large click followed by the whirring of big fans from the unit under the window. The air stirred the drapes behind Cass, and for a moment I felt like she was a ghost.

I don't know why that thought scared me.

Cass reached back, hit something on the panel of the unit. The force of the air scaled back, the bottom of the drapes stopping flying around and just fluttered a bit. The whirring of the fans became a low-lying hum in the air.

Her head turned back to me. "Blake told you that story." Not asking, but saying. Maybe even accusing.

The mention of Blake always threw me off. Like a physical yank. As if out of nowhere, someone had slapped me. It took a minute for me to figure out what Cass was saying.

"The story about the stars?"

Cass nodded.

I echoed her nod. Blake was the only person to really get it, when I tried to explain what I did. "Yeah."

She snorted. "I figured out what you were telling me, later. About how big the universe is. I think I understand it, maybe."

No matter how big the human mind thought the universe was, it was always bigger than that. Something in our brains kept us from that realization. Kept us from truly understanding infinity.

With enough time, we could grasp any size, no matter how big. No matter how small. Because as big as the universe was, it also was infinitely small. There was something smaller that made up molecules. Something smaller that made up an atom. Something smaller that made up an electron. Hadrons and quarks and other things even smaller, which we haven't discovered yet.

We could grasp a size, once we understood it. And we could understand the progression to that size, the *growth* of something. But we couldn't understand infinite growth. However big we thought something was, it was always, *always* bigger than that.

Blake had loved the concept. We talked about it a lot, deep discussions I had never had with anyone else. Something in her had just gotten it, maybe even better than I ever had.

Maybe it was her father. She had loved their trips to the fields, in the middle of the night. Staring out at the stars. Knowing that as many as she could count, there were always more. Countless more. And that, if I wanted to, I could see them all.

"Think how amazing it would be," Blake had said to me, one time. *"What you can do, what you can see, what you can do... it could be everything. It could all tie back to you."*

At that moment, we both had been lying in bed together. Blake across my chest, her eyes staring deep into mine, her soft hair brushing over my skin. Almost... intense.

I liked it when she was intense.

Back in that moment, I had grinned at Blake. Held my hands out to either side, like I was flying. *"I'm king of the world..."*

Blake had slapped my chest. But grinned back. I was maybe the joker in our relationship, she was the one with vision. The driver. I lived in the moment, she lived for a future. Which ended up being ironic, with me living on, and her gone.

But back to the memory. Back to her soft hair on my chest. Her soft skin, silky and warm sliding against mine. The smile in her eyes, the promise of wicked things to come, the *intensity* that was all Blake.

We got to the more intense stuff.

And as I've said, I kind of liked her when she got intense.

Cass's voice interrupted the memory, her tone sharp, her words clipped. "You're thinking of her right now, aren't you?"

It wasn't quite an accusation. But like the mention of Blake's name earlier, it yanked me back from the memory. Back to the present. Where Blake was forever gone.

Dead is dead, after all.

"Yeah," I said. Then added, for some reason. "Sorry."

Cass moved in the chair, a shadowed reflection. Maybe it was a shrug of a shoulder, maybe it was a wave of one hand, as if saying, *forget about it.*

Whatever it was, it started a long moment of silence. Then Cass shifted again. As if she was uncomfortable. Her next words were a surprise, as if she had decided to confess something. "I used to hate her, you know."

I wouldn't have guessed that in a million years. When Blake had introduced me to Cass, her younger sister had taken an immediate dislike to me. As if she had been protecting Blake. Which, as it turned out, she had been right to.

I had the feeling they had developed their bond over time, that both Cass and Blake felt like it had been the two of them against the world. Which maybe was true. When the world starts changing around you, and no one else remembers the previous reality, well that kind of thing has a way of bonding people together.

You ever have a brother, or sister, who remembered something from your youth. Could remember the exact moment with an intense clarity, about when you snuck in and stole some cookies from the cookie jar? Or borrowed your parents' car keys? The sister (or brother) could describe it exactly how it happened.

But you couldn't remember. That part of your brain was blank. Like the moment had never existed for you. But it had for them, and it had *meant* something.

I felt like that was the world today. People who could remember, and people who couldn't. People who had stayed when I stole reality, and people who hadn't. People whose memories remained, and people who had never had that memory to begin with.

Knowing that, I could understand the Remainers. Who they were. Why they banded together. Why they struggled to keep certain memories and knowledge alive.

I just didn't like the part where they tried to kill me.

Still, Cass hadn't liked me, even before Blake had told her who I really was. After Blake had mentioned that, Cass had exploded. Like a volcano. Or a storm.

Thinking about it, I didn't know why she was with me now. Not really. It wasn't like she cared whether or not I got revenge for Blake. And Cass would get her own pound of flesh, with or without my help. As I had just seen, she was capable. And she was that kind of person.

So maybe some of those thoughts showed. Or maybe just the surprise. "I didn't know."

"Yeah," Cass said. Her voice soft. "Growing up, a long time ago. Her and Pop had a special relationship. Something I could never get with him. Maybe it was because my mom wasn't Blake's mom. Or maybe it was just me."

She went silent for a moment. As if her memories now were the ones taking her back, to another time and place. As if she was the one lost in the past, now.

"My mom was young. A little shallow, and used how she looked to get what she wanted. Used me, too, I guess," Cass's voice got thicker, the longer she talked. "And she didn't want a farm. She wanted city life. Bright lights, stores and shopping, fancy restaurants."

"Pop sold the farm. I think I was three or four at the time." Cass took a breath then. It was one of the shuddering ones, that you took when you faced something you didn't want to see. "I never got to see the stars. Not like Blake. Not with Pop holding my hand, listening to the crickets chirping around us, staring up into the night sky at the stars…"

She swallowed. It was a loud sound, easily heard above the hum of the air conditioning. Like she was forcing something back down inside her.

"Girls and their dads, right?" she said, too quickly. As if she thought she needed to beat me to the punch.

Still, I hadn't been thinking of a joke. I had been wondering about a girl who had desperately wanted the kind of relationship her big sister had, with a special kind of man, a father who had spent time with his girls, and had loved them both. Who had tried to do one thing with Blake, and maybe had tried something else for Cass, thinking what Cass's mother wanted was what Cass had wanted, too.

I was supposing there. Maybe putting myself into his place. Because we would never know. I had robbed Cass of that. Blake too, by stealing reality around them one day. Something large enough that their father had forgotten both of them.

I pushed that thought away. Blake had told me about it, about when and how the two sisters had discovered they were Remainers. The day their father had forgotten about them both and walked out the door.

Just taken off.

Blake had told me they had found him. Years after he had left. Years after he had abandoned Blake and Cass. Pops wasn't back at his original farm, but he had found one nearby. As if, not being able to go back to the last place he remembered, he made do by getting just close enough.

The man didn't remember them. Didn't acknowledge the pictures they showed them. Was polite, but confused. And kept telling the girls they had the wrong man.

Cass had been heartbroken. He had been polite in his denial, but it had cut Blake's sister deep. Blake had taken it better, but she was older. She had already understood some of how the world worked.

And not the worst thing, in Blake's opinion, but Cassie's mother had forgotten them too. Blake thought maybe that part was faked, that after their father had left, Cassie's mom didn't want to be burdened with either of them.

That part struck me. I could see why Cass was the way she was now.

A killer. Probably someone who didn't want fancy restaurants or shopping days, but someone who fought to do things that mattered.

Cass spoke again. Her voice still thick. Slow. And still somehow soft. "I figured I saw your scars... You might as well see one of mine."

I'd argue they weren't the same. The scars on my skin, they were all surface. I thought I was more like Cass's mom, than her dad. Because the things that were deeper, the wounds that never healed, I refused to acknowledge those.

There were just too many, if I thought about one, they would all overwhelm me.

The worst thing about a long life was the long list of regrets it came with. So many of us do things at the time, without realizing what the real consequences of that action would be. The result of a bad choice usually comes long after the test.

I had had many tests. And a long list of regrets. And no way to fix anything I had done. If you had asked me, right then, if I would have gone back and returned the reality I had stolen, whatever I had done at the time to keep Blake's father around, keep Cass and Blake in that reality, I would have.

Not just for Cass, but for Blake, too. Maybe that one decision would have kept her alive. Maybe it would have kept them both away from me.

But, what's done is done. We haven't talked about this as much, with me getting shot at and almost dying, but I might as well introduce you to Rule Number Five. In case you need the refresher, here's the first four, again:

#1 – I can't bring anyone back to life

#2 – I can live forever (but I can also definitely die – this last one was... close)

#3 – We all can change reality, in some way

#4 – Dead is dead

And Rule Number Five, there's no time-travel for a guy like me. No traveling whatsoever. I can't steal myself to a different universe. I can't go back in time, there's no reality where I can go to the future and see if a choice I've made has royally fucked me. There's no universe where I can go back in the past and change a bad decision. Time and place only flows in one direction for us all.

What's done is done.

CHAPTER SIXTEEN

I had told you I liked etymology. Maybe I even told you why. Like me, some words kept a part of who they were, long after parts of them had changed. I liked to look at a word, almost weigh it, and wonder how it had changed, and when.

I remembered parts of my life, but it was hard to remember them all. You're probably the same way. The important parts of your life, the parts that matter, probably are crystal clear. But the smaller moments, those start to fade, especially as time increases the distance between you and that moment.

The problem is that those smaller forgotten moments start to matter. Because as they gathered together, as you lived them, they steered you in a certain direction. A path you took without realizing. Like revisiting a new city, a place you hadn't been in a while. You thought you were heading the right way, you took a left here, a right there, went straight for a while, took that last second turn you remembered was always a bitch to get to, but still you ended up in the wrong place.

And you wondered what mistake led you there.

Words and me, we were the same. Where we had begun and where we were now weren't the same. And I couldn't tell you about the little moments where we changed. I mean, it had been a long time since I could remember my parents. My birth. They were lost to me now.

A lot of words were the same. People used them without knowing the moment they had been created, what they had been created for. Without understanding the changes they had underwent over time. Without even knowing if they were being used correctly, or if their meaning had changed.

Where's this talk leading?

The Remainers. The group Cass, and at one time Blake, had belonged to. People who realized, after reality had shifted, that they remembered something different from others. Who remembered a time where the Challenger had made it into space. Who remembered a time where that bomb hadn't gone off in Grand Central Station in New York, killing a few hundred thousand people.

If you're not a Remainer, what would happen? The best I can gather it's like you've forgotten something. You're just not sure what. The closest thing that you might remember is a weird passing of time. Maybe you're sitting at your desk, look at the clock, and wonder where the past few hours went. That time was a blur now, and you just can't believe those hours are gone.

Anyway, why Remainers? Why that word?

To me it felt right.

You have the word in old French, *remanoir*, which means to be left out. In mathematics, its meaning is anything that's remained, after a separation or removal.

In Latin it had been the word *remanere, "to remain, to stay behind, to last."*

But my favorite was what I fancied was the word's origin. As back as far as the fourteenth of fifteenth century. The word *remainen*: to be left after a loss, to survive.

The Remainers were survivors. They were what was left, after parts of their world had been stolen from them. They were what remained, time and again, as I had stolen parts of other universes and swapped them out with what existed in this one.

But they were more, now. They were protectors of what remained. And not just killers. Not today. They had grown into killers. Predators. Hunting the one prey who, by his existence, had created them.

I wondered if they ever thought about what might happen if they killed me? Not in the *what would happen to all the realities* type of way, but in the *what would happen to us, if we kill who made us* kind of way.

I wasn't sure Remainers thought that far ahead. Which was odd, seeing as they worked so hard to preserve what they had lost, in the past. People always said those who didn't learn from history were doomed to repeat it.

I wondered what that lesson would inevitably be? Would the Remainers remain? Would the word? Or would the meaning of the word change, as they did? Like all words did, over time.

See, etymology's interesting to ponder, right?

No?

Eh. You get it or you don't.

I struggled to get up out of bed, but quietly. Cass was asleep in her chair, her head tilted funny. She would have a heck of a crick in the neck when she woke.

I felt... okay. Not strong, but not weak. My side ached like a bitch, but I had endured pain like it before, and I would again. There was some itching, where the threads of the stitches rubbed against my skin. Sports tape was wrapped around my waist, medical tape over that, and there was a bulge on my side where extra pads might be.

There was a part of me that wanted to lift up all the bandages and look at the wound, but I knew what I would see, and I didn't want to re-wrap everything. Like I said, I healed fast. Part of the perks of taking a bath in the Fountain of Youth.

The steady hum of the air conditioner came from under the window. It was getting to be early morning, sunlight was bright behind the closed drapes of the room, and the temperature was rising fast. The fan was working hard to keep the temperature constant in the room.

I padded over to the chair, taking the lumpy blanket from the bed and laying it over Cass. I reached out to tuck part of the blanket underneath her chin, but thought that might wake her, so I didn't. Just left it draped over her chest.

I opened the fridge and grabbed one of the cherry sports drinks. It went down quick, tasted as delicious as it had the night before, and I felt immediately better. Stronger. Kind of crazy, how replenishing your body with just a little liquid could make you feel a little jolt of energy.

The drink made me hungry, though. My stomach almost stung with emptiness. There were packaged cakes next to the sports drinks, the small cylindrical chocolate-covered cakes with a cream-filled, swirly center. Ho Hos.

I thought the company that had made those went bankrupt. Has that happened in your world? Just my reality? Maybe I was wrong, because there the treats were, packaged up in the mini fridge.

I couldn't picture Cass eating them. But there were some wrappers in the trash can. It was just a strange choice for someone like Cass, I felt like she ate bullets for breakfast, and finished it off with a nice blended drink of sandpaper and shivs.

I was hungry, but I didn't grab the cakes. The plastic would be loud, and crinkly. I didn't want to get shot. Or, at the very least, threatened to be shot.

Cass really needed her sleep. Yesterday had been rough, tense, full of adrenaline highs and lows. Shooting, and killing. Running. And then there was me, almost dying.

I was used to all of that. And as practiced as she had looked, as smooth as she had looked, moving with her gun, taking out the cell of

Remainers, I wondered how many situations like that Cass could have practiced.

Not as many as me, that was for sure.

I remembered her back at Bubba's, leaning back against the bar, breathing in and out rapidly, almost psyching herself up for what she was about to do.

She did need her sleep. Really needed it, I thought. And to be honest, sleep was something hard to get sometimes, in my life. Part of me wanted to move her from the chair, it couldn't be comfortable, with its hard arms and straight legs, but I kept going back to not wanting to wake her.

My stomach rumbled. I was starving. I didn't want to find out if this place had room service, or what it might call room service. I found my clothes hanging in the hallway closet, the ones all hotels had right next to the bathrooms, and put on my slacks, the t-shirt, and the dress jacket overtop the t-shirt.

I buttoned the jacket. The t-shirt for some reason still had the seahorsey monster prints all over it. Little spiked unicorn heads, with some kind of funny grin plastered on their faces, as if they knew something about their world I didn't, and they were all kind of laughing at my lack of knowledge.

No one likes a critic. Especially a few hundred of them mocking me from a t-shirt. But there was nothing I could do about it now. Like I said, the more I switched realities, the more it all became... fuzzy. The reality I stole never quite fit the reality I was replacing. Sides of square pegs, the edge of the round hole, it all got trimmed when I jammed them together, splinters fell off, things from both worlds blended and became something new.

It was just my luck that this damn seahorsey shirt was one of those splinters.

It looked like Cass had everything cleaned. At least the clothes smelled fresh. A little too lavendery, but fresh. The t-shirt was clean, but it still had a stain where I had bled on it some, I just hadn't bled enough to cover all the little monster prints. Unfortunately.

I found my wallet on the dresser and looked to see if I had any cash before tucking it into my back pocket. There was a hotel card key stuck in the side of the wallet, as if Cass had known I would be getting up before her.

I was a little low on funds, and there were wallets next to mine. Three of them, from the Remainers trying to kill us. One had a good bit of cash in it, and I tossed that wallet in my jacket pocket. That was better than pulling more of my money out of an account, or switching realities for more.

Especially the latter.

Cellphones were next to all of them. One was a flip-top one, with its battery pulled out. Two others were smartphones, (like a phone could be smart), and both of those were powered down, completely off. I grabbed the flip phone, guessing the not-so-smartphones probably had some kind of passcode I'd have to figure out, which I could probably do, but again that would involve switching realities, and I was trying to avoid that. So the flip phone got tucked next to the wallet in my jacket.

I'd have taken everything, but then my pockets would be puffy.

My vanity popped up at the oddest moments. I mean, I was wearing seahorsey t-shirt, for heaven's sake.

Anyway, I thought I'd get some breakfast, sit down and look at the things I had grabbed. See what I could figure out. Then come back and see if Cass was awake. I'd bring some breakfast back, trade it for some Ho Hos, and the two of us would look at the other two wallets, and phones. Maybe play a game of guess the passcode.

There was a pad of paper on the nightstand next to the lumpy bed. Right next to the phone. The pad had the hotel name at the top, and a few words in the fake cursive script, the script that's digitally printed instead of signed, saying *We're happy to have you staying with us.* There was a cheap pen, white with a blue plastic cap. The cap was on so tight I struggled to pull it off the pen.

Which I did.

Barely.

Man, I was weak. I hoped breakfast would speed up the recovery.

I wrote a quick note in blue ink on the cheap stationery. *Going to get some food. Let you sleep. Will be back soon.* I looked at the clock by the bed, an old cheap alarm clock with red digital letters. *Left @ 8:37 AM.*

I quietly left that piece of paper tucked into the frame of the television set, so it would be the first thing Cass saw when she woke. Then I turned up the fan, so that the air conditioning would be loud and mask the outside noise as long as it could.

All thoughtful things, I thought.

And man, was I wrong. But that's the thing about the choices make. Large or small, remembered or forgotten, you don't know if you've made a wrong one until long after you make it.

Until long after the scar.

But all I knew now was I was hungry, so I walked out the door.

CHAPTER SEVENTEEN

I HADN'T REMEMBERED MUCH ABOUT THE HOTEL ITSELF. Stepping past the door, I saw why. Not just because I had been out of it, but this place could have been one of a thousand I had stayed at in the past.

The carpet was dingy, made of cheap tan nylon threads, thin as I walked on it, so that my feet felt like I was walking on concrete. The walls were a blank white, no pictures adorned the walls, no prints of landscapes or drawings of the sea. Just a dirty tan floor, whitish walls, and lights that didn't seem to be quite bright enough.

A few doors down a metal blue can lay horizontally on the floor. A tall blue can, twenty-four ounces, with the name of a beer company scrolled diagonally around the can. There was beer left in the can, some of it had spilled onto the carpet before the door, and I could smell a kind of skunky scent.

There was never a time that stale yeast and hops smelled good. I took a quick breath and held it in, holding my breath longer than I should have as I walked, at least until the hallway opened into the lobby.

The young man from yesterday was gone. The desk was manned by a young girl today, her nametag said she was Lucy, a slightly overweight girl with long red hair tied back in a ponytail. Kind of an odd combination. She was kind enough though. I stopped by and mentioned we might stay another day, she asked my room number, I told her, and we exchanged a little cash.

Lucy asked if I wanted maid service. I told her no, that my friend would be sleeping in. She nodded with a knowing smile. As if understanding what might keep two people busy late enough that they had to sleep in.

I'm sure I didn't look too awake, but I didn't have the heart to correct her. And besides, if I did, word could get back to Cass. And then Cass might shoot me.

So, I nodded back. Purely in the interest of self-preservation. And then I asked Lucy about some good food places nearby. Places with a hearty breakfast. She gave me Cup of Joes, a waffle house type of place a few blocks back from the beach. I thanked her and headed outside.

There were still signs of the storm yesterday. Actually, a lot of things. Torn scraps of umbrellas, white poles sticking out of the dunes here and there. All the little flotsam and jetsam from a hurricane-level event. Coolers, clothes, bits of Styrofoam cups, white like bones, sticking in the sand. A mass of trash on the beach.

Big things were left, too. One of the taller hotels north of me, a nicer one, with glass windows shimmering and reaching high into the sky, that hotel was missing a good part of its face. Like the wind had sheered it off. The whole beach area in front of it was roped off, and even as far away as I was I could see furniture hanging of all the open rooms, beds and chairs and even in a few cases a dresser. On one of the top floors it looked like a piano was dangling precariously, two of its legs holding on to the floor, the top of the piano open.

I winced. Holy moly. I wished I could have put the storm back faster. But it had been strong. It had resisted me. And I had been tired.

There was a lot of junk underneath the hotel. Large piles of the collapsed wall. A few emergency vehicles, lights and sirens off. People walking around and pulling up bits of rubble, as if looking for someone. Or someones.

These were the bad parts of stealing a reality. And maybe you think I should feel worse, but I had seen a lot of death in my life. A lot of pointless death. It kind of got to a place where I was used to it, where a callus had built, thick scar tissue, over that part of my brain. Because I knew if I kept thinking about it, where those thoughts would go.

And besides, sometimes it all seemed pointless. At some point I might wonder if my vengeance was worth the cost. Probably a long time from now, when the true cost of the decision would come home to roost.

All I could do was make a decision. Move forward. If I wasn't doing the right thing, I was doing the thing I thought best at the time. When you live fifty or sixty years, or even eighty or ninety, a lot of times you don't get to see the consequences of all the bad choices you've made.

When you live a few thousand, you get to see them all.

That's how calluses get built. From repeated motions, to protect against the tiny rubbings of life that wore you down. The worse the friction, the longer the abrasion ran, the thicker the callus.

And hey, I'm not defending myself here. Or maybe I am. It sounds like I am. But I've tried to be better, once I understood what was happening. When you look at it, at least lately, all I did was switch around tiny pieces of universes. All I did was steal a suit, a lime, a bottle of good whiskey here and there.

I wouldn't bring a storm if someone wasn't trying to kill me. If someone hadn't killed Blake. I wasn't the Remainers, people who opened fire into a bar, on a crowded street, just on a chance they might kill me. I wasn't some person who used their power to rule the world, the universe, to have all of this reality answer my every whim.

I just wasn't the type.

And what would you do, in my place? Are you saying you wouldn't try to stop a school shooting, if you could switch out that reality? You wouldn't try to find a world where the shooter had a healthy home, had grown up adjusted, had someone that helped them as they grew, supported and nourished them, so the kid didn't feel like he needed to grab a gun and go on a shooting spree?

Surely that reality was one I should change out, right? I could find the reality that was the reverse, find the one reality where a well-adjusted kid lived in a bad family, and switch the well-adjusted kid out with the shooter? Put the bad kid with the bad family, and hope the well-adjusted kid would make it better here?

I mean, why the hell could I do what I do, if not for that?

It was a damned if you do, damned if you don't, kind of situation. So, calluses get built. Because otherwise, all death, everyone around me, can be laid at my feet. It's my fault for stealing realities. Or it's my fault for *not* stealing a reality.

That's why thick calluses get built.

I am *responsible*, in both cases. Either way. Whichever choice I make. And there's nothing I can do to change it, and there's nothing I can do to stop it. All I can do is make the best choice I can at the time. It's why I once had desperately wanted a purpose.

Because when I steal realities, right or wrong, it fuzzies the world up. More splinters peel off. And more Remainers get created. More hunt me.

They find me faster.

So, I have to steal more realities just to stay alive.

And create even more Remainers.

Wow, it really does go round and round.

And yeah, I have these kinds of conversations a lot. They're pretty circular, and tend to go nowhere. But I usually have the time.

They just leave me feeling a little more hollow inside.

Speaking of hollow, there was an empty stomach to fill, and a Cup of Joes somewhere ahead. I walked inland. It was still early, and after the storm not a lot of people were coming to the beach, so the streets were fairly empty.

Lucy's instructions were spot-on. I found the diner on the corner, where she said it was. It did look like it had been a Waffle House, once. The sign on top of the restaurant was square, stretched the length of the front, illuminated, and looked like it had been yellow once. The sign was orange now and perched overtop the tall windows wrapping around the front of the restaurant. Inside was a bunch of booths around the windows, and four-chair tables further in, scattered around the floor.

The door had a real bell at its top, and it *ching-a-linged* me in. Inside smelled like roasting coffee and hash browns. Like outside, there weren't a lot of people here, either. Just an old couple, to my left, tucked into a booth. A family of four, a few tables away from that booth. One of their chairs had been replaced with a highchair, and a mother leaned over, trying to feed some of her pancake to a two-year-old that wasn't quite feeling it.

Which was odd, because I thought pancakes were one of the universal constants of life. Everyone loved them. Or should.

An older guy hung out behind the counter. I knew he was old because of the gray hair, short around his head. A yellow pencil was tucked in the gray hair, behind one ear. He had a white coat on, buttoned with dark orange buttons, and a nametag proclaiming the was Joe, maybe the Joe of Cup of Joes. He held a pot of fresh coffee loosely in one hand, the pot was steaming, and he watched the whole pancake-gate scene with a small smile on his face.

In front of the counter were stools. Four-legged things with a round brown cushion on top. But I didn't want to sit at the counter today.

I stepped closer. Joe shook his head, pulling himself out of a memory, maybe, and glanced at me. Filled a white porcelain coffee cup in a practiced motion and slid it over as I walked up. A second practiced motion, a nod of his head, showed me where the cream and sugar were.

Today I felt like both of those things. So, I opened a couple of the plastic containers, popping them over the coffee. Then I tore a few packets of sugar in, stirred it with a spoon, and took a sip.

As good as the sports drink had been, fresh coffee would always beat it. Hands down. The dark bitterness, the sweat cream, the hint of sugar —it all tasted just right. Especially when you desperately needed it.

Joe saw it in my face. Made an incorrect assumption. Which I always felt, like all of those types of things, ran in threes. "Hell of a storm, right?"

"Yeah," I said. "Came out of nowhere."

"City was lucky," Joe said. "I been in one, the waves washed out the first few blocks."

I shrugged. "I guess." I took another sip of coffee. Whatever else Cup of Joe could do, he could brew a mean cup.

"Menu?" Joe slid a small laminated piece of paper over on the counter.

I shook my head. I knew what I wanted. The hash browns smell, the fried potatoes on the grill, smelled fantastic. And the pancakes the kid didn't want looked fantastic. "Can I just get a large stack?"

Joe smiled and took back the menu. "Sure," he said. "Just syrup and butter?"

"Definitely," I said. Then second thought it. "Maybe a plate of hash browns as well."

Joe's smile grew wider. "You got it," he said. "More coffee?"

My cup was more empty than full. So, I finished it off. "Please."

He tilted the carafe over the cup. Steam rose up from the pour, the coffee was thick, black, and hot. The smell was rich and roasty. I did the same dance with the cream and sugar.

"You guys really should be busier," I said.

"Got lucky," Joe said. As if explaining. Gave me a look like he had seen worse.

I wanted to tell him I agreed. And that maybe luck was all life was about. Both good and bad. Instead, I took my cup and found a booth. Away from the family and the old couple.

CHAPTER EIGHTEEN

I remained in the booth and waited on my food. The padding of the bench was worn but comfortable, I kind of sunk into it and enjoyed my coffee. Every now and then I'd stare out the window.

The sun kept rising above the buildings in the east, the hotels I had passed as I headed inland. Yellow god-like rays broke through some of the clouds remaining from the world of the storm, dark stains scattered over the blue skies of this world. The rays flashed over the windows at Joes, illuminating the table, the brown vinyl, the bottles of ketchup and mustard resting next to the window side of the table.

I drank my coffee and ignored the clouds. Instead I relaxed under the warmth of the sun on my skin, took deep breaths of the fried potato scent, listened to smacks of a spatula against a pan, the sizzles of a hot griddle, the conversation of a mother and the father and a two-year-old that for some reason did not want to eat pancakes.

A small part of me wondered, briefly, if the reason was me. If the young boy was a Remainer. If the world had changed around him, and he no longer felt like he knew what the world really was. If his family was really his. He was just too young to have the words to say it, to figure it out, to know what was going on.

Like I said, I understood the Remainers.

The brief wonder flittered away. It was easy to blame myself for anything. Too easy, sometimes. People dying, people killing other people, people not liking pancakes, all these things happened in any reality, with or without me. There was a reason I had thick calluses. Maybe the kid just didn't like pancakes. Even though I could imagine most children liking them, there had to be one that didn't, right?

The pancakes came on a warm white platter, Joe holding the plate on the corner with a tiny white towel. He set the pancakes in front of me, a hot little tin pitcher of syrup next to it, and a small plate with a large hunk of butter on it. He left, came back with a deep white bowl of hash browns and another fresh pot of coffee, and refilled my cup for the third time.

Joe left the pot.

He was starting to grow on me.

I dug into the pancakes. They were big and filled the entire plate, a tall stack of four, soft, but also with the crispy edges on the side that come from tiny trails of batter being cooked in a hot griddle. The syrup poured thick from the tin pitcher, spread in little waves across the face of the pancakes. The butter slid across the surface, leaving little rich swirls of cream and syrup. The warm maple scent was comforting, it was a sugary scent I just took in. My fork slid through the syrup and the butter, the pancakes gave with just a tiny press of the edge of my fork, and it was all delicious in my mouth.

They went down quick.

The hash browns were less sweet. More substantial. Plenty of onions and garlic, and seasoned aggressively with salt and pepper. There were bottles of ketchup at every booth, and I mixed a little in mine, and the sweet tomato flavor mixed perfectly with the fried potatoes.

I inhaled everything. The pancakes, the potatoes, the pot of coffee.

After it all I felt like a new man. I almost could feel my body take all the food and caffeine and fire itself up, like little workers had taken everything I had eaten and drank and started rebuilding tissue, skin, blood. Working double and triple time.

I hadn't eaten this well in a week or two. Most of my meals had been of the liquid type, usually around eighty proof or so. So, this stuff all felt like heaven to me, it warmed my body, my soul (if I had one). It's hard to describe, unless you've been there, starving and needing real food, real nourishment, and then getting it.

It didn't take long to finish everything. Joe came by right when I dropped my fork into the empty bowl of hash browns, took the empty plates, asked if I wanted anything else. I asked him for an order to go, maybe bring it by in a bit. In case Cass was hungry. But I kind of hoped she wasn't. I felt like whatever was rebuilding my body would want more.

Joe grinned like he got that all the time. And he probably did. It was a really good, down-home breakfast.

I leaned back in the booth, as if stretching my stomach out would make it feel less full. Took a large breath or two. It was time to do a little work.

I took the wallet and flip phone out. The phone had a tackiness to its back, as if a sticker had been ripped off and left some gluey residue. The kind of residue that easily transferred to your fingers, but for some reason was hard to get off the surface of the phone.

I slid the battery into the phone and waited for it to power up. A little digital display resembling a galaxy (a little bit of irony here, right?) came on the tiny screen, a little tiny universe all in light whitish-green pixels. The pixels spun around the galaxy, and then the phone came on.

I wasn't expecting a contact list, and I wasn't disappointed. Flip phones were what people bought when they wanted cheap and quick. A lot of these types of phones were pay by the month, I think they call them no-contract. Even though you have to give your credit card to get them working.

So, there was no number under a big picture of a guy with a bald head, maybe his pinky finger at the corner of his mouth, called Doctor Evil. No Master Planner, no This-is-the-guy-you-should kill. Maybe I'd have better luck with the cellphones.

There was a number in the phone, under the most recent tab. Just one. Not a local area code.

I was tempted to call it, but I'd save that for later. After I looked at everything and knew as much as I could. Otherwise, all I could do was ask "Hey, are you that person sending all these people to kill me?"

That didn't sound like it would go anywhere. Except for more people getting sent. And maybe someone laughing at the end of the call.

So, the wallet was next. I had seen Wabbit Hunter and his backup, the young kid, what's his name. Reed. I think it was Reed. Or Reid. However it was spelled.

Anyway, this wallet wasn't either of theirs. It was the sniper's. I hadn't seen him, though I had seen he was good at shooting, he just hadn't been at Cass's level. Of course, not many people could have made Cass's shot. I grinned at the thought that maybe she was from another world, one where people are born in battle, where a handgun was their first toy handed to them in the crib, where they could shoot snipers through the eye from a block away.

Back to the wallet. The driver's license was kind of what I expected. A middle-aged man, late twenties at the youngest. Clean-shaven, strong jawline, pronounced cheeks. His face was all sharp edges, like he was a weapon. His haircut was the classic military high-and-tight, shaven on the sides, short on the top. He was army, I thought.

I say was. I guess I should say, had been.

His name was (had been) Clyde. Clyde Worthington. He had been six-foot tall, blonde hair, blue eyes. And was not an organ donor. The picture didn't show it, but he had recently acquired a bullet hole. I was guessing in the face somewhere. His license was from Mirtle Beach. I chuckled at the misspelling. It was a bad forgery.

I took all his cash and thanked Clyde for his donation. Seven hundred-dollar bills and a few twenties and tens. As if he had bought something with an eighth hundred-dollar bill, like a flip phone, and had a little change.

I tucked one of the hundreds under my empty plate. Thought Joe had earned it. The pancakes definitely had. I put the rest of the cash in my wallet, careful to leave the photo of Blake tucked behind my driver's license. Even took a second to look at the picture, the film thin between my finger and thumb, before letting it go.

Miss me Yet? xoxo...

A deep breath, one my full stomach resisted a bit. Back to Clyde. From Mirtle Beach. There was no way for me to find out where he had come from. All there was in the wallet was the forged license.

It felt likely—to me—that this guy was head of the group we had found. Maybe Cass and I had gotten lucky. Maybe, however the Remainers tracked changes, Clyde had been the first to get the call. Him and Reid/Reed and Wabbit Hunter. If that was the case, then we could get out of Charleston alive.

That was a new thought, for me. I didn't travel with others much, anymore. But Cass and I were stuck together now. She was right, someone somewhere would have the video of her helping me down the street, of us being together, so whatever bridge could have brought her back to the Remainers was burned now.

Likely burned the moment she had fired her first shot. Maybe when she had walked into Bubba's. Maybe even when I was making the first finger motion that morning, turning the knob like I was turning a channel of reality, and brought the storm.

Still, it was a difficult thought. The world had become a solitary place for me the past hundred years. Even Blake, we had met at places, vacation spots, beaches, big cities, mostly east coast. New York and

Boston and Chicago. We never traveled together, both of us were worried that some Remainer somewhere would see us together, so our meetups had felt almost clandestine. It had lent them the intensity I had liked. Not that Blake had needed more.

But that kind of hiding had also kept us from all the other things. Getting to know someone, in a way that people who traveled did. Knowing bathroom schedules, favorite things to eat, what kind of music or soda or toothpaste they liked. Political and religious leanings. All the things people talked about, which I hadn't talked about with anyone, for a long time.

Clyde's wallet had been pretty empty. Other than the cash, the man hadn't had much. A medical insurance cross, with a blue cross at one corner. A coupon for a local fast-food place, some kind of deal. A five-for-five thing. Five sandwiches for five dollars. Seemed like an odd thing to have for someone rolling hundred-dollar bills in their wallet. An insurance card, and a coupon to one of the chain hobby stores that sat in the big parking lots. Twenty percent off his next purchase.

Odd.

I put the coupons and the license and the medical card back in the wallet, and the wallet and the phone back in my pocket. I made sure to take the battery back out of the phone, first. Then I took a second to try to wipe that gluey residue off of my thumb. Seriously, what the hell was in that stuff?

Joe brought the to-go box. A big square, white Styrofoam container. It was heavy with the food inside it. I thanked him, told him the food had been great, and gave him a pair of twenties for it. I'd let him find the hundred later.

A good place with good food and good service was rare these days.

Then I headed back outside. The humid air, the salty smell of the ocean, the sun all hit me as soon as I left Joe's. The warm rays felt good though. I felt rejuvenated. And although I was no closer to finding out why Blake had been killed, or who had killed her, I was at least making it out of Charleston.

The next step would come, well, next.

I was careful with the Styrofoam, holding it with one hand, underneath. The container was heavy and warm on the bottom. The smell of the pancakes and hash browns alone would wake Cass up.

I thought she'd enjoy the breakfast. But when I had walked out of the hotel, my plan had been to trade this for some Ho Hos. I wasn't sure that was a fair trade, anymore. Maybe I'd hold back a pancake or two. Just to keep things even.

CHAPTER NINETEEN

I wasn't sure what had warned me, when I had opened
the door and stepped into the hotel room. After all, the room was dark.
Almost pitch-black. The drapes had been pulled shut, tight to the wall.
So, the room felt pretty much the same as I had left it.

I guess my subconscious had seen something in the *pretty much the
same* that my conscious brain had missed. In my defense, the sun had
been bright outside. It wasn't hot and humid inside. The hallway was
cooler, and we humans tend to huddle a bit more as we walked, scurry
quickly from place to place, have a little more narrow field of view, when
it's cold.

So, back to my opening the door. Lucky me (saying this a little
surprisingly), the card worked on the first try. The door lock beeped,
there was a clicking sound in the knob itself, and it unlocked. I turned
the knob and stepped inside. The air conditioning unit was loud, like I
had left it, though the room still smelled a little musty. The hallway was
dingy but still fairly bright, and like I said, I had left the room pitch-
black, so it was going to take a moment for my eyes to adjust.

I couldn't see Cass in the chair. I couldn't see the chair, actually.

The shadows in the room made everything hard to make out. And like any hotel room, I didn't have the right feel of the space. I didn't intuitively know which blob was the chair, which blob was the corner of the dresser, and which blob was the bed.

Still, I stepped in, letting the door shut behind me. The heavy springs on the door pulled it shut fairly quickly. I looked for the light switch, turning this way and that, my free hand snaking up and down the wall next to me.

Then, for some reason, I *ducked*.

You don't live as long as I do without developing some reflexes. Some intuitive premonition, constantly sensing the world around you, responding at an almost primal level. Some part of me thought that was why I had taken that last drink at Bubba's. Right before Clyde's bullet had grazed my cheek. It was why I had turned a little, at the last second, before the guy had stabbed me.

I was sure my subconscious took in everything around me, sights and sounds and smells, snapshots of people outside, and had put together action plans, based on an intuition I had developed over thousands of years. Overdeveloped, maybe, with all that time. Some part of my hind brain was always working on a plan, seeing threats, and getting me to move. Usually it would do the first part, and allow me to work out the reason why later. After it had kept me alive.

So, for some reason, I ducked. And the reason, like it usually did, became instantly obvious.

Someone had been hiding in the bathroom. Was hiding in the blackness of the open bathroom door. And they had swung something, intent at the very least to knock me into the next day.

But—sadly for them, and thanks to my overdeveloped hind brain— I ducked. Usually one of the first of my action plans. A tried-and-true method for getting me to a safer place.

Still, the *something* they swung grazed the back of my head. Actually connected with the base of my skull enough to cause a flash of light.

Accompanied by a sharp burst of pain, which seemed to be happening a lot to me, lately.

The hard something thumped into the back of the hotel door. It was a heavy thump, like a bat, or a pipe, or maybe the butt of a gun.

My hind brain put action plan two in place. Or maybe it was the flash of anger, that always came with getting thwacked in the head. The primal response to anything that threatened your life, to the pain of that threat. So, I dropped the second breakfast from Joe's (maybe with a little regret), spun, and jumped into my attacker. Before they could start Swing #2.

Sure, I wasn't great at fighting. But I also wasn't bad, either. Stick around for a few thousand years, and you learn some things. I wasn't going to take people who fought their whole lives, like Mike Tyson in the ring, or Royce Gracie on the circuit, and I wasn't going to ever shoot with Cass, but against most people, hand-to-hand, I was going to come out just fine.

My attacker was bigger than me. A man. A flash of worry, or fear, came over me. Wondering where Cass was. What had happened to her. If she was dead in the chair, if I had left her to sleep, and by doing so, left her to her death.

There was no wondering about this man. He wasn't a mugger, or a thief. He was a Remainer. Which meant there were two more, somewhere.

Another cell. That somehow had found us. Far sooner than we had hoped.

And that meant I had to finish him quick. In case his buddies were in the room with him, waiting with the lights out for me to come back.

The struggle was short. Like all fights, they seemed much longer in the moment than watching them from the outside. Adrenaline slowed the moments down, so that each ticked by slowly, and I almost pondered every action before I did it.

He was a big man. And it was a bat in his hand. Maybe he had it because it was easy to carry around in the street. A metal bat, which was too bad, because professionals used wood. At least, the people getting paid in baseball used wood. I wasn't sure what mugging professionals preferred when trying to take someone's head off.

Maybe metal cleaned up better.

Anyway, both his arms leaned down and away from me. Bringing the bat back up, after his big swing. That made his height a non-issue. It was easy for me to step into him and swing my elbow, a little up. My right elbow, so I could keep my left side away from the man. Protecting the wound and the stitches there.

My elbow cracked into the side of the man's face. The other side of his head hit the doorjamb of the bathroom. He grunted, and since he was awake enough to grunt, and since he was big enough to worry about, I hit him again with the elbow. His head hit the doorjamb again, a little more violently this time, because I had put a little more into my swing.

The man sagged a bit, his hands dropped the bat, but he still stood. So, I kneed him in the groin. Ten times out of ten, that puts someone out of action.

He fell to the floor. It was a heavy thump.

I flicked on the lights. Quickly. The chair was empty. Cass was gone. The blanket I had put over her, thrown to the side. The room was empty. There were no other Remainers. Just me and a guy breathing really funny on the floor. Kind of a moaning, high-pitched rhythmic groan.

Then he tapped out, fading into unconscious-land.

I grabbed his bat. A Wilson. Silver aluminum metal with red wrapping around the handle. I thought it was actually a softball bat, it seemed thicker than a baseball bat, but what did I know.

I dragged the man back into the room, still careful I didn't pull my stitches out. My side still ached. His eyes fluttered, as if he wasn't quite out. I was able to work him into the same chair Cass had slept in, then walked over and tore the phone cord out of the back of the hotel phone. Got the curly receiver cord as well. I tied each hand to one of the arms of the chair, tying the cords tight enough they dug into his wrists.

Other cords in the room were next. The lamp cord, the television cord. I tied his legs to the legs of the chair. The whole time, he stayed out.

Then I went back to the bathroom, turned on the light. Found a hand towel and pressed it to the back of my head. It came back with a smear of blood. Not a lot, but not a little either.

Great, another scar to add to the bunch.

There wasn't any ice in the room. I ran the cold water as long as I could, and ducked my head into the sink, rinsing it. Then held the towel on the spot. There was a little bump there, puffy and soft, under my fingers.

I found a bottle of rubbing alcohol that Cass had bought yesterday, more empty than full. I dabbed a healthy amount of it on the towel, in a spot not stained by blood, and pre-winced before holding it against the base of my skull.

The pre-wince never helped. Rubbing alcohol always stung when washing out a cut. So, it was bound to hurt a lot more on a piece of skin opened up by a bat.

The pain made me angrier. I pressed the towel harder against my scalp, and worried about Cass. My guess is, that two of the cell had taken her somewhere, and left their minor-league softball player buddy to take a swing at me.

I'd figure that part out.

At some point, the wound stopped bleeding. Always a good sign. Unless, of course, it's because you're out of blood.

But for now, I had plenty. Or, at least enough. Even after yesterday's bleed-out.

It was time to figure out what I was going to do next.

I sat the bat on the bed and searched the man, careful to not tug on my stitches too hard. I pulled a phone and a wallet out of his pockets, set those on the bed next to the bat. The wallet had a decent amount of cash in it. No cards. The phone was a flip phone and had the same single number in it as Clyde's phone had.

To me, that meant this man was the head of his little cell of three Remainers. It made sense. I needed to learn more, as soon as he woke.

I grabbed a sports drink out of the fridge. Drank it and liked it. Decided to go back to the breakfast I had brought Cass.

The Styrofoam container had opened. Some of the hash browns had fallen out. I was still hungry, but I wrote those off, as it had been way longer than five seconds and the hotel room floor was questionable, at best.

Part of a pancake hung over the lip of the container though, and it maybe touched the floor, but I'll admit I didn't check that closely. Those things were delicious, so I just quickly tucked the pancake back inside. It was surprisingly still a little warm. I brought the container back to the bed, rolled the bat aside a bit, opened the container and ate the food with my fingers. Watching the guy. Waiting for him to wake.

I was hungry.

I remember a line in a movie about second breakfasts. Some group of people on a mission to defeat a dark, oppressive evil. I think the people ate a lot, even though they were smaller than humans. The whole crowd had laughed at one of the guys complaining they hadn't had second breakfast yet.

But maybe they had the right of things. Because the pancakes were just as warm and fluffy as at Joes, the leftover hash browns and onions still just salty enough to balance out the sweetness of the round pieces of cake-like heaven. And another sports drink washed it all down.

I thought about what I was going to do next. The opportunities are endless, after all, when you can steal a piece of an infinite number of realities. It just came down to how far I was willing to go.

When I had first learned of the Remainers, why they existed, I had tried to stop what I did. Slow down the number of times I reached into another universe and pulled something back. Even reduced the magnitude of the theft. Things like a single lime became more common, trying to prevent shootings less.

But the Remainers had kept coming. And I still had to keep pulling from other realities, just to keep myself alive. It seemed like we had reached a point of no-return. No matter how little I tried to steal from other realities, or how few times I did perform the theft, more and more Remainers kept coming. Almost like they bred faster than I stole, now.

Maybe it was time for me to go another way.

I kept eating me some second breakfast. It was delicious. And eating the second breakfast, thinking of that movie, I decided I was going to have me a chat.

As I recall, those little guys had been hounded the whole time. Split up. Battered, until a pair of them had crawled up the side of a volcano. Until a single one of them had been left, standing on a jut of stone, a rocky lip under which fiery lava bubbled and burned.

I didn't want to be hounded until I got to that same place.

These guys were going to start understanding that whatever it was they didn't like about me, there could be a lot less for them to like. I felt like I had tried to be nice about this, but they had killed one of their own. They had killed Blake. They had come after me, and they were gunning down innocents hoping to get me. And now, they had Blake's sister.

Whatever it was I had done to them, it was far from what I *could* do.

It was time these Remainers found that out.

CHAPTER TWENTY

FINALLY, THE STYROFOAM CONTAINER WAS EMPTY. I TOOK the side of my finger and wiped the inside, catching all the grease and butter and syrup that was left of second breakfast. I licked my finger, what was left was gooey and salty and sweet. I had come down off the adrenaline from the fight, but second breakfast had fortified me a bit, enough so I wished there was such a thing as third breakfasts.

I went to wash my hands. The mirror in the bathroom showed a haggard face, thin, much like I had looked yesterday. The face of a man who hadn't slept a lot. The face of a man who drank too much and had lost a lot of blood. A man chased, harried, and who kept losing.

The face did look a little healthier though. The eyes were focused. The jaw set. Maybe it was the food. So as bad as I looked, I had the face of a man with a purpose, now. Or at least, I had made a decision.

I dried my hands and walked back to the room. The man was awake, now. He was a big man, used to getting his own way, and even though he was tied up it didn't look like he was afraid. He looked like someone that expected to break free, like in the movies. That somehow he was going to tear through the cords binding him, overpower me, and win the day.

I was about to disabuse him of that notion.

I sat down on the edge of the bed. Turned to face him. He had dark sandy hair, thick on his skull. His eyes studied me, held a hint of derision. Maybe I didn't look scary enough to him. I wasn't a small man, but this man looked like a defensive end, or linebacker. He hadn't faced many things he was scared of.

Fear was funny though, Usually, it wasn't something that just instantly happened. I mean, people were afraid of things, like stepping on a nail, or there being a snake in the grass, or a hornet buzzing around their room. But it was hard to get to the kind of fear I wanted. That kind of fear had to start small and be grown. Like watching a scary movie, you had to get the person in the right state of mind, before the monster popped out with a jump-scare.

I flipped through the man's wallet. David Brown. From Myrtle Beach. Six-four and two-fifty. He looked all of that. Thick with muscle.

He was thirty-two years old. Young enough to still think he could conquer the world, but at just the right age to start understanding there were things out there that could stop him. He would know, now, that there were things he couldn't beat by being stronger, or bigger. That knowledge was always the beginning of fear. Fear that would grow, the older you got. When knees started aching, backs got thrown out. Until, for some reason, these chest pains wouldn't go away.

Not that I understood those same fears. But I understood the principle.

His wallet had a couple old photos. I was surprised to find them, most people kept photos on their phones now. But David seemed to be a little like me. His pictures, my photo of Blake and me together, they were things we wanted to be real and close. Not some digital image that was one among a million other snaps.

Just thinking about the photo of me and Blake brought the moment back. Sitting in the photo booth, her sitting in my lap, her back warm against my stomach, it was a feeling I would never let go. Could never let go.

I had to push it away now. So, I did. And turned back to David. To the man who had kidnapped Cass. And tried to kill me.

The first was a black-and-white picture of him on a farm, with an older lady and man standing behind him. I'm guessing his parents. The boy was holding a bat in two hands, and the bat rested on one shoulder. The parents were tall, I could see where David had gotten his height. Gray hair, as if they had had him late. Farmer's clothes.

Working the farm had likely given David his build. He was a thick boy, what they call country strong. Thinking of that, of a farm, of being out in the country, brought Blake back to my mind. Cass too, her voice thick, talking about her dad taking Blake out to count the stars.

My eyes flashed to David. He sat there angry. I didn't think he knew angry, not really. He couldn't have. He was too big to have experienced real fear, real frustration.

His second picture was a color photo. He stood in the same area, though he was much older in this one, not far off his age now. And the grass was taller. Greener. It was easier to see the fence behind him, built from railroad ties, thick stalks of corn poking out in the distance.

A lady stood next to him, someone blonde with long hair, around David's age. She didn't wear coveralls, but a nice set of slacks and a summer blouse. A young boy stood in front of the pair, with a bat in his hand, like his dad had stood thirty years before. The bat was just on the other shoulder.

I smiled.

"Want to tell me where you took the woman?" I asked. "The one sleeping here?"

The corner of David Brown's lip turned up, slightly.

I nodded to myself.

"You guys know why you're chasing me?"

The curl of the lip remained. He was going to wait me out.

Which was fine, I was just setting the stage.

A good fear needed to be carefully built. Crafted. You had to steer a person to the edge of the cliff and show him what waited below.

"You're awfully quiet, if you know who I am," I said. "What I can do."

"I know, whatever you do, I'll Remain." he said. He pronounced the last word like it was a religion. His voice was thick and rumbly, it came right from the center of his chest.

"Sure," I said, nodding. "Sure."

The anger seemed to sharpen my thoughts. The anger of Blake's meaningless death. The anger of Cass's kidnapping. The anger of the lack of purpose I felt in my life. What I could do, why, when what I did caused things like the Remainers.

Anyway, for once the boxes of universes seemed clear to me. It was easy to find what I was looking for. Everything I wanted lay in the same factory, on the same line, in the same box, one reality packed right after the next. The first universe I wanted was right on the top of the container, ready.

I wish I knew how that happened. Regardless, I'd use them. I'd use them all.

I picked out the first. Smiled at David. "Tough guy, huh?"

He matched my smile, then shrugged. "Tough enough, I guess."

So modest. Easy to be tough when you're bigger than everyone else. Easy to carry on like nothing can hurt you.

A lot of times, those same people are the easiest to break. The bigger they are, etcetera, etcetera. I thought that was because they've never been tested.

And speaking of tests...

"I've been wanting to do this for a while," I told David. "I've never really known what I can do, around you guys. To be honest, I've never really had the opportunity..."

I paused. Let him see the pause. Then picked my next words carefully. "I've never really *taken* the opportunity to test what I think. What you guys can sense and not sense. What you can feel. What makes you guys so special, that you Remain."

I made sure I pronounced the word like he had. Then I waggled my fingers. Letting him see the motion. (It makes sense to do it, right? Even when I don't have to. It's all part of the show.)

"You should hurry," he said. "Before my friends come back."

"Sure," I said, like I had plenty of time. Nodding, with a small grin on my face. Like I was unconcerned. "Sure."

I waggled my fingers. Letting him see the motion.

Then I waited. *We* waited. The big man looked around. His eyes flicked back and forth, as if he expected to be in a different place. Or he expected something different to be around.

Then he grunted. Like a laugh. His eyes rested on me, narrowed. As if he had faced the worst I could bring to the table and survived.

"So, you didn't feel anything?" I asked. Interested. Curious. The Remainers, well they *remained*, when I sent a piece of our reality to another universe. I wondered if I could bring a part of them back though. If I could steal the smallest bit of them and exchange it.

One more flick of his irises around the room. As if wondering what to expect. Or wondering if I had done something he hadn't noticed.

The big man tested the straps holding him down. Flexed his fingers. He tried to move his feet and looked around. David was wondering what I had done. So, I walked to the hotel door. Opened it. Let him see the number on the front of it. *432.*

No longer the room on the first floor.

Just a subtle change, but it was setting the stage. Letting him see what I could do. Switching the room we were in out with one on a higher floor, basically just finding a reality where the room Cass had chosen was higher, and swapping that room out for the first-level room.

It was something that would buy me a little time. A few minutes, if his friends actually were coming. Enough time, because I could feel that this was a man I could break. The stage was set. The mood, developed. The cliff, just a few feet away.

I just had to lead him there.

"Curious, you didn't feel that," I said. I let him see me thinking, as I shut the door. "For some reason I thought you guys could feel it."

He moved around a bit. Like maybe he had felt *something*, but hadn't been sure what it was. Maybe some Remainers felt more than others. Or maybe I was just in his head.

I walked over, sat next to his chair. "Maybe you're not so special, right? Maybe you guys remain, but that's just it. That's all. So, maybe I can't send you away, but maybe, just maybe, I can pull something different, something from another reality, maybe I can bring that here to *you*."

David wasn't looking at me. He was listening though. Hands and feet moving a little. Testing the bonds.

"There's an infinite amount of Davids out there in the universe," I said. "All living different lives. I wonder what will happen if I pull one of their lives to you? What do you think?"

His eyes flicked to me quickly, then looked away again.

"Let's find out," I said. Holding my hand in front of him, waggling the fingers.

He jerked a little that time. He didn't want to, but he did.

"Pretty tough," I said. Smiling.

His jaw clenched, and though he didn't look at me, I understood he was bracing himself to hold out.

Which he couldn't possibly do. Not against me. After all, I had been around a while. I had seen a lot. And one thing you learn, living as long as I had. You learn how people break. "You didn't feel that?"

The tendons in David's neck were taut. His jaw line stood out sharply. He must be gritting his teeth together, tight.

He didn't move.

"This picture here," I said, showing him the black-and-white one. Where a bat rested on the kid's left shoulder. "You're left-handed, right?"

I saw him hold his breath. His chest paused, as if he waited.

"Funny," I said. "You seem to be right-handed now."

His chest never moved. But I saw his right hand flex, then stop, then ball up into a fist. Then release. Then the fingers of his left hand moved. Cautiously. Slowly, each finger moving as if for the first time.

He was trying to feel it. Feel the change inside him. This time though, I hadn't done anything. A part of me didn't want to take my test that far. I didn't want to lose what made David remain, because if I did, then I might lose where his friends had taken Cass.

But I knew his hands were strapped tight to the arms of a chair. So tight that his wrists were dark red with the blood trapped there. So, I knew he wouldn't be able to feel his fingers, not really.

All good magicians start this way. With a piece of truth, to set the lie. Showing the door, that I *could* do this, and then taking the next step. Leading the audience into a realm where they *had* to believe what they were being told, what they were seeing. David Copperfield taught me that.

His jaw set. I got the feeling he had told the fingers of his left hand to move, and when his right hand had jerked first, he had realized something inside him had changed. Something small. He had tried a few times, to get his left hand to move, but each time his right hand had responded.

"It's a small thing, right?" I said. "Actions you've performed your whole life. Things that had once been automatic, now irrevocably different. Forever. How you swing a bat, play a game of pool, pick up a fork and eat..."

I let my sentence die off. Let him think about it a moment. Think about all the things in life I had "changed" for him.

All small things.

And fear starts in the small things.

The feel of that fear was thick in the air. It came off David in waves.

People think they know something about the world, about what they could endure, about what I could do, but knowing and seeing, knowing and *believing*, those were very different things.

I smiled at the guy. Like we were best buds. I pulled out the black-and-white photo again. Made the little motion with my fingers.

Flipped the photo to me. It was hard to tell, in a black-and-white photo, but the lady's hair had subtly changed color. From a gray to almost black. She was shorter too, rounder. Her cheeks more plump, with a dark apron tied around her waist. Not the tall thin lady that had been in the picture before.

One hand still on the young kid in front of her.

But a completely different person.

I showed David the picture.

Waggled my fingers again.

Changed his father, right in front of his eyes. Shorter. Thicker. Thick black hair, not the rugged brown of David's.

"Crazy, right?" I said. "How people you've known your whole life are just gone now. I mean, you'll remember your other parents, because you remain. But you'll still have to learn these new people, right? Maybe you even live with them, out on the farm. They'll wonder how you got to be so tall, what kind of recessed gene jumped out in your gene pool. They'll never know you really aren't their kid. But you will."

David had gone from not breathing, to a rapid breath. In and out, in and out, faster and faster. He started jerking against the cords on the chair, started bouncing up and down.

That got him a bat to the stomach. I had been ready, and got him right in the solar plexus. His breath whooshed out, and David fought throwing up.

But the chair stopped bouncing.

I pulled out the next picture. The one of the young lady. His wife. And his son.

"Now," I said. My voice as guttural as I could make it. As serious. I smiled at David, but I made sure the smile never reached my eyes. "We get to see how committed you are."

David fought to breathe. He stared at me, the anger, the certainty in his eyes, all gone. The irises were like a wild creature, trapped. Not knowing what else to do but fight, but knowing the fight would cost him, dearly.

I held the picture right in front of his face. Held my other hand right next to him. Went to waggle my fingers.

"No," he finally spat out. "Please." He wrestled more in the chair, but his heart wasn't in it. He was staring over the cliff, realizing what waited below.

I shook my head. "The magic word isn't going to help you here."

"*Please!*"

I waggled my fingers. Let him see the change begin in the picture. Something simple, like the bat disappearing from his son's grip. If he believed his son would be the same as him, that his son would remain too, I wanted him to know that wasn't the case.

David screamed. Spittle flew from his mouth. He writhed in the chair. The scream turned into two words, over and over, before it became a sobbing.

I leaned closer, until I could make out the words. A long trail of saliva hung from the corner of his mouth.

"Folly Beach," he was saying, over and over. His eyes were pressed together, tightly, and the words mixed with sobs and hiccups and big, shuddering breaths. "Folly Beach, Folly Beach, Folly Beach..."

I leaned closer, spoke into his ear. Softly. "I need an address, Dave."

He gave it to me.

I left him there, sobbing. His friends would find him. Or someone would.

Maybe you think I liked doing what I had just done. I didn't. I never had. But the Remainers, I would never convince them I wasn't evil.

I mean, there was a time, long ago, that I had pulled things from other realities, changed people, changed things, changed *lives*. But I hadn't understood what I was doing then, not really.

And when I had, I had stopped. Mostly. Sometimes, like the storm, things happened. But those usually happened because it was a them-or-me type of situation, and believe what you want, but all of us, in those times, usually pick the me side.

There were accidents, occasionally. Sure. Because everyone wants to believe what they can do, who they are, has a purpose. So, I have done things I wouldn't be proud of, in search of that purpose. Because power ultimately means responsibility. You may have heard me say it once, but I've tried to find out what that responsibility should be for a guy like me.

With not much success.

But finding out that what I did had real consequences. That pieces of this world didn't fit right with others. That people Remained, and I was affecting other's lives, that had changed me a little. And as narcissistic as I was, I still tried to avoid hurting others, when I could. Maybe the only last good thing about me.

So—if I had a choice—I wouldn't steal reality in a way that hurt innocents. I didn't care a thing about David, but I wasn't going to hurt his wife, or his son. So, I hadn't changed a single thing in David's life. I had lied to him about his hands, and then I had changed two pictures in front of him. Pulled the picture from another David in another universe.

Pretty easy. Set the stage. I had made him believe I could and would do anything. And he had bought it, hook, line, and sinker.

I wasn't the monster the Remainers wanted me to be.

Though innocents did get hurt. Sometimes there were no good decisions. So, while I didn't go out of my way to hurt bystanders in the war between the Remainers and me, I also didn't put them at the top of my "be careful" list.

Because the Remainers had grown over time. Become greater in number. More violent, and more opportunistic, in the ways they tried to end my life.

Maybe David was a nice enough fella. Maybe he was just a believer on the other side of a war, a war that had gone on for centuries, now. Remainers seemed almost a religion, to me. David himself believed at that level.

Those kinds of people needed to be shown the error in what they believed in. That worse things can happen to them. Before the believers became martyrs. Before the religious became a mob.

It's why I left his pictures there. Still changed. I wanted Dave to always know it could have been worse. That it *would* be worse, if he picked up his bat and came back against me. That I could always go back and get his family, if he made that choice.

Remainers needed to know I could hit close to home too.

I felt responsible for Cass. I had gotten her caught. Because Blake's death had sent me into a spiral, and I had called a storm. Gotten a lime. On the day we were supposed to meet.

She was an innocent. Or had been, until the Remainers had shot up a bar in an effort to kill me. Until they had shot up rugby fans, a bartender, people outside, to try to take me out.

Their fervor, their hate, seemed a little much to me. It was hard to justify that killing, just for me. I wasn't sure what drove them to those lengths.

Cass had helped me when she hadn't had to. In all likelihood she had saved my life, twice. I wasn't going to repay that by allowing the

Remainers to kidnap her, torture her, even kill her, in their attempt to get to me.

Blake had believed I lacked real passion. The truth was a lot of who I was, and what I felt, was just buried deep. Under thousands of years of living. But anger was a good shovel, and I could feel the emotions stir in the back of my brain.

I was showing David just a small part of what I could do.

Since I found out what I was doing affected others, I had tried to avoid hurting the innocent. But I still wasn't really a turn-the-other-cheek kind of fellow.

CHAPTER TWENTY-ONE

Outside the sun was shining. It was still midmorningish. Humid with the promise of more heat to come. I'd be sweating again in a moment, and left my jacket unbuttoned to get a little air, even if the little seahorsey monsters showed prominently on my shirt.

The sky was blue, speckled with the remaining bits of black clouds, and though the waves washed peacefully up the shore, not many people wandered the beach. The few that did walked tentatively, they took a few steps and then looked around. They talked in low voices. There were none of the shouts and screams of fun from the beach, not like yesterday.

A storm like that did that to people. I'm sure they had woken up yesterday, checked their weather apps on their phones, had the news on, getting ready for the day. They had seen a beautiful sunny day and got ready for the beach.

Then a hurricane, a tempest, had appeared. From out of nowhere. A storm out of the blue that hadn't been on any news channel, any app. A storm of fury and vengeance, something that came with an immediacy and an urgency, something unexpected and surprising on an otherwise beautiful day.

Something deadly.

People had woken up yesterday with an excited feeling, had run around on the sands, maybe dreaded having to count one more day off their vacation clocks.

And they had come home scared.

Sudden storms did that to you. They were something... out of this world. Elemental, in their fury. In their vengeance. An unnatural tempest.

So, the beach was mostly empty today. Maybe a few more people were around now, than when I had left the hotel this morning. Like a turtle, they were slowly poking their heads out from the relative safety of the hotels and homes they stayed at. A few wandered the beach, maybe looking for something they had lost, fleeing from the storm the day before. Maybe just looking at all the damage, all the trash that had blown around, pieces of walls, roofs, boats.

I gave it all a glance, headed down the alley. Away from the shore. To one of the main streets running parallel to the beach. A number of cars and trucks sat at meters there, and I picked one that I liked. A larger olive-green truck, one of those that had four-door cabs. At first I thought it was a truck, but it was a Jeep. Or a Jeep-truck with big tires. Something called a Gladiator.

I liked the name. I tried the door. It was locked.

So, I thought about it. Tried it again. This time the door opened. It's amazing in how many universes people leave their doors unlocked.

There were keys lying in one of the cup holders, with a tiny black fob thing on one of the rings. The Jeep-truck had one of the push-button starts, which I wasn't a fan of, but it did make it easy to start. The engine fired up with a press, the frame vibrated with a good rumble. Ready to roll.

I took a second and adjusted the seat. Pushed it back a hair.

Adjusted the mirrors. The navigation screen came up on the dash, and I typed in the address David had given me. It was in Folly Beach, an area I knew well enough.

I pulled the Gladiator into the street. It started slow, but with a lot of power, like the Jeep-truck was stretching itself before getting ready to roll. Like a lion, taking a long step or two, before getting ready to pounce.

I was headed south. I knew Charleston a bit, the whole city mirrored the shore, had grown inland over the years, across the swamp-like areas and the finger-like tributaries that stretched to the ocean. Folly Beach was south of where I was at, I'd have to circle west a bit to get across a few bridges, then head south and back east.

Luckily enough the streets were fairly empty. It felt a little weird, like someone had instituted a quarantine, telling everyone to stay indoors. Occasionally I'd have to take a detour, as emergency crews worked removing a flipped over car. Or cars.

I found Folly Beach Road, got on it, headed south. Followed the blue arrow on the navigation screen. I knew the highway ran south-east through the city, through some marshy swamps, over a few bridges, and ended up directly at Folly Beach. Probably why they called it Folly Beach Road.

The swamp areas were a lot less marshy today, more like lakes, dark with mud. The water levels were high, as if the storm had pushed every-thing up a bit and held it there. Everything was flooded, and only the tops of the reeds showed there was any marsh there at all. Here and there the water was high enough to crest over the road, just an inch or two of the ocean, leaving long lanes of shimmering wetness to drive through.

Which was perfect for the Jeep-truck. It split the water like a lion running through a stream, pads splashing with every step.

There was a lot more traffic heading north than south. Away from the beach. Cars and trucks of vacationers, heading home early. Fleeing the destruction of the storm. Mile signs flew by underneath the occasional billboard. I made good time.

Folly Beach, coming up.

I pulled out Clyde's phone. The flip phone with the one number. I didn't want to use anything of David's. I wanted whoever answered to believe he was still waiting for me back at the hotel.

I pressed dial.

It rang just once. As if on the other side, someone had held their phone. Waiting.

"Ah, the Reality Thief," the voice said. It was deep, with an accent, something elegant. A little clipped, and maybe British. Whatever it was, it was the tone a guy smart enough to know the person calling him wasn't Clyde.

"Good to hear you've heard of me," I said.

"I can't say what I've heard hasn't been easy to believe," he said.

"They say seeing is believing," I said.

"I know that," he said. "Now."

I started the misdirection. "So, I'm on my way. Figured I'd call. It's rare I get a chance to talk to the people trying to kill me."

The voice didn't say anything. Just subvocalized a grunt. Maybe he was wondering if what I told him was the truth. His first question was something I didn't expect.

"You steal a car?" he asked. "A Gladiator?"

I was shocked enough that I let off the gas a bit. In the background of the call were voices of other people, as if the man stood on the side of the street. I thought I could even hear the beach.

Was he next to the motel? Had I passed him somewhere? Had he left Folly Beach? Why?

Too many questions, but maybe a bit of good news as well. It might mean Cass was still alive, if this man was at the motel.

"What's it matter?" I asked. "Stolen. Bought. It all takes me out of Charleston."

I definitely did not like the town. The heat. The bugs, the "palmetto bugs" people pretended weren't cockroaches. The humidity that caused me to sweat through every suit I tried on.

"I hardly believe you will leave your friend."

I was more relieved than I would have thought, hearing Cass was still alive. I didn't let that relief touch my voice though. I wanted to give this man a reason to keep her that way.

"Ummmm, I *did* kind of leave her." I made sure to sound surprised.

"Hmm," the man said. The subvocal grunt, again.

"Why? You guys find her?"

The man didn't say anything. I wondered what he was doing. And my mind couldn't help but drift to how this man had discovered what I had stolen. And if that same process helped him to track me now.

Hopefully, it was just the little theft I had done. Stealing reality so I could grab the key. Maybe this guy could locate where I did my little trick. Talked to whoever was around that thought they had locked up the Jeep-truck. Gladiator. Whichever.

"She doesn't talk much," the man said.

I smiled. She was alive. And pretty much being Cass. "Well, now you know why I left."

Silence from the other line. A muffled sound, because I could hear something. Like the man was talking with the phone speaker covered by the palm of his hand. Then he returned, and when he did, I thought he was testing me.

"So, me killing her won't bother you?"

I was good at apathetic. I almost didn't have to pretend. "One thing I've learned, everyone dies on me at some point."

He did the subvocal grunt thing again. Man he liked doing that. Like he thought with his throat.

I slowed down the Jeep-truck. Saw a billboard of a store I wanted to stop at. Took that exit off of Folly Beach Road, swung around the off-ramp, turned right, and found the store. Parked right in front of it.

I felt a little urgency now. The stars were aligning, and that always worried me, because that didn't often happen in my life. I knew Cass was alive, and I knew where she was at. And I knew the guy who wanted to kill me wasn't there.

Still, this man was the guy trying to kill me. I *felt* it. And this might be the only chance I had to learn more about him.

"You still there, Jeeves?"

He sounded amused by the name. "Quite."

"You the guy leading the charge?"

"For now. If it matters."

"Well, these things kind of do," I said. "I've got to know who to kill."

"Hmm," Jeeves said. "Is that really true? I would think someone that does what you do wouldn't have much of a conscience."

That wasn't really fair. "You know I wouldn't have to do anything, if you guys wouldn't keep coming after me."

"It would be interesting to figure out," the man said. "Is the cause the real cause, or is it just the effect?"

That was a fancy way to say chicken and egg.

"I think we both know each other. What we've done," Jeeves said. "We know that you won't let me go. And I know that I will kill you. It's just a matter of time."

That seemed dire. And the way he phrased it was confusing. I wasn't aware what he knew about me. And I knew even less about him. Unless all Jeeves meant was that he had killed Blake. In which case, what I wanted to do, *needed* to do, was clear.

The man remained quiet. Like I had given him a piece of information that I was unaware of. Something unexpected for him. Perhaps even dangerous.

"Look," I said. "I'm about out of this town. Just wanted to check and see if we couldn't call a truce on this thing, before I left."

There was a little pause. "What if I said yes?"

Well, that caught me out of left field. I got the feeling I didn't know enough about this man. And that the knowledge I lacked might come back to bite me.

"Well," I said. "It'd be nice not to have to worry about getting stabbed."

He chuckled. As if that should be the least of my worries. As if he knew something I didn't and was thrilled to find that out. "Let me ask you, how long have you lived? How many years?"

Well, Blake would have defined the word *lived* differently than me. And just thinking of what the word meant, long ago. Hurt.

She would have thought of lived as a way to spend your life. Not just a way, but the way. *Live* your life. Make it have meaning. So, her number for me would have been a lot less than any number I came up with.

But an old root of the word was German. Leben. And it meant something like leave. To leave.

So, Blake, I guess we were both right.

I finally replied. "Long enough."

"Hmm," Jeeves said. "On that we agree."

"So. No truce then." Not that I had hoped for one.

He chuckled. "Time's running out. I almost had you once."

It had been him, in the alley.

The thought scared me more than anything he had said. I even almost glanced around, looking for him behind me, ready to punch me in the side with the dagger again. And fear for me led to anger. Exactly what I needed.

"You sure?" I let my voice get serious. Spoke low. "I mean, *you* might be ready, but surely you have people around you that aren't. Mother? Wife? A favorite puppy? Because if we get into this, you should know that's where it's going to go. Everyone you hold dear will be fair game."

He was silent. The line was silent. I almost thought he had hung up. "*Who* are you?"

I didn't know what he meant. And we were measuring each other.

So, I felt like a threat would be the proper way to end the call. "You keep following me, you're going to find out."

I snapped the phone shut. It closed with a click. It didn't feel as good as I wanted it to, not like slamming a door, or screaming, but it was what I had.

I closed Clyde's phone. It was a quick motion. Flipping shut with a snap.

The Jeep-truck was still running. I held its button down until the truck powered down with a slight shudder. I missed the days of keys and ignition switches. Engines felt more powerful with the turning of a key. Like you were unlocking something.

A button could never quite capture that feeling.

And then I let out a breath. Cass was alive. And hopefully would stay that way for a bit longer. I thought Jeeves was at the hotel we had been staying at. Maybe he'd find David and stay there a bit.

Which meant I had a window. I just had to be careful. If he could sense me stealing reality, however the hell that could happen, then I'd have to do this the old school way.

Which is why I was in front of this particular shop.

I would do this right. If I got there and Cass was alive, I would save her. If I got there and she was dead, I would be... vengeful. Because I already had put Blake on their tab. If they killed her sister as well... they had yet to understand a real martyr, and I was the type of guy to cut off his nose to spite his face.

The people who had taken Cass would regret it.

I turned the phone off. Then got out of the truck. Looked at the store in front of me. *Swords of the East.*

I liked the line. I think we've all seen the movie. So, I thought it appropriate.

It was time to get medieval on some motherfuckers.

CHAPTER TWENTY-TWO

I'M SURE YOU'RE ASKING YOURSELF, WHY NOT JUST CALL UP A sword? Or steal a nice knife from another reality? Easy, right?

Actually, I bet the real question you're asking is: why does this guy want to bring a sword to a gunfight?

Let me tackle the second one first. I've mentioned that I haven't practiced fighting as much as I should. Especially lately. But there was a time in the past that I had.

Guns are relatively new. And they are, if I'm being honest, relatively scary. A single bullet could kill a person, from a mile away. You might never hear it. You might just walk out the door one morning, feel a *pop*, and then fade to black.

That kind of thing scares a guy who has lived a long time. It's just too easy. There's no effort to the killing. Everything was easy to make nowadays, guns were no exception, and it's a relatively simple process: point, then *click*. For a guy like me, ending it that fast was terrifying.

I mean, I know I don't have a real purpose for existence. But I'd like to keep up the search. Just in case, you know, there is one.

A sword though, that was a weapon you had to be up close and personal to use. You saw the person trying to kill you. They saw you, as well. And if you were good enough, lucky enough, or some combination of both, you survived.

To be honest, for thousands of years that's how people killed. They got up close and personal. With a blade.

It's hard *not* to become good at a thing, living that long, over that period of time.

So, swords, knives, these things had been around a while. It made sense for me to have more practice with those, just due to that length of time. So, I was a fair hand with one back in the day. I could stand with some of the better swordsmen of the various eras.

(Is it swordspeople now? Swordspersons? Hell, I didn't know.)

Anyway, back then swords were also hard to get. Hard to make. So, when a person wore one, they were probably good with it. For thousands of years wearing a sword was a sign of *don't fuck with me.*

That was kind of handy.

So, I started wearing one. And I started getting good with it.

I mentioned being in Japan around the time Dracula had been around. That I had missed that whole thing. I was there because I'm a fan of elegant things. And one of the things I had found most graceful, most refined, was the katana.

I spent some time with the Samurai. I enjoyed the code of honor, the rigid culture, the dignity. There was a purpose there, I felt, behind all of those things. Learning from them. There was this sense that I felt like I could be a part of all I might have been.

That's faded now. But it had been there. The feeling of being.

I admired their ability with a sword. Swords. The Samurai called the pair they carried daishō. Everyone today knows the longer sword, the long single-edged blade, as the katana. There's a mysticism to that sword today, I loved how the movie *Kill Bill* revealed that power of the sword. Of the commitment to master it. The mystery. The elegance.

And if you really committed, there was some magic to it. You could do some amazing things. Things that seemed almost mystical, like carving up fifty or sixty bad guys in a restaurant.

Not a lot is mentioned about the second blade Samurai carried. The wakizashi. It was smaller, maybe a little more curved. No movie really singles this blade out, though a samurai usually wore the wakizashi even in places where they were made to give up their katana. Whenever the shorter blade is in a movie, you see it used for seppuku, when a person kills themselves over some point of honor.

I spent time learning the katana. I got to be pretty good with it. And while back then I couldn't have held my own against the Samurai I had learned from, today was different. Today I was probably a god with a blade.

I mean, today they talk about the ten-thousand-hour rule. If you spend ten thousand hours learning something, you got to be a master at it. Ten thousand hours is little more than a year in total time, four hundred and sixteen days.

So, if you extrapolate those hours over a lifetime like mine, you could say I'd had a little bit of practice at it.

And as practiced as I was with the katana, I was even better with the wakizashi. It was more of a dirty blade, used for infighting. For small rooms and crowded places. Close up and personal. Something I had a true natural talent for, oddly enough.

I didn't carry a blade today, oddly enough. It's funny, how almost anyone today could pack heat, carry a gun, anywhere they went, but strap on a katana and people would look at you funny. I mean, it's so much easier to kill someone with a gun than a blade. So much easier to do the point-and-click, than stare someone in the eyes and push a sword through their heart.

Anyway, here I am drifting again. You had a second question, which was actually your first. You wanted to know why not steal a sword from another reality? Just have one appear?

The first reason is obvious. I didn't want to clue the Remainers in, that I was closer than they thought. I wanted them as surprised as they could be. They had found some way to know when I stole reality, I couldn't tell you how, but it was more than just people passing along word that reality had changed now. There were immediate responses. And I kind of had a feeling Jeeves was behind those.

The second reason just goes back to when I learned how to use a blade. Guns are easy to kill with, even if they don't feel right in the hand. But they are hard to master. I wasn't as good with them, and I was far out of the league Cass was in.

But a sword, that was different for me. To use it right you had to *feel* it. You had to hold the blade in your hand, test the balance, know it was something you could work with. So, if I picked one from another reality, the balance might be off. The handle too long. The blade too heavy. I would have to try a thousand of them, maybe, to find one that works.

A lot easier to walk into a store and pick one out.

And that's what I was going to do. Lucky for me South Carolina was one of the states that didn't require all kinds of permits to have a blade. So, stores like *Swords of the East* were a dime a dozen.

I walked in. The door had no bell, but there was a guy behind the counter. Flipping through a magazine on the counter in front of him, which was actually a long glass display case with a register on top.

The guy was short, thin, with long black hair tied loosely behind his head, and a patchy beard. A loose blue button-up shirt hung from his shoulders. Behind him on the wall hung all kinds of swords, each blade lying horizontally under the next. They were arranged in eras, there were curved blades from the middle east, longer, straighter two-edged swords from Europe, and what I was looking for to one side. The katanas of Japan.

"Help you?" the guy asked, his voice a lot deeper than I would have guessed, as small as the fellow was.

"Yeah," I said, nodding to the katanas. "Looking for a pair. The katana and the shorter blade."

"A fan of the daishō?" The man smiled. "Most people just want the katana."

"I like pairs," I said. I looked in the glass case. In there were more modern knives, the K-Bar of the military, other longer hunting blades. I think I saw a bowie knife, the blade larger than my forearm. "I don't see any of the wakizashi though."

The man shrugged. Flipped through a page of his magazine. Looked like a gun magazine, funny enough. "Not a lot of call for those."

I understood. Not a lot of call for a blade that people used in the movies to kill themselves over a point of honor. A lot more desire for a weapon to kill another, just because.

I walked over to the wall. The katanas were mounted in their wooden scabbards, hung one over the other. The scabbards were called *sayas*. All the blades had the same length and shape, long with a very slight curve.

I didn't ask the man, just started pulling them down one after another. There was something innate in the human touch. We all instinctively know whether we like something or not, just by holding the object in our hand. How our fingers cupped it, how heavy it felt, whether the object was too warm, too cold, or too squishy.

So, I went through the katanas fairly quickly. I paused at the ones I liked. I'd grasp the hilt in one hand, the saya in the other. Slide the weapon out and feel the weight. Feel how it felt in the hand. Feeling the smoothness of the blade, as it slid in and out.

Most of the sayas were black. A few had ornamentations on them. A few of the hilts of the katanas were decorated as well, with tiny diamonds etched into the wood, or patterned with the leather. Which traditionally, if the hilts were bound with true samegawa, should be shark skin.

Back in the day, that was how you would identify who had made the saya, by the patterns of the samegawa, just like you would identify the swordsmith who had made the katana by the signature on the blade. The *mei*.

The third blade that I tested was good enough. I stopped there. The saya was a brown wood, almost maple-colored, with black cord tied around the hilt end. The samegawa was a white leather, the handguard black, and the blade itself had a beautiful silver sheen when I pulled the sword out.

It slid out and in with a whisper. Like the smoothest of bearings. It wasn't a blade from *Kill Bill*, but it felt good. Perfectly balanced in my hand. I took a few practice swings, short chops, then held the sword with both hands. The balance and heft felt great. I even tried the one-handed twirl thing they do in all the movies but makes no practical sense.

The man grunted behind me. As if he approved of the pick.

"Lucky you," he said. "That was a special order. I have the pair."

He disappeared for a moment. Around the wall behind the counter. I heard him rummaging around, then coming back with the wakizashi.

It was much shorter. The blade was a foot in length. The hilt maybe half that. But the samegawa, the saya, the curve of the blade, it all looked the same. Just in miniature.

I took out the wakizashi, quickly slid the blade out, grunted (I could do it too), and slid it back.

"I'll take both," I said.

The guy looked at me, nodded. Looked at my shirt. Then focused on the rib area, where there was a washed-out stain of blood.

He tilted his head a bit. Shrugged. "Grand for the pair."

I smiled. I happened to have that on hand, in cash, thanks to Clyde and David. And it wasn't my money, but I liked to bargain. I looked at the case below me.

"Throw in a K-Bar and the leg strap, and you've got a deal,"

He grunted, more I feel to one up me on them, and then nodded. Pulled a black K-Bar knife out of the case, along with a rig people strapped along their upper leg, so that the knife would ride alongside the outer quad.

I pulled out the cash I had taken from Clyde and David and handed it over. The man took the cash and nodded. Didn't write me a receipt, just went back to flipping through his magazine.

I wonder if he knew what I was about to do. Maybe he felt, after the storm, people were just getting ready for the end of days. Maybe he was getting ready too, by moving on from the close-and-personal swords he carried, to something that killed with a point-and-click.

Whichever it was, it was time to get moving. I headed back out to the Jeep-truck. The Gladiator. It waited on a quiet street underneath a blue sky, with just a speck of black or two remaining from the storm. Pieces of the storm that refused to leave.

It was time to get medieval.

CHAPTER TWENTY-THREE

The Jeep-truck rumbled up with a push of the button. The button press still felt wrong. But the rumble felt good. It was the rumble of a lion in the wilderness, a hunter stalking its prey. Letting the antelope know—at the last second—their demise was on its way.

Appropriate, right?

I got back on Folly Beach Road. I had a mile or so left as the highway lay through the rest of the swampland and tributaries. The last part of it was crossing over Folly River, swollen now, before the road turned into Center Street. Which, as its name implied, cut through the middle of Folly Beach.

Folly Beach was... damaged. The storm had done a number on it. Pieces of roofs and walls lay everywhere. Umbrellas and chairs and tables scattered. Pieces of clothing, t-shirts, towels blown everywhere.

Places built at the beach always seemed temporary, like they weren't built to last. I felt like that's why, if you watch the news when a hurricane hits somewhere in Florida, you see the corrugated metal roofs flying everywhere in the wind, the composite-built walls tumbling over, until it was all flotsam and jetsam in the water. People living on a beach knew the power of nature. Instead of building fast against it, they built in a way where they could rebuild quickly. And cheaply.

So corrugated roofs lay everywhere in Folly. And parts walls. Some of those stucco, some plaster, drywall broken in pieces here and there. People walked everywhere, picking through the garbage, uprighting white plastic tables with a hole in their centers, finding the table's lost umbrella pole.

There weren't a lot of people. Not the tourists and the rest that I had seen headed out of Charleston. But these people were who lived here, the shop owners and bartenders and other people who had bought a home, maybe a beach home at one point, and then a place to live.

A young man stood at the corner of a street, holding a splintered surfboard vertically, one end of the broken board on the sidewalk. Others walked around holding towels and big black trash bags. A few were carrying one of those big tent stands out of the road, the kind you can rent to put over your chairs on the beach. There were a number of the chairs themselves, blue and red webbed things, blown everywhere. Like a giant hand had grabbed a couple hundred of them and rolled them down the street, as if they were dice.

I passed restaurants, north and south of Center Street, all closed now. Lost Dog Café, with palm trees around it. The Crab Shack. Wiki Wiki Sandbar. And on the corner of Center Street and Ashley Avenue, Rita's Seaside Café. A place I had always liked because her name was written in white cursive letters on a red round sign, kind of like Coke. Which was my favorite non-alcoholic beverage.

I made a left at Rita's, got onto East Ashely Avenue. Slowly navigated around a person collecting chairs there, stacking a red on top of a blue, then finding a blue to put on top of the red. The man was shirtless and shoeless, just wore a pair of khaki trunks, and stared at me like he thought I was heading the wrong way. His hair was black and wild, and his eyes kind of matched it, like he thought in some way I was responsible for what had happened here.

And, I kind of was.

But I was heading to the real culprits.

Maybe it was the guy's eyes, but I started to get angry as I slowly navigated the road north. Worried. Cass wasn't really a friend, but she had saved my life, twice, and I didn't really have a lot of people in my life that would do that kind of thing. I didn't really have any friends. It got to be too hard to keep them after seeing them age and die.

That's probably why I was like I was now. A drifter. Never really belonging anywhere. Never really not belonging, either. Stuck in some weird place in the middle. Maybe relationships were what kept us going, what helped us face the future. I've doubted whether I have a purpose, in fact I had given up on finding it, and living a long life had tilted me in the direction where the point of it all had been hard to find.

Blake had been someone I had connected with. Deeply. As deep as I had ever connected with anyone. There had been something about her, something that understood me, what I could do. I felt like she had been a key to unlocking the puzzle about me. About my purpose.

But now Blake was dead. And her sister could be too. May already be dead if I didn't hurry. Anger and frustration swelled in me, like rhythmic waves beating against my chest, making me push the gas pedal down more. Drive over the broken drywall in the road, instead of driving around it.

Funny how emotions can get to you. You can tell yourself that anger leads to rushing, and rushing leads to mistakes. You can repeat it like a mantra. But the emotion keeps washing over you, like the ocean beats against the rocky shore. It wore you down and uncovered something real. It got to you, at some point. It washed away the sand and the silt and laid your rocky shore open to the world, naked and bare.

It was then that you knew the truth.

I kept the gas pedal down. Swerved around the obstructions in the road. People stopped to watch me fly down the street. Crunch over wreckage. Knock the webbed chairs and plastic tables aside.

Jeep-truck handled it all.

To the north, in the distance, Morris Island Lighthouse poked out, like a red and white peppermint pencil, all by itself. It became my focal point. On my right was the ocean, shimmering under the sun, millions of shining waves, the waves with glittering tips, or crests, as if an army of blades was washing to shore. To my left was the beach, the stores and shops, some blown down, some flattened, others standing as if nothing had touched them.

I drove down the middle of it all. The knife-like waves to my right, the destruction to my left. The sun high overhead it all, an impartial yellow judge in a blue sky. And those damn specks of black.

I got under control enough to slow down a few blocks away from where I needed to turn. I didn't want to warn them I was coming. Parked the Jeep-truck on the side of the road, buttoned up my suit, and grabbed the katana. It had been awhile, muscle memory allowed my hands to wind the around the saya in a way that allowed me to sling it around my back, and the leg-holster was easy to strap up around my pants for the K-Bar. The wakizashi I just held, in its scabbard, in my free hand.

Then I took the fob out of the Gladiator and locked it. Took off running. West. Into the beach and down a few blocks. Keeping a building between me and the house I wanted to get to.

There was a lot of destruction here. A lot of homes that were now pieces of homes. I ran by one where an entire wall—the length of the house—had been torn away by the wind. I saw inside the entire home, the living room with a couch and television, the galley kitchen, the bathroom and bedroom, the bed frame part of an old rowboat.

I wondered where all the people were. Wondered if they had left when I had brought the storm. If they were in another reality somehow, and all that was left here were Remainers.

That thought made me a little more cautious. I peeked around the corner. Roofs torn off homes and tossed into the street. More walls blown down. Couches, chairs, even a long wooden dresser in the street. A car here and there, parked amid the wreckage. But no people.

The house I wanted was a lucky one. It was whole. I saw the number on the mailbox, one of the few still remaining on the street. Like all beach houses, it was single level. A pale blue home with pink shutters. Stucco walls. A low-angled roof, with a garage. With a frickin' pink garage door, of all things.

The house next to it was in pieces. I snuck around to that side and worked through the destruction. Crawling over some of the rubble, the wakizashi tight in my hand. My side ached with a quick, sharp pain, as the rubble shifted underneath me, and I stretched a bit too far to steady myself. My foot got caught in what I thought was a big toy fire-engine, and I had to work to get it off.

Then I heard a scream. Cass.

At that point, all plans evaporated.

I slid down the other side of the pile. Stood by the blue wall of the beach house, right by the garage. There was a pink door there, with a tiny four-square pane of glass at the top. I broke the glass with the hilt of the wakizashi, reached in, and unlocked the door.

There was truck in there. Well, a sports utility vehicle. A large black Land Rover, with tinted windows. Something you might see in a Bond movie.

British people. Always have to have a little class.

The Land Rover was so big I had to work my way around it. The garage was that small. It took a little more time than I would've liked, and so I made it to the door to the inside of the house at the same time another guy did, coming from the other way. A young man, with a backward hat on, and some kind of blonde scruffy beard.

It was convenient and timing for me. And not so convenient. Scruffy Beard had a gun, already forward. I was a step or two away. He was already pulling the trigger by the time I was unsheathing the wakizashi.

By all reports, bullets are faster than knives.

I think I've said this before, but the one thing about adrenaline is that it ramps everything up. Every thought and action. Every reaction.

I can always seem to find the reality I need in the middle of a fight. Far easier and faster than when I really was looking for something. And if the reality wasn't particularly tough to find, like trying to find one where Scruffy Beard carried a water gun instead of a Glock, then I could make the switch in less than a heartbeat.

I stole a different door. Something harder. Metal. From a reality where break-ins were common. It still had a window at the top, smaller, with bars in it.

Scruffy Beard fired. The door held up. He hesitated for a brief second, then fired again.

That had been enough time for me. The wakizashi was out by then, and the blade was sharp. It split the glass, passed right between two bars and then right through Scruffy Beard's face.

Who dropped pretty quickly.

I opened the door and stepped over the man. The young man. Boy. Well, they were all boys to me. I made a flicking motion with the knife, snapping the blood from it, before I sheathed the blade.

All of my motions were from memory.

I had been pretty good at this once.

But there was no time to stand around and pat myself on the back. The gunshot I was sure alerted everyone in the house. I rushed through the kitchen, something mostly white with a lot of pink backsplash. Small flamingos, little statues, stood on the windowsill above a sink. For the love of heaven. What was up with all this pink?

A hallway led away from the kitchen. It had been where Scruffy Beard had come from. I rushed down it, passing a cupboard with a glass front, showing the world all kinds of garishly colored china plates. I don't have to tell you the theme. Or the color.

There was another scream. Louder. Cass again. And a snapping sound. The scream came from the far end of the hallway, which stretched the length of the house, from the kitchen to a closed door. Other doors were to the left and right, I guessed leading to things like bedrooms and bathrooms. Every door shut.

To my right the hallway opened up. A living room of sorts. No one was there, just a big fat blue couch and a television that wasn't on. I crouched down and ran down the hallway, as low as I could. To me, speed mattered more than safety.

I was still bringing a knife to a gunfight.

A shotgun blast echoed that point. I was passing the door to the first room on my left when pieces of drywall exploded over my head. The sound of a shotgun firing was unmistakable. Bits of plaster splattered everywhere, leaving the hallway dusted in a cloud of talcum white.

I paused, still in the cloud, blinking the dust out of my eyes. Everything tasted like the acrid smell in a shooting range. My ears were ringing but I could still hear the heavy ratcheting sound of someone reloading.

Never a good sound.

I moved as soon as I heard it. My left hand reached up over my shoulder. Grabbed the hilt of the katana. Unsheathed the blade and swung it around in an elegant, quick motion. Thrusting it through the open hole.

There was a grunt. A heavy sound, a thumping of a heavy piece of metal on carpet. Like a shotgun being dropped.

Then another scream came from the room at the end of the hallway. I could barely hear it from my ears ringing. It was less a scream, more of a shout for help.

It cut suddenly off.

Cass.

I pulled the katana out of the wall (and whoever was on the other side). Then I thrust it back again. One more time. A little higher, so I had to push it through the wall. The sword slid easily through the sheets of drywall.

I was rewarded with a second grunt. Barely audible. The katana pulled up in my hands as the blade took on the weight of a man's body. The hilt jerked a bit, then got suddenly light. Like the body had slid off the blade.

The door at the end of the hallway opened. The room holding Cass. I was still in the talcum cloud drifting like smoke in the hallway. A man stood in the open doorway, someone in a jean jacket and jeans. The Springsteen look. He had blonde hair and his face had tiny spatters across it, like blood.

I was ten feet away. The katana still in the wall. Too far for a knife.

The Remainer pulled out a gun. It was small and black, a forty-five or 9mm. Probably a nine. All the kids liked those today, maybe from all the rap videos. The gun was black and semi-automatic, it would fire as fast as he pulled the trigger.

There was no time. I let go of the katana. Left it stuck in the wall. Tucked my head underneath my jacket. At the same time, I tossed the wakizashi, scabbard and all, at the man.

Then I ran at him.

Trust me. I know you can't throw one of those knives. I know they're not meant for that. But I was just looking to get the man off his aim. Give me a second or two. Ten feet is a long way to run at someone with a gun.

It wasn't something I would normally do. Neither one of those options, running at a guy with a gun, or throwing a knife, were my top choice. But it was all I had.

I ran at him, screaming like a madman. My head down, tucked under my jacket, not seeing anything, praying the material held. The man swore, loud enough for me to hear. My scabbard clattered against the wall. Maybe he had batted it aside. Maybe I had an extra second or two. I moved as fast as I ever had, thinking... *I probably should have tested these suits out before doing something like this.*

I know. You really should test the things out that your life depends on. But in my defense, the suit was kind of a last line of defense for me. Something for when I wasn't paying attention, maybe. Not something to hold in front of my face, like a matador held his cape in front of a bull.

I guessed that analogy was off. The Remainer was the bullfighter. I was the bull, running at the man, with a cape over my head. Hoping it would protect me but knowing that it could just be hiding what was coming next.

The inevitable stab of the bullfighter's blade. Or gun. Whichever.

I kept up the charge. Feet stamping the floor. I took one last breath, waiting for the blast of the gun, the bullet to stab me, and the final *Olé* from the crowd.

Something bounced off my head. The back of it. Not dead on. The shot had been altered some, though a flash of light burst over my vision, and I could feel the force of the bullet furrowing over my skull, along the suit.

The jacket did its job, though.

It still hurt like a motherfucker. You ever walk into the edge of a low ceiling? Or stand up, so your head smacked into the side of a door? It hurt like that, only a thousand times more. Like a cabinet moving towards you at the speed of light.

The flash of light remained. A bell rang. A loud bell that didn't stop ringing. I almost fell, stumbling, keeping my feet churning, and somehow kept moving forward. I hit the Remainer just as a second shot went off and took him to the ground.

For some reason the light in my eyes was tinged with red. My jacket got caught over my head, tangling my arm up. The Remainer and I fell to the ground, the man punching me with one hand, moving the other one done. Maybe trying to get his gun pointed somewhere in my direction.

All I could do was wrestle with him. Roll around the floor, trying to get my arm untangled. Acting more on instinct than anything else.

And as I've said before, I had a well-developed instinct. Honed with thousands of years of situations like this.

Fury burned through me. Adrenaline. The two of us kept rolling on the floor, wrestling. I ended up on top. My arm freed. My head broke out of my jacket. The Remainer swung his fists, hitting me on the back of my shoulders with the butt of his gun. I kept my left arm up enough on that side to keep him from hitting my skull again, trying to grip his wrist, trying to keep him from pointing the gun at me.

I finally got the wrist. I pinned the guy's arm against the floor. He pulled the trigger a time or two again, firing the gun across the room. I didn't, or couldn't, hear Cass at all. Everything was hard to see, everything was still clouded with that flash of light, everything was tinted in a pulsing red. For now, it was just me and the Remainer.

He pulled the trigger one more time. But that was it. Mostly because my right hand had reached down along my leg, pulled out the K-Bar, and plunged it up into the man's side. Right under his ribs. Up into his heart.

Where a man had tried to kill me, not so long ago.

The third Remainer gurgled under me, until he stopped gurgling. It didn't take long when you do it right. When your blade is long enough.

Then that was it.

CHAPTER TWENTY-FOUR

I took a deep breath. Everything still tasted like acrid gun smoke, but there was a new addition: the salty taste of blood. I pushed myself off the man. Got myself kneeling a bit. Wiped my face with the back of my sleeve and looked around the room, waiting for the flash of light to go fade away. For the bell to stop ringing. For the pain in my skull to recede.

Cass was sitting off to the side. Still in the white shirt and blue jacket I had met her in at Bubba's. The Remainers had tied her to a chair, like I had done with David. They were better prepared, though. Thick black wire ties held her wrists and legs to the chair, an old wooden thing, well-constructed, with thick spindle-like legs, curved arms, and a hard straight back.

Her eyes were closed. Her head lay down at an angle. The bob of black hair she had tied up at the back was loose now, and some of the hair fell forward, over her face.

I slid over. Saw her chest rise, slowly. Cass had been beaten, pretty bad. Her temple had a gash in it. Her nose leaked a trail of blood. Her cheek had gotten puffy, and later, after she had been punched enough, had split open. Blood ran freely from all three places: her temple, nose, and cheek.

The red remained in my vision. An angry cloud at the edges of my sight. I took a deep breath and shook Cass, gently. Trying to wake her.

She didn't wake though. I wasn't going to slap her, like you see in the movies. I was happy she was alive. Even tied to a chair, I didn't want her to wake up and somehow shoot me.

I needed to hurry though. Jeeves would know where I was now. He had an ability to know where and when I stole reality. So, I had to get Cass out of here. Quick.

I went and got the K-Bar out of the Remainer. Cleaned the knife before cutting the wire ties holding Cass, making sure she didn't fall after she was freed. She slumped a little in the chair, but still didn't wake.

That worried me a bit. Especially if she had a concussion. But alive was better than not.

I collected Springsteen's wallet. Went back and collected the katana and the wakizashi. Cleaned the katana, put it back into its scabbard, slung it back around my back. Found a way to slide the wakizashi and its scabbard inside the K-Bar leg rig and tie it there.

Here you may wonder why I didn't just change reality during the fight. Steal a toy gun and replace the 9mm. Change the shotgun out with a squirt gun. Find a house with something in the hallway, like a small fridge being moved between rooms or something, so I could hide behind it.

It's a good wondering. A good question. I'll just tell you it's pretty tough to do. Especially when milliseconds count. I can't just grab any squirt gun from anywhere, the reality has to be close to mine. Same area. Same place. Same people-*ish*.

The Remainer is going to stay. That's a fact. So, I have to find some kind of reality where a person is standing in the same place, with a squirt gun. Or something. And there's one out there, in the infinite number of universes, but finding that one is going to take some time. Rolling through all the realities, opening up all the boxes, looking for what I needed, that's going to take a millisecond or two. It could take even a second or more. Or a minute or ten.

When you're betting your life on those seconds, you need to make sure they all count.

I hadn't been able to come up with a rule for this yet. All I can say is I can't do things like stealing the Eiffel tower from Paris and move it to London, or Chicago. But I can stand in the middle of a city and switch out an apartment building on a block with a pizza place from another reality.

Yeah, I know.

You'll bring up the knife earlier. The stabbing I took. And it's a good point. All I can say is then I knew I was a sliver of an inch from dying. I could feel it. And so, lucky or not, I immediately stole what I needed. I had found a guy holding a shorter knife nearby and been able to steal that knife and replace it with the one I had been currently getting stabbed with.

But I couldn't even remember looking for the smaller knife. It really just kind of happened. And that's the way it works. At least for me. I mean, I *am* still figuring these things out. I have my rules, but for the most part this has been a trial and error type of thing.

And there's been a lot of errors to get to now.

I studied the first two people I had killed. The Remainer I had stabbed through the wall, and the one by the kitchen door. The first guy wasn't a guy, but a thickly built woman. Maybe it had been sexist of me to assume it had been a man. She had been older, with a lot of gray in her hair.

Part of me felt bad about killing a woman. I had been born during a time where those things weren't done. In fact, chivalry had been a large part of my life. The social equality movement was kind of relatively new to me, but I was trying to catch up to the times.

I guess Remainers came in all shapes, sizes, and colors. And today was all about equality. Nothing said equality more than equal-opportunity killing. So at least I was conforming to the social norm.

Still, I couldn't help feeling bad. But I moved past it. And into the kitchen.

The Remainer there lay where I had left him. The young boy in the backwards hat, and patches of scruffy blonde beard. Neither the woman nor the boy looked British to me. And the guy dressed like Springsteen didn't strike me as British either. I collected the man's wallet, and the woman's purse, a thick canvas satchel thing.

I put what I found on the blonde kid inside the satchel, slung it around my shoulder next to the katana. Told myself it really wasn't a purse. It's a man's shoulder bag. At least, that's what I saw on a show once.

While I was in the kitchen, I poured a tall glass of cold water. The water was not really cold, just cool, and had a rotten egg smell to it. Little flecks floated in the water, swirling in the cup under the tap. Beach water.

There were keys next to the sink, with a fob on them. I tossed them in my pocket. I carried the glass back to Cass. Put my fingers into the top of the cool liquid and flicked it at her. Just a few spots at a time. Letting the water hit her face.

It took a few flicks, but her eyes began to flutter. I waited, then flicked some more, until the lids finally opened a bit. The eyes behind the lids were on autopilot, they looked confused, but there was anger behind the confusion. I could see Cass trying to force herself awake. To push through the confusion and get into war mode.

I spoke to her. Said her name. Tried to make her understand war mode wasn't necessary. Let her know she was safe, for the moment. Until we found British guy, at least.

I pulled one of her hands up, wrapped the fingers around the cool glass. I took more water and let drops of it fall onto her forehead. To

The water mixed with the blood there, made little red twirls on her skin.

Her eyes cleared. Her fingers tightened around the glass. She went to move out of the chair, like she was trying to stand.

"Easy," I said, leaning forward. Letting her lean against me. Her head fell a little on my shoulder, and the glass of cool water lay between us. I was surprised at how slight she felt. "Easy."

She muttered something, but it was guttural and unclear. The words a violent whisper.

"What?"

"Gun," she may have repeated. Her free hand found my arm, and her fingers dug into my wrist.

"Let's get you standing first, Cass," I said. Fearing terminator mode. "Before we weaponize you."

"*Gun.*"

Who was I to argue with a walking terminator? Cassinator? Herminator? Eh, probably just going to stick with what first came to mind. And not mention it aloud.

I gently leaned her back in the chair. Set the glass of water to the side. Went back to Springsteen and peeled the pistol out of his hand. I had been right, it was a Glock 9mm. Almost no one uses the forty-fives, anymore. At least I didn't think they did.

Cass took the weapon. It seemed like as soon as she had the gun in her hand, she got stronger. Like something came over her. She took a deep breath; her hands went through the checks all people made when picking up a gun. Slid the magazine out, checked the bullets remaining. Moved the slide action. Checked the safety. Or safeties. I think Glocks had a few. Like the company was saying *here, have something that'll murder someone, but check and make sure you've filed all the appropriate forms before you do.*

Like I've said, I don't like guns. I'm getting better with them, but they are just too easy to kill with. Too impersonal. It's so easy companies that make them have to instill all kinds of ways to keep people from "accidentally" killing someone else.

I mean, multiple safeties, right?

Cass held the Glock tight in her hand. She pressed her eyes tight together and took another deep breath. Then opened them and tried to stand.

It took a moment. She grabbed me as she waved, her knees not locked. She was very light, lighter than I had thought. Like the clothes Cass wore weighed more than Cass, herself. Weird I hadn't noticed that yesterday.

But then, yesterday Cass had been carrying me.

"You good?" I asked. Checking.

Her eyes found Springsteen. And then she shot him, once. The hole appeared in the direct center of his forehead. His head briefly bounced up in the air, and at the same time a red liquid pool splat out from under his skull, blowing his blonde hair out around his head.

I felt like that meant she was good.

"Was there a guy here?" I asked. "British accent?" I thought.

The urgent feeling grew inside me. But I wasn't going to rush Cass. Especially with how she felt right now. She took a slow moment to kneel next to Springsteen. Went through his jacket until she found a couple of spare magazines and put those into her coat. Her voice was still low. Still raw. "He left, not long ago."

I didn't think I'd be that lucky. Jeeves was still out there. Maybe with more people. There was no telling how far, or how close, or how many. Maybe he had run out to grab lunch. Maybe he was getting more things to torture. Maybe he was getting a scratch-off ticket.

No way to tell.

Part of me wanted to wait for him to come back. Surprise the bastard. But looking at Cass, I wasn't sure we should. Or could. I was just coming off a day of almost bleeding out myself.

We had to move.

And I found out I hurt a lot more than I thought. It was a bad time to start coming down off the adrenaline high. My head hurt like a bitch. My ears sounded plugged, but there was some ringing still.

And my side ached. I couldn't tell if I was bleeding, mainly because my shirt was covered in Springsteen's blood. But I didn't want to check. I wanted to power through, until we were somewhere safe.

I got us to the Land Rover. Jeeves knew about the Jeep-truck, so I had to leave it. As much as I liked it.

Plus, we were in a hurry. And I had a new fob, which made things easier to steal. Even British things.

The Land Rover was parked too close against the outer wall, so that I couldn't quite open the passenger door enough for Cass to get in. We had to take a little bit of time opening the driver's side and working Cass over to the other seat. She was hurt and tired, and I was hurt and tired, and neither one of us wanted to push ourselves too far and end up, well, *more* hurt and tired. Like the dead kind.

She buckled her seat belt. It snicked together. I snicked mine, took a moment to arrange the seat and mirrors. (Yeah, I wasn't sure why, I wasn't going out and doing a driver's test.) Then I pushed the button to start the Rover. It powered up quick, a smooth transition of the engine from off to on, feeling nothing like unlocking anything or unleashing a lion. But I guess that could just be me and my preconceptions. I had liked Jeep-truck.

Then we both sat there in the Rover. Cass looked at me, and there was a hint of the old Cass in her expression. The slight arch of an eyebrow.

The garage door was still shut.

It was an old garage. Wooded slats ran horizontally in front of us, thin pink boards weathered by time. A rope hung down from overhead and brushed the top of the Land Rover's hood. There was no button to press. No remote for it hanging on the sun visor. You had to get out and pull the door up and down yourself.

Which didn't sound that appealing in my current state.

And we *were* in a hurry.

Fuck it. It wasn't my truck. It wasn't even my house.

I slammed my foot down on the gas.

Turns out, those doors are more substantial than they look. Even old pink wooden ones. But the Rover lurched through it after a try or two.

CHAPTER TWENTY-FIVE

THE SUN WAS STILL BRIGHT OVERHEAD. THE SKY STILL BLUE. The remnants of the storm, the black specks of clouds, still dotted the eastern horizon. Hanging over the ocean like the darkness was waiting. Watching.

I turned left out of the garage. Headed north. Even though I knew there was nothing that way, no way to drive off the island. Folly Beach had one bridge, and that was back on Center Street. Knowing that detail, and knowing that Folly Beach was kind of closed with the storm, I figured I might run into Jeeves that way. Maybe he was waiting and would recognize the Land Rover.

As much as I might want to meet the guy, neither Cass nor I was really up for it. Not right now. We might be able to power through a gunfight, or an exciting car chase, but I fell back on my tried-and-true. When in doubt, run.

So north was safer in the short term. Away from the Folly Beach bridge. North to the edge of the beach, south of Morris Island and its lighthouse.

Cass slumped a bit in her seat, like the seatbelt held her up. Her hand tight on the Glock. Her head laying against the side window, as if she was using the window to hold her head steady. Her eyes though, were alert. "You're not heading the right way."

"Nope," I said. "I'm not."

Her jaw shifted. As if she wanted to say something else but thought about it. Or maybe she was just tired.

"I've got a plan," I said. "Trust me."

The jaw shifted again. But Cass stayed quiet.

I navigated the neighborhood, swinging around anything in the streets too large to drive over. It was empty, and my feeling that everyone here was gone returned. That all that was left was destruction, me and Cass, and the Remainers.

I pushed the button for my window to go down. It wasn't too long ago, at least for me, that you had to crank a handle to do the same thing. But now everything was a button. Engines, windows, sooner or later maybe even spaceships. No countdowns, no booster rockets, just a quick press of a button and a launch into space.

There was an odd feel in the air. It was humid and thick and quiet. Even with a fairly clear sky and a bright sun overhead, there was a feel of a storm. The black dots of clouds stayed in the east, as if the darkness there knew the pause was just a momentary lapse. As if everything around me waited for yesterday's tempest to return.

I didn't like the feeling. It was more than a storm. It was the feeling of something coming. Something unpreventable. Something world-ending.

Maybe that was me though. Knowing things weren't settled between me and the Remainers. The feel of them, all around me. Cells of them scattered through Charleston, at Folly Beach, surrounding Cass and I, pinning us in Folly Beach. All of the cells and Jeeves, with his fanaticism.

But really, what could one guy do? One guy with an accent and a hard-on for killing me? I mean, the worst that could happen was me dying.

Maybe.

I've been blamed in the past for an overactive imagination. But I felt like my feeling of fear was accurate, at the here and now. Things were coming to a head, and I couldn't understand why. The Remainers had been around hundreds of years. Maybe even thousands. Maybe since my first theft of a reality, so long ago.

Their numbers had grown since then. Since whenever my first theft had happened, and then the second, and the third. Maybe it was just the natural order of things, for the Remainers to gather and grow, to get to a certain number where they seemed to be everywhere. Like any tribe that grew to a certain size, like any two groups of competing philosophies, the Spartas and the Athens of the world, they were ready to take out the thing that threatened them most.

Which happened to be me.

But it felt like more. I couldn't tell you why. But it felt that way.

I got us to one of the roads leading out of the neighborhood. Turned left onto East Ashley Avenue. Which was an odd way to name a road that ran mostly north along the coast. The neighborhoods faded, the road became mostly a highway that split one level homes on either side of the street. Beach houses, mostly, of all the different colors that beach homes come in. Pale blues and yellows, some whites, one or two more pink buildings. A few of these buildings blown down from the storm, revealing broken interiors, scattered furniture, loose-lying sheets. One of those had a teddy-bear, sitting by itself on the front lawn, facing the street.

More and more though we saw the water. The ocean and its waves, with shining knife-like crests glittering under the sun. Cass remained silent but alert, her eyes open, keeping lookout. I left the radio off, so there was just the hum of the engine and the muted rumble of the tires rolling along the asphalt.

There were a few more cars on this road. Most of them heading south, opposite us. They drove slow, like turtles. Maybe the air was too thick and too humid for anything to be fast today. Maybe these people were just poking their heads out of their shells, looking around after yesterday's storm. Maybe they were all Remainers, and only let us pass because we were in the Land Rover.

We stayed on course, north-northeast. The thin pencil of Morris Lighthouse grew larger in front of us. It poked up out of the water, the tall building striped horizontally in large strips of red, then white, then red, then white. A dark hat of maybe stone or steel sat on top of the lighthouse.

That wasn't where I was going. I was looking for something specific. I could sense Cass wanting to ask the question, but maybe she just didn't have the energy.

Then I found what I was looking for.

Folly Beach was an island, running north and south, long and thin. The sandy coast of the beach faced the ocean to the east. Folly River looped around behind the island, so the west was mostly swampland and marsh. A bunch of little tributaries cut inland from the river, little branches here and there, fingers of water stretching from the river into Folly Beach.

Atlantic Ocean was to the east. Folly River to the west. All kinds of hidden little waterways. And with Folly Beach being an island and all, there were bound to be boats.

Jeeves might know where I was at, even though I hadn't stolen any reality here. He might be waiting at the bridge, even now. But I didn't think he could or would watch all the waterways. The Remainers couldn't follow us onto the ocean. Well, they could follow us, in some kind of high-speed boat chase, but I thought finding a boat and hitting the ocean would give us time. We could find somewhere to hole up and heal up.

So, I watched the homes to the left. The homes built next to some of the small fingers of water connecting to Folly River. I was looking for a home that had been destroyed but had a boat behind it. The first couple of homes I had seen, there had been a pier, but no boat. One had a boat floating hull-side up behind it. Another had some people heading out to their boat, coolers and suitcases in hand.

Finally, I came to what I needed. A home halfway destroyed. The house was a dark yellow, maybe a light tan, it was hard to tell because most of the front of it was missing. The roof had fallen in there, in pieces. The rear of the home still stood, and behind the house was a long pier with a sailboat tied up next to it.

I pulled into the driveway.

Cass saw the boat, looked at me. I wouldn't say her face looked happy. "That's your plan?"

I held the button down on the Land Rover. Let the engine switch off. Nothing like a lion. "It gets us out of here, doesn't it?"

"You can sail?"

A corner of my lip turned up. "I've been around since sailing was invented."

"That's not an answer."

"Yeah," I said. Answering. "I can sail."

I wouldn't have to sail though. We were looking at a good-sized craft. Thirty feet, I thought. Single mast, but it would have an engine.

Cass didn't get out. And she didn't look at me.

"Look," I said. "I'm worried. They seem to be everywhere. There's one road in and out of this place. So, I'm trying to do something unexpected."

"I believe you," Cass said. "I just don't like the water."

Then a moment later, she clarified it. "The ocean."

"You'll be fine," I said. "There'll be life vests and all, in case."

She rolled her eyes.

"I can swim," she said.

"So, what is it?"

"The water," she repeated. "I just don't like it."

"You'll be fine."

Her jaw set. "I'd rather shoot it out."

I waited, not sure what we were going to do. I could see the boat in front of us. It sat high in the water, maybe a thirty-foot cruising yacht. Small enough to take through the branches leading to Folly River. Not something you used to race, something with a pretty broad beam and a lot of room inside.

It would be a great place to hide.

Cass seemed to read my thoughts. She blew out a breath and opened her door. Swung out and climbed out of the Land Rover, holding onto the door to steady herself, the Glock still in the other hand.

I hesitated. Wondering if I was breaking some kind of Cass-rule. "You sure?"

"Come on," she said. Her voice short. "At the very least, if something goes wrong, I'll be able to tell you I told you so."

I had thought I had a good idea. It might not be great, but it was good. A way to get off the island without confronting any more Remainers. Without worrying about where they might catch us. And even—with a good amount of luck—finding a good place to hide and heal up.

Suddenly though, I wasn't sure. Cass's words had sort of a premonitiony feel about them. They were hard to ignore, they kind of lodged in the back of my spine, like a big knot. I wasn't looking forward to hearing that particular *I told you so*.

When, and if, that time came.

CHAPTER TWENTY-SIX

I helped Cass to the boat. The *Isla Marie*. It was an Island Packet cruising yacht, white with light wooden rail around the deck. One center mast with white sails, the pale canvas edged in blue trim. A jib colored the same. The sails were stowed, but a light breeze stirred the loose edges, blue edges flapping weakly in the air. Four square windows lined up next to each other along the side, called ports, right in the middle of the boat. A hatch there where people could descend into the cabin, be out of the sun and relax.

It sat high on the water next to the pier. It was a little bit for me to jump over to it, the *Isla Marie* rocked when I did, and then it was a little bit more work to get Cass over. She pulled back initially when I reached out to help her, and then finally forced herself across. Looking down at the dark river water below, the boat rocking and shuddering the whole time.

We went aft, climbed down the short ladder to the cabin inside. A sink and small kitchen area sat in a galley immediately off the entrance, there was even a microwave and a small fridge. A saloon had two couches placed against the bulkheads, one to the left and one to the right. A narrow hallway ran the length of the cabin to the front of the boat, with a couple of doors on the sides, likely to small closets. There was a small bathroom compartment (sailors call it a head, however that came about) in the center of the ship. The head even had a shower.

I sat the man-purse of stuff I had collected from the Remainers in the galley. Cass sat on one of the couches. She wasn't pale or anything, just weak. I remembered she probably hadn't had much to eat, that I actually had eaten the breakfast I had bought for her, and that the sports drinks and Ho-Ho's back in the hotel room—what she had planned to eat—was still back in the room with the Remainer I had left there.

I quickly checked the cabin out, then the rest of the boat. Everything looked in good condition, though it was a bit old. The bed in the v-berth was clean. The engine wasn't going to outrun anyone, but it was topped off with fuel. The kitchen area had utensils, plates and cups, some bottled water, but not much else. Nothing in the fridge.

I twisted the plastic cap off a bottle of water, then handed it over to Cass. She grimaced a thanks and took a few sips. "We leaving?"

We weren't really stocked to go far. "Soon," I said, checking the cabinets again. Seeing if I missed anything. I was planning on running into the halfway destroyed house and do some foraging. Hopefully find the keys to the boat as well. "Be right back."

She gave me a look.

"We don't have much food," I said. "And you kind of look like you could use some."

Cass wanted to argue, but finally nodded.

"Hold the fort," I said.

I climbed up the short stairs topside. Jumped back over to the pier. Trying to hurry. The air, hot and humid earlier, felt lighter now. As if whatever had been holding it down had let go, allowing the moisture to burn off.

Maybe that was a good thing, but the muggy heat reminded me of watching a cat play with a mouse. How the cat would hold the mouse down with one paw, then release it. Catch it again, hold it down again, and release it again. Until on the final release, right before the mouse made it to safety, the cat pounced and gobbled it up.

I shuddered. Not because I felt sympathy for the mouse. But because I had heard things like the quick squeal of sudden death, I had seen the last spurt of blood, the light crunching of bones, and those kinds of things stick with you.

Anyway, back to the foraging. The back of the house by the pier was still standing. There was a rear door there, white with four small square windows in a single frame. The roof actually stretched a good length of the house, it just looked like the front of the house and the far side of it had collapsed under the storm.

I tested the door. Locked. But the home definitely had no power, and I didn't see anyone inside, so I punched out a square of glass with my elbow and unlocked the door. I stepped into a short area, like a mudroom, but for beaches (you can tell because there's always a little grit and sand on the floor).

From there I found the kitchen. Which was perfect. The floor was white tile, a little old, a little soft, a little yellowed. My steps were soundless against it. The cabinets were all white, and a nice dark oak-colored counter ringed the wall.

A white refrigerator rested off to the side, a photo stuck to the front of it with a yellow butterfly magnet. A metallic magnet hook sat next to it, with a pair of keys. The boat keys. I grabbed them. Easy-peasy.

The picture was of a young man, standing on the *Isla Marie*. He was young, with long dark hair and tanned skin. He had a great smile, leaning over the stern of the ship, towards the camera, with two thumbs-up.

I wondered if that kid was still here. Still in the home. Back in one of the rooms that had collapsed under the roof. Or if the storm had whisked him away.

Hopefully he had been out. There wasn't a car in the driveway. So maybe he had been lucky. Or maybe he was just gone. It was hard to tell, because past the kitchen and towards the front of the house the roof had collapsed, bits of broken wood and black shingles all piled together, under a clear blue sky.

I tested the fridge for food. It was a quick nope. There was no power, so the smell when I opened it was pretty much rancid everything. Spoiled milk, rotten meat, and moldy cheese.

So... on to the cabinets. And found what I needed there. A lot of packaged items. Cans of soups, little cans of spaghetti with bits of meatballs or hot dogs in them. Some of them had pasta spelled out in letters, which was weird to me. Others had a sloppy-joe like sauce in them.

The next cabinet over had packages of bread and buns. The classic jars of peanut butter and jelly. Cans of tuna-fish, and a plastic bottle of mayonnaise. And a bottle of Buffalo Trace, the amber liquid dark under the label, the etching of a wild buffalo frowning at me.

I looked through the house. It was hard to go anywhere. The living room was under the roof. So were the back bedrooms. There was just an office right off the kitchen, and a hallway that ran just far enough to get to the bathroom.

I looked through the bathroom first. Got some shower stuff, soap, deodorant, and a nice find: a good-sized first aid kit. I grabbed it all and took it to the kitchen. Peeked back into the mudroom. There was a toolbox there, and a couple of buckets. A square bucket, with two sides that would hold a mop. And a big five-gallon bucket, blue, that you might use for cleaning.

I took the buckets back to the kitchen. Loaded as much of the food up as I could. The five-gallon bucket grew pretty heavy. The square one was hard to fit stuff into, and I ended up packing the bread on top of it so the loaves wouldn't get squished. I tucked the Buffalo Trace next to the bread (you knew that was coming along), and then I ran the first load out there.

Cass was lying down on the couch, facing the hatch, Glock still in hand. The barrel also facing the hatch. Her eyes narrowed when she saw me. Or maybe it was when she saw the bourbon. Probably both.

I handed the first aid kit to Cass. Told her I'd be right back. She kept up her glare and I was beginning to think that was her normal face. But she took the kit and started going through it. I ran back to the house, planning on going through the office and then coming right back out. You never know what you might need when you head out to sea.

The office was small. Little bigger than a closet. A small desk and a chair. A tiny window looked out over the Land Rover I had parked outside of the house. The front grill of the truck was cracked, and the bumper had a broken piece of pink slatted wood sticking up.

The desk held a laptop on top of it, and a smart phone on top of the charger. Seeing the phone there made me think the guy who owned this place wasn't coming back. No one left their phone at the house. At least he wasn't lying around here somewhere. The smell of a dead body always ruins a good scavenging.

Oh well. His loss, my gain. I took the laptop and the phone and their charging cords. Packed them in a small duffel bag beside the desk. Took out the other phones I had. David and Clyde's. I turned on Clyde's phone real quick, to make sure I knew the number.

As soon as Clyde's phone powered up, it rang. A shrill, repeated beeping sound. I looked at the number, knowing what it was going to be. Knowing who would be calling this phone.

Jeeves.

Dammit. The one time you actually want a telemarketer call, right?

My first instinct was to turn the phone off. Disconnect the battery. Or destroy it. A fear ran through me, I worried Remainers were lined up around the corner of this house, like a SWAT team, ready to charge in and take me out.

It was too late now. If they had me, they had me. I thought about answering. It was about fifty-fifty. Maybe it was just human nature, because I just couldn't seem to leave well enough alone. You would think, after a few thousand years, I would know better.

Apparently, I didn't.

I might as well see what Jeeves wanted.

I answered the call. Trying out an Italian accent. (I can speak the language fine; actually, I can speak many languages fluently, but somehow accents seemed beyond me. I always butchered them. My Italian accent usually sounded like a video game character, like I was impersonating Mario.)

"Papa's Pizza Shop," I said. "You buy 'em, we slice 'em."

"Stop," Jeeves said. His voice hard, but I still could hear his clipped British accent. I wondered how he pulled it off.

"You no like-ah the pizza pie?" I asked. Maybe grinning a bit. Playing the bad accent up. Enjoying the moment, even if there was a SWAT team hiding around the corner.

"*Stop*," he repeated. His voice somehow harder. Somehow more British. Commanding.

Then a moment of silence. I waited. He waited. I got the feeling, like I had outside the sword shop, that he was listening to what was around me. And again, I knew that was wrong. But he was doing *something* and that bothered me.

I waited long enough. I tried my British accent. It wasn't any better than my Italian one. "Bugger me... something up your knickers?"

He didn't say anything. Still listening, maybe. I felt a tension from the other line, a swelling anger, a rising tide. Something Jeeves had trouble holding back.

"You're there now, aren't you," he finally asked. Well, *said*. In clear, cold words. I could almost feel his realization, as if he stared at a radar, watching the green sweep of the hand revealing a big blinking dot that screamed *Folly Beach*. Like I worried, he had some way of sensing what I did. He had seen me steal reality when I had switched out the door at the beach house to something more bulletproof.

It was my turn not to say anything. The conversation felt more like two people talking to themselves. He talked, I said nothing. He talked, I said nothing.

It was a weird back and forth. More like a forth, I guess. Like a tennis player lobbing the ball over the net, waiting for the return, when they were the only player on the court. Both of us waiting for the ball to come back. There was an emptiness centered between us. A fulcrum, a midpoint. A weird balance of emotions, a seesaw of anger on his side, and the slight amusement on mine.

The seesaw tottered then, and finally tipped.

"You don't know me—" Jeeves started to say. But I cut him off.

"I know your type. I've seen versions of you for thousands of years. Always angry. Always wanting to settle the score. You can't imagine how many times I've heard this speech. That I don't know you. I don't know what you're capable of."

While I talked, I walked around the inside of the house, taking a few peeks out the remaining windows. The collapsed front of the house. Looking for the SWAT team, just in case. "You know what, Jeeves? There is no score to settle. If you're angry, be angry at the world. For being born. Because whatever you think I did, whatever it was, I can't apologize for that, but I'm sorry it happened."

The pause lasted a long time. His side of the teeter-totter, high in the air. And his response, when it came, confused me. The voice was almost wondering aloud. "Who do you think I am?"

"I think you're some guy who wants revenge," I said. "Some guy that feels like I did him wrong. Who climbed to the top of a bunch of other people who think I did them wrong, and all of you want to kill me for whatever it is you think I did."

"Hmm," Jeeves said. Still in the wondering tone. "Fascinating."

This guy. I had no idea what he wanted. And he confused me, and I was too tired, too beat, and too... stabbed to want to deal with any of it.

"Yeah, well fascinating is all you get," I said. Peeking out the kitchen window. Looking at the *Isla Marie,* bobbing in the water. "Because whatever happened, I can't bring it back. I can't bring them back. If it's your mother, your kid, or your wife, if they lost their memory, or maybe they're just gone... I can't do anything about it."

The rules were the rules, after all.

"I wonder," he said. Which was his tone, after all. "I wonder if I can trust you. What you are saying."

"It is what it is," I said. "Whatever I did, it wasn't malicious. It wasn't something I did on purpose."

Hell, whatever I had done to Jeeves, likely it was something the Remainers had even caused. Most of the things I had done lately, at least the *world-changing things*, those realities had been pulled because I was running for my life.

Just like the other day, when I had been stabbed, and pulled another building from another world just so I could get away. "Chances are, you can blame your little group Jeeves. Usually I just do the things I do because they show up."

"So, you say," Jeeves said.

"Yeah, so I say."

"So, life's been tough for you?"

You could say that. Blake being killed. Getting stabbed. It definitely wasn't peachy.

"Well, look around sometime," Jeeves said. "Life is tough for everyone. So, take a ticket. Look in the mirror. And own what you've done. What you keep doing."

The image of me in the mirror, just a day ago, came to mind. All the scars. The dark, hollow eyes. Reminders, of how long I had lived. All the people I had left behind. The numbness that was my life.

Especially now that Blake was gone.

Jeeves wanted me to own what I've done. Whatever it was that I did to him. The other Remainers. But I didn't know how to do that in a way to satisfy them. Other than letting them kill me, which I kind of had an issue with.

The truth was, I was trying to own my past. I was trying to make amends, in the only way I could. I *mostly* didn't steal reality in big ways anymore. I had given that up, given up finding out why I existed. Given up on my purpose. Given up believing I was on this Earth for *something*.

So, it had been awhile since I had tried to save a school full of kids, or change the course of a ship headed for an iceberg, or save the Two Towers. I—*mostly*—had stayed away from world-changing events.

But the storm yesterday had been me. At least, the first time I had called the storm, it had been all me. It had been the act of a drunk man, full of despair. A sad man, who maybe had found his purpose, his *other*, and before he had realized it she was gone. And he didn't know how to go on.

Could purposes be people? Maybe Jeeves and I were more alike than I thought. Maybe I was his purpose now. Maybe he could be mine. And maybe I wasn't entirely blameless for whatever had happened to him. I certainly was responsible for what had happened to this world.

Still, if Blake was alive, I wouldn't be *here* right now. I wouldn't have had to rescue Cass. I wouldn't have had to call the storm at all. So, I put the blame back on the Remainers. At least enough to look in the mirror. After maybe a drink or two.

"You guys are making me do this, you know," I said.

The wondering tone was back. "What are we making you do?"

I let out a breath. Spelled it out for him. "Steal reality. I'm trying not to do it anymore. Can't that be enough? I don't want to kill anyone, anymore. I even left your man alive."

"David?" Jeeves said. "Funny, you say that. I'm with the man now."

He must have gone looking for David, after finding out I had stolen the Jeep-truck. I heard him grab something where he was at. Then I heard the big man I had left in the hotel room. David. I got the feeling he was still tied up in the chair. Asking what was going on. Asking

Jeeves what he was doing. The voice getting panicked. Shouting, "*No, please no. No, no, no, no, no—*"

Then a gunshot.

Then no more sobbing. No more pleas from David. No more playing baseball with his kid.

Jesus. They grow them hard in the Remainers.

"Let me illuminate you," Jeeves said. His voice clipped again, short. As if he had made a decision. "I'm not who you think I am. I don't think you are, either. And while that fascinates me, in the end, it really doesn't matter."

I had been around awhile. I understood people like this. I had met them, and I had buried them. Though sometimes the burying was tough. Guys like Jeeves stayed around for a reason. They were dedicated. Too much so.

"You say you have seen a thousand of me," he said. "You will understand one day soon, that you have not."

I felt like we had reached the end of our conversation.

"That's it?"

"Until we meet again," he said. "There's nowhere you can go that I can't find you. And the one second you slip up, the one second you're staring up in the sky, thinking about how nice the day is, that's the moment I'll slip a knife into your heart."

I froze, holding the phone in my hand. My gaze locked outside the kitchen window at the boat bobbing by the pier.

It had been him, in the alley.

The thought scared me more than anything he had said. I even almost glanced around, looking for him behind me, ready to punch me in the side with the dagger again.

And then I realized, really realized, what this man was. A killer. A stone-cold killer who stopped at nothing to achieve what he wanted. Who had been hunting me for the past half a year, while I had not even known the man existed.

My brain leapt to another conclusion.

I almost had you...

Jesus, he hadn't been talking about the knifing at all.

"Were you in Chicago?" I asked. "Recently?"

I could feel his smile from across the line. Well, cell phones didn't have lines, but you get my drift.

"I think the question is," Jeeves said. "Were *you* in Chicago?"

I almost dropped the phone. I was surprised, but also angry. Shocked, tired, yet filled with violence. He had shot Blake. And he had thought that was me.

Something wasn't right in that thought. But I was too angry, too tired to realize what it was. There was something I was missing, and I still let it slip away.

This man was different. He wasn't like the others. He wasn't like anyone I had outlived before. And not only different, not only committed to his cause, there was something he had, knew, some friend or program or piece of electronic gear, that could find me.

I wondered who he had been, before whatever had happened, and Jeeves became the man over the phone.

He chuckled. "Still feel safe?"

I swallowed. "Safe enough."

"Sure," he said. "Sure."

My world changed. I couldn't outlive him. I couldn't keep running, find a place to hide. For the past few decades the Remainers had been something like a fad to me. Something I thought would go away if I just stopped stealing reality. If I just left well enough alone.

That wasn't the case now. Wherever I went, Jeeves could find me. He had thought he had found me in Chicago. He had followed me to Charleston. And he knew I was in Folly Beach. He was listening to something, *someone*, and whatever or whoever that was, they were accurate.

"So," Jeeves said. In a perfect American accent. "Something up your knickers?"

Ha. Boy was this guy funny. Though, if I'm being honest, turn-about was always fair play.

I had been ready to run. The boat was the plan. I was going to run the *Isla Marie* out to a place to hide. Some island somewhere. Allow Cass to heal up, maybe trail down the coast. Find a place to land and flee to another country. Maybe South America. Maybe Africa.

That wasn't possible now. Jeeves would find me. And he was going to bring everything he could to the party.

The feeling of dread, the world-ending fear, rose up in me.

I no longer had the advantage of time. Of outliving. Of outlasting.

I was going to have to face this man.

Jeeves scared me. I had no shame in admitting it. But beneath the fear was anger. He had killed Blake because he had thought she was me. As bad as I was, or had been in life, as many lives I had taken, affected, lost with stealing reality, none of those had been *meant*. If I killed someone, I did it up close.

My teeth were clenched so hard my jaw ached.

So, I was scared, but I was angry too. And fury was a good tonic for fear. I needed that anger, because I could no longer run.

I was really good at the 'revenge is best served cold' thing. I could wait with the best. But I had also killed a lot of people. Hard not to do when you live forever. And when there was a person to kill, there wasn't a better person for the job than me.

So, I harnessed the fury. Stoked the flames. Built them up so that fire towered over the fear.

There was a man to kill.

I was ready to do it.

Jeeves was quiet. Maybe watching something. Maybe listening. Maybe looking at the mess he had made of David with a quiet smile.

"You think running around shooting a man in a chair will impress me?" I asked.

"Impress you?" Jeeves said. "No. I doubt things impress you, anymore. Me either." He pronounced it *I-ther*. "I'll tell you I'm curious, but I've been curious before. It'll pass."

Whatever I had done to this guy, it had left him scarred.

"I understand," I said. "We done here?"

I know I've been talking pretty dismissively. I mean, I *have* outlasted or outlived everyone and everything that's tried to kill me. That kind of ability does build up a certain... ego, I guess.

But this was different. Jeeves was going to be difficult to kill. He had a focus, an intensity of purpose that carried him over and through any obstacle he faced.

An intensity I lacked, for the most part. Even now. Even with Blake's death. His revenge seemed to have more of an edge than mine. After a few thousand years the world was more blurry to me, than sharp.

Still, the sharpest edges can also be the most brittle.

He chuckled again. A dry type of chuckle, like he was going through the motions. Like he was angry as well, like he was stoking up his own flames and gearing up for what would inevitably be one of our ends.

Time was wasting. I needed to get back to Cass and the boat and get out on the ocean. Get some distance between me and Jeeves. Give me a little time to figure out what to do.

So, I hung up on him.

It didn't feel as good as I'd hoped.

CHAPTER TWENTY-SEVEN

SHE WAS LOOKING OUT THE WINDOW. NOT CASS, BUT BLAKE. Staring into the dark night, the apartment buildings across the street, tall dark structures with illuminated panes of glass sprinkled here and there, like fireflies. In the moment, I remembered one of the illuminated panes fading into black, as someone turned out the light.

I was back in a memory. The last memory I had of Blake, alive. The last time we had spoken. I was in the middle of my Chicago condo, standing next to a little drink table, where a few glasses lay scattered around a decanter of tequila and a silver bucket of ice. It was a big room, the couch nearby where the two of us had spent rainy evenings in. Across from the couch there was a television hanging on the wall above a mantel, muted, and a fake fireplace under the mantel, with its fake fire fake crackling.

I remember her standing in tight blue jeans and a tan jacket, something just thin enough to be warm in the Chicago windy nights. Her arms wrapped around her, one hand loosely holding a book. I think I even remember its name. The one by Douglas Adams. *Hitchhiker's Guide to the Galaxy.*

I wasn't sure if Blake was looking out at something or catching her reflection in the glass. I caught her doing that sometimes, looking at herself. I didn't think it was vanity. It was as if she was surprised by the gaze staring back at her.

I did the same. I had seen my face a million times in the mirror. But sometimes, usually in a glimpse of a reflection, I would pause, struck by the hollow eyes staring back at me. The weariness behind the gaze. I would wonder about the sadness, and what I would find if it all just went away.

Then I would blink, the glimpse would disappear, and I'd bury all those thoughts until the next time.

So, I watched her, watching herself, and I wondered what she saw in herself, in these times. And my words, spoken softly, still seemed too loud for the room.

"What are you doing?"

Blake started. As if she hadn't been thinking, not of me, not of us, not of anything here. Her head was tilted up, just slightly, as if she had been wanting to see the stars, when all we could see was the lights of the city.

Her smile was wistful.

"Just looking for flying saucers," she said.

I smiled back. I knew the story. "Green ones?"

She looked away.

What was the next part? "Something about the end of the world coming, right?" And drinking. Which I could get behind. Or beside, since the liquor table was right next to me. "Drink?"

There was more silence. More fake fire cracks. More of Blake, looking at her reflection, like she had never seen it before.

"Have you thought about Shangri-La?" she asked. Her voice not carrying its usual intensity. More of a hushed tone, words with just enough life in them to reflect off the window in front of her and drift their way to me.

This again. She was into that stuff. Science fiction. Fiction. Fake realities, fake dreams of authors from the past. Wondering dreams of the future from authors of the here and now. Always searching for lost knowledge, real or imagined.

I wondered which way the conversation would go. If it would move on to Atlantis. The lost library at Alexandria. Nostradamus or El Dorado. Or if it would move into space, about a man-made ring of steel circling some star out there. Mars and Alpha Centauri and the Milky Way.

Or maybe this was just about Shangri-La, today.

"You know I haven't," I said. "You know I won't."

A pause. Phony crackles and pops from the fireplace.

"I don't understand you," Blake said. Again, the words barely making it back.

What was there to understand? How could I convey thousands of years, of life, of everything I had done and been. She was young. I was old. And there is no bridge in the world to cross that gulf, that will gift someone the jaded knowledge of experience.

No matter how much you want to. "I know."

She was torn about something. That I knew. What it was, she wouldn't tell me. Maybe there was a wide gulf for her too, a place where she was, a place she wanted me to be.

But she couldn't build that bridge either. Maybe I had burned that one behind me, a long time ago. Whatever the place was, wherever she was at, I couldn't get there.

Of course, I wasn't willing to try.

"I thought I would," she said. The words a little stronger. Not drifting their way back to me now, but digging into me, like darting arrows. "I thought, with enough time, I would get to know the real you."

There was nothing I could say here. I had lived this a hundred times. A hundred times a hundred. Every time, it would come to this.

I wanted Blake to be different. She *was* different. But I wanted *this*, this thing between us to be different too.

I just didn't know how.

"Maybe you do," I said.

Crackle and pop. Crackling and pop. Then, Blake swore.

"*I don't believe it*," she said. Sounding angry. Like she found herself wrong about something.

Blake was always intense. And she was most intense about the things she believed. So, I understood the passion, when she thought she might be wrong.

"Trust me," I said. "I wish I could be different. I wish I was the man you thought I was. You think I was. Am." I was really messing this up.

She turned around to face me. Still standing by the window. Still holding herself, But her head moving side to side in little motions of denial.

Then a memory inside this memory. Something I remembered clearly, standing there. Her finding me, at the beach.

"*What are you looking for?*" I had asked.

Maybe you...

Six months later, here we were. At the end. The flame that burns brightest, burns quickest.

Still, I clung on. I found a glass in my hand. I tossed some cubes of ice into it, listened to the chinking rattle. And poured a little amber liquid from a decanter. And then more than a little. It was an extra Añejo tequila I favored, something that was a little sweet.

"Why do you keep asking about Shangri-La?" I asked. "*Why?*"

Her smile was sad, as if she knew what I was doing. But she played the game.

"Why not Shangri-La?" she said. "Why not Atlantis? Why not Mars or Alpha Centauri?"

I took a sip. The glass wasn't warm in my hand, and it wasn't cool either. It was just there.

"I don't know," I admitted.

"You keep saying that," she said. Forceful. "But you *should*. You can do all these things, you have all this power. You look in all these realities, find all these universes where anything can exist and happen, and still... you stay *here*."

I fought a shrug. "There are the rules."

"The rules, the rules, *the rules*," she said. Really angry now. Her eyes flashing. She threw her book down, it hit the floor with a slapping kind of thump. "You have these rules, have you ever asked yourself *why*?"

"They aren't my rules."

"How do you know?"

Quiet then. Here we were at the impasse. Her face so intense it hurt for me to look at it. So, I took another drink.

How did I know the rules?

Experience.

Something Blake wouldn't get, until a long time from now.

If then.

"You tell me you want a purpose," she said. "Your body is dying for it. *You* are dying for it. And yet, you don't look for one."

"I told you," I said. "I've looked."

"Here," she said. "*Always here.* What if here isn't all there is? There are literally an infinite amount of worlds you can reach into. What if your purpose is out *there*? What if it's out there *in the universe*? What if Atlantis exists, what if your purpose is there? Shangri-La?"

"It doesn't work like that." I couldn't go anywhere. I stole reality. I couldn't travel to other worlds, just pull pieces of them here. And Blake knew that.

She knew it. And she knew this talk would make me angry if it went long enough. So, she poked, one more time.

"Says who?"

I threw the glass. Heard it shatter against the wall, the drink splash over the edge of the dark wooden mantel, the glass tinkle down over the fake fireplace. "Me Blake. Dammit, *me*."

She stood there, still intense. Her whole body screamed with the effort to correct me. To tell me I was wrong. But she didn't. She just stood there and looked at me with the same face I caught in my own reflection. Hollow eyes. Sadness.

Disillusionment.

"Says you," she said. Nodding. Turning her face away from me, as if I had failed at something. Some test.

Crackle and pop. A dripping sound too, drops of amber liquid hitting the fake wooden floor.

"I wish I could be different," I said.

"You *are* different." The words hushed again.

I knew I was different. That I was unique. That the power I had was some cosmic joke, maybe even some random genetic sequence I had no one else did. Our whole relationship had devolved into this. "I meant something else."

Crackle and pop.

"Me too," she said. Moving to walk past me. "It's time."

I hated the words. The definitive marking of a moment from where there was no retreat. No going back.

My free hand reached out, but I pulled it back.

Some things you had to let go.

She was going to do her thing. I thought it was something with the Remainers. The thing that I thought she wanted me to be a part of. Some meeting or gathering here, in Chicago, she had to make. Something Blake had put off for some time, but finally felt the need to go.

The anger fled out of me, it had flickered like a comet in the sky, blazing at first, and now gone. Leaving me empty. And a little broken. And the words sounded that way. Desperate. "Want me to come along?"

There was a long, long moment, filled with the emptiness between us. A crackle and a pop. And a few last drops of tequila, tapping on the floor.

"I did once," she said.

The silence in the room was heavy. Oppressive. The windows reflected her and I, standing in the center of the room. Her looking towards the door to the condo. Me trying to see past my reflection.

There was another glass on the table. I tossed some cubes of ice into it, from a nearby silver bucket. Poured more tequila in it. All muscle memory.

She neared. I could feel the warmth of her body. She leaned into my side, and my hand found its way to her hip. Her head nestled against my shoulder, her cheek against mine, her lips next to my ear. Her hair tied tight behind her neck, the taut strands on the side of her head pressed against my face.

"You leaving?" I asked.

"I don't want to give up," she said. A real whisper now. A real breath of warm words against my ear. "On any of this."

And her last words to me. "I'll be back soon."

My breath caught, something deep in my chest. Goosebumps rippled over my arms. Maybe I was wrong. Maybe she wasn't leaving tonight. Maybe there was some part of me she still believed in. Maybe six months would make it to six months and one day.

"Okay," I said. Just as low in sound, as if the word had barely escaped me. A word I said but couldn't feel, I wasn't okay, not at all, not with her leaving, but I was afraid of what might happen if I broke the lessons of a thousand lives and said something else.

My hand had tightened on her hip instead. Pulled her closer against me. Felt her body press tight again, for one moment that seemed to last forever.

She pulled away.

And then was gone.

CHAPTER TWENTY-EIGHT

The kitchen seemed too quiet after the call. Like the house was in the center of a storm. The midpoint of some soundless, all-seeing eye, winds whipping wildly around it, unseen currents that tossed and toppled and raged in the distance.

Still, everything felt dead in the house. The tile floor was too soft, the white cabinets too muted, the light coming in from the window a little dim. The temperature even felt limp, lifeless, not too hot, not too cold. Just there.

A heavy pressure could be felt, though. From the storm raging in the distance. Not the storm I had called, but Jeeves. I could feel that one head my way, drive me to run, like an invisible wind pushing hard against my back. My spine tingled with it. The need to flee.

I wasn't one to ignore those feelings. My instincts were honed. Sharp. I had lived a long time by them. So, I tossed Clyde's phone in the sink. Add David's phone. Took a dark coffee mug and slammed both a couple of times. Then turned the faucet on and let it run, the water splashing over the cracked digital faces. The same slight rotten egg smell came from the tap.

It was what I could do. Jeeves would find this place anyway. I felt like he already knew where I was at, and even if he didn't, the Land Rover probably had some kind of technology in it telling Jeeves *I'm here, I'm here*, as a little beeping dot on a map.

But why take risks? It wasn't like I'd have to pay the water bill. Or buy another phone.

I hurried though, grabbing the last bucket of food. And the bag with the electronics. By the time I was out of the house, I was running to the *Isla Marie*. My side ached with the pain, and I was careful with the stitches.

Outside, on the boat, I could feel the wind. The edges of the canvas flapped with it, beckoning me to open the sail and fly. I ducked into the hatch, set the bucket and the bag down. Cass was in the water closet, in front of the mirror, stitching up a cut on the side of her forehead. One hand steady with a needle, the thread taut between it and the tiny flap of skin tugged out from her temple.

"We're taking off," I said.

Her expression didn't change, but she nodded.

"Careful with the stitches," I warned. The *Isla Marie* would bob some.

Cass rolled her eyes. She still wasn't happy about the boat thing. "It's not my first rodeo."

Man was this going to be a great trip. Cass and me stuck together for who knows how long, running from Jeeves and however many Remainers he brought to the party. An older braver me wanted to say something about it, talk to Cass about trying to get along, but I'd seen her shoot. So, I went back topside instead.

Like I've said, finely honed instincts.

The boat kept bobbing, like it was eager to leave. The mooring lines were loose. It was easy to cast off. I pushed us off the pier a bit with my leg, then a bit more, getting a little more distance between the small wooden deck and the boat. Then I went to the helm, placed a hand on the wheel. It was old and wooden and smooth in my grip.

I turned the keys and felt the engine crank up a bit and then sputter out. It was diesel. The gas tank was full, so I worked the choke and tried again. The third time was the charm, and the engine turned over.

There was no roar to the motor, just a guttural rumble, but still we were off, slowly moving our way through the water. The engine was more of a puttering thing than anything with real power. But it was enough to get us moving. Enough for us to navigate down the channel a bit until I could swing the boat west and get to Folly River.

There's no where you can go, that I can't find you...

Jeeves wasn't lying. And each time he missed me, he got a little bit closer. I wish I knew how he did it.

I almost had you...

I was worried about being able to kill this man. He was good with a knife, but I didn't think Jeeves would accept a challenge to a sword fight. The only thing I thought I had was that he wanted to kill me, and he wanted to be close when he did. He wanted to see it and feel the death.

You don't know me...

And I knew then I didn't. I was afraid of this man, with the world-ending dread feeling he brought with him. I was going to have to ask Cass what she knew about this man. Let her know I had found who had killed Blake. But right now I wanted to go faster. The boat seemed to top out around six to eight knots. Which was slower than walking. But it was what I had. So, I stayed patient and steered us down the channel.

The water was smooth. We glided along it. The boat bobbed up and down, ever so slightly. Occasionally the breeze would pick up and flutter the sails, still rolled up.

The sun was hot. Somehow on a boat, out on the water, the sun always felt hotter. More intense. Maybe because there was nowhere to really hide from it. I looked around and found a ball cap tucked by the seat, blue with a marlin on the front with a line hooked in its mouth and a fishing pole off to the side.

Houses passed by on my left. Slowly. They all seemed empty, at least the ones still standing. No one looked out the windows, no one waved from a backyard. There was an open grill in the back of one home and what looked like hamburger patties still on it, a long metal spatula on the ground. As if people had been having a cookout. I wondered how the grill had stayed upright during the storm.

My head hurt. The back of it, where the bullet had shaved me. The jacket had saved my life there, the cloth had actually torn a bit under the graze, and that area of my brain was tender. Especially with a bat having connected with my skull a little earlier.

The channel was clear and straight. Wide open. Nothing stirred around us, and the *Isla Marie* moved at such a slow pace, it felt like we were sitting still on the water. I mean, we were moving, but it was real slow. So, I ran down the hatch real quick. Leaving the topside unattended. Breaking one of the cardinal sailing rules. Just add it to the list.

The water closet door was closed, Cass still inside. I thought I heard the shower. But the first aid kit lay on the couch, closed. I shuffled through it until I found a bottle of aspirin. Took it and some water back topside.

It all looked the same. We were still center channel. Puttering along. I took four or five aspirin and swallowed the bitterness down with the warm, tepid water. The bottle crinkled some as I drank.

The aspirin was bitter. The taste stayed on the tongue, no matter how much water I drank. I told myself to call me in the morning if I still had the headache. Then I found that hilarious and chuckled.

When you're a few thousand years old, you take the laughs wherever you can get them.

The houses got thicker along the eastern bank. Every now and then they became a neighborhood. Then they would turn back into fields of scuff. Then all that disappeared, and more commercial buildings popped up. The restaurants and tourist places I had originally passed on my way here. Well, not the same restaurants, those were likely blocks away. But close enough that I worried about being seen by the Remainers.

Jeeves had me scared.

Which was probably a good thing. I didn't want to be daydreaming again, or moping, or whatever it was I had been doing when he had stabbed me. I wanted to be alert. Aware. And ready.

The channel began breaking west. Away from Center Street and the rest of the restaurants and tourist shops there. I swung the boat that way and kept it center channel. Just a guy heading out, maybe going fishing. Maybe just getting away from all the destruction. Nothing to see here. Move along, people. These aren't the droids you're looking for.

Cass came up. She had a small Band-Aid on her temple. Her cheek was still swollen, but the cut there looked small. She had a bottle of water in one hand, and gripped the rail leading up out of the hatch pretty tightly with the other. She wore the same clothes she had before, but her hair was wet and tucked under a ball cap, a big red *C* on the cap. Once she got topside, she looked around at the water with a wary expression, but let go of the rail and sat on one of the cushioned chairs aft.

"You good?" I asked.

"Fine," she said. A little short. Then, a moment later. "I probably should thank you."

"For what?" I asked. "Coming after you?"

"Yeah," she said. Frowning. I couldn't tell if she was frowning at me, the world, or whatever she was thinking. Like I said before, I kind of felt like it was her natural expression. "I didn't expect it."

That stung a bit, but I didn't blame her. I'm sure I didn't look like the hero type. Not even a reluctant one. When Blake had introduced us, I'm sure Cass felt like I was just some guy having a bit of fun with her sister. Living up life. Which, honestly, was kind of how Blake had made me feel.

It had been so long, until that moment I had seen her.

For a while we had hung out occasionally. Here and there. Then Blake had told Cass who I really was and what I could do, and that hadn't gone well. That was the sum of the relationship, between Cass and I, until Blake had been killed.

Until yesterday, really.

"Well, I kinda owed you," I said. In fact, I kind of owed her twice.

Cass nodded, as if that was something she understood. A trade she could make. She sipped on the water and watched the homes and the beachy restaurants slowly scroll by. There were still people walking around, picking up stuff. Every now and then a person was stopped in the middle of cleaning up some of the destruction, holding a piece of corrugated roof, a section of wall, a chair. I even saw a guy dragging a mattress across a back alley, the soft bed bent over his back, almost like a big, puffy cape.

Ahead was Folly River. To the south, in the distance, Center Street ran out over the water and became Folly River Bridge. The bridge was a tiny line barely high enough to cross over the river, and too close to the water for the *Isla Marie* to sail under it.

Maybe she could before, but not now, especially with the water level after the storm. I might have been able to get a powerboat to fit, but I wasn't lucky enough to find one of those. Just this slow boat.

I had another way out. Something the *Isla Marie* could swing. I thought. I was going to head north on Folly River, until the river split into a lot of muddy flats and swamps and thin, finger-like channels curled so tightly they almost doubled back on themselves.

Maybe you've been there. Maybe you think there's no way to get a sailboat through. If so, I'm not sure how you're reading this. I mean, you can't be in the same reality as me, because I knew in this one I could make it.

It wasn't just the high-water level after the storm. I knew the waters here. I had been this way before. It had been three or four hundred years, and I'm sure the exact same channels didn't exist today as it had then, but a way out would be.

In case you weren't aware, or maybe you're in some other reality, in this one, three or four hundred years ago, the Folly River had dead-ended in some swamp. Charleston—*Charles Town*—had been a happening place then. There had been privateers and pirates and colony ships and the occasional visit from the *Queen Anne's Revenge*.

I might have been there then. In the town. Maybe enjoying the life of a smuggler. Sometimes I did things like that. I might have found myself trapped between my ship and a couple cutters out of Charles Town, and back then I might have stolen a reality where the river connected to the Atlantic, through a maze of waterways and swampland that would be hard for my pursuers to follow.

I'm saying might have. Hopefully you get the drift. (Here I'd say "get it?" but the word choice was bad enough that I'm guessing you do.)

So north was an option. Especially because I wanted to stay away from the bridge, from where Jeeves might be waiting with a sniper rifle, waiting for me to cross to the mainland. The one point he thought I would have to cross.

He wouldn't know about this. Or I thought he at least wouldn't guess it. Or maybe he would, just too late to do anything about it.

By the time he figured it out, we could make it to Morris Island. Then sneak onto the Atlantic. If we didn't get stuck on a mudflat or a sandbar. It would be tough going, the *Isla Marie* had a full rudder, it wouldn't maneuver as easy as some of the more modern sailboats.

I kept us headed north. The whole time feeling the southern horizon calling to me. Maybe because we were fleeing. Like a bird fleeing the winter, the safety of the south beckoned us on. There was an urgency to its call. It felt like escape. The wind even blew that way, fluttering across the deck of the *Isla Marie*, stirring the edges of the sails, washing along my face.

Jeeves would feel the same thing. Something told me that. He would know where I was headed. Like he knew where I was, I knew where he was.

At least, that's what I hoped. Likely it was going to be a fifty-fifty-ninety thing. We just had to get the right fifty. Neither one of us, Cass or me, was in good enough shape to fight anything out. Not right now. Not with Jeeves and his maniacal obsession.

Cass watched it all. Quiet.

"Want to talk about it?" I asked. My words coming out a little... uncomfortable.

"Not really." Her shoulders made a little motion. "Not much to talk about."

Well, I tried.

"Actually, there was something," Cass said. Which surprised me. She looked over at me, with a calculating look in her eyes. As if she was trying to add things up. "I got the feeling they were surprised to be there."

"Folly beach?"

"Nah." She shook her head. Sipped the bottle of water. "Charleston."

Well, maybe they didn't like the place any better than me.

"One of the people there argued with the British guy," she said. "The Brit kept saying it was moving around. And I got the feeling he didn't understand it. That whatever it was, it was moving, and that it shouldn't."

It must be me stealing reality. Which told me they had a way to track me. Well, Jeeves did. But the whole moving around thing, that I didn't get. Didn't understand. I'd been doing this for longer than anyone's been alive, and I'd always moved around. I've lived just about everywhere on this Earth, and stole reality everywhere. So, that didn't make sense. Well, nothing made sense. Jeeves killing Blake. Hunting me. Telling me my time was short.

"What do you know about Jeeves?" I asked. Cass looked puzzled, so I clarified. "The British guy."

She smiled then, a real smile. Surprisingly, it turned her face beautiful. "That's what you call him?"

"Yeah."

"To his face?"

I shrugged. "The phone."

She laughed. "Oh that's rich. He's got to hate that."

"It was hard to tell," I admitted, "but I was hoping."

Cass chuckled some more. Her eyes looked worried. She finally explained. "If he's who I think he is, he's bad news."

"How bad?"

"Bad," she said. "Couldn't get worse type of bad."

"Why's he got it out for me?" I asked.

"He had a daughter," Cass said. "Six or seven years old. Needed a heart transplant. She was actually on the table, in the middle of the procedure, when the doctor forgot what he was doing."

I tried to imagine that happening to me. Having a child dying in the operating room. The act wasn't hard to visualize, but it was hard for me to really *feel*. The calluses were just too thick.

And as long as I've lived, I've never had a daughter. Or a son. I vaguely remembered my parents, and the faint connection there, but like everything else, that familial closeness had faded with time. And like I had said, I had kind of learned to stay away from the real close connections. When you live this long, everyone you know always dies.

There was a part of me that wanted to go back and undo the whole Fountain of Youth thing, if I could. I had already swapped that reality back, a long time ago, but that hadn't fixed me. I still lived on. I knew I had once had the feeling of family, and maybe a small part of it remained, hidden inside me, a small part buried in the feeling of a family, of closeness, of having each other's back until the both of you closed your eyes one final time and drifted away...

But the larger part of me just kept moving on.

I could imagine how Jeeves had felt, losing his daughter. But just intellectually. Not where most people felt things, on the inside. It wasn't something I had anymore, I didn't think. Not likely.

"Apparently he was there, watching it all," Cass said. "Saw the doctors and the nurses all kind of look at each other, look at his daughter, and panic. I think some of them even ran out, almost screaming. Wondering where they were."

I couldn't remember doing anything around a hospital. Not in the past few decades, not after the school shooting thing. I had learned my lesson there. I guess there was always the case that some reality I had stolen had some odd side effect, some weird combination of square peg in a round circle.

"At least, that's what Blake told me," Cass said. "She had some fascination with the man. I could never understand it."

That was news. An irrational sense of jealousy came over me. Which didn't make sense. But then, jealousy rarely did.

"Was it here?" I asked.

Cass took a little more water, shook her head. "Some hospital in Europe. Probably England. Some heart center somewhere."

Weird. I couldn't remember being in England, or Europe. Not in the past decade or two. And definitely not six months ago, or even a year.

I must have done something though, and then some splinter had peeled off, some butterfly effect had carried the splinter overseas, so whatever it had been that I had stolen, a jacket, a lime, a bad movie, whatever it was had started this chain with Jeeves. It had steered him this way. To me, and his path of retribution.

Speaking of steering, I swung the wheel. Felt the engine rumble, the prop dig into the water, as I guided the *Isla Marie* off the small branch of water onto Folly River. The waves pushed against us, forcing us south, and the motor of the boat didn't make a lot of headway. And as I swung the boat north, it made even less.

It would be slow going.

The canvas flapped, but I knew the sail wouldn't catch if I opened it. The wind was blowing almost directly south. The river headed north here. It would take a bit before I could use the sail to help move us along. I would just be tacking back and forth against the headwind, I felt it'd be better to trust the motor for now.

"You look like shit," Cass said. She hadn't said it seriously, it was more of a comment between two soldiers. Two people who had fought a battle and come out alive. The words meant something like *can you believe we survived that?*

So, I grinned. "You saw yourself in the mirror, right?"

Two comrades in arms. A weird feeling for me. She hadn't directly said it, but Cass had to blame me in some way for Blake's death. And Cass had never liked me, anyway. Maybe saving a person's life helped them get a different perspective on you.

I kept the grin up. I did look like shit. And felt like shit. My side ached, although it wasn't open again. My head ached, a low pulsing throb from the back of the skull. I was sure I had a concussion, maybe two, if people could actually get a concussion on top of a concussion.

It would all heal. Hopefully sooner than later. I had been through worse. And likely would again. Like relationships, pain would fade away in time.

And while the fading happened, I needed to catch Cass up.

"Jeeves killed Blake," I said.

Cass started. Tilted her head briefly before nodding. Almost to herself. As if it made sense.

But it didn't. Not if Blake was *fascinated* with the man. Putting that with him hunting me, and wanting to kill me, telling me my time was short, Blake being with me, well when she wasn't out in the field, none of it made sense.

Maybe Cass would know more. I told her about the conversation with Jeeves. Just the highlights. Not a lot of information, really. Basically that he wanted to kill me, he was going to hunt me down until he did so, and the feeling of dread I had talking to him.

And how I knew he killed Blake.

Which was the clincher for both of us.

"We're killing him, right?" Cass asked.

"Yeah." It was what we both wanted. Although Jeeves had me worried. "I hope so."

Cass looked at me funny. It was a *did you really say that* kind of stare. Maybe you know what I'm talking about.

"He scares me," I admitted.

And he did. Now that I said it out loud, I was comfortable with thinking it. I felt like it was a good thing, to have a bit of fear. It would keep me from underestimating the man.

Cass had no such reservation. "If he bleeds, he dies."

Well, when you're a walking terminator, I guess that's what you think.

I was still unsure though. Just a week or two ago I had been with Blake. Felt her warmth against me. The cold spot she had left behind. "Be nice to know what Blake was doing."

Cass cocked her head. "You didn't?"

I shook my head. One hand light on the worn wooden wheel of the boat. Steering the *Isla Marie*.

"I thought it was something she was doing for you."

The wheel jerked a bit. Something hard grabbed the rudder. A current of water maybe, something underneath the surface, pushing against the boat.

My fingers tightened around the wheel as I held the boat straight in the river. The hardness in the water, the dense cold pocket of water, whatever it had been passed underneath us. Maybe Blake had died doing something for me, but it wasn't something I asked her to do. Or even wanted her to do.

She had walked her own path.

"You know Blake," I said. Not correcting the past tense. At least, not out loud.

Cass barked a laugh. A short, bitter thing. As if that had been something the two of them had often fought over. In addition to arguing about me. She took a sip of water and grimaced. "Yeah."

Blake had never done anything she didn't want to do. But I knew Blake had been worried. That she was meeting someone, and that she had put off the meeting for quite some time. Months.

Since she had met me.

Why was she worried? The worry I felt talking to Jeeves kind of felt like the same kind of thing. But that thought didn't make sense.

Let me clear something up. Cass and Blake *were* Remainers. But when I say that, I mean they would stay around when I stole reality. They remembered changes.

They weren't part of these cells. Not the ones with Jeeves. Those people were a different kind of Remainer. That had been a relatively new thing, the cells, in the past year.

Maybe I should come up with a different name for Cass than what I called the Remainers. Seeing as that's kind of a thing with me. Words, that is.

Remainers, though, seemed to fit. It wasn't like they were a military organization. Or deeply placed terrorist cells. They were loosely formed, loosely organized. At least, they had been. Before Jeeves.

Had Blake been working with him? Meeting the man? If so, why? What had been so important that she had risked her life?

I didn't know. And I hadn't got it then. Not even when she had been asking me about Shangri-La, or talking about Riddick, or any of the other questions Blake had for me.

I had thought they were tests, that Blake wanted to know how much I could do. Or what I was willing to do. Maybe not so much what I could do, but what I *would* do.

Now, I was starting to feel they had been something different. I had been wrong then. So wrong. But I had thought it right at the time.

"Think we should ask Jeeves?" Cass said. "Before we kill him?"

It was a good idea. Except killing Jeeves might be harder than we thought. He was smart, cautious, driven. A dangerous combination. Maybe it would be easier to go somewhere under a flag of truce.

What would Jeeves say, if I called him and asked for a meeting? He'd probably laugh, and tell me he'd find me anyway. Hell, he was probably already right behind me.

"If we can."

"Shouldn't be hard," Cass looked at me like I wasn't thinking. Like it was simple. Or I was. "Get somewhere in the open, let him come at you, and let me take him out."

It hit me. Cass's plan. Simple, like I said, but the best plans usually are. It all unfolded in my mind like a flower. Cass was right, it would be easy. Almost too easy.

Jeeves hated me. With a real vengeance. Any kind of meet-up I could or would plan with him would be taken with suspicion. There was no way I could call him and set that up. Even if I offered Jeeves a one-on-one fight to the death.

He'd know it was a trap. Even with the opportunity to kill me, he'd sense it. I mean, a child would.

But Cass's plan was more subtle. I'd have to do it right. I was already doing part of it by running. I just needed to keep fleeing until I found a place where I felt good about Jeeves cornering me.

That would be the tricky part. Some place with long sight lines for Cass. But not a place he would be suspicious of.

Plenty of places like that in the south. Long stretches of beaches. I thought about heading to Florida, some beach around Jacksonville.

Run long enough that it would look like I felt safe and was stopping for a bit. Then set up there. Find a tall building for Cass, and have me walk along the beaches, the tourist shops, the restaurants, just a guy waiting to get stabbed.

Just like in Charleston.

It felt perfect. It's exactly what Jeeves wanted. Having me walking the streets, looking at the stores, gazing up and the sky and daydreaming... Jeeves would take the chance there. He wanted to be up close and personal, so he could plunge the knife in. He'd risk getting that close for the satisfaction. That was something he would kill for.

Something he would kill me for.

The timing of it would be dicey. Close. Jeeves had an intuition about me, what I was doing, how I was feeling, where I was going. He had an advantage there of knowing when I stole reality, and where. And he was deadly quick. Almost supernaturally fast.

I would just have to hope Cass was faster.

And I'd have to trust her. Trust she didn't want me dead more than Jeeves. She had never really liked me. Never really liked me and Blake as a thing.

Maybe she would let Jeeves kill me, then take him out after.

That thought came out of nowhere.

And it wasn't like I could bring it up and ask her about it. *Hey Cass, about this shooting Jeeves thing, is there just one bullet you're going to fire? Is there a plus one on that list of people you want dead?*

Did Cass want me dead? She was always grouchy, but maybe that was just around me. Maybe she was just with me to get revenge for her sister.

But it didn't make a lot of sense. I mean, if she wanted me dead, she could have left me in the alley. She didn't have to stitch me up.

Still, there was a new, nagging worry in the back of my brain.

Cass held the bottle of water against the side of her face, as if the water was cold (it wasn't) and she was using it to keep the bruise there from spreading. And she had a small smile on her face, like she knew exactly what I was thinking, and maybe even was enjoying it.

She had saved my life.

And I had saved hers.

Maybe that meant less than I thought. Maybe that just made us even. Maybe she wanted me dead just a little less than Jeeves.

Damn nagging worry.

All I could do was smile back. Try not to think those thoughts. Cass was a bit abrasive, and maybe a pain, but I still liked her. Even if she wasn't that fond of me. We were brother soldiers in the trench, the two of us against the world, and that was enough for me. Even if she was all I had left of Blake.

I guessed that would pass, though, in time. Memories of Blake. Of Cass. I knew, like no one else could know, that this moment would be some blurry memory of the past. It would fade and jostle around and mix with others, so that Cass and Jeeves and even Blake would disappear into the black hole of my past.

Still, they were what I had now to keep me going. Keep me feeling alive. Keep me feeling like my life meant something to someone.

The waves of the river ran down from the north, following some dark current. The swells pushed past the boat, and the engine struggled a bit to make headway against them. The wind rose, stirring the sails, the edges of the canvas snapping in the breeze. Every now and then a cold pocket of water would grab the rudder, as if wanting to turn as around.

Even as we headed north, everything else seemed to be pushing us south. To a place and time where Jeeves and Cass and I would settle this. Like Mother Nature had already known the plan. As if she was fast-forwarding through the movie, rushing to the end, eager to see who would live.

And who would die.

CHAPTER TWENTY-NINE

The sky that morning had started out a deep blue, and lightened as the day went by. Now it was the color of old, faded blue jeans. The water shimmered with the reflection of it, a pale blue sky painted across a muddy brown canvas. Even the *Isla Marie* even appeared in that mirror, the ripples of the water waving across the image of her white hull.

Cass and I talked some. I wanted to know more about Jeeves, but she had never met the man, she hadn't heard much in the beach house. And the rest of it she only knew from Blake and the meetings. The ones I had spoken about, the ones like any other Anonymous meeting.

Blake, though, had been interested in the leader. Jeeves.

Maybe it was the topic of the conversation. Maybe it was the bobbing of the boat. The slow heading north. Likely it was the hot sun above us, but the conversation died off, leaving just the tiny whispers of a fluttering breeze and small laps of water against the boat.

I stayed at the helm, keeping us north, fighting the wind and the current and even what felt like the sun. The rays beat hard on the white topside of the boat, warming my skin to the point where it was uncomfortable. Like we were in the middle of a fiery white oven.

I took off my jacket, even though I wanted to keep the bulletproof cloth wrapped around me. But I was sweating too much, sweating through my shirt, and that came off too. It left just the bandages around my side, which thankfully weren't completely soaked with red, just one large dot in the center of the white cottony wrap. So, I was healing.

Cass stripped down to a small, ribbed tank top. White. She had more curves than I thought and looked better than I would have suspected. Especially because she seemed to always wear clothes that masked her shape, loose-fitting shirts, jackets.

Interesting. Blake had been taller, thinner, more angles than curves. Though she could still be pliable and soft when she wanted to be. It was odd to me. The sisters couldn't have been more different. Blake with long blonde hair, Cass with curly black tangles. Blake's sharpness had hidden a delicate inside. Cass's curves were softer. It was her inside that projected the hard outer shell.

Funny, where thoughts go.

The breeze wasn't enough to cool us down. It wouldn't be until I could open the sails. And that took awhile. Cass went belowdecks and came back up, holding a bottle of suntan lotion. We took turns lathering ourselves with it, though she seemed tense when my hand ran over her back. Like she expected a knife.

Even after the lotion, the sun felt hot. Beads of sweat ran down us both. Cass kept up a steady supply of bottled water, as I throttled the *Isla Marie's* motor down. Ahead the river split up into little fingers, channels running like strands of spaghetti. I picked the largest one and steered the boat that way, struggling to pull up what I knew from memory.

A lot can change in four hundred years. They had shored some things up north of here, and that had altered some of the currents, so what I remembered and what was reality was a good bit different now.

There were some points where I really had to throttle the engine down, ask Cass to run up to the bow and look ahead. We made some good guesses. There was a tricky spot, where the boat wouldn't quite work its way through a narrow channel. Damn full rudder boats. But we caught a lucky break, snuck out and hit a larger channel east. Big enough to open the throttle back up.

Morris Island Lighthouse came back into view. Grew larger, with its foreboding black as iron top, its square black stone windows, its thick red and white horizontal stripes. As we passed, I saw the stone was faded and dark in places, stained with time, eaten by age.

The lighthouse sat offshore now, in a shallowish patch of ocean. I guessed it wasn't operational anymore. And that no one had come back to repair it. Or even paint it. It was just some stone historical site attracting the occasional tourist now.

Part of me wondered if what I had done back then had led to the death of the lighthouse. If stealing a bit of reality back then, raising the water level so I could escape a few Charles Town cutters, had led to the ocean sweeping in over the centuries, swallowing the lighthouse. People said it was construction, jetties in Charleston for the harbor there, but every time I saw the lighthouse I couldn't help but think it was my fault.

You never know what splinters fall off the peg, as you pound it into its hole. You never know what the little things you do will lead to. And what the bigger things you do will cause. The lasting effect is always something that surprises you.

Maybe that thought is true for more than just me stealing reality.

Cass wondered aloud about what it might have been, back in the day. She stood off to the portside, staring north at the old monument, ancient stone worn down by the constant washing of the sea. Another bottle of water in her hand.

I remembered when they had built it. I remembered the light clear in the night sky, blazing over the hidden ocean waters. A beacon in the darkness.

I tilted my water bottle to the lighthouse. A little salute between old acquaintances. An acknowledgment.

Time wears on us all.

We passed Morris Island. Or what was left of it. And finally the ocean opened up before us, a large dark expanse of water, wide and endless, spreading to the east.

I let the boat center itself in the current, shut off the engine, and then opened up the sails. The center mast first, then the jib. Felt them pop and catch the wind, taking us on south on a broad reach. Felt the *Isla Marie* surge under the motion and soar from the river to the Atlantic. And finally, *finally*, felt a cool breeze wash over us. Maybe a little late, with the sun descending to the west, but later was better than never.

Cass took a large breath and let it out. I felt like doing the same. The wind was so cool it shocked me, the breeze was frigid against my skin. I shivered for a moment, at least until my body found a balance between the heat of the yellow sun and the invisible coolness of the air.

I didn't have to worry about navigating our way around other craft. The ocean was almost empty. A few powerboats cruised it, parallel to the beach. Not as many as usual. Maybe people weren't trusting the weather, or maybe they didn't trust the big, wide expanse of dark water looming underneath us all.

Speaking of which, Cass took one look at the waves and headed below. Telling me she was going to rest. Giving me the fisheye the whole way down, as if warning me what might happen if the boat sank while she was sleeping.

Like I had control of that.

Well, I kind of did. But still, that was a lot to expect from a guy.

I tacked us south. The wind was steady, and the sails eagerly pulled the boat along. I shut the motor off, hearing it chug a quiet death, and let Mother Nature take us.

And then I did let out a big breath. Feeling the cool air deep in my lungs, letting it escape me. Goosebumps trickled along my skin.

There was a freedom to the wind. To sailing. To letting a breeze take you wherever. You didn't need to pump gas into the sails, or fire up a combustion engine, or plug the boat in and let it charge. Just the canvas and the wind.

There was a song I heard once. By some guy... Christopher Cross? I think it was *Sailing*. It captured everything I loved about a boat and a sail and the open sea. I had first heard it in the middle of the United States somewhere. Maybe in the seventies. I think I had been driving, oddly enough. I had pulled off to the side of the road and let the radio play out, waiting until the DJ told me the name of the song.

I didn't know if it was a special song. But somehow it captured a moment for me. And moments were special to me. So many of them blurred in my past, that when one stood out, I captured it. Like the song. Like the sails.

I let the wind carry us south. We had started late in the day, but it would still be a little bit of time before night fell. I'd find an island somewhere, a sandbar off the beach, and anchor us there. Let the night go by. I didn't need to get to Jacksonville that fast.

And we needed to figure out a plan.

The helm had a wheel brake. A little nut I could tighten, and keep the wheel (and therefore the *Isla Marie*) somewhat straight. I waited until we were far enough out, where it was just us and the rippling flat surface of the Atlantic, then I pointed us south and tightened the brake.

I ran below. Grabbed one of the packs of bread, it looked like hamburger buns. The jar of peanut butter and jelly. A plastic plate and a knife from the utensil drawer. A few more bottles of water.

And the Buffalo Trace.

Then I ran back up. The *Isla Marie* hadn't made any wild course corrections while I was grabbing food, so we were still headed south. I stood by the helm and made a few PB&Js, using the hamburger buns as bread. The buns were a little stale, but the peanut butter was fresh and smooth. Not chunky, which I was happy about. To me, chunky peanut butter was what they made after someone quit halfway through making smooth. Like the factory had just called it a day and shipped the rest of the jars out half-blended, throwing a chunky label on them.

I layered the peanut butter on thick, the stale hamburger buns crumbled a bit under the knife, and then scooped out the same amount of grape jelly and tried to make equal layers of both the peanut butter and jelly. It got messy. The stale buns kept breaking, and the knife cut into the jelly more than smoothing it. Little purple blobs kept dropping off and splatting to the deck, I had to wipe them off with a finger.

At least those purple blobs were delicious.

Matter of fact, peanut butter and jelly sandwiches were delicious. But then, peanut butter and jelly always were. Even on stale hamburger buns. So, I made a few more and munched on them, letting the breeze flutter past me, keeping an eye south, looking for a good place to anchor. Occasionally I sipped some water, which never seemed to wash the peanut butter out of my mouth, but always took the taste of jelly away.

Then I made more sandwiches. Sue me. They were good. And I was hungry.

And still had a headache, despite the aspirin. The wound under my ribs still stung with a deep ache, even if it was healing. Food was good for both.

The sun had lowered some to the west. The sky was getting darker. Pale clouds streamed above us, tiny wispy things reflecting the last of the day. It had taken some time navigating our way past Morris Island and out to the Atlantic, and it would be night soon enough.

I ate another sandwich. It seemed like weeks had gone by since I had stared out at the beach in Charleston. Since I had called the storm. Right before I had gone to meet Cass at Bubba's.

It had been a day.

Blake had been dead less than a week.

I stared south, felt the sun on the right side of my face, the shadows on the left. The breeze seemed to chill me more, now that the sun wasn't beating down on us. I had unlocked the wheel brake and one of my hands rested casually on the helm, feeling the rudder steer us through the Atlantic. Feeling the little shakes and pulls that come with the popping of the wind in a sail.

I had been standing a week ago, in a similar pose. One hand holding a glass with ice and something alcoholic in it. The other resting casually on Blake's hip. She had been leaning into me, her warm cheek next to mine, her lips next to my ear. Her hair was thick and blonde and tied tightly behind the nape of her neck, but I still remembered the feel of each taut strand where it lay against my face.

I'll be back soon, she whispered. The words warm on my skin.

A thrill had run through me then. I had feared she wasn't coming back. That she was leaving for good. My hand had tightened on her hip. Pulled her closer against me. Not wanting to let her go.

A moment later there was a quiet snick of a door shutting. I was alone. Only a cold spot remained on my hip, along my side, where the warmth of Blake had just been.

I kept coming back to this moment. It felt important to me. Not because of what had happened to Blake, but because of everything leading up to that.

We had argued most about me having a purpose. About me giving up. About Blake telling me maybe it was *out there.*

I kept telling her what I did didn't work that way.

And she had asked me how I knew that.

How do you know...

Blake's words burned in my brain. It had been a mantra with her, while she had been with me. Always questioning me. Always wanting me to do more. Always believing I was capable of something great.

It was nice, having someone in your life that believed that of you.

But she had believed in many things. Atlantis. Shangri-La. The Lost Library. She had been fascinated by others, civilizations on Mars, giant arks of spaceships, a huge metal world shaped in a giant ring. Hell, what was the book she was reading, that last night? *Number of the Beast*? Of traveling a million different worlds? A story of multiverses, if that was even the word?

No, that hadn't been it. She had read that one, but the last one, the one she had been holding, that book had been *Hitchhiker's Guide*.

Just looking for flying saucers...

Something rung in me then, deep inside. A tolling bell. Like I had struck a truth. But I couldn't for the life of me see it. Maybe it had been the argument. Maybe I was too close, and just remembering our fight. I mean, I kept saying the rules were the rules.

Says who?

Me Blake, dammit. Not just me, but time. Experience.

You are *different...*

Says you Blake, says you...

I drifted along those thoughts much like the *Isla Marie* bobbed across the water, with bigger and bigger waves rolling in from the eastern horizon. I felt the bobbing in my knees, and I steadied myself against the helm. It was just some passage of some big ship, leaving large ripples of its passage in the ocean, a hollow wake. Ripples that ran on for far longer than the moment of its passage.

I smiled. It wasn't a happy one. More of something built of regret. Took a drink of the bottle of Buffalo Trace. It wasn't as sweet as the jelly, so all I felt was burning in the bottom of my throat.

I had given up the search for a reason I existed a long time ago. Mostly. Finding a purpose. A reason. A design to my existence. I was a freak, a party trick, an act at a circus. There was no real rhyme or reason to my existence, except that I kept living it.

Past conversations with Blake ran through me, past thoughts, arguments, always about the same thing. Kisses on a couch, then the argument. Holding hands at a carnival, and then the argument. Leaning against each other under the stars, arms wrapped around each other, warm slick skin against warm slick skin, and the argument.

She always pulled back just a little, and her eyes bore into mine. Irises so green, like the greenest of summer lawns. It was as if she was probing deep inside me, looking for what made me tick, wanting to figure me out. Figure out what was different in me, from others she had known.

Like she already knew.

The bell inside me took another ring. Another truth I had stumbled upon, out here on the deck of the *Isla Marie*. A truth recognized far too late to do anything about Blake.

She had known. Blake had known something about me that I didn't.

How?

You should *want* to know, she had told me. She had almost screamed it at me. But I had been so deep in what I already knew, in my *experience of life*, that I knew it all and even had *lived it all*, that I had missed her point. I had missed what Blake had been hinting at.

You are *different...*

I shook the bottle of Buffalo Trace, swinging it wildly at the night.

How, Blake? *How?*

The bells kept tolling inside me, tolling truthful rings, each echo resounding through me, telling me there was something I needed to know. Dammit if I could figure it out. Dammit if I knew. And fuck, it had been so long since I had really looked...

Tens, hundreds, thousands of years. Centuries had moved by. I had seen the bow come around, the arrow. The gun. The cannon. Rockets. Nuclear bombs. I had seen Columbus sail out on the Santa Maria, and I had also seen John Glenn take a step on the moon.

I took another drink. The bourbon swished around in my mouth. It was sweet now on my tongue, like I had forgotten the jelly.

Time was what I needed. Just time. Time to forget all of this, like my tongue had forgotten the grape jelly. A minute, a month, a year. Just time to forget this. Forget Blake and Cass and Jeeves.

And then, a hundred years from now, maybe I'd forget about all of it.

God, I hoped so.

The bottle was half gone, so I finished my last sandwich, figuring it would soak up what more I drank. I recognized where I was going, so I tried to drink just a sip here and there, letting the bourbon wash away what was left of the peanut butter, letting the burn steal all the sweetness of the jelly.

You would think after a few thousand years of drinking, I would be immune to being too drunk. And for the most part that was true. But sometimes even a body as used to alcohol as mine could tip the scale. It wasn't hard to find a reality where an empty bottle of Buffalo Trace became a full one.

Seeing it without seeing it, I watched the sunset. One hand on the unlocked helm. Heading south. Tacking occasionally. The boat sailed through the water, easy, there was very little tugging on the rudder, it seemed like even the currents, the winds, everything was excited to move us along.

On my right was the burning glow of the dying red orb sinking below the horizon. It would be night soon, there was a chill in the air now, and I looked inland for a nice place to anchor for the evening. A nice little cove somewhere to tuck the *Isla Marie* in for the evening.

It was nice being out on the open water again. Thoughts of Blake and her arguments of me and the idea of a purpose went away. There were more immediate things for me to concentrate on, such as I could, since I was on a second bottle. I think.

Cass had given us the framework of a plan, and I needed to put a few more details in to make it believable. Jacksonville could be made tomorrow. Or even the next day. I wanted to make the trap seem real, like I was really fleeing. Staging everything.

Drawing Jeeves in.

I found us a cove. I little half-circle of land, trees circling the thin strip of sand that might be called a beach. From muscle memory I brought us in. Lowered the sails, allowed the boat's momentum to die out, for the *Isla Marie* to drift to a stop. I dropped the anchor, making sure to let out plenty of line, feeling a slight tremor in the line when the anchor thudded into the mud. I took a quick moment to start up the engine, back the boat up and feel the anchor catch, then power it back off. Then I headed down to the cabin, saw one of the doors was shut to a room. Heard a slight snore from behind the door.

Funny that Cass snored. I thought she would hate knowing that. And then maybe shoot me after I told her.

I was a little drunk. I could tell because my feet weren't going exactly where I wanted them to go. Still, I carefully put away the peanut butter and jelly. And what was left of the package of hamburger buns. Only so much Buffalo Trace that stuff could soak up in my stomach.

Carefully, I cleaned off the knife at the galley sink. Washed my hands, splashed my face a bit. Ran a few drops through my hair. Took a deep breath, my hands on either side of the sink, feeling the tape of the bandage pull against my ribs. The ache there. The pain in the back of my head. Thinking I was glad there was no mirror in front of me.

Maybe you wonder what all this is about. I think I would have told you yesterday, but getting shot at kind of changes your plans. It had been a busy day or so. But maybe now it's time. Time to go back to the beginning of this part of my life, to where this had began.

To where I first had met Blake.

CHAPTER THIRTY

Okay.

That was the last word I had said to Blake. The word haunted me now. The blending of everything I had been, every memory I had, the churn of what I had left behind, everything I was now all mixed with some bleak darkness that was just *okay*.

I'll be back soon...

Sure you will Blake. Sure you will...

Maybe you're tired of me talking about this. Maybe you wonder how a person could get so *meh* about their lives, about their memories, about all the highs and the lows. I'll ask, how many of you remember every moment along your drive to work this morning? Or recall every step you made walking around town. Everything you've ever said to your neighbor, every Monday morning, for two hundred Monday mornings, when you both pull your trashcan to the curb?

Now take all that and expand it a couple thousand years.

Hopefully you get it now.

And that's just a small part of life, when you live forever.

It all becomes a blur. All of it. The highs, the lows, the big moments, the terrible heartaches, all of it and everything. It all blends together in something called the past. Something I had lived. Something I remembered, from time to time. In odd occasions, when a certain song hit, or a scent, like fresh apples. But all of it was something I rarely *felt*, anymore.

It was all meh.

It was all... okay.

That was the word. Something drifting after you in some kind of apathetic cloud. A cloud that never left, but touched upon you and everything you passed, in some kind of mind-numbing invisible mist.

Haunting, right?

I sipped on the Buffalo Trace. Still straight from the bottle. There was a slight sweetness to the burn, something left after the bourbon had gone down, something that lingered long after the pain. I wondered, after tasting the jelly, how the memory of sweetened grapes could be erased, forgotten. Just that quickly the memory of PB&J sandwiches were gone, replaced by a different sweetness of the bourbon, a raw burning sweetness that ached deep in the pit of my stomach.

For some reason I was at the bow. The foredeck. The very front of the boat. My legs dangled over the side, I leaned forward a bit, my arms folded over the hand rail. The currents had spun the boat around a little on the anchor, and the *Isla Marie* faced east. The boat and I stared out over the dark ocean and the black night. Though I wasn't sure the *Marie* was contemplating pasts and futures. She likely just was happy in the moment.

Boats, right?

The moon was hiding, maybe it was just that time of the month. I thought it could be scared of what was coming next. I knew I felt that way, the world-ending fear, the something wicked this way comes. And I'd hide from it if I could. If I didn't feel the need to fix what I had broken, with Blake.

At least the stars were out. Just a few in the beginning, braver little dots of light here and there. More came as the night had descended, as the dark thickened around me, until the sky was scattered with clumps and clusters and wispy bits of plucky lights.

It was beautiful. And serene. Just the thing to drink to. I raised the bottle and toasted the night. Took another sip and listened to the waves wash against the hull, little lapping sounds coming from overboard, like a watery sprite tapping, tapping, tapping. Wondering if anyone was home.

I seemed to be around the beach a lot lately. Not just now. Not just a week ago, but for the last few decades or so. I found a peace here, there was a timelessness in the crashing of the surf, the washing of the waves, the constant rolling motion of the water combined with the permanence of the sea.

Like me, the ocean had been around a long time. The waves in themselves were temporary, yet also somehow unchanged. The water composing each wave was different, but every wave still crashed against the rocks, every wave always withdrew from the beach, always left faint remnants of the ocean in puddles and wet patches of sand, stealing tiny pieces of the shore. The motion was the same, the rhythm of it the same, even as every part of it was completely different.

Something in all of that echoed to me.

A bird cried out. I thought at first it was an owl, but it sounded like a seagull, and I wondered what the creature was doing out so late. There was a heavy flapping of wings, and a splash, and then it was gone.

Gone.

Blake.

I had met her at the beach. Not far from here, actually. Hilton Head Island. The *Isla Marie* had passed it on the way down. Kind of a fancy place, had a nice golf course. I liked it because there was some law there keeping people from hanging advertising signs out on the roads. So, as you drove the island, the windows down, there was nothing but trees and the feeling of the beach along the road. No gaudy signs trying to draw your attention, no blaring blinking names on electronic billboard. Just the wet feel of the air, the cool sharp salty breeze.

Though every now and then the trees would open up to the side. You would see a grocery store, or even the outlet mall, or a crab shack or two as you drove on. The trees would swallow them up again, and it was back to being you and the trees, the rumbling of the car and the smell of the beach.

Anyway, I liked the place. There were enough people around, enough locals manning the restaurants and the shops, that they usually remembered you. At least, they remembered me. I would stop by every year or so and make sure to get a pitcher of white sangria from this one place, which seemed to taste just right. A sweet wine, sweet fruit, and just a hint of alcohol.

So, I was in Hilton Head again. I had picked up a pitcher of white sangria from the restaurant (it was close by, right off the beach) and walked it home. Not a home per se, but the condo I usually rented out. I liked getting something close to the beach, something facing the surf and the sand, and sit out on the patio and watch the moon rise over the ocean.

I'd sit and drink, and if the mood took me, I'd sometimes hop over the rail to the patio and head down to the beach. Jump into the dark water and lose myself in the chilly coolness of the sea at night. Tumble around in the current and see where it took me.

So, there I was (back then), sipping on a pitcher of white sangria. Leaning back in a chair, one of the rocking beach chairs that have this nylon net material you sat in, so that the netting supported you almost like a hammock. Feet kicked out, the arch of one bare sole on the cool metal rail of the patio fence. I rocked a bit, watched the dark ocean, the moon rising up in the east, and the white sand, illuminated by the moon's light.

A figure walked the beach. Someone tall, slim. Lithe, I thought the word was. Thin but athletic. Long, straw colored hair hung behind her head, tied up in a pony tail. The figure would take a few steps, look at something in her hand, maybe her phone, look around the beach, and then take a few more.

A weird little dance. I wondered then if she had lost something. Maybe she had one of those apps that tracked what she was looking for. A watch, or something.

I sipped the sangria. A piece of grape floated into my mouth, and I rolled the jelly-like fruit around with my tongue. Tasting the sourness of the flesh, the sweetness of the grape, and the small bite of whatever alcohol they had mixed with the wine. I did so while watching the woman walk back and forth, little arcs across the beach, each arc bringing her closer and closer to my patio.

Finally, she looked away from her hand. The moon was behind her, so she was still a shadow, just tall and lithe with glimpse of straw hair, but I could have sworn our eyes met. Could have sworn those eyes had lit over me with interest, and maybe excitement.

I swallowed the grape. "Looking for something?"

"Yeah," she said. I sensed, more than felt, a smile. "You."

Brazen. But that was Blake. Or, that had been Blake.

She put her phone, whatever it was, in her back pocket. She kept coming closer, and I could see she was younger than me. I mean, everyone was younger than me, but with her and I it was more relative than actual.

She wore something like a set of chinos. Pale tan color pants, with a white wispy shirt. The shirt so sheer it was almost see-through. Enough that I could see there was no bra. Like she had thrown something on in the middle of the night, just to go on some search.

Something in the woman resounded in me. Some call of like-to-like. Something rare, even for me.

The feeling thrilled me, but it also scared me. Enough that my immediate reaction was trying brush her off. Which was odd, for me. "I'm probably too old for you."

This is a memory, or not quite a memory, but a story I'm telling you. I want to mention here I could see her smile, still see it as I'm saying this, perfect white teeth revealed as full lips curved deliciously, wider and wider.

I won't ever forget that smile. I saw it even as her eyes stayed locked with mine, and wouldn't let me look away. "You think?"

You ever had that person who understood everything about you? Where you were strong, where you were weak? Who knew when to be the strength when you needed it? And when to be weak, when you needed that too?

I'm telling you, for me, that had been Blake.

I had been around a long time, and I had never met anyone like her.

She crossed over the banister that night, onto my patio, into my life. Took the pitcher of sangria and drank from it. The drinking led to talking, the talking led to talking standing closer, side to side, until she was leaning into me, her shirt thin against the back of my arm, until the shirt was gone and we were inside, on the bed. In the bed. She had been intense and curious and her skin was warm and smooth and glided across mine...

I shied away from the memory. Took a deep breath and let it go. All of it. The closeness. The understanding. The curiosity. The smile. Blake had always been searching for something the night I met her. The night I lost her.

And there was something about her, some feeling she had about me. Some knowledge. Something she wanted me to learn about myself.

How could she know that? Internally, I knew there was no way she could. No way she could understand the lives I had lived, the thousands of years, the breaking down of the spirit and the world of meh.

But she said I was different.

And I wondered how. How I was different. How she knew I was different. How could she possibly know that about me?

Unless it was just a feeling from her. Just a belief she had about me. A belief that ultimately had been wrong...

I think.

God, why did all of this have to be so difficult? Why couldn't I just move on, like I had a hundred times in the past? What was different about here and now, what was different about Blake?

Okay, I breathed out again, into the night air. Trying to lengthen my breaths, feel my chest rise in and out. Feel my heartbeat slow, the splashing of the seagull, the washing of the waves against the boat. Trying like hell to feel the word, be the word, even though I was probably the furthest I had been from okay in a long, long time.

Okay

Okay.

Okayyy...

"Hey," a voice startled me. Enough that I jumped and almost lost the bottle of Buffalo Trace.

Cass. She took a seat next to me on the bow. Dangled her legs over the side too. Glanced over at me. Then, seemingly surprised, glanced again. "Are you... crying?"

I wiped my cheeks with the back of one hand. Took a sip of the Trace. "What, you think I can't?"

She took the bottle from me. "I never said that."

"You don't have to," I said. "I know what you think of me."

It's what all Remainers think. It's what they pass along in their meetings. Some soulless man fucking up their lives, who stole pieces of their reality and forever ruined what they had. Cass would grow up the same way, except that I had gotten her sister killed. Well, her sister had been killed because of me. Likely the same thing, in Cass's mind.

"Do you?" she said. She glanced over again, her eyes narrowing. Then she shook her head, as if at a passing thought, and took a large sip of the bourbon herself.

So, the two of us sat there, quiet. Passing the bottle back and forth.

Sipping together, but alone in our thoughts. There was just the washing of waves, the occasional tapping of the water sprite against the *Isla Marie*, and the random call of a lonely, hungry bird.

The moon in hiding, nothing but us and the night and the stars. The bright ones, larger and brighter now, enough that we could see the entire Milky Way trailing across the sky and over the horizon. We sat and drank, shoulder to shoulder, like I had watched soldiers do in a trench, before gathering up whatever courage they had and charging up over the lip of dirt into enemy fire. The two of us drank and stared at the stars, the patchy pinpricks of light rising above us, swelling into rich, illuminated fields against the backdrop of night.

"So many…" Cass said. Her voice drifted off as she looked up at the night sky. At all the stars and the constellations.

I pointed out one or two to her. Funny enough, it was Cassiopeia's bright *W* that we first saw rising above the horizon, her belt of stars standing out brightly among the cloudy background of the Milky Way. I wondered if that was who Cass was named after. If so, she couldn't be more unlike the queen in the myths, but her father had loved stargazing.

"Is it always like this?" Cass asked. "The stars look so bright over the water."

I nodded. "Out in the ocean, it feels so different. Every star feels closer. Brighter. Like the stars and the moon have been placed, staged in a certain way, like it's all there just for you …"

And they were. Every star glowed with an inner light, out over the water, that I never found on land. The moon always loomed out over the sea, brighter and bigger than on the beach. The universe itself felt wide open when I was out to sea, in a way that I never felt anywhere else. Like anything and everything was possible.

"Hmm," was all Cass said, her face turned up to the sky.

More constellations surfaced, the night was rich with them. The winged Pegasus. Perseus, the warrior looking across the pin-pricked field by his steed. Pisces and Aquarius, rising from the depths of the horizon. Off to the side, Aries, the stubborn ram.

I talked about them all. The myths as I had first heard them. The heroes and villains. The world I had grown up in, survived, outlasted, until all that was left were bright pinpricks of stories, illuminated dots scattered across the night.

Cass listened and drank. Her face rapt with dreams of stars and possible planets around those stars. Of places and peoples and times she had never met. Of constellations of places she would never go.

I talked about Ptolemy, one of the first to give stars a name. Others who had dreamed of what was out there. People like the Egyptians, Greeks, and Romans. People like Blake.

Curious people. Driven people. People who wondered, who looked out into the evening sky and thought about possibilities, much like Cass and I were doing now, gazing over the wide expense of black water and blacker night, with the moon nowhere to be found, just the two of us and a field full of stars.

We both drifted into silence. Cass handed me the bottle. I drank. I handed her the bottle. She drank. A nice rhythm developed. I was lost in my memories of Blake. Cass likely the same. The two of us had both been close to her, but Cass and Blake, they had been closer than I had seen any pair of humans in my lifetime. Like they had fit each other, like some puzzle had clicked into place with the two of them.

Maybe Cass had been for Blake what Blake had been for me. Both of them had passion, the emotion came out in different ways, but it was there in Cass, like it had been in Blake. Both of them intense, just Cass more terminatory-so.

I hadn't ever been what Blake wanted, but I hoped I had been close. She had been so driven. Always searching. Always curious.

I had lost that part of me a thousand years back or so.

I took the bottle from Cass. Found it empty. I did a little finger waggle. It was full again. Not Buffalo Trace this time, but a bottle of

Gentleman Jack. A whiskey, maybe a bit more mellow than other whiskeys, but a little rougher than the Trace, maybe. Not quite a gentleman. Which was better for my mood.

Cass frowned at the motion, but took the bottle from me and drank anyway. Grimaced. "Could have picked a nice gin."

I grunted. Finger-waggled and traded her a different bottle. Times like this, finding another reality with an *Isla Marie* and a different liquor was as easy as shooting ducks in a barrel. Which was a saying I never got. It sounded easy though. If you could somehow get all the ducks into the barrel first.

Her frown remained, but she looked at the bottle before opening it. Hendrick's Orbium. I could smell the botanicals in the air, but Cass took a nice sip and smiled. She had a nice smile. The frown seemed just for me. Or maybe because I kept stealing little pieces of reality right now.

I would have explained, but it could wait. The silence was comfortable between us, no need to disturb it with the plan I had come up with. Not one she would like, with the ocean underneath us, but one I thought would work.

Jeeves could track me, somehow. The Remainers could track me, seemingly after I had stolen a little piece of reality. So, I would lead him south this way. Small thefts of reality, like breadcrumbs, leading him south. To a beach north of Jacksonville, a place I knew.

Then maybe a little storm. Something that would drive us ashore. Maybe sink the *Isla Marie* and leave us stranded. Breadcrumbs drawing Jeeves in. An island with a storm surrounding it. One way in or out.

Cass wouldn't like the whole sinking the boat part. I'd get her past it. We had a couple of days, and I'd talk her into it tomorrow.

Tonight was for drinking. For stars. And for Cass and I, different memories of the same person.

CHAPTER THIRTY-ONE

I MAKE IT SOUND LIKE BLAKE AND I WERE THIS GREAT couple. Like among the great couples, Beniffer. Brangelina. Ashmi. But the truth was, we fought some. We actually fought quite a bit.

Mainly about me. I guess it was about us, about the one difference we had.

After that first night, the two of us remained together. We had woken up on the patio, fooled around again, took a shower together, kind of became inseparable. It wasn't long before I shared who I really was, which I did with just a few of the women I had spent time with. Women, I thought, would be around a while.

She took it all in stride. Never questioned it. I showed her a few tricks, and if I'm being honest, Blake hadn't seemed to impressed. Some of the tricks excited her, but like I said, she was always curious, but always *intense*. There was a sense that she had always wanted *more*.

The two of those had combined in wanting something more for me.

She couldn't get why I wasn't curious. Why I hadn't dug deeper. Why I hadn't tried to do more with what I was given, *achieve* more. As if I was born with something that could make me king of the world. King of the universes. King of all the realities of all the universes.

I laughed and told her that the power didn't work that way.

She frowned—the one thing that Cass and Blake had in common—and asked me why I thought that was a fact.

I guessed I didn't. Just a few thousand years of experience. I tried to explain the square blocks and the round hole theory. The other things I had encountered. I tried to explain how it felt, all that time passing, how it all blurred together into a gray past.

I could tell Blake didn't buy it. That she felt I had given up. To some degree, that was true. I could also tell she wanted me. That she was driven to find out what I didn't seem to want to know. Or that I was—maybe in her mind—too lazy to search for.

I wish now I had taken a greater interest. But I thought at the time that as exciting and refreshing as Blake was, she would be gone like all the others in time. She would grow older and hate that I stayed the same. Even if she loved me like Juliet had loved Romeo, that love would twist and fade and betray with age. I knew it. I had experienced it.

So, I had filed her passion away. Put it away to Blake being Blake. Let her do Blake things. Which is what had led her to getting killed.

We had argued a lot that week. She had found out something. Some piece of knowledge of the Remainers. Something only the oldest of them kept secret. Maybe just a single person, whispering a few words in the next person's ear right before death, person after person through the ages, maybe even from the very first Remainer.

She thought that could be it. The reason I existed. Or some piece of knowledge I needed to become king of all the realities of all the universes. Some *purpose*.

I had laughed at her and filed it under Blake thinking Blake things.

Man, had she gotten angry then. Some inner fire had lit her. Some passion I lacked. Some *fury*.

"Blake," I had said. Hand holding my drink. My other hand on her hip, feeling her sharp pelvic bone against my thigh. Feeling her pull away. "Let's just enjoy our time together."

"You always say that," she said. Both of her hands pressed against my chest. Pressing her body away from me, slightly. Enough that I had to really hold her hip to keep her near me.

"I do always say that," I smiled an empty smile and took a drink. The glass had a layer of perspiration over it, cool to my lips, colder still for my fingers holding it. I always say it because I knew our time was fleeting. A week, a month, ten or twenty years, all of that time was a drop in the bucket of my life.

Twenty years to Blake would be half of her life. She would be close to forty. She would look ten years older than me, and wondering if I was looking at other women then. She would feel age creep up on her, joints crack getting out of bed, pluck through gray wisps of hair, frown at the lines appearing on her face.

Twenty years to me would be nothing.

So, I always told her let's enjoy our time together. I knew she wanted more. I knew how me saying that would feel to her. But I couldn't escape how everything felt to me.

And god, I just wanted to feel *something*. And this thing with Blake *blazed*. I would feel it for centuries, I thought. So, I wanted to ride this comet with her as it burned through the atmosphere, ride it as long as I could, until it crashed into the Earth and ended.

To a man who lived forever, even a Blake only happened once in a lifetime. A long lifetime. So, I wanted to spend what I had with her, all the seconds and minutes and hours and days. Because I knew one day she would be gone, and I would keep going. And I knew then, the time I spent with her would carry me on.

It was the one thing I couldn't make her understand. She seemed to feel like we would be together forever. Every passionate relationship started out that way. The two people together felt the electric glances, the hot touches, the inability to keep your hands off each other. Maybe you know what I'm talking about.

It was later on, after the passion fades, that Blake would get worried. Worried about her age, how she looked, how I kept looking so young…

I tried explaining that to her once. How Blake would feel in ten or twenty years about me, about us. Let me tell you, I'll never do that again. Never, ever tell a woman what she will think.

Ever.

So, I learned to let the argument go, when we got into these fights. I let it all wash over me and just responded with a smile. Responded with the same word, *okay. Let's just enjoy our time together.* Even now, even if she had found some rumor, passed through the centuries through some kind of Remainer grapevine. Of some secret she thought I needed to know. She was *driven* to have me know.

"Don't you want to know?" she asked, for maybe the thousandth time. *"Don't you feel you're owed something? An explanation? A reason?"*

"Blake," I sighed. It was some wild-goose chase. I had no purpose. I had been looking for one forever. *"I'm happy to be in this moment. It's enough for me, now, with you."*

Honestly, what were the chances this one Remainer would know it? That this one ancient guy had figured it out, then passed it on? Why wouldn't they let all the Remainers know? Seemed like something they were doing more for their protection, than anything I should know. Than anything about me.

Blake grabbed my glass. Finished it. Held it out, until I sighed again and finger-waggled another glass into existence. Which was a neat trick, the never-ending glass. Easy to do.

It was always five o'clock somewhere.

She let me take a drink, and then finished that one off too. As if what she was about to say was final.

"I want it though." Blake, leaning back against my hand, pushing away

from me, her eyes vividly green. I think this was the core of who she was, the archeologist in her, the need to find old things, buried. The reason she read all her books. The need to find the past, the drive to discover the future, trying to make all of that work with the present. *"I want to know."*

And a pause then, "You should too."

She said it like her wanting it should be enough for me. Like she couldn't figure out why I wasn't interested. But I couldn't get it across to her, like I knew I wouldn't be able to. The seconds passing as minutes, the minutes passing as hours, the hours as days and the days as thousands upon thousands of years.

Just a blur. Just a big blur of gray and black, where an occasional memory would surface. Of a smile, from a person who may have been my mother. Or she could have been someone selling pastries from a store window.

I had given up trying to figure who was who.

"Okay," I had said. The glass was back in my hand. Empty, except for a few pieces of ice. Little slivers that slid around in the base of the glass, melting even as I watched.

"I'll be back soon," she said. Then pulled away. Leaving that hand empty too.

"Okay," I had said again. Finger-waggling a new bottle into existence. That seemed to be what I used my power most for now. I ignored the look in Blake's eyes. Ignored the guilt I felt, even then, by not realizing how passionate she felt about this. About me. About whatever secret the Remainers held...

The boat rocked gently underneath me. A splash from a night bird, hunting. Cass leaned against my shoulder. I thought she was still awake, still gazing out over the stars. The night air carried a chill, the breeze fluttered around us, so different from the heat of the midday sun, and I couldn't stop a shiver from running along my spine.

Okay...

CHAPTER THIRTY-TWO

Some time passed. The Earth rotated underneath us all. Cassiopeia marched across the night sky, headed west. Perseus and Pegasus and Aries followed. The light breeze had died down, everything was quiet, the lone bird had finally settled in for the night. Neither Cass nor I had moved in a bit, we still sat in the bow of the *Isla Marie*, our legs dangling below us, our arms folded over the handrail. I had my shoes off, and the ocean radiated a chill that cooled the bottom of my feet.

Cass gasped.

There was a blooping splash below us. Her bottle, now sleeping with the fishes.

The thought had me chuckle.

Cass frowned at me, like I had been responsible for her falling asleep. Or her dropping her bottle. Whichever. Maybe both.

Being Cass, she went on the attack.

"You never told me," she said. Her words slurring a bit.

"Told you what?" I asked.

"How she died," Cass said.

Oh.

I hadn't told anyone that. Maybe it was something you were waiting on. But it was something I was trying to forget. It wasn't something I wanted to remember, much less pass along to others. Easier to just check the box saying Blake was dead and get to the revenge part. Easier to do than feel.

Easier didn't mean better though. Usually, it meant the opposite. Usually we avoided the things that we needed to say or do. At least, that's been my experience.

Maybe that's just me.

"You going to tell me?" Cass asked me again. Or demanded.

Yeah, it was probably me. Cass seemed to be someone that lined things up and knocked them down. Through, rather than over or around.

I had lived long enough that around was plenty fine. I had plenty of time, there was no need to rush in most of the things I did. I had discovered that in time the question, the answer, both of them would fade.

Even the desire to find them would fade. The urgency to *know*. Whether or not I had found what I was looking for, I knew it would all go away. It just took time.

So, why was I here now? With Cass? Looking for revenge?

Okay...

I was here because some things were my fault. Some things still felt like I couldn't shake them. Blake's death had hit me harder than anything I could remember. And I knew it would haunt me, long after the memory of it was gone, when the only thing left was the sudden abrupt jerk out of a cold, dead, sleep, when my body was covered in a chill sweat and a deep fear ran through me, from something in my past that would never, ever let go.

Blake had been different. She had awoken something in me, something I had thought long dead. So, she deserved something different from me. Something different than my normal move along and forget about it.

At least, that's what I was telling myself, right now.

I took a drink. I'd say the Gentleman Jack burned my throat, but honestly I was numb to it by now. Drunk to it by now. I couldn't taste the charcoal mellowing, the hint of vanilla or oak. It was just a liquid that warmed my stomach a bit, after the swallow.

Cass took the bottle from me. Drank and grimaced. Saw that I didn't want to talk. "Chicken," she said. The word coming out like *sshhiken*.

Like she could know. It wasn't that I was chicken. It was just that I was tired. Tired of the flash of passion. The brief burning in the night. Tired of the passing of someone I cared about. Of watching them age, or of watching them get taken away in a flash. Tired of it all.

Though Blake had been different. Felt different. Somehow.

She hadn't been gone long. I had still been drinking from the same bottle. I think. In some fancy hotel in Chicago, overlooking the city. We had gotten a room at the very top, so I was out on the balcony. It had been cold, with the winds so strong that I kept one hand tight on the rail. They didn't call it the Windy City for nothing.

Highrise buildings had rose in front me, like tombstones from a grave. Silent, mostly dark. A few windows still lit, here and there, given the faces of the buildings an eerie Halloween feel. Like someone had carved a pumpkin, put a candle in it, with the eyes and the nose and the teeth in wrong locations. Like you could see the face, you knew what they were going for, but just barely.

The moon had been out, but it was cloudy. The Windy City, right? Banks of clouds, dark overhead, flying by in a silent rush. Like the Earth was turning faster underneath the night. The clouds hid the moon and stars above, hid the constellations. It was just a blanket of darkness covering all of us below.

Then a scream.

A gunshot.

A couple more.

The scream stopped.

There was commotion below. So far down I couldn't see. Just flashing red and blue lights on the street, as sirens spun up around me.

For some reason, I had known then. Some heavy feeling had descended on me, the kind of feeling you get when the phone rings late at night, rings over and over, with your hand paused over it. Not wanting to answer, because *you know*.

I set the bottle down. Walked outside the room. The hallways and elevator were just bright lights to me, fuzzy. I didn't remember much until I got to the base of the hotel. The lobby. People were gathered there, at the doors. Even this late at night, there was a nice crowd. A lady dressed in a nice suit, with a badge having her name and the name of the hotel, was there waving people back.

I walked past her. Past them.

The lady tried to stop me. Told me there was a shooter outside. The red and blue lights strobed out there, along the streets, as more police cars appeared. Cops, hiding behind the doors.

A body lay on the sidewalk. Right in front of the lobby. A long, lithe form, with blonde hair tied tight behind her head. A dark pool spreading out beneath her.

I pushed past the lady, opened the door. A cop screamed at me to get back inside. Yelled at the crowd to get away from the glass doors of the hotel. Someone was still shooting, potshots from down the street.

I ignored the cops. Went to the body, placed my hand on the side of Blake's face. Her skin was a little warm, but also cool. Cooling fast. Her eyes open, sightless. Blank.

Okay...

One of her hands was balled up. I opened it, put my fingers through hers. They were just a little stiff, maybe from one last clench of her fist, one last heart-breaking moment of Blake trying to stay alive, take another breath, another second of life. And then she was gone. But the muscles remembered.

I sat there like that for a long time, the cold concrete seeping into the backs of my legs, while the screaming cop settled himself down. He got what I was doing. Who she had been to me.

I sat there and searched all the realities. It felt like it took forever, but I'm sure it was only a moment or two. I opened all the boxes, looking for one that could bring Blake back. One in which I had gone with her and kept her alive. One in which she didn't go on her foolish mission to try to find something to give me purpose. One in which she was alive and vibrant and laughing in my arms.

Nothing.

She was nowhere to be found. Not my Blake.

Dead is dead, after all.

All the sounds became muted in my ears. The sirens, the gunshots, the screams and the panic. Like I had gone deaf.

An ambulance showed up, its lights off, its siren silent. Just a ghostly wagon. Other cops too. They moved me away, kind of like moving a puppet. In stages, getting me up, tugging an arm here, tucking it around their shoulders, then pulling the legs along behind.

I could tell them I had seen more death than they knew, more death than anyone else alive, but they wouldn't understand. Right then, I didn't understand.

They covered Blake with a black tarp.

That was the last I had seen her. Would ever see her.

Senseless to me then. Senseless to me now, telling Cass. But apparently something I was going to figure out.

CHAPTER THIRTY-THREE

———

Of course, Cass being Cass, she didn't like the story. Hell, I didn't like it. I didn't like me.

We stood face to face. Her eyes were tough to discern in the night, the starlight didn't quite illuminate her face, but I could feel her anger. The boat rocked gently underneath us, from some unknown swell rolling in from the ocean. Unknowingly, her hand reached back to steady herself against the rail.

Being Cass, she started with an accusation. Wanting a fight.

"You weren't even there."

I wanted to look away, but didn't. "I know."

"She wanted you to come, and you didn't."

I shook my head. "She didn't want me to come. She wanted me to *want* to come."

A distinction without a difference, maybe. Cass thought so, as well.

"It's the same thing," she said. Thought it came out funny. *T'ssame thing.*

"It's not the same thing," I said. I had never quite figured that part out. Blake and I had been great, but when we had fought, it was always about that. About her wanting me to want more. About her wanting me to want it all. And me telling her it wasn't worth it. Wasn't worth the cost. Stealing reality changed too much, but what it didn't change was everyone else dying. Everyone else fading away. All of it and everything becoming this crazy black hole in my memories, as more and more images, sights, sounds tried to pack their way in.

What more could I want? King of the World? What could that do for me? Why? Just to sit around and tell others what to do?

There was no purpose to my power. No higher calling. No lower calling either. After all, what is the meaning of ruling the world, if you could change any part of it you wished? There's no sense in it. When everything is temporary, there is no meaning. Nothing to *build*. Like a child at the beach, I could destroy any sandcastle I built, whenever I wanted to. I could change it. I could steal whatever reality I wanted to live from any world I wanted, and when I tired of that I could just steal another.

You kind of run out of things to want, after awhile.

You see what happens to others, when you live that way, after awhile.

You realize there's no point to it. No meaning.

Blake never got that. And it looked like Cass wouldn't either. At least not in a way where I could convince Cass of my side of the argument.

When you're the only person who can do what you can do, it's tough for other people to see your side. They never understand. Cass didn't. At least not now. Not while she was drunk.

"Chickenshit," she said. *Shhikenshit.* Her eyes flashing, even in the shadows of the starlit night.

"Cass," I said, and reached out, wanting to calm her down.

She punched me.

Hard.

I didn't see her fist, it connected with my jaw. A sharp quick punch.

All I saw was a different kind of stars. Part of me shook my head, my eyes closed tight, still seeing the flash of light that happens when someone lands a good punch.

Her other hand pushed my chest. Pushing me away. Only I weighed more than Cass. And, regardless of the amount of bourbon I had drank, I was steadier on my feet.

I felt her presence disappear.

Then there was a splash. A big splash. Followed by frantic paddling splashes and a quick scream.

Cass had gone overboard.

I blinked away the stars. Looked for a life preserver, or a life jacket. Didn't see one near me, not among the shadows of the deck.

I took a breath, kicked off my shoes, and jumped overboard too. Far enough away not to land on her. The ocean was icy cold and immediately soaked my pants. Soaked my bandage under my ribs. My pants made me feel heavier, the soaked denim tugged on my legs as I moved through the water.

I was close enough to swim over to Cass. She was frantically paddling, it looked like she had forgotten how to swim, and her head was bobbing below the surface of the water. She would sink down, then thrust up out of the water to take a big gulp of air, then bob back underneath. Her eyes were frightened and saw me, but didn't see me.

A person like that could drown the person rescuing them.

"Cass," I yelled out, kicking my legs out to keep me afloat. Feeling my pants drag through the water. "I'm here. Relax. I got you."

She did anything but, though. It was like Cass didn't recognize me as anything but something floating in the water, something she could use to try to stay afloat. Her arms jerked out to me, and latched onto my arm. Pulled me down in the water with her.

I was able to get a deep breath before we went under.

Her grip was tight. Her other arm latched on as well. I tried to pull away, but she had a death grip on me. Maybe literally. Because without three arms, no matter how hard we kicked, we weren't getting back to the surface.

I cursed myself for not taking a moment to look for a life preserver. Or a jacket. Something to help us stay afloat. I had jumped in, thinking I could ease Cass back to the boat. Thinking that the splashing I had heard was more of a surprise splashing than real fear.

So, I grabbed Cass instead. Shook her, underneath the water. Hard. Enough that she paused, maybe not out of her fear, but enough to wonder what I was doing. It wasn't like I could tell, with it being night and dark, the water was a miring blackness, absorbing all light.

I didn't need light, though. I was looking through realities. Looking for something specific.

For some reason, maybe adrenaline, things became clearer to me in times like these. When I was stabbed, or bullets were flying, or I needed something *immediately*, the reality I needed was right next to me. It was as simple as reaching out and grabbing it.

Going back to the factory analogy. If I was searching through all the factories with all the conveyor belts carrying all the boxes stuffed full of all the universes, usually I could never find quite what I needed. It took a lot of effort. A lot of searching, to maybe find something that would work.

But now, with Cass dragging us down into the depths of the water, with the blackness of the cold ocean surrounding us, the reality I needed just happened to be right next to me. As if I stood in just the right factory, next to the right box on the right conveyor, and the universe I was looking for happening to be right on top of the box.

Maybe it was some kind of zone, some kind of clear thought process that came around when the adrenaline was high and all the nerves were firing. I couldn't say. I knew what it felt like though. It felt like a fine-tuned engine, when you pushed the gas pedal all the way down and the car responded by surging forward, eating up the road.

It was kind of a high. An excitement. A *this is it* type of feel. And I had it now.

What I needed was right there.

I grabbed it. Stole the reality. Pulled it into our universe. Switched what was there with what was here, with me and Cass and the *Isla Marie*.

It took a moment, but I could feel the realities blend. Feel the square edges shave off, as I pulled one reality through another. Feel the peg not quite fit, until I forced it in, tugging and pulling until all of a sudden one thing *slipped* through another.

And just like that, our world was different. The continental shelf now was a little higher. I had pulled from a reality where plate tectonics were a little different, the land masses a little more prominent, the end result being that the continental shelf below where Cass and I were now was shifting, growing higher underneath our feet.

Not too far out though. Just enough of the reality around us, the cove where we had anchored. Not the entire southeast coast.

Well, it *was* a continental shelf. So maybe I had changed the shelf in a few miles in either direction. Maybe more, maybe a few dozen, or hundred. It was always hard to tell.

The moment crystallized. Cass still remained motionless in my hands. Whether the movement just felt long to me, or she had given up, I couldn't tell. I just knew the cold water wrapped us like a thick, cold gelatin, as we sank the thirty or forty feet to the bottom.

Thirty or forty feet became twenty or thirty. Then ten. Then five.

My feet touched bottom. The mud was soft under my feet, but still hard, like wet clay, squishing between my toes. Then my head broke the surface of the ocean, as the water lowered around us, and in front of me I saw Cass's face, covered in black, stringy hair.

Her eyes were wide open. Her face was blank. The ocean drained off of her, off of the two of us, as the water level continued to lower. As the ground continued to rise. Until there was maybe a foot of it around us.

There was a large groaning in the night. A creaking of wood. Then a shuddering splash. A thin wave of water sprayed us as the *Isla Marie* tipped over. Thankfully falling in the other direction, revealing a white belly-like hull thick with streaks of dark mud.

Then the night was quiet. Except for the washing of water. Some splashing around us, from fish flopping in tiny pools of water along the shore. Like giant tide pools.

I stood there, holding Cass with both hands. Waiting for her to get a grip. Waiting for the fear to pass and her brain to start processing.

The lone bird returned. The owl, or the seagull. There was a *hooing* call high over the water, then more splashes as the predator found easy early morning snacks.

Cass blinked. Shook her head. Said something softly. I thought it was *what the hell*.

But she was processing. So, I took her to the shore, tugging her along behind me. We were both wet and cold and she was shaking, so I pulled her close and let our body heat team up and try to warm us both up. The mud kept sucking at my feet, there were sharp rocks and shells in it, and it was a relief to get to a beachy area, something with soft, dry sand that felt warm to me, after the cold ocean.

It was hard to tell, but it felt like the ground was still moving underneath us. Little shakes and shimmers. Like it was scared, or trembling. But that could have been just me.

I sat Cass down there, asked her to stay. The shore was a lot sandy, a little rocky, with a tall brush mixed with trees behind it. There were no lights, no homes, no people that I could see or hear.

I went back to the *Marie*. Tired. Exhausted. Usually stealing realities didn't affect me. Maybe this time I had more reality than I thought. Stolen more than I had before. Moved more shelf or sea or world. Maybe it was just a long day after a long day after a long week.

Hell, I didn't know, but I was drained. But also happy. This was what I had wanted, in a way. I wanted to steal a little reality here and there, lead Jeeves this way like breadcrumbs. Let him track me, without knowing that's what I wanted.

I had been thinking about pulling in another storm. Leaving the *Isla Marie* sunk somewhere. Give Jeeves the idea that we had run aground and had to flee south. Where we would be trapped on Tybee Island. Try to lead him to our ambush.

That might have been obvious though. This was much better. Jeeves would see this and wonder what had happened. The *Isla Marie* looked like it had been dropped in the middle of a muddy swamp. He'd know that I did it, but he wouldn't know why.

A storm and a sunken boat might look like a trap. Jeeves wouldn't figure this out. It wasn't obvious.

At least that's what I hoped. Wondering was good. It would make Jeeves question, and questioning, he may miss the obvious. He could miss the trap.

So, I was tired, but I was also happy. All I had to do was get a few things from the boat, something to feed Cass and I, something to warm us, some new clothes. Then we'd make our way to Tybee. Leaving one large crumb behind us, a beacon blazing in the night, for Jeeves to stumble upon.

CHAPTER THIRTY-FOUR

THE SHAKING OF THE GROUND CONTINUED. I COULD FEEL IT in the boat. The *Isla Marie* trembled with little shakes and shimmers. Every now and then the boat would rock and I would have to reach out a hand to steady myself since everything was sideways.

I was standing in the galley. Literally maybe on the galley, my feet resting on the wall right next to the sink. I was squatting down and going through the cupboards, pulling out the food that I had pulled out from the cupboards back at the house in Folly Beach.

Déjà vu, anyone?

The lights were out in the boat. Something had happened to the battery when the *Isla Marie* had tipped over. I had a flashlight tucked underneath my arm, the beam rocked as I moved and never quite rested where I needed the light to shine. I had to steal it from another reality, after not being able to find anything outside on the deck to illuminate the dark inner belly of the boat.

I had grabbed some spare clothes for both Cass and me. Shoes. A blanket. The first aid kit. The peanut butter and jelly. Bread. The laptop and spare phone. Water. Stuffed as much of it as I could in the back-pack. Tossed the blanket over my shoulder.

I found a gym bag, started filling it too. Found the 9mm, the wakiza-shi, the katana, and my jacket. The bulletproof suit one. It needed clean-ing. It was rumpled and dirty and stained with dark drops of dried blood. But I'd worry about that later. It had saved my life before, and I thought it might come in handy again.

I put as much of it as I could in the second bag. Slid the katana through the handles on the top. Felt like I had as much as I could carry. A collection of things to get us through the night.

All through the night. Hah. I snicker-giggled. I did like the song.

I was getting a little loopy. Definitely needed some rest.

Chuckling, I pulled myself out of the below decks portion of the *Isla Marie*. Grabbed the backpack I had stuffed and hopped down on the muddy shore the boat was grounded on. Or was it an ocean bed? I didn't know, but I took a last moment at the side of the ship and patted the hull. The reverberation felt hollow.

I felt bad for the *Marie*. She had been good to us.

Definitely getting loopy. My plans had changed. I originally had wanted to find a tiny island somewhere and wait Jeeves out. It was what I normally did. It was easier for me to wait others out. I had the advan-tage of time.

Having Cass along had changed that. Just like having Blake in my life had changed it. Maybe there was a reason I preferred being a solo act.

I worked my way through the mud, navigating around the wet puddles, dark tidepools left as the shoreline had risen, the flashlight reflecting back from the black surfaces. The thin layers of water slapped under my feet. The ground no longer shook, or I couldn't feel it anymore. Just like I couldn't feel my toes or the water's temperature with my feet, and I hoped it was because I was just used to the cold. I hadn't wanted to put on my shoes until I got back to land. I just had the one pair.

Cass remained where I had left her, though she had drawn her knees up to her chest and circled her legs with her arms. She rested her chin there, between her knees, huddling for warmth. I sat the bag next to her, pulled the blanket off my shoulders and laid it around hers.

She nodded a thanks.

I grabbed an older shirt and rubbed my feet. Feeling the warmth as I worked the soles, and grateful for it. Then I tugged my shoes on and went looking for firewood.

The brush was thick, it made tiny *swishing* sounds as I worked through the tall grass heading towards a clump of the trees. The night was quiet, as if everything still waited and watched the shore. Even the bird was quiet. Wondering what had happened, what had changed, what might still change. The flashlight was a tight beam of light, illuminating nothing in the brush, until it finally picked up old pieces of wood as I neared the trees.

I gathered old branches. A big piece of driftwood. Whatever I thought would burn. Then I brought it back. Made a big pile by Cass. Set some of the bigger pieces to the side. Gathered some old brush and dead grass and set it on the pile.

Then looked at it.

Fuck.

I didn't have a lighter. I hadn't seen one in the boat. And it wasn't something I normally carried.

Well, in for a penny, in for a pound. If Jeeves could track me by me using my powers, it wasn't like he would miss what happened with the shoreline here. I waggled my fingers. Reached into the front of the backpack and pulled out a lighter. A little Bic with a loud click when I flicked it, leaving a little flame standing over my thumb, waving a bit in the night.

I moved the lighter to the dried grass, waited until it caught, then nursed the small fire until the flames grew large enough to remain on their own. The red and yellow tongues licked at the air, flowed from the grass to the little branches, consuming them in tiny pops and crackles.

And then one of the larger pieces caught. The little tongues of flame swelled together into one or two larger tongues, reaching high into the night. A little smoke drifted away, something that smelled grassy and mossy with maybe a hint of cedar.

Cass slide herself a little closer to the fire. We sat opposite each other, and her eyes shone in the firelight. They were open and glassy, almost wet, and she didn't have her usual frown on.

"Sorry," she said. More of a mutter, I guess. Though she no longer sounded drunk.

I smiled. "About almost drowning us?"

She shook her head. Waited a moment. A bit of breeze kicked up, stirring the flames between us. "About calling you chicken."

Oh.

"It wasn't fair, or right," she continued, her gaze lost in the fire. "I guess I just miss her. Miss how she made me feel. Miss who I was around her."

What she left unsaid is that she would have gone with Blake. Would have demanded to. It would have been fair to say that to me, but it was nice of Cass to leave it out.

Although we both knew that truth.

I couldn't remember the last time someone had apologized to me. Seems like it had been decades, with me running from the Remainers, and trying not to steal any reality. Trying to live a quiet life with no meaning. Just existing.

So, I didn't know how to handle it. I shrugged it away. Along with how Blake had made me feel. The excitement, the intensity, the searching for purpose. "We both miss her."

I was tired, but I knew for some reason I wasn't going to sleep. I could lie down, but I'd be restless. So, I pulled out the laptop and the phone.

"I tried those earlier," Cass said. "They're both locked. Need a password."

I had ways around that. It's why I grabbed them. What I did rested a little on probabilities. If I went into the factory and started looking for boxes, trying to find a reality where there was a laptop and cellphone around that I could use, it could take me forever. Especially on the coast of Georgia.

However, if I already had a laptop and cellphone on me, it seemed to be a lot easier to find a reality where I already knew the password for both. There were a lot of realities "closer" to me, when that reality was more like the reality I was in. So, it was nothing to switch those realities out. Steal the laptop and the cellphone I could use, and swap those out for the two I couldn't.

Another waggle of the fingers.

"You're doing something," Cass said. "Or you did something."

So, Remainers could sense what I did. I had wondered, back in Bubba's, if Cass had guessed or if she had known that I had used my powers. Before the whole shootout. Maybe that was part of how they tracked me. Or maybe it was the start of something they did.

"Yeah," I said. Opening the laptop, turning it on. The cellphone too, setting up a hotspot. "What's his real name? Jeeves?"

All I could remember of him was that he was gray. Seemed gray. Felt gray. Gray slacks and trousers, the lighter color, like a stonewash. Something that would drift along and fit in to most places, without standing out. I think he even had gray hair. Or, if it was salt and peppery, it was mostly salt. The only thing that really stood about the man was a small flash of yellow on his chest. Right over his heart.

Cass smiled at the Jeeves comment. Just a small one. But it looked like she was coming around after almost drowning.

"I think it's James," she said. "James Bennett. That's it."

I worked the laptop to get online. Started a search on the man. "How do you know him?"

Cass still had her knees pulled up to her chest, and though the blanket hid her motion, it looked as if she rocked a bit back and forth. Thinking. "Blake would tell me things," she said. "She talked about him a lot."

Then she paused. Looking at me. Worried? Or wondering?

"When did it start?" I asked. "Six months ago?"

Cass thought more. Or maybe she was still working through the gin. "Sounds about right. I remember her being upset one day, out of the blue." Her shoulders lifted and lowered. "It felt like a bad relationship to me. Like if someone had come into your life that you hoped you never saw again."

Then she fell silent. I knew, just like she did, we both were thinking about things we could have listened to. Could have responded to. And maybe, if we had, Blake would still be alive.

It wasn't a name that stood out. There were a lot of hits, when I first typed his name into the search bar. I went through LinkedIn posts, social media hits, twitter accounts, and started entering in more information. London. Hospital. Death.

Then I found something. A tiny article in a newspaper. The Daily Telegraph.

The picture was the guy I remembered. The guy who had stabbed me. The gray man with a flash of yellow on his chest. A gray suit. Gray eyes. Looked like we both like the color. Maybe neither of us dealt in absolutes.

In the picture he was younger, but still with the ghostly hair. Salt and pepper, with more salt. A serious face. Focused. Still a splash of yellow over his breast pocket though. I must have commented on it out loud.

"It's his thing," Cass said. "His daughter's favorite flower."

It made a kind of sense, wearing your daughter's favorite flower over your breast pocket. Even if she was dead. A little morbid, if you asked me. But it fit Jeeves. In many ways it was like the picture in my wallet of Blake and I. It was something to keep her around. Something that would always bring that moment back in my mind.

I swore then.

Pulled out my wallet. Sopping wet, from the trip overboard. Fished the photo out where I had last tucked the picture, carefully folded.

It was floppy, and soppy, and I had to work to peel it apart. The ink blended and smeared and much of it was just a blob. A colorless thing. A smudge, a stain that would never again be what I needed.

Her words though remained on the backside. Hard strokes, firm against the white background.

Miss me yet? xoxo...

I wanted to scream. Maybe I did scream. Cass certainly looked at me funny, with wide open eyes over her folded knees. I got the sense she pulled back a bit, though the blanket hid her motion.

She was gone to me now.

Forever.

No picture of her and me together. She would never again rest her head on my chest, tucked under my shoulder, smiling and turned towards me. The memory of her would fade in time, like all the others, and I would never have anything to remember her by.

I knew I would never forget this moment.

My hands shook, and I couldn't put the photo back. Couldn't fold it right again. The picture fluttered in my fingers, I had dropped my wallet, and all I could see was this blueish smear across the front across the photograph.

Like I had said, I could find another. It might even look the same. But it would never be my photo. It would be something I stole from another world, maybe even another me. Not something Blake had given me, with a smile and a quick kiss on the side of my cheek. It would never be truly *mine*.

Did Jeeves have the same moment? When his daughter had first pulled a daffodil from the ground and waved it at him, the bright yellow head flopping around on the thin green stem? Was that the moment that stuck with him, the memory? Was that why he kept it on his breast? Was it a badge, a symbol, or just a reminder?

Maybe he and I were closer than I thought, in that. Driven by a moment of a memory. Clinging to something before it disappeared forever into the past. The flower. The picture. Different. But the same.

"Hey," Cass said, loudly. Like she had said it a couple of times.

I looked over at her.

"You okay?"

My hands still shook. My fingers still held the photo. My eyes seemed to rove over the world in front of me, the smudged picture, the hard lines of Blake's words, the flickering flames of the fire, the gray tendrils of smoke twisting in the air, masking the stars, leaving just the dark, dark night above me.

It had been Cass's fault I had lost this. Her fault, starting the fight. Falling into the water.

I'm not sure what my face looked like, but Cass flinched, so I looked away. Not answering her. I wasn't sure I could speak, or what would come out if I did.

I forced my hands to steady. Found my wallet. Put the picture back the best I could. Tried not to scream in rage as the wet paper folded and smushed behind my license. I grabbed a breath, then another, inhaling the dry bitter scent of burning grass, dirty bark, inhaling the ashy taste of dead limbs long since fallen from the tree.

I struggled to put the laptop back in my lap. Focused on Jeeves. There was no article about his daughter's death in there. Nothing at all.

As if she never existed.

It talked about the new lord in Parliament. The Field Marshal. Some military position.

Which meant Jeeves was a dangerous man.

I searched for a long time, looking for something I might have caused. Some event, some splinter from a reality theft I had done, ten years ago. Twenty. There was no other article there. Nothing mentioning a daughter at all. Nothing about a hospital or doctor causing a death of a young girl anywhere in England. Or Europe. Just the man's recent elevation.

Nothing I had done to have this man try to kill me. Nothing I had done that would cause him to come after me. Come after Blake.

Cass had turned away from me. From the fire. The blanket was wrapped around her. Maybe I had hurt her feelings.

I finished my search. There were a bunch of links and photos on the first tab of the browser, under the article of Lord Jeeves being the new Marshal.

The clickbait every website seemed to have. Something there caught my eye, and I clicked it. The title read: *Earthquakes along the Eastern Coast.*

I knew I wasn't going to sleep anytime soon. So, I clicked on the clickbait. Read through the article and grunted. There were a few fault lines in the south-east of the United States. Something called the Eastern Piedmont Fault System. Whatever I had done had apparently shifted things under the Earth's crust, enough that a few minor quakes had rolled through the coast, the trembling felt as far as Augusta, Georgia. As far north as the Appalachians.

More clickbait underneath that article. Speculations. Even this late at night people were freaking out. Reports of people heading to the store, buying up all the water and milk and bread. Other links showing people heading out of town for a bit. And one wild article about a scientist wondering if there was a super volcano about to surface somewhere in the southern states.

She pointed to similar shifting plate tectonics out by Hawaii and Iceland, something about even though the east coast was older and more "settled," didn't mean that something couldn't still erupt from underneath. That we didn't really know what lurked beneath the surface.

That was as a true statement there as any I had read that night.

I'll add this here, because I know you might be thinking it, but I'd never done anything in Hawaii. So, don't put that on me. Volcanos, earthquakes, storms, these things are natural things. They happen. They don't need anything from me to destroy what's around them.

Though I admit to some blame here tonight.

Cass was truly asleep now, I thought. At least, I heard her tiny snores, the rhythmic breathing of someone lost in slumber. She had moved a little away from the flames, streaks of mud clumped with brush and sand staining the blanket tucked around her.

I closed the laptop. Turned off the phone. Put all thoughts of Blake and the picture behind me. All thoughts of Jeeves and wondering on why he felt like he needed to kill me, and focused on what I needed to do tomorrow.

We'd have to find a place to clean up, first thing. More clothes. And then we'd have to look for weapons. Get set up on Tybee. And hope Jeeves took the bait.

I mean, he couldn't miss it now. Not with all the little thefts of gin and tequila. Not with the *Isla Marie* on its side in the cove. Not with the earthquakes.

I wondered if I was being too obvious.

I put a couple of the larger logs on the fire, and tried to find a comfortable place to lay down myself. The sand itched over my skin, and I rolled several times. I was too hot close to the fire, and too cold just a few inches away. I thought about sharing the blanket with Cass but didn't. I thought about Jeeves and wondered about a man who wore his dead daughter's favorite flower.

I thought about Blake and wondered what she had been searching for so desperately. All the times she had left to some dig. All the things she had wanted to save. I wondered why she had looked for old things,

things that had meant more to her than maybe they should. Way she had wanted to save them.

Why she had wanted to save me.

Oh god, the fights we had over it. Why I didn't want more for myself. Why I didn't want to *do* more with what I had. She couldn't understand me, and I couldn't convince her that what I knew, what I had lived, the length of life I had, was what proved her wrong.

And I started to question myself. Wondered if I was missing something. Wondered if there was some proud part of me that had never listened to Blake, never opened up to the possibility that my experience was *wrong*.

I lay there. I kept laying there. Not sleeping. The flames crackling next to me. The dark sky overhead, masked by wisps of smoke that twisted in the breeze, revealing some of the brighter stars of light, like someone pulling a hazy gray drape across the night. The ground still trembled underneath me, light shivers and shakes, as if something had awoken deep underneath us all, some long-dormant power, rising and ready to erupt.

CHAPTER THIRTY-FIVE

Of course it's always at the last second you fall asleep. After lying in a place for hours, tossing and turning, exhaustion hovering in the background of my body, of my soul. Getting more and more frustrated, turning some more, asking for just a moment's sleep. A moment's peace from thoughts twisting around each other in the night...

And then you drop off.

Somehow I tumbled into the darkness of rest, to the washing of the waves, the crackling of the flames burning the wood, the whisper of the wind through the brush and the trees. To the black night resting above me, only the brightest stars showing over the twists of gray hazy drapes, the flickering light of the fire.

It was a dreamless kind of slumber. And while I didn't exactly dream, a fuzzy awareness still ran in the background of my mind. Shapes moved around me, muted shapes, things I could sense more as a lessening of a pressure than actually seeing any real outline. Almost as if, in the blackest of nights, there were lighter shapes of blackness pressing in upon me.

You probably know this already, but when you wake from those kinds of sleeps, you feel like someone hit you with an anvil. Like the anvil even still held you down, resting on your chest, so every movement feels weighed down by hundreds of invisible pounds.

Your head is heavy. Your thoughts are slow. Your body moves sluggishly, and responds long after you tell it to get up.

I was warm though. Not from the fire, but from the blanket. It had been tucked around me sometime during the night, and I was lying on my side, facing away from the fire. Enveloped in my own body heat.

The first thing I saw was the sun. Or part of it, a yellow sliver on the horizon, beginning its rise over the ocean. The sky was blue and clear and cloudless around the sun, though a burning orange reached out to either side of the orb, small tendrils of a brick-like color, warning me of the day ahead.

The second thing I saw was the boat. The *Isla Marie*. The tide had come back in while I slept and stolen the ship. It floated on its side, further out than it had been the night before. I thought the water was still low enough that I could walk out to the boat, but maybe not.

The third thing I saw was Cass. Standing at the edge of the water. Her arms huddled around herself. Looking out over the water. Staring at the boat.

I went to get up.

Then I tried again.

Like I said, it was tough, after that kind of sleep. I let out a groan and pulled myself into a sitting position. The blanket fell and the enveloping warmness disappeared with it. The fire was out, the sun wasn't high enough to heat anything, and the morning air carried a chill.

Cass turned at the sound, looked at me. Her face was still bruised from yesterday, and her temple still bandaged. Her voice was soft over the sound of the waves and the breeze. "We're a mess."

Whatever had passed between us last night, she was going to forget.

I guess me too.

I groaned again, got to standing. My legs felt stiff, like stilts. All I could do is agree with her. "Yeah."

"Where are we?"

I looked inland. "Close to Savannah." Savannah was a large city, just north of Tybee Island. I had found us a little cove, with no houses or homes by the beach, and now I wished there was something closer.

We'd have to hike a bit today, until we found something. A home, a house, a hotel. A trailer. Something. From there we'd have to clean up, then put together what we had and get ready for Jeeves.

Who was likely already on his way.

"You know where we're going?" Cass asked. As if reading my thoughts.

I repeated myself. It was that kind of morning. I needed coffee. "Yeah."

She stepped away from the water. Moving slow too. I guess stilt-legs were what people got, sleeping on a beach. "We probably should get moving."

I didn't want to say the word again, so I just nodded.

Cass didn't look great. She looked worn down. Tired. Beaten and hungover. I probably looked the same. I know I felt the same. At least the beaten part.

She was looking back out at the water. At the *Isla Marie*. "I didn't know you could do something like that."

When she said something like that, she meant the continental shelf. Raising the level of the land around here. Enough to get us to safety.

Hell, though, I didn't know I could do that. There seemed to be no limit to what I could bring over from another reality. No limit to the mixing I could do between worlds. It wasn't something I thought about, or tried, and to be honest the whole shelf thing had been in the moment. Cass had been drowning, she had panicked, and she was taking me with her. I just had done the first thing that had really popped into my mind.

I mean, when you're sinking, you just want your feet to feel the bottom. It had been that thought. It had been that easy.

Blake's voice echoed in my thoughts, *Don't you want more?*

I didn't. I really didn't.

We packed up the little things we had. Two bags. Cass shouldered one and I shouldered the other. I was hungry but didn't want to stand around making another peanut butter and jelly sandwich, and making one while we walked seemed like too much trouble. Cass solved it by digging out a plastic spoon and eating the peanut butter.

We moved through the light brush and weeds behind the sands of the beach. Into the woods. Walking along a path that seemed like other people had walked before. The leaves left fluttering shadows along our feet.

Cass handed the jar of peanut butter to me, like a buddy sharing a beer. I took a couple of spoonfuls of it. The peanut butter stuck to the roof of my mouth, and I had to work it down with a bottle of water. Still, it beat down the hunger. At least for now.

Cass took the jar back, ate some more with a wince. "Not the best hangover cure."

I had already forgotten how much she had drank last night. Well, how much we both had drank. Like I said, though, I really didn't get drunk anymore. Or at least, after a few thousand years, I didn't really feel it the same way the next day.

"You're not hung over?" she asked around the peanut butter in her mouth.

"Nah," I said. "The fountain thing seems to have fixed that."

Whatever that had been, whatever had been in the water of the Fountain of Youth, it kept me the same age. Healed me a little faster. I guess my liver underwent a constant battle, bathing in alcohol, then getting fixed or repaired by the magic fountain water, then bathing in alcohol again.

"I'd jump in that right now," Cass said.

"You might," I said. "And a thousand years later you'd regret it."

I wasn't in a talkative mood. Cass felt it and stopped asking her questions. We headed through the woods in silence, with just the morning calls of birds above us, tiny tweets, here and there. A little rustling of the leaves in the wind. Snapping of dead branches as we stepped on them.

The world I had found the fountain in, it had been a quiet reality. A universe without humans, I thought at first. The fountain had been hidden in the woods, with no one around. No city nearby. I sensed buildings, lost among overgrown trees and forbidding mountains. Homes and houses, broken down and decrepit.

But no people.

I had wondered about that.

Let's say I somehow could find the reality again. Bring the Fountain of Youth back to this world. Allow anyone to jump in it. What would happen?

Well, then everyone would live forever.

And we know people. The more of us that are around, the less we get along. The more of us that lived longer, the more we would fight about.

I had thought about this a lot. I mean, I had a lot of time. I suspected there were those in the fountain reality who wanted to be king of that world forever. Maybe a few that wanted to be left alone. Maybe a few, like me, who just didn't care either way.

Maybe our short lives just limited the amount of damage we could do. If we could live forever, we'd end up like that other reality. An empty world, with the forests and the trees overgrowing anything we had once built. That we had once been.

Mother Earth, taking back what was hers. Eliminating our existence, until all that was left was our bones, deep underground. Just a few layers above the dinosaurs.

Certainly, I could see that happening. Just looking back at my own life, and wondering what would happen if there were a hundred me's. A thousand. Billions.

There had been a time I had wanted more. That I had experimented with my power. It had been hard to turn away from, but I had.

If there were a hundred of me, maybe ninety-eight of them, ninety-nine, wouldn't have done the same.

"Are you always this quiet?" Cass asked.

I glanced at her. The bandage over her temple was dirty, grimy. Sand clung in her hair. I was sure I looked the same.

Maybe I was always this quiet. At least sober. I had run out of things to say a long time ago. It felt like everything I could say, I already had said, thousands of times. "Pretty much."

Cass grunted. Then shook her head. "I'm surprised Blake was interested in you."

Well, that stung a bit.

"Not being mean," Cass said. "But you seem like you really aren't her type. Solitary. Quiet. Kind of a loner. Not really gung ho about anything. Not really exciting."

We walked a bit. A few branches snapped under our feet. I could hear a little bit of traffic ahead, a car engine in the distance.

Blake had been driven. Had wanted more for herself. For her life. I thought that was why I had liked her. An opposites attract kind of thing. Or maybe she appealed to a younger me, one of the ninety-nine that wouldn't have chosen the life I had. "I guess we never can pick who we fall for."

Cass's eyes narrowed a bit, at that. But she kept looking at me. And the stare made me feel uncomfortable, so I walked a bit faster. Getting ahead of it.

Ahead, I could see a few buildings. Well not buildings, but trailers. The kind of place that existed in the middle of nowhere, near enough to a beach and a city to always be full, but with the kind of people that couldn't afford life closer to Savannah.

The car engine I heard was at the trailer closest to us. I stopped and held out a hand for Cass to stop. The trees and brush around us kept us a bit hidden.

A family came out of the trailer. A man and a wife holding a baby. A smaller kid, a boy in a red and black baseball cap, following. No one locked the trailer, and the screen door swung shut behind them as they all headed to the running car.

The wife was yelling at the husband, who was quiet. Taking his due, maybe. She held the baby tight in a pink blanket. The blanket was long and dangled from her arm. The boy was quiet too, standing behind the man. Looking at something square and black in his small hands, likely a cell phone.

The husband opened the back door of the car. An older four-door tan sedan with a big dent in the rear bumper. The wife got in the back and put the baby in a baby seat. Yelling at the husband the whole time as she buckled up.

The boy walked around and got in the passenger seat of the car. The man got behind the wheel. A couple slams of car doors, and the four-cylinder car purred away.

It was still early. I doubted anyone else was in the trailer. Which gave Cass and I a chance to clean up.

The family would come back from wherever they were going and find out they had left the trailer unlocked. The wife wouldn't like that, and I felt bad for the husband, but that was life. Sometimes you can't pick the ones you're with.

CHAPTER THIRTY-SIX

The inside of the trailer was clean, organized. Not what I expected, watching the family leave. The door opened to the living room. There was carpet on the floor, the tan carpet had the zig-zag stripes you always see after someone vacuums, and a nice couch, facing a small flat-screen television on the opposite wall. The couch was a bit older, and a dark wooden coffee table was placed in front of it. The coffee table had tiny scratches across its top.

As soon as we entered both of us took off our shoes, then our socks. The both of us felt dingy and dirty, and even our feet were going to leave small tracks of mud and bits of sand in the trailer.

So, we tried to be quick. I let Cass take the first shower. The kitchen was behind the couch, with a tiny breakfast bar that held a bowl of fruit. Apples, oranges, and a couple bananas.

I took a banana and peeled it. The skin was a nice yellow with very little black, and the fruit was sweet without being too sweet. I finished the banana and wanted more, so I opened the fridge, found a gallon of milk, and went through the cupboards for a bowl, a nice dark blue piece of stoneware.

One of the cupboards had a few boxes of cereal, I picked out one with squares dusted with cinnamon and sugar, and poured the cereal into the bowl, the cinnamon squares rattling against the stoneware. The cinnamon squares rattled in the bowl. The milk splashed over the squares and drops of it hit the counter. I found a spoon and took a bite.

Nothing like a nice bite of cinnamon and sugar, with a little taste of cold, full-fat creamy milk. I savored the first bite, then finished the bowl quickly. Poured out a second bowl and did the same.

Cass came out. Her dark curls wet and stringy, her face still a bit mottled and puffy from bruises. A new bandage on her temple, one of those slightly larger than normal band aids. She was dressed in some of the older clothes I had saved from the boat, and she scrubbed her hair vigorously with a dark towel. She frowned, looking at me.

"None of that is yours," she said.

"I'll leave money."

She let out a sigh. As if I was a two-year-old. "There's no hot water. Not sure the water heater works."

Well, I couldn't have that. Below the counter, I waggled my fingers a bit. Finding a reality where there was a working water heater. Which took a bit longer than I expected. But I made the switch.

Cass's frowned got deeper, her brows furrowed. Sensing that I was doing something.

"Your face is going to stick like that," I said. And smiled, thinking maybe it already had.

She let out another sigh, and then looked like she regretted doing it. It seemed to be tough for her to not get on me about things. But she knew we wanted the Remainers here. Wanted Jeeves to follow us.

"I'll be quick," I said, walking by her to the shower. Grabbing my bag as I did so.

I tried to be quick. But the shower water was hot and I let it soak through my skin, warm me to the core. I was in long enough that my skin burned and started to itch.

The water drilled into my scalp, and a sharp pain radiated from where the bullet had furrowed along the back of my head. I healed faster than most, but sometimes it still didn't feel fast enough. Isn't that always the case?

I soaped up everywhere. Peeled my bandage off, looked at the angry twisted scar tissue. Less red than yesterday, more pink. I was just happy to see it closed and clean, I had been a little worried that the ocean water might infect it. I took the dandruff two-in-one shampoo and scrubbed my hair and let out a deep breath. Feeling better than I had in a few days.

A hot shower was a great healer.

I toweled off and put on some other clothes, a t-shirt and jeans. Found my bulletproof jacket and put it on, trying to pat out the rumples. Then I piled the dirty clothes I had been wearing into the small trashcan by the toilet, and pulled the plastic bag out.

Cass and I had messed the bathroom up, leaving spots of mud and sand, but I wasn't going to clean it more than taking the trash out. I didn't want to waste that time. I had wasted enough in the shower.

Cass had cleaned up after me in the kitchen. There were two bowls in the dish rack next to the sink, and when I saw the box of cinnamon squares in the kitchen trash I smiled to myself. But didn't say anything to her.

The television was on and turned to the news. A man and woman sitting behind a desk, the front of the desk had a peacock on it, and there was a big number three super-imposed on the bottom right corner of the screen.

The woman was talking about the earthquakes. There had been some damage in Savannah, and a lot of general fear, because they had come from nowhere. There was more specific fear, as the male anchor talked about the vicious storm that had hit Charleston, as well as the earthquakes. Apparently, some seismographs were showing a little movement deep underground.

People were leaving. Others were headed to the store to buy out all the milk and water and bread. Geologists and climatologists were headed to Augusta, Savannah, and Charleston. The woman anchor talked about the President of the United States issuing a state of general emergency for both Georgia and South Carolina. There was talk about sunspot activity and wondering if that had been the cause.

"This was us, wasn't it?" Cass asked.

I didn't think it needed an answer. I found my wallet, ignored the clumped whiteness of the photo behind my license, and pulled out some of the dwindling cash. I left a hundred dollars on the counter, tucked under the bowl of fruit. I debated leaving more but thought that would be enough. I was leaving them a nice new water heater, after all. That seemed to be a fair trade for a banana and a bowl of cereal.

Cass was still watching the television. The woman was going on about some of the older buildings that had partially collapsed, about the number of people that had been injured, though there hadn't been any deaths. At least none reported. "You should have just let me go."

"Maybe," I said. Though there was no way I was going to. Just like there was no way she was going to leave me in Charleston. The two of us had a task, and we both were going to see that task through. Soldiers on a mission.

And Cass had grown on me a little. She had always been Blake's younger, annoying sister. The sister that didn't like who Blake was dating. The sister that got on my nerves, every time we hung around each other.

Blake and I argued. But there was a passion there between us. The arguments were almost a dance.

When Cass argued, it was straight-forward. Like she was lining up her shot. There was no dance.

I couldn't help feeling for the girl who had only wanted her dad to take her out to the field at night. The father who had never pointed out the stars to her, like he had her sister. The girl who had become hardened and tough, when the man who had been her dad had forgotten all about her. Because of something I did.

In the end, I had learned to live with that. The unknown consequences of what I did. I had tried to limit the pieces of reality I stole. I had learned that life was unforgiving to everyone, and that whatever anyone did, they could never really know the effects of their actions, until they actually did them.

So, I did the best I could. Made the choices that seemed right to me at the time. And I lived with the consequences of those choices. Cass would have to learn how to do the same.

"How do you live with it?" she asked. Her voice angry, her eyes wet. Maybe wishing she hadn't drank so much. Fought me. Fell overboard.

She hadn't understood yet, that was just life. You don't mean to hurt people, and you feel bad if you do, and you make amends where you can. And if all that fails, you just power through.

Cass was all I had left of Blake. The only friend I had left in this world. Maybe she didn't understand that meant something to me. So, I put it in terms I thought she would get. "I've learned to just take the next step. Not too far ahead. Not too far behind."

It was what life was too me. I couldn't remember everything from thousands of years ago. And I didn't want to remember the pain of recent events. So, I tried the best I could to put it all away, put it deep in a well, deep inside of me, and hope it never surfaced. Focused on the next thing.

"Right now, that step is doing whatever it takes, until we get who killed Blake."

Cass wouldn't look at me. But she was listening. She was watching the television, wondering what the cost of her life had been.

"Whatever it takes," I said. "So, if you feel bad about the earthquakes, the storm, just put it on me. Put it all on me. I'll take that blame."

I'd shouldered that load for a long time now. It would just be a few more pounds to the scale. A little more weight to carry.

So, I turned off the television. Gave Cass a moment to let that sink in. Picked up my bag and looked over. "Ready?"

She paused a long moment, still not looking at me. Then grabbed her bag.

I waggled my fingers. Car keys appeared on the kitchen counter. I knew another sedan would be outside, an older beat-up blue four-door car with a crack in its windshield. And I knew the keys on the counter would start it up.

Easy to find another reality where beat-up, older cars existed in a trailer park. Millions of those universes exist. It took no time at all to make the switch.

Cass had been watching me, and now had a funny look on her face. She grabbed the keys. Maybe wanting to do something. Or not wanting to think about things like earthquakes. We locked the trailer up as we left. I didn't know if the family had taken the house keys when they had fled, but it was likely, and I thought locking up was just a nice thing to do.

I wasn't perfect. I wasn't even a particularly nice person, anymore. But like the hundred dollars and the water heater, I tried to make amends where I could.

CHAPTER THIRTY-SEVEN

ONE THING ABOUT PICKING A BEAT-UP CAR, YOU NEVER know what you might get. I should have been more selective, when I had been searching. Because I didn't get anything nice. The car smelled of cigarettes and burned oil. Cass shook her head and started the sedan. The engine had a little high-pitched whine to it, and plumes of smoke puffed out the exhaust, gray with hints of blue. The maintenance light was a bright red warning on the dash.

And a tire thumped sometimes, at certain speeds. I could hear it because I had cracked the window to try to get some fresh air in the car. It must have been out of balance.

"Nice," Cass muttered.

It was no Jeep-truck, but beggars can't be choosers.

Cass had driven us through the rest of the trailer park. Not a lot of people were outside yet. It was early still. A baby's cry made it into the car, from inside one of the trailers, kind of a low repeating thing with a few hiccups in it.

Cass's head had turned towards the trailer as we passed it, and maybe we both wondered the same thing. Hoping someone was just sleeping in, and that the baby wasn't alone. That I hadn't caused someone else to disappear.

The tires had crunched on the sand in the lot. The sedan springs needed replacement, the sedan bounced as we drove over all the bumps and holes in the lot. Then we had pulled onto the road. Cass pushed down on the gas, the engine whined louder, the sedan belched a big plume of smoke, and we were away.

Somewhere on that road Cass looked at me. "You know where we're at?"

I shook my head. "Somewhere between Charleston and Savannah."

"Great."

I left it at that. There was no need to remind Cass I hadn't planned on coming ashore here. And though she hadn't been the one to shift realities, to raise the continental shelf and flip the boat over, she was taking the blame.

The road felt like a country road. Sand and weather had worn it down. The yellow lines faded, the white stripes painting the sides of the road broken up here and there, where the asphalt had cracked and crumbled. As we drove, Cass kept the sun at our back, taking us west, where we hoped to find a larger road that would take us south.

I tried the radio. It didn't work. I turned the knob and tried a bunch of channels, and all I got was static.

"I almost saw what you did," Cass said. "Back when you made the keys appear."

Her face had the funny expression on her.

"What do you mean?" I asked.

Her shoulders made a little shrugging motion. She was focused on the drive. "I can always feel it, when you switch the reality. It's like a funny feeling, in the pit of my stomach. I was watching you though, when you made the keys appear, and I almost saw it happen."

Interesting. No one had told me that before.

"There was this shimmer, like when a bright light hits a prism. All these rays. And a darkness too. All swirled together, for just a split second. Flashes of things."

I never saw anything. At least, not in the reality. Like I said, the searching for it felt like digging through an infinite number of universes. When I tried explaining it using the factory, with all the boxes and all the conveyors, that wasn't something I *saw*, it was more something I *felt*.

The closest I came to seeing anything was during the switch. Flashes of the existence of one universe. Flashes of a blue sedan in a trailer park. Flashes of the storm. Flashes of a larger beach. Like people say when they "see their life flash before their eyes," what I saw was just brief images, one overlaying another, like someone flipping quickly through the pages of a picture book.

But mostly, it was a feeling as I made the switch. I selected what I wanted, pulled the square peg out from that universe, and made it fit the round hole in this one. I felt the edges of the peg, as the round hole shaved them off. I felt bits and pieces of the one reality fall away, as I made the piece fit. But I never really saw those pieces.

"You ever wonder if those other realities ever really exist?" Cass asked.

"What do you mean?"

"Like, are there really an infinite number of worlds?" Cass said. "Or are these other realities just figments of your imagination. Other places you dream up. Like fake dimensions. Something that exists only because you think of it."

I had never thought of it that way. The realities always feel real to me. But now that Cass had brought it up, I didn't know. I couldn't answer it.

I had always pictured it like the factory analogy I told you about. The boxes and conveyor belts and factory after factory. I knew that's not what it really was like, that's not how my power really worked, but it was how I envisioned it.

Though it had been awhile since I had really looked at it. I had stopped doing big things. I had stopped looking for a good reality to replace the broken one around me. Everything I did lately was more reflex.

"They seemed like dreams to me," Cass said. "The flashes. There was the shimmer, and flashes. It reminded me of when I was a kid, and when I used to doodle on all the pages of a notebook, so that when you flipped through them the doodle moved."

Cass saw the flashes too. Interesting. I wondered if the other Remainers could see them too. Would Jeeves want to search other realities? Would he look for one where his daughter lived? Did he know the rules, that dead was dead?

"Almost felt like déjà vu," she said. "Like I almost knew what you were doing, what was going to happen, before it did."

I had thought the same. I wasn't surprised Cass had said that. It was one of the rules. Everyone steals some reality sometimes. A lot of those times the person felt something like déjà vu. Cass seemed to have seen more. Felt more. Which was curious.

I had always wondered why I had never met anyone else. I had wondered if there were other worlds, each with their own thief of reality, where some of the things that happened here were due to someone else taking something from our world. Like the Bermuda Triangle, all the planes and ships that had disappeared there. Or the Loch Ness Monster. Maybe those things had existed, at one time, and for whatever reason had been pulled away to another reality.

I didn't know. And I couldn't say if this world was the only world, or if people really existed in the others. It was something I would never know.

The other worlds felt real to me, though. But maybe a part of me needed them to be. Because if they weren't, then maybe this was all I had. Maybe there were no others like me. And that would mean I was truly alone, and that I really had no purpose.

And what would the point of that be?

I've talked a lot about having a purpose. About searching for one. I thought that part of me dead. If not dead, then settled low in the depths of my subconscious, after thousands of years of not finding the reason for my existence. I thought I had given the search up.

But that part of me stirred now. I could feel it moving, deep under the alcohol and apathy I had buried it under. Because if Cass could see the flashes, then I felt like they were real. That these other realities existed, and weren't some figment of my imagination. Some dream.

And if they were real, and if they were infinite, then there would be one where there was a reason for what I could do.

I almost jerked at the thought, and braced one hand on the dashboard. Goosebumps ran along my arm. Tingling ran down my spine. Senses I thought long gone, woke.

Cass drove along. Lost in her thoughts. And I became lost in mine. Scared of what had awoken in me. Because I could feel something coming, my thoughts shot along to the target, like an arrow shot from a bow.

It had started at the hotel. With the light fading from Blake's eyes. Her blood pooling over the sidewalk. I had sworn then to figure this out. Not to find what Blake had been looking for, well, not only to find that, but to extract revenge.

That led to now. To Jeeves, chasing me to Charleston. The storm. Earthquakes. As if the world was falling apart by the minute. The very earth trembled with the knowledge, the air was showered with it.

Now people fled South Carolina and Georgia, as if something heavy hung over the horizon. Something looming, a sliver of something now, a crescent-shaped darkness, thin but growing, like the dark slice of a moon that was about to eclipse the sun.

Maybe some things aren't natural. Maybe my realities were déjà vu like dreams. Because that black line out there, the small evil light-absorbing darkness, sure felt like the storm from a day ago.

The thought had surface. And now I couldn't shake the feeling.

That everything was related. That Cass and I were on some pre-ordained path, that had nothing and everything to do with both of us. With Jeeves and his daughter. With the Remainers. With Blake.

Something wicked this way comes.

It not only came, but *rushed* towards us. Towards Tybee Island. And whatever it was, I couldn't help but feel my purpose, the thing I had given up looking for long ago, was tied up with it.

CHAPTER THIRTY-EIGHT

At some point, the small road became a larger one. The white lines became more solid, were less broken up by sand erosion and less worn by the weather. More traffic inside those lines.

Things were coming to a head.

I wanted to laugh.

What things? And what could I do about it? I switched pieces of a world with another. I could never just push something from this world to another. I couldn't just take something from another world and put it into this one. I couldn't take my problems in this world, whatever they were, and push them into another.

It may seem that way to you. For instance, I couldn't just magic the knife away Jeeves had stabbed me with, I could only swap it out with something else. Maybe *anything* else, but for me it was always faster to find something similar in shape and size. I mean, life and death were on the line (it usually is), and when seconds make a difference it was best to go with what was easiest.

But going back to what I was saying. The thing is, it was never just me stealing something from another reality. It always had to be a swap, and it always had to be for *something*.

You saw I had stolen some limes earlier at the bar. But I hadn't stolen just the limes, that wasn't how it worked. I actually had stolen a drawer holding a couple limes in another universe and swapped that out with the empty drawer in this one.

You would think that was a difference without a distinction. You'd be wrong.

I could never just look at a car and push it into a different reality. I would have to always swap it. So back at the trailer park, I hadn't just made a car appear. I had exchanged a trailer with a family that had owned one car with a trailer owned by a family with two cars.

Still not seeing a difference?

Well, ask the family in the other universe how they feel.

There was some scale that kept what I did honest. Almost like the law of conservation of mass or energy, or *something*. Just tweaked a bit here and there for a person with my particular abilities.

I tried to put a name on it. Maybe I could call it the law of conservation of infinity. It seemed to fit what I did, but did conserving something like infinity really make sense? Could it?

Whatever I stole, or exchanged, always had to exist in some form in both places. At least, the *idea* of it had to be the same. It was a weird contradiction in my mind. It was hard to picture a closed loop of an infinite number of universes. I mean, how could something that went on forever have an end?

Still, it was a real thing. It's how it worked. And if it wasn't one of my rules, it was only because I was still trying to figure it out. There were the four:

#1 – I can't bring anyone back to life
#2 – I can live forever (but I can also definitely die)
#3 – We all can change reality, in some way

#4 – Dead is dead

#5 – What's done is done

But Rule Number Six didn't quite exist. The law of conservation of infinity. Maybe I could label it an addendum. Or maybe a postulate. That made a weird kind of sense. Number Six was just something I assumed existed, in some form, in some way. And you know what they say about assuming.

I hadn't fully tested the theory out. I had tried, in the beginning, but no longer. Because if there was some scale to what I did, some balance, then it meant there was a reason for my power. I existed for a purpose. So, me testing out Number Six was also me trying to figure out that purpose. And a person can only go so long when that purpose never appears. A guy can only hang on so long to the phone, when no one answers on the other side.

Tell me... No matter how much you scream the words, there's never an answer. You can trust me on that one.

Many times I used my power, switching things. Stealing. But not items. Not things or places or people, but more like *concepts*. Maybe that's why the edges of the realities always shaved off, because the idea of what I was stealing from another reality didn't quite fit the same idea of what I was replacing in this one.

I couldn't tell you. But part of me desperately wanted to figure it out. Because knowing how might also give me the *why*.

And the why had been important to me. Maybe it was still important. Even if I had set it aside, even if I had let it go after all the years of searching. The call of finding out my purpose came back now, and the call was powerful.

So, back to #6. The rule that wasn't a rule. That I deal more in stealing concepts of reality, than realities themself.

The storm!

I hear you saying it now. That was something I obviously had stolen from another reality and pulled into this one. There was no storm here, in this universe, and then I had made one appear.

And I understand it. I don't just steal concepts. But I do steal the idea of a thing, more than the thing itself. It was hard to explain. It was like I wanted something, and looked for it, and when I found it, I stole it from that universe. Pulled the thought of it into this reality. Replacing it with the concept of what I wanted to trade.

I understand it's confusing. Maybe just trust me. I had to think of the something I wanted before being able to steal it. I had to *conceive* it existed, then find it. And when I found it, I could steal it.

So, I thought about the idea of a thing, rather than the thing itself. I didn't look through a car lot of cars until I found the broken piece of shit we were currently riding in. I looked for a car, the sort of car that might exist in a trailer park, and then stole the idea of that car and replaced the concept of a family with two cars by their trailer with the idea of a family with just one.

Confusing? You bet. Differences without distinctions to most. But hardwired in my mind.

Back to the storm. So, the concept there was me looking for a tempest, a real storm, something that would echo my mood that morning, and something that would hide Cass and I a bit later. Something dark and black and unforgiving.

That concept was easy. And then, I was just trading the idea of it for the idea of a bright sunny day. I was just swapping the weather. Blue skies and clouds in this one, white and puffy and friendly before I switched it all out, black and angry and violent after.

And in that way, I could make the switch. It was easy, once my mind settled on the idea of the switch. Once I found a reality where I could steal something, swap something, all I had to do then was make it work in my mind.

To appease the law of conservation of infinity, there always had to be a balance.

I know it's kind of a delicate thought. It doesn't make sense. It doesn't balance in the brain.

After all, there's a certain weight to the storm. Like a million more clouds. How could I trade the few solitary white clouds for something like the monster that hit Charleston? How could an empty drawer be switched for a drawer with limes in it?

Like I said, I'm still figuring it out. There's definitely a rule in place. Or a postulate. A hypothesis. I've narrowed down what I can and can't do, at least to a certain area of things. It's definitely not something like I have to exchange the same ten clouds in one universe for the same ten clouds in this one. It's more of me trading... concepts, or images, or thoughts.

Yeah. It's weird. And maybe I'm completely wrong about it all. When you find another person who can do what I do, you can maybe ask them.

Cass tapped me on the arm. Interrupting that train of thought that may not have been going anywhere. "Hey, you've been out a while."

She was right. That train had been going on longer than I thought. An hour or so. The sun had gotten on her side. We were heading south on an interstate now. I-95. The car bounced along the highway, that damn tire thumping against the blacktop.

Some traffic headed in with us, mostly big rigs mixed with smaller trucks and sedans. Though there were more cars heading opposite us, heading north. Out of the city. Signs for Savannah exits rolled by to my right, big and blue with little pictures of fast-food places and gas stations and arrows pointing out which way they lay.

"You look invested," she said.

That was a strange word. It had been around a while, since the sixteenth century or so. Invest had started out meaning something like wearing a piece of clothing to signify rank. Wearing something that meant power. Though lately, it was more a reference to using money to make money. But Cass hadn't meant either of those.

She had meant engaged. I looked involved. Emotionally. Physically. All in. *Invested*.

Although there was a different connotation to the word that most people didn't think of. It didn't immediately come to mind. A military meaning. To besiege. To surround with hostile intent.

More traffic rolled around us. Cass had to punch the gas and work the sedan around a slow truck. The burning oil smell in the car grew stronger.

More people, headed into Savannah. I wondered why they weren't headed the other way. The traffic closed around me, like a funnel. The cars pressed in, like a trap. Some of them were emergency vehicles, yellow lights blinking. Power trucks, plumbers. A few Humvees, painted in that light desert camouflage. The National Guard, maybe.

I thought of Jeeves. Of what was coming. Of the something dark this way comes. And I could feel myself gearing up to meet it. Rising to the challenge. Finding out the *why*.

So yeah, maybe I was invested. It seemed as good a word as any.

Or maybe I was just trying to talk myself into something.

Either way, it was coming to a head. Seemed odd to me. Felt like something was ending. It was a long road I had traveled, thousands of years long, and finally I was coming to an end.

I should be more excited. But all I felt were the nerves. The fluttering in the belly that let you know you weren't really ready for what was coming. The juice that fired you up and made you unsure all at the same time. The feeling that had you excited, and at the same time close to throwing up.

I hated that feeling.

I had avoided it for so long. Even when Blake and I fought about it, about finding the purpose of my powers. Of finding the why. I had avoided it with her, and avoiding it, I had caused her death.

I didn't want to do that again.

Cass and I weren't friends, I didn't think. But we weren't enemies either. And we had Blake between us.

I glanced over. Cass's jaw was set as she maneuvered the older sedan through the traffic. Her face was still bruised, she had a fresh bandage over her cheek where she had stitched it up. Her black hair, so curly, so unlike her sister's blonde hair, tumbled over her forehead. Her eyes were the only thing that reminded me of Blake. Cass's eyes were blue, Blake's had been hazel, but they both had the same glint in them. They both had flashed, Cass's eyes flashed even now, with determination and grit. A *see-things-through.*

I could go into a fight with worse.

I wondered what would have happened in our world if Blake had lived. But I knew, ultimately. Because I would live forever, and Blake, Blake would have been someone whose memory faded in time.

"She would have grown old," I said.

Cass looked over. Frowned at me. The eyes flashing. Then she glanced back ahead, tapping the brakes as we came up on another truck. "What?"

"Blake," I said. "She would have grown old."

The truck kept slowing down, and Cass swore. Put on her blinker and looked in the side mirror, trying to find a gap in the cars next to us so we could get around. "What are you telling me?"

"We fought some," I said. Well, admitted. "Blake and I. She wanted me to figure out my purpose. Why I had the powers I had. Why I could do what I do. It's why she left that night."

"Okay."

"I couldn't tell her," I said. "I couldn't tell her what would happen. That I'd lived these kinds of relationships before. That she would grow old and start to resent me. Hate me, even. So, I pushed all that away. Pushed her away maybe. I think that's why she wanted to figure it out even more."

"Lived these relationships before," Cass said. "Are you telling me my sister wasn't special?"

Cass didn't understand either. She was living in her world, her moment. Maybe people with normal lives couldn't really feel what it meant to live forever. All the loved ones you left behind, scar after scar, until all you had left was thick, hard tissue where your heart used to be.

"She was," I said. "She was unique. I thought she really understood me. She was the first person I thought that really got me."

And she had. I had felt that. But I had ignored it. The feeling had hit the thick wall I had placed around myself and knocked, but I had ignored it. Maybe the one person who could have really understood me. Wanted me. Wanted things for me.

Maybe that was what I had ignored. Maybe I had been scared of feeling too much. Of wanting too much with Blake and watching her grow old. Maybe I had been pushing her away, even then.

"It's why she didn't want me with her that night," I said. "I just wanted to get that out there, for some reason."

Something wicked this way comes. Not just wicked, but terrible. I had no idea what it could be, but I knew it would be terrifying in its reveal.

At least, terrifying to me. A man who had lived a pretty closed life, for a long, long time.

Cass finally swung around the second truck. Got in front of it. The lane ahead was empty, the truck was just slow to be slow, for some reason. She stepped on the gas.

"Well, since we're telling the truth," she started, then stopped. Then started again. Keeping her eyes on the road. "Sometimes I was jealous of her."

"Jealous?" I asked. Then I compared the two. Blake, elegant, tall. Driven. Fun. Passionate. A blonde surfer's body. A smile that you couldn't look away from.

Cass next to Blake would look a little mousy, maybe. Shorter. Not stocky, but more compact. Muscled. Rounder, in the places that women should be rounder in, but not too much so.

And maybe it wasn't even that. Maybe Cass wasn't jealous about looks, or personality. Maybe she had been jealous a long time ago, when their father had taken Blake out to a field late at night and counted stars. And gotten over that in time. Or buried it deep inside her own well.

"Your father?"

Cass glanced over. The flashing in her eyes had gone soft. The blue was more liquid now, almost a shimmer. The corner of her lips turned up in a tiny smile, as if she was remembering something funny, yet sad. "Yeah."

She looked at me a long time.

"Yeah." Cass focused again on driving. Talking for a moment, her voice soft, but then firming up. Like she was getting it all out. "Sometimes I hated her. She was driven, but I was that. She was tall and such a model, and I could get over that. She was bossy sometimes, like older sisters are. But some things I couldn't have, and she could, and some of those things were like a cold spike between us."

She took a big breath, let it out. "Those spikes stayed. I felt them like nails. I could never get over them. But we *were* sisters, we loved each other, and in the end it was always us versus them."

I got it. And maybe I got a second point. That sometimes you have to give in to love. Let it ride you. Let it crash and burn when your loved one passes away. Sometimes you have to be the passion, and allow it to guide you, no matter that you know where it leads. You have to hope, even when you *know*, that this time it could be different.

You have to hope, even if you know it could never be different.

Otherwise, you end up like me.

I stayed quiet. Feeling the tire of the sedan thump against the highway. Breathing in the smoke of the sedan. It felt like the cabin was full of it, suddenly, and I cracked a window.

"I hate this car," I said.

Cass barked out a laugh. It made me smile. The blue signs hanging over the shoulder of the road announced the next few exits were for downtown Savannah, and one of them mentioned Tybee Island. People headed in and out of the exits, cars running the looping of the ramps, everyone blissfully away of how this day might end, just concerned about their own corner of their lives. Jobs. Family. Food. Friends. The recent earthquakes. The storm, up north.

We were here.

I took a breath, like Cass had earlier. It was loud enough that she glanced over, a question on her face. I didn't know how to tell her. Whatever we were going to face, whatever was going to happen, it was going to happen today.

I could feel it.

CHAPTER THIRTY-NINE

Cass took the exit for Tybee. We passed through the north side of Savannah. The sun was overhead, but we were still driving into it, so it was still before noon. The traffic thinned out, we slowed down from the interstate speed, so it was easier to hear the occasional soft thumping of the out-of-balance tire. Especially with my window open. I shifted in my seat, ready to get out of the car.

"I'm going to need a gun," Cass said.

I had gotten it, I thought, back in the *Isla Marie*. "I packed your nine."

"No," she said. "A rifle. Something with some distance. Unless you want to take the chance of me missing."

Well, that made sense. I hadn't thought that far ahead, I guess. Maybe I was too focused on what was going on around me, instead of what we were planning.

I opened the phone. Found a few places in the web browser. There was a shop along our way, in an area of Savannah called Thunderbolt. Which seemed an odd, and ominous name.

"What do you need?" I asked.

"I'd like an M14," she said. "But I'll be okay with anything with a scope."

Cass said it nonchalantly. I wondered what her life had been like that she had practiced so much. Had she been a ranger in the army? Marines? A navy seal? I had no idea. I found it a little scary, and a little comforting.

At least she was on my side.

I was pretty sure.

We hit a state road, US 80 or something like that. Took a few turns into Thunderbolt, got onto something called Victory Drive. The roads were straight and the blocks were square, most of the buildings were older brick, and most of the lots had green grass. We passed small banks, little shops, a sports bar.

Blake and Cass were so different. Both driven, but in different ways. I wondered what had happened that the sisters had diverged. Blake, athletic, graceful, fun. Elegant, long, lean. Cass, focused, surly, a pain in the ass but a hell of a shot.

We found the gun shop. It was just opening. It had plenty of weapons. Even some knives, but I had what I wanted. A short man with a white beard asked us if we were looking for something in particular, and I nodded to Cass. His eyebrows raised, but the two of them started talking. He pulled a few rifles off the wall behind him and let her handle them.

I left them and walked around. Looking at all the different guns under the cases, but not really seeing them. I couldn't shake the feeling that something big was happening today, and I didn't know how to prepare for it. Other than just being there.

Maybe I should run. Maybe I should talk Cass out of this. I had plenty of time. I could come back and find Jeeves myself.

Part of me was swept up in this. In vengeance. And I had seen a lot of people get killed for that.

"Hey," Cass said, coming to find me. "He needs money."

"Found something?"

"Yeah." She paused, really looked at me. I didn't know how I appeared, but she saw something. Cass placed a hand on my shoulder. It felt stronger than she looked. But it also felt awkward, like Cass wasn't used to offering comfort. Or maybe I wasn't used to taking it. So, her hand ended up falling off.

"You're not who I thought you were," she ended up saying.

I was surprised to hear it. Not because of what she said. But because she had said it. I wasn't who people thought I was. I was different from what they thought. Because they couldn't imagine the life I had. Not what I could do, everyone could imagine that. But the length of it. What you carried with you, through the years. What, and who, got left behind.

"When we first met, I was sure you were some self-absorbed drunk," Cass said. Her eyes were a little unfocused, as if remembering. Going back in time. "I thought you were some guy taking advantage of my sister, doing things you wanted, ignoring other people."

She was talking about back in a club. A trendy place in downtown Chicago. A city I liked to hang out in. It had a good history, for only being around a few centuries. Parts of it had sank under the earth, buildings sunk through the dirt and the mud, buried over the years. Part of me had liked that.

"You were kicked back against the bar, and you were looking at Blake," Cass continued. "And I don't know how to describe it, but part of your eyes were alive, and part of them were... were still kind of dead. Like the flashy part of yourself was hiding something else."

I was surprised Cass had seen that in me. Not the dead part, everyone kind of got that. But the live part. I smiled, but it wasn't a funny smile. Or a happy one. It was sad, and my lips turned a little down underneath the weight of it.

I remembered it differently. I had remembered Blake wanting to go dancing. She had pushed me into it. We had gotten into one of the fancy clubs with the driving beats and the flashing lasers and the bodies on the floor, grinding together to the sounds. It wasn't me, not really, but Blake loved it, loved the techno poppy sound. Some song called *Sandstorm*, with no words, just frantic beats and a pounding rhythm.

Cass had shown up. Blake had been surprised. I was drinking something at a bar and watching Blake dance by herself on the floor. Then Cass was next to me. I had never met her before, but at the time I remembered Cass ordering a drink, striking up some small talk with me (I don't remember what I said, it's why they called it small talk), and sometime during that she stopped. And just watched me watch Blake.

Maybe that was the moment she had decided she didn't like me.

"I always thought you someone who was all about themselves," Cass said. "But you're not like that."

Then a pause. "Not at all."

"Yeah," I said. I felt on the edge of something fragile, in myself. It wasn't a feeling I was used to. But something wicked this way came, and it had me off balance. "I don't know what I'm like, anymore."

Our eyes caught for a moment, until I looked away. "So much has passed. I've lost so much of who I was, who I grew up as, who my parents were..."

A truck rolled down the street. It was a dark shadow through the tinted glass of the shop. But big enough and rumbly enough that I could feel its travel in the air, on my skin.

"I just don't know," I ended up saying. Not able to explain it. How I was feeling. Or hell, even who I was. I had these rules, and that's all I seemed to have anymore. Rules, and what I could do, the Remainers, and the consequences of thousands of years of what I'd done.

I guess, if I had to go down, if I had to die, maybe it could be for something. Maybe it could be for Blake. Maybe I could help Cass get her revenge.

Though I probably would live. I always seemed to. Even when others fell.

Cass patted my shoulder. They were awkward pats. Trying to comfort me, which felt odd, because she wasn't good at it, and to be honest, I wasn't good at receiving it. I never really let anyone get that close, and what was there had been buried for a long, long time.

"You know, Blake was always Blake," she said. "She was always going to do Blake things."

I didn't know what that really meant. I understood the gist of it, maybe, but not really what Cass was trying to tell me.

Cass saw that. A little smile appeared on her face, just her lips curving slightly. It changed her face from the perpetual frown to something more... lively. Happy. Fun. "I mean, Blake was always about Blake. As much as I loved her, as much as we were sisters, what Blake wanted always came first."

I caught her eyes again. They were less frowny than normal. More open. As if Cass was trying to press a point. Something she had discovered in her life, that she wanted to pass on to mine. "Chances are, Blake was where she wanted to be. Doing what she wanted to do," she said. Talking about when Blake had been shot. "And if she wanted you there, you would have been there."

Cass was trying to comfort me. The whole experience felt weird. I had been so used to the other woman. The irritable one.

I shrugged. I couldn't help but feel like I had missed something important with Blake. That she would have meant something more to me. That I had given something up before understanding what it truly had been.

But hell, that's what regret was. The odds were what I thought they were. She would have grown old. Hated me for staying young. Maybe I would have tried to find the fountain again. Lord knows I had tried before. But somehow, I could never find that box of realities after finding it the one time.

Maybe I knew better.

Maybe I should have known better, before sipping the first sip of the fountain.

Cass's smile slipped away. Her eyes grew serious. Intense. Almost uncomfortably so, enough that I looked away, at her chin, instead.

Her voice was soft. "You put a lot on yourself, Gavin. Maybe you should let people take the blame for their own actions."

I looked away then. Out the tinted, dark window. And wiped my eyes a little with the back of my hand. Not because they felt watery. Definitely not because of that.

"Some women may not want forever," Cass added, her voice light, almost grinning. As if she was talking about something she knew, a secret she was sharing with me. "Some may just want to enjoy the ride."

I laughed then. More of a harsh choke, or chuckle. A huckle. Which had Cass sniggling, and then me laughing, and then her laughing too.

Man we were tense. Both of us. It felt good to laugh at anything.

I walked over to the counter. The man there had one eyebrow raised. There was a Browning X-Bolt rifle on the glass countertop in front of him. I knew what it was because it had a tag on it. The entire gun was camouflaged in a desert-like tan and green, even the scope. It was long, with a weird stock at the end of it.

"You folks get caught in the earthquake?" the man asked. His voice much higher pitched than a short round man's should be.

"Yeah," I said, pulling out my wallet. Some of the hundreds were still not quite damp from the dip in the ocean. Other hundreds had been in a roll in the bag.

"Look like you've been smack in the center of it," the man said.

Cass snorted. I nodded at the man. "Yeah. Funny things happening, right? Going to go head inland, a little place we got stashed."

"You a prepper?" The man grinned, then held his arms out over the shop. Encompassing all the weapons. "Me too."

Funny man. I let the man check my license, then handed over the money, let him make change. It was more than I thought, a few hundred more than the tagged price of the rifle, and I realized he had a little box next to him.

"Earplugs," Cass explained. "Bluetooth."

Ah.

Made sense to have some kind of communication going between us. With me walking the street, and her scoping for Jeeves. Maybe obvious, too. But the plugs were small, and hell, everyone walked around today like a jackass talking on their phones.

So maybe it wouldn't be obvious.

I picked up a rain jacket too. Just a slicker, black and long, a thin piece of plastic-like substance that would cover up my rumpled bullet-proof jacket and hide the wakizashi. With the hood, I might even be able to wear the katana too. If I worked it right.

I felt like details mattered now. But I was a little frozen, not sure which detail to pick. Which way to go. Maybe that happened to every-one, as they neared the end of the road. Maybe everyone looked left and right for the right off-ramp, for some kind of dirt road that would let them escape the ending that waited for them.

But I had chosen this. I had placed the two of us in this time and place to wait for Jeeves and whatever was coming with him. If it was going to end, then it was going to end in Tybee Island, on this day.

I thought Blake was worth it. And if I came out alive, then I thought I would know my *why*, and that would be worth it too. So, it was a gamble, for all the marbles.

The thing about gambling though, is that you don't recognize the real cost until the final throw of the dice. Until the final card was flipped over on the river. Until the final marble tick-tacked its way along the wheel, slower and slower, until it found its home.

CHAPTER FORTY

THE SUN OVERHEAD. THE WATER HITTING THE BEACH. Waves washing the sand, long flops of white crests hitting the beach and slowly pulling back in a dragging froth. An endless rhythm, a motion that had been happening since the world had began.

Tybee Island. Where this would end, one way or the other. A feeling of dread, something I had lived so long without, pounded in my chest. Not just dread, but a world-ending fear.

The island itself was shaped like a knee. Like a bent leg, the city of Savannah on the inside of the knee, and the beach on the kneecap facing east. Facing the doom on the horizon.

The thin line of black clouds had remained over the eastern horizon. Not just remained, but had grown. Swollen. Like someone had taken a razor and slit open the sky, like a ragged mouth had opened and all that was behind the mouth was darkness, a bleak, black world-eating kind of vacuum.

The beach was littered with *Beach Closed* signs. Some of them said it was due to strong currents. Other due to sharks. A few said due to inclement weather. I thought they should at least all agree on the reason, but maybe that's what happens when the world's about to end.

One long road, Butler Avenue, ran north and south behind the beach. The road was littered with older single-story homes and occasional bigger buildings, like a bed-and-breakfast, a motel or two, a restaurant near the water. Most of the buildings were a block off the beach, behind Butler Avenue, but some of them, like one of the motels, sat in the tall grass behind the sands.

A tall lighthouse, old and painted red and white, stood at the north end of the beach. Right above the kneecap. The more south you went, the more cluttered the buildings. The beach shops selling umbrellas and towels and sunglasses and souvenirs, older homes, rental agencies. Seafood shacks and bars by the bazillion.

Maybe I shouldn't find the black clouds strange. After all, the storm had been tough to remove, for whatever reason it had been harder to push the square block of its reality into the round hole of the reality I was trying to put it in. Surely some of the edges had shaved off, left a bit of the storm here.

And there were white puffs directly overhead. Which felt normal. The black clouds stayed in the distance, hanging. Waiting.

I faced it all. Felt the hammering of my heart. Watched the dull green and black surface of the water shimmer a bit under the sun. A slight breeze came in, low over the small waves, bringing the scent of salt and the slight hint of something rotten. A red tide kind of smell, fishy and dead.

Cass had wondered if the other realities were dreams. Illusions. Flashes. She had mentioned she had felt déjà vu when I had stolen some reality.

She was wrong. They were real. I had stolen pieces of so many other worlds, switched those pieces out with pieces of this reality. I couldn't have done that if those places weren't real. Because then this world would be real and fake. Real, in the ways that it had been before I had come along. A fraud, in all the holes I had removed the real world, and replaced it with a stolen fakeness.

So, either all of those places were real, or all of those realities, including this one, were a dream. Because we can't replace what was real with a dream.

Or so I thought.

I mean, if it was fake, why would I have this dread? This fear? What was coming would shatter this reality. The world would break into a million pieces. I could feel it like others could feel a storm coming on. I could feel it like *the* storm.

That thought frightened me. I held my cell phone, tapping it against the palm of my hand. Thinking. Wondering.

The phone had a browser. I had searched the internet, about what was going on off the coast of Georgia. All kinds of weather prognosticators were predicting all kinds of things. Most of them agreed there was a sudden depression where there shouldn't be, and that a storm was forming in a place where a storm shouldn't be forming.

There was all kinds of fear-driven news. So much it was hard to discern what was real and what was adjective laced click bait. You know, the alliterative titles you see in big bold letters, like Sudden Squall Shreds Charleston, or Tremors Terrify Savannah, or even Cataclysmic Climate Change Causes Concern.

Well, that last one I might have made up. But you get the idea. It was like they flipped open a book of synonyms and just put the worst words they could find together. As long as the first letters were the same. Alliteration at its finest.

Still, after what had happened in Charleston, and the recent earthquakes, there was a real fear. You could see it in every headline. Although, to be honest, I wondered how many people paid attention to them now. I mean, you could only cry wolf so many times, right? So many of the people reading the internet right now might not even believe what was happening.

I knew better, though.

I knew what was happening, and I needed no alliterative click bait to capture that fear, no Climate Crisis, no Storm of the Century, no Terrifying Tempest kind of headlines to be afraid.

I was afraid already. To the bone.

What would Blake do right now? Cass? What would Jeeves do, in my place? Hell, what would I have done, thousands of years ago, before I became the person I am now? While I was still searching for the person I wanted to be.

I thought I knew.

So, I made the call.

And Jeeves answered on the first ring, a rhythmic kind of beeps.

"Tybee Island?" he said. "This is where you want it to end?"

The way he said it caused me to wonder. Had I led him here? Had he planned this all along? Was I leading him, or was he driving me? Was Jeeves the reason for the fear, or was he just a part of it all?

I thought all of us now were wrapped up in this moment. There was certainly some force behind it. Something that had led to him and I meeting here. On this beach, a bit out of Savannah.

And whatever or whoever that was, it was too late now to back out. This was going to play out, one way or the other. And if I survived, maybe I would find out then, what it had all been about.

"It is what it is," I said.

Something in the back of my mind, some tingle rang through me. As if I still could change this. As if the world didn't have to end.

Silly back of my mind. Always the optimist.

"Well, there's no running left," Jeeves said.

"Maybe," I said.

I think it was my voice. I know how it sounded. Like I had lost the taste for revenge.

Had I?

I didn't think so. But the cost of a thing like revenge, it was something that needed to be measured. And I wasn't sure what that cost ultimately would be. I just knew I was scared of it.

"Come on now, friend," Jeeves said. He sounded... off. As if wanted me to be angry, like I had before, and now that I wasn't, he didn't know how to respond. "You and I both know this needs to get sorted out."

"Maybe," I said, again.

The black, gaping maw beckoned over the horizon. I could almost see it opening, the large mouth of darkness, ready to swallow us all. Ready to eat this world and everyone in it.

Was my revenge worth that? Was anyone's? Was what Jeeves wanted worth this? I mean, whatever it had been, it hadn't even rated an article on the web.

I started. "Look," I said. "I don't know why you killed her. I don't know what I did to you. If it was your daughter, then I'm sorry. I wish I could bring her back. But I can't."

There was a silence on the other side of the phone. As if Jeeves was surprised. Or stunned. Maybe even contemplating what I said.

"*What?*"

Wait, what? I didn't understand. What did Jeeves mean, what?

"You think I killed her for revenge? For something *you* did?"

His voice *was* stunned. Jeeves *was* surprised. I started to get a really bad feeling. One of those goosebumpy feelings that turn your stomach inside out and make you want to throw up. Like someone was just told you that yeah, you're in the hospital, and it's bad, and everyone here is sorry, but there's just nothing more we can do.

That kind of bad.

There was a sound on the line. Kind of a sputtering sound. I didn't think Jeeves was the type. "You think this whole thing is about you? About your world?"

And the bad feeling got really worse.

Oh god (Between you and me, part of me did kind of want to believe, here), did I fuck this up?

Jeeves was quiet. Putting things together. I was just as quiet. But finally one of us had to talk. "It isn't?"

His question was from out of left field. His voice cold. Like he had turned all the thoughts in his head and buried the result. "Where's your machine?"

It was my turn to be surprised. "What?"

"The machine." His voice was so cold, clipped, chill, that I wanted to shiver. "What you use to steal your little worlds. Where do you keep it? How can you possibly use it, walking around like you do?"

And Cass's conversation came back. From when she had been kidnapped. How the people there had complained about something always moving around. Realization stormed through me, like Clyde's license. And what I had thought was a misspelling but had been spelled accurately. Accurately for a different world. A different reality.

Mirtle Beach.

I *had* fucked this up. Was his accent even British, or was it something else? Some other accent from some other reality? How the hell could I know?

"We should call this off," I said. Scared. "Maybe talk about it."

"There is no *calling this off.*" Was he talking about him and me? I wasn't sure. But his laugh was loud. His voice still clipped. Angry, maniacal even. But resolute.

If I had guessed wrong about many things about him, I still had nailed his type. Men who commit to something with such a single-minded focus it didn't matter to them how many corpses they had to climb over. They just kept climbing.

"I'll give you a chance," Jeeves said. I could sense him, holding up his index finger. "One chance. You give me your machine, and I'll let you walk away."

I looked over at the storm. Understanding now the depth of trouble

I was in. That the world could be in. This reality. I smiled a little, but it was kind of a sad smile. Whatever Jeeves was bringing, whatever he had, I had Cass, so I liked my odds surviving Jeeves. It was what happened afterward that scared me.

I guess, maybe, I should focus on the now.

"That can't happen," I said. Because I didn't have a machine. Because I was different, then anything Jeeves had known. Maybe I was the one page in the infinite book that could do what I did. Even if there were others that could do the same, using some machine.

"That is too bad," he said. Misunderstanding me.

"Yeah," I said. I sighed. The breath was long and seemed to echo with the washing of the waves. The escaping of a breath, the frothy crest pulling back into the ocean, leaving a dark expanse of dark sand, littered with tiny white bones of rocks and shells. "I figured."

I wondered how close he was. He sounded confident. And that confidence should scare me, but it didn't. Not while I looked at the horizon and the Terrifying Tempest out there.

Damn hyper-aggrandized weather reports.

Part of my mind reached into the millions of realities that surrounded me. The boxes and boxes, trying to see if there was a reality open, some thread tying this one to another, that might keep the storm here. Something I could cut, and maybe remove the storm. At least keep it from growing.

There were so many I quickly lost track. I would need time, time I didn't have right now. "Look Jeeves. I guess I wanted to try this, and I guess it's not going to work. So, you're going to get your shot."

Somehow in his past, in another reality, Jeeves had lost a daughter. And somehow, that had led him and his jolly crew of Remainers here. Had led his quest for revenge to this Earth. Where he had killed Blake, which was something I wanted revenge for.

Maybe in life, it just comes down to the simple things. Anger. Hate.

Revenge. Our showdown was going to happen, world-eating tempest or no world-eating tempest.

And if it was about revenge, then that's what Blake deserved from me. Whatever it meant to this world. Whatever the cost. Whatever it meant from other realities or other worlds.

When you find someone worth everything, then that's what you give.

"Good," he said. "No more running, then."

"Nope," I echoed. "No more running."

I wondered if it was about a daughter anymore. This machine sounded important. I'm guessing that Jeeves thought I used something to do what I did. Which had me wondering if there was a machine that could do what I did.

Blake knew, though. She knew what I could do. She knew there was no machine. All the questions about what I would do, what I could do, took on a different understanding now that I knew what I knew now.

She was trying to get me to see it. Trying to get me to want more. Not because of something in this reality, but because of something that came from another. And maybe I would have come around, with enough time. Time Blake thought she had, but also feared was running short.

The hammering in my chest took on a different tone. Became less the pounding of fear, and more the pounding of a drum. Like someone going to war. So what, if this reality was about to be swallowed by some otherworldly storm? If everything and everyone was about to be blown away by a universal tempest?

Was Blake worth a world?

She had been to me.

And that's all that mattered, right now. The switch had flipped. Fear to anger. I had gone from trying to settle things, to someone ready to get medieval on some motherfucker.

I had tried. And if, at the end, Jeeves wanted to finish things, I'd be happy to oblige him. If it took the world with it, well, Blake was worth that. To me.

"So be it," I said. The words thick.

"So be it," Jeeves echoed. And laughed. A maniacal, crazy, clipped British laugh.

I hung up on him in the middle of it.

It felt about as good as the first time I had done it.

Still, I had tried.

CHAPTER FORTY-ONE

I turned around, phone in hand. Cass stood there, an angry expression on her face. Her arms folded across her chest. It wasn't her normal angry expression, not even her terminator-like angry expression, but an incredulous kind of fury.

"You were going to let him walk?" she asked. But it really wasn't a question.

She had overheard the conversation. And had gotten the wrong impression. Because she had only heard my side. So, she had gotten the right impression, but for the wrong reasons.

"It's not like that," I said. Wanting to explain.

"It's not like what?" she asked. "What the fuck are you scared of? Mister Lives Forever?"

"It's not like that, Cass." And it wasn't. She didn't have the advantage of the inner monologue I had with myself. She didn't know about the world-ending fear. All she heard was me trying to settle things with Jeeves.

And I didn't know if I could explain it to Cass. I mean, she thought the other worlds were dreams. Illusions. Would she believe the feeling I had? The intuition, developed over thousands of years?

Blake would have understood, though. She had gotten it. Gotten me. Like she had been there.

"She died because she was with you," she screamed. "Because she was *with you*."

"It's not *like that*," I shouted back. Anger flooded through me, and I went to throw the phone.

At the last second I stopped, realizing how dumb that would be. Because I needed the phone and the earpiece to talk to Cass. I stopped, paused, and almost smiled at the stupidity of this moment. Holding the phone and staring out over the wet sands.

She punched me. It was a good punch, right under the chin. There was a flash of light, a shot of pain, some blackness interweaved with the light, and found myself on my ass in the wet sand.

Cass stood there, chest heaving. Arms braced like a boxer, as if she was ready to wade in and keep punching.

I just sat there. I felt my jaw, right next to my chin, and rubbed the sore spot. My tongue stung, and I spit out a little blood. I must have bitten it.

"This is about *revenge*," Cass hissed. "This is about taking revenge for a woman killed because she was *with you*."

"Cass, look," I said. "I know what this is about. I'm here too, you know?" And I was. I was here for Blake. And maybe you could argue I was here for me, because of how I felt about Blake, but to me, it was all wrapped together.

Still, even facing Cass, I could feel the storm at my back. Feel the blackness spreading over the horizon, a thick dark ink of clouds. Ready to swallow us all.

"But maybe it's about more than that," I finally said. Knowing Cass wouldn't understand.

"There's nothing more than this," she said.

"Look—" I started, but Cass interrupted me.

"No looks." For a moment she looked at her arms, as if wondering what to do with them, now that she wasn't beating the life out of me. Then she just focused on me. Her eyes shimmering with anger. "No explanations. No excuses."

She would never get it anyway. So why try?

"Fine."

"I got to trusting you," she said. "I got to *liking* you. I thought I finally knew why *she* liked you. You and your scars. Your life."

Her eyes shimmered, she was so angry. A wet shimmer, like the surface of clear, rippling ponds. A tear rolled down her cheek, and she swatted it away from her cheek.

I sighed. This conversation felt much like one I just had. Sometimes the emotions got the best of all of us. Sometimes they created a chasm so wide, no bridge could cross it. Still, I wanted to try. "Cass, I'm here. He's still coming. We're still killing him."

Her chest rose and fell in deep, fast-paced breaths. She stared past me, out over the ocean, at the dark murky water she feared. Maybe not even seeing the storm, over the horizon.

It was a long moment. But finally, she spoke.

"Is he here?"

"No."

"But he's on his way?"

"Yeah."

Little words, small gestures, falling into the empty gulf between us. I was sadder than I would have thought.

"Good," Cass said. She stepped back from me. It felt worse than I would have thought. But maybe, when you're down to one friend, that's what you get.

She nodded to the lighthouse. "I'll be there."

I thought that might be too obvious. But it made sense. It was, by far, the tallest thing around. A tall brick-like building with a nice walkway around the beacon. Glass windows for three-hundred and sixty degrees. A sniper's perch if there ever was one. Maybe even a place that could hold off an army.

Not that an army needed to storm Tybee Island.

But if they did, Cass could probably hold them off.

"No one's there?"

Cass rolled her eyes. "Beach is closed."

Yeah. Inclement weather. Rip tide. Sharks. End of the world.

Take your pick.

It took a second for me to stand. My palm sunk into the wet, chilly sand as I tried to get up. My legs still felt a little rubbery. Cass didn't help.

Nothing like getting punched in the jaw to get you ready for a show-down with a maniacal British fellow.

"Okay," I said. Wherever Cass wanted to go, that was fine.

Cass still stood there. Cheeks wet. Not looking at me, but not *not* looking at me. You know the look. Where someone's eyes are on you, but also distant?

"I can't get it," she said.

I waited. She wasn't going to illuminate it for me. "What?"

"Blake trusted you," she said. "And I thought I had figured it out. The scars. You coming back to save me. And you talking about the stars. I could see what got her. The pain. The hidden hero. The lost dreams."

Cass had gotten that from *me*?

"But I was wrong," she said. Wiping more tears from her cheeks. "I think something in me made it up. Made it up for *her*. Maybe I just needed a reason."

You are *different...*

I stood there. Rocked by the realization. Not what Blake had said, but by what Cass had thought of me. I had never gotten that from her. Except maybe from the awkward pat, back in the gun shop.

I didn't know what to say, either. I wasn't anyone's hero. I hadn't been, for a long, long time. The scars I carried, most of them I couldn't remember what they were from. I mean, the one I could remember, for god's sake, I had fallen into a man-sized blender of margaritas.

Where had Cass gotten that?

Had it been from Blake, or something she had thought of on her own?

Whatever it was, it stirred something in the back of my soul. If I had one. My spine almost tingled with it, like it had woken up to a dream long dead.

"Look," I said. Wanting to say something. Put a coherent thought together. Take the next step and see where this thought led.

Cass interrupted me.

"After I kill him," she said. "That's it for us. We're through."

That surprised me. Stunned me, for some reason.

We're through? What the hell did that mean? I didn't know, but like I said, it hurt when the only person who knew you, who had seen your scars, when the only soldier that has been in the trench next to you, just walks away.

"Fine," I said. Angry. Part of me, the crazy part, wondered if that meant I would be next on her hit list. But there was nothing I could do about that. I thought we still trusted each other enough to see this through.

And honestly, I had seen her shoot. If she wanted to kill me, I wouldn't even hear the shot. There would just be the fade to black.

It'd be worth it, though, if we got Jeeves first. "Just make sure he's dead first."

That made her even angrier. As small as Cass was, she seemed to swell with it. Finally, not looking at me, her eyes keeping up their shimmer, she said, "That's not who I am."

It was good to know Miss Terminator had rules. Like my rules. I wondered if she would find out hers might not cover everything, like I had just discovered. Which, all in all, was a weird realization to me.

And a relief, to some degree. I could concentrate on avoiding a certain knife from a British guy, plus however many other Remainers Jeeves brought, and *then* possibly keep this world from getting eaten by that tempest hanging over the horizon.

Cass leaned over, picked up my phone. "Make sure this is charged."

She was back to being the Cass I was familiar with, with the mom tone.

"It's not the first time I've used a phone."

"Just keep it charged." The tone again. "Keep the earpieces in. Talk occasionally, comment on the weather, whatever, so I know the line is open. Just don't talk to me."

I looked at her. How the hell was I supposed to talk, if not to her?

"And stay on the east side of the buildings," she said. "Don't go into any alleys, or stores, or anything like that. Don't get out of my sight."

"How will I know if I do?"

"Look back and see if you can see the lighthouse, dolt."

Ah, old Cass, I missed you.

And what she said made sense. If I could see the lighthouse, she could likely see me.

I took a breath. Looked Cass in the face. Willed her to look back at mine.

There was a weird feeling of finality here, on the beach, on the wet sand. With my jaw aching and my rib hurting. With her face bruised and bandaged, and her eyes looking past me out over the ocean.

All I could say was, "You know what Jeeves looks like, right?"

She just rolled her eyes. She was good. She had done her research, knew her target, how to identify him. Like she had been a trained sniper. Or assassin.

So that was it then, between us. We would do this and be through. Cass and me.

A week ago I had said goodbye to Blake, without knowing I was really saying goodbye. All I had left of her was an image, her sightless eyes on the sidewalk, her blonde hair strewn over her forehead, the ends of the strands lying in a growing pool of red. My fingers tangled in her cold ones. A cold, lightless ambulance pulling up in front of us.

And now I was saying goodbye to her sister. We would kill Jeeves, and she would leave. Or Jeeves would kill me, and I wouldn't worry about any more goodbyes.

Still, it seemed odd, with me feeling that the world was about to end, that I felt bad that this goodbye wasn't going a little better than it was.

Soldiers should have a tighter bond.

She walked away. Through the sands, towards the lighthouse. She probably already had her new gun up there somewhere.

I followed her. Not really following her north, but moving off the wet beach, to the dry, softer sand. I had one of the bags there, with my gear next to it. Such as it was.

I strapped the K-Bar knife on my leg. Tucked the wakizashi and its scabbard inside the strap, but on the outside of the my leg. Right behind the K-Bar. The strap tightened a bit and my leg complained, but I told the leg to quiet down.

The suit jacket was next. It was still a bit rumpled, and there was a tear in the fabric from the earlier fight in the house at Folly Beach, right around where a certain bullet had attempted to funnel through it, but the tear was small. I buttoned it, just the bottom two buttons, and then threw the katana in its scabbard over my back.

I'm sure I looked funny. I know I looked funny. But there was no one else on the beach. It was just me. So, I thought I'd avoid getting pulled into a police station for questioning.

There was a bottle of water in the bag. I grabbed it and walked over to where a few cars sat against the side of the road. Two gray, four-door sedans. Like the same person had bought the same car twice.

I emptied the water into my hands, splashed my face. Did my ritual.

Cupped some of the water and ran it through my hair. Then looked at myself, in the side window of one of the sedans.

The reflection was see-through. I was transparent. Maybe fading from the world. My eyes were more hollow than a couple days ago. Darker circles ringed underneath them. My skin lighter in color, more pale. Like I was a ghost.

I took a serious look. Today could be the day it all ended for me. I had had a nice run, a few thousand years, give or take a century or two. I had looked for a reason, and found nothing. Then I had played around with a power no one else had, at times I had acted like a god, and, over the millennia, I had become *this*.

What reflected back at me. A transparent, fading image. The remnants of a person I had once been, a long time ago. Just a kernel left, really, as bits and pieces disappeared from me, over the years. In such a slow fade, I had never known what was happening to me.

For a brief period of time, a special person had brought some of that back. Someone unique in my life who had gotten me. Who had reached out and for some reason tried to pull me back from the brink I stood over.

And she had almost done it. We had just needed more time. Time we hadn't had.

Dammit, Blake.

I shifted my shoulders, moved the strap of the saya so that the katana sat a bit more comfortably on my back. Felt the anger stir, the comforting emotion we all fell back to, that we all used when nothing else was left to fuel us.

Maybe I faded more, in the window. Maybe my image solidified some, in the side window of the sedan. Maybe anger would be enough. I felt like it would need to be. The man looking back at me would need it to be enough, with the sparse grass of the beach behind him, the shimmering crests rippling on the surface of the ocean. The engorged black clouds taking over the horizon, until the edge of it was lost in waves of darkness. Until the horizon itself was just lost.

Oh.

Shit.

The storm. A lost horizon.

The Lost Horizon.

A world-eating tempest, on the edge of the world. Something I could no longer send away, something that had left little pieces of itself here, enough that those pieces had spread, like a cancer, eating anything and everything around it.

What had been Blake's question? Back in Chicago, when it had been just the two of us, and the rain spattering the windows. It seemed so long ago now, but it had just been a few months. The middle of the summer. The Windy City. A night inside.

What would I do if a storm came raging in?

It all hit me then. Blake. Why she had been unique. Who she had been. What I thought she had been trying to do, for me. Her tests and questions and hints.

Not only had I missed what Jeeves had been.

I had missed it all.

CHAPTER FORTY-TWO

It's not a storm. Just a little rain...

Not something like this. Something... otherworldly.

Like a hurricane?

I could remember how she felt. A little pulled back from me, on the inside. Like Blake had been thinking, but what she really had been doing is *recalling*.

A hurricane that spreads out and covers the world. Such a storm that rages, on and on, until all human things are leveled in some vast chaos.

Blake had seen this storm. She had known it was coming. Maybe even knew why it was coming, what caused it.

Had it been me?

What would you do?

Are you asking me to send it away?

Would you? Could you?

Could I?

I started running. I needed a bookstore.

How hard could that be to find at the beach?

Turns out, pretty hard.

I ran down Butler Avenue until I got to the touristy area. I kept touching the earpiece in my ear as I ran, making sure it stayed in. Tybee Island was more of a family beach, so it didn't really have a boardwalk, but there were some shops and restaurants put together in a few blocks off the beach.

I ran past the first couple restaurants. There were very few people around the area, but more than on the beach. Likely, like on Folly Beach, the people who lived in the area. Congregating in each other's shops, wondering to each other about what was happening.

I stumbled on the sidewalk. Caught myself against a wooden wall of a restaurant. Some seafood place. The wood was rough and splintered from the weather, and a few splinters shoved their way into my palm.

I didn't notice. I was caught in another memory. The very first one, in fact. Where I had met Blake.

What are you looking for?

Maybe you...

Oh god how I had I missed all of this?

I'm probably too old for you...

You think?

Blake. Blake. Blake. Why didn't you *tell* me?

But I knew the answer. Standing there. Chest heaving. Realization after realization hitting me, like blasts of a shotgun, so loud they were impossible to miss, impossible not to feel them. Hard, fiery explosions from the back of my brain.

She hadn't told me because she wasn't sure. She could only go by what she saw. Who she saw. And for the longest time, she had seen what I just recently did.

A fading image of a burned-out man. A man who had told her he had sent storms away, back in the day. A man with the kernel of something good, but also something broken. A damaged man, who Blake had been finding out more and more about, but also a man who could be the cause of everything going on.

I guess, when you're talking about an infinite number of worlds, you have to be certain about these kinds of things.

Dammit.

I started running again. I needed a bookstore. I crossed a little street, a little road with old blacktop heading back east, winding back into a neighborhood. A few shops hung out there off the sidewalk. I paused and looked at each one.

While I did, I called Cass.

I heard her answer. Short words, conveying nothing except maybe a mild… distaste wasn't quite the word, but something like that.

"I'm not in position."

"You need to get there," I said.

"I know my job."

Great. We were still doing this. We didn't have the time.

"I know you know, Cass," I said. Or shouted. At least my voice was raised. "Listen, this is going to sound funny, but I have a question about Blake."

Her sigh might have been as loud as my shout. It sure sounded that way. "Fine. What?"

"You said she used to walk out with your father, out and watch the stars, right?"

"Yeah."

"And one day, they walked out, and he didn't come back?"

"You really going over this with me? Now?" Her voice was angry. Pained.

"This is important," I said. Not knowing if I could explain it. Not knowing if I believed it myself. But all the pieces fit.

A long moment on the phone. The first store I looked in was the standard beach shop. An older man sat behind a counter, packs of cigarettes behind him. Sunglasses on a spinning stand next to the counter. Beach towels and umbrellas and inflatable rafts everywhere.

I wasn't sure what Cass was doing, but her breathing had caught once or twice before she answered.

"Yeah."

The second store was much the same. Just different color towels and umbrellas and rafts. A surfboard in the corner. With another old man behind the counter. I wondered how the both of them stayed in business.

Cass had told me about the cold spikes between her and Blake. The little points of pain, how some of them remained. But she had said then, firmly, that the two of them were sisters, and sisters just had that kind of bond.

There was no way I could explain this to her. Not in a way that she would believe. But I needed to know. "Did Blake seem different, then?"

"Gavin," she said. "I was *three*." Her tone somehow conveying that she thought I was currently that same age.

"I *know*," I said. The third store was closed, but it looked like a little coffee and dine-in shop. I looked through the window, past my faded reflection there, inside. The counter inside was rounded, and a large expresso machine sat on one side. Next to the machine was a rounded bubble of plastic, and the bubble held shelves. Little lights under each shelf illuminated muffins and pastries. A little stand held a few old newspapers, magazines, and what looked to be a couple books.

I paused there.

Time was critical. I wouldn't find a bookstore here. No Barnes & Noble, no Books-A-Million. So, this was going to have to do.

"This is important, Cass," I said. "*Think*."

Another long moment. And when she spoke, she sounded like she was humoring me. But she answered.

"I don't know if she was different," she said. "But I remember her coming into my room that night, and holding my hand. I think she'd been crying."

Blake somehow had been part of a reality switch. The Blake Cass had known had been stolen, and replaced with the Blake we both knew. And doing that, then, while her father and her had been looking at the stars, had caused the man to forget everything.

Why?

I thought I knew, looking back over the water. At the oncoming storm.

I thought I knew, waiting here for Jeeves.

Waiting for this moment. The world-ending moment.

Blake had been looking for Jeeves. For the person who brought the storm. And she had found me. And, finding me, thought maybe she had found a person who could fix the very thing she had come to prevent.

Could you?

I took a breath.

Broke the glass window. Broke my reflection in the glass. Watched the glitter of broken shards dance on the sidewalk. Reached through and unlocked the door and stepped in.

I didn't know. But I sure like hell was going to try.

CHAPTER FORTY-THREE

"I don't see you," Cass said.

"I know. I'm in a shop."

"What are you doing there?"

"Figuring something out." I walked over to the little stand of magazines and old books. "Let me ask you something else."

"Do we have time for this?"

"We need to make it," I said. "We both thought Blake was a Remainer. But you said she kept you from them. Did you ever see her cell?"

"Her phone?"

"No, her cell," I said. "The other two people who should be with her."

"Huh," she said, and went silent. "I never thought about that. I always thought she was protecting me from them."

Keeping them from me, Cass had said on the boat. Protecting me from them. Or maybe, she had said, a little sad then, protecting them from me.

"Exactly," I said. "She was never a Remainer."

A longer pause. "I don't get it."

"She was pretending to be one," I said. "Working her way up. Taking you to all the meetings. Waiting. Watching."

Blake had known there was a Jeeves out there. She was here, watching for him to appear. Which told me there was a group of Blakes, trying to stop this man. Someone who sent her here, someone who might have a machine.

Maybe she was looking for him that night on the beach. Maybe that's what she had in her hand while she was walking the sands in front of the hotel. She hadn't expected to find a *me*. She was expecting to find Jeeves.

Had she gone to meet him that night? Had she confronted him about what he was doing? Tried to talk him out of destroying this world? Was there something I could have done, was Blake just unsure enough about me to not bring me to that meeting with him?

Because I had no doubt who really had brought the storm here. Dead is dead, but Jeeves would search a million worlds to find his daughter. Like I said, I knew his type.

I was coming into this late. I was just figuring out things now. There was too much out there. Too much I didn't know.

But I knew now, what I should have known then. What Blake had been trying to find out, with me. What she had wanted me to say, the door she wanted me to pick, with me having no idea what lay on the other side.

Why Blake? *Dammit, why?*

My train of thought was way off the rails. I was lost. But I knew how Blake had tested me, the questions she had asked. All the hints in the books she had been reading. In the little conversations we had. She had been trying to bring me to the brink of a wide gulf of knowledge, some deep chasm, and waited, kept waiting, for me to take the plunge.

So, I stood there, in front of the little stand of magazines, newspapers, and some books. *Coastal Living, Power & Motor Yacht, Latitudes and Attitudes.* The *Savannah Morning News,* with its motto of *Light of the Coastal Empire and Lowcountry.* Whatever the hell *Lowcountry* was.

The books were sparse. There was something by Anne Rice on the bottom shelf, its front cover folded and a bit torn, leaving half a picture of a southern mansion in a dark night. *Black Cherry Blues* from James Lee Burke, looking brand new for some reason, as if someone had recently bought it and left here. And an *Odd Thomas* novel by Koontz.

I could work with that.

"What are you doing?" Cass asked.

"Hold on," I said. I needed to concentrate. This was going to take some work. I dug deep into all the realities around me, opening all the boxes in all the lines and factories around me.

Hard to picture? Imagine having to do it. Infinity is a bitch sometimes.

I noticed, searching around, the lightly veiled threads again. Tiny, fragile things, like the thread woven by a spider. A lot of them led away from me, some of them came back, like a twisted cat's cradle by someone with a million fingers on each hand. All the interconnected realities.

Some of the threads seemed stronger than others. Some I knew were from me, realities I had stolen and switched. But other threads were thinner, they waved in the imaginary air of the factory. Some of them broke as I watched.

And some of them were eaten.

I could feel the storm, even here. It pressed on me, a darkness, the kind of blackness no flashlight would penetrate. It hovered over a box, just a few feet away, and in my imagination I could see the sides of the box broken, aged, the cardboard so dry it seemed desiccated. And even as I watched, the box crumbled, and little bits and pieces of realities fell to the floor.

The blackness connected back to other boxes, other realities, not quite like a thread, but more as an absence of anything. A line that wasn't a line. A line that never existed. As if nothing could exist in the path that had traced the storm's past course.

I pulled back. Looked at the factory I was in. (Keep in mind, there was no real factory, no lines of conveyor belts, no boxes, it was just how I organized these things in my brain.)

Like I've mentioned once or twice, I was kind of winging it here. It wasn't like someone had taught me how to do any of this. I mean, my brain was trying to handle an infinite number of realties. And as we've said, that's not an easy concept for anyone to *get*. So, my brain was interpreting it in ways I could see it.

I had started with boxes a long time ago. Wooden-slatted things. Over time those had migrated into the cardboard boxes in my imagination. Sometime in the twentieth century, the images had become factories in my brain, with all the conveyor belts and boxes I had told you about. All the moving belts, the arms packing the boxes with reality after reality, each line stretching far into the distance.

The factory was a ruin now.

It looked like one of the buildings you see in an old mining town. Something in West Virginia, or Pennsylvania. The factory was old, falling apart. The roof sagged. A long wall had fallen in along one side. Lights flickered in the parking lot, and they illuminated a path that wasn't a path, a line that wasn't a line, an absence of a thread leading from another factory in the distance.

That factory in the distance was black. Trails of smoke left from a fire long dead, there was nothing left of it but ashes and blackened bones of walls that used to stand tall. A collapsed roof. And nothing else. Just a black, smoky memory of what used to be there. Just emptiness, with all those realities the factory used to hold *gone*.

Jeeves. Somehow. A daughterless reality to him, so just another page ripped from the infinite book.

I followed the thread that wasn't a thread back here. The darkness led closer and closer to my factory, the reality I lived in now, the blackness trailed over the fallen wall of the factory and along the conveyor belts. The nonexistent thread touched a box here and there, a line here and there, and everywhere that path weaved, the boxes were gone. Nothing left but desiccated remains of imaginary cardboard holding infinite amounts of universes.

Just emptiness, and crumbled boxes, as the black cloud wandered its way closer and closer to my world. A belt that had stopped moving, under arms that no longer packed the boxes. Just one box open there, holding one world. My reality.

I had asked Blake once, on a rainy Chicago night. *Do you want me to send it away?*

I remembered almost laughing back then. Wondering if Blake had wanted to go to the club that night. Or if she wanted to see what I could do, something to show off my power.

God, the immaturity of a man who had thought he knew it all.

Would you? Could you?

Holy shit, Blake, I didn't know. I had never seen something like this. I realized then, and the realization shook me, that even though I thought I had seen it all, *been* it all, there was so much more out there to experience. To find. To discover.

I mean, I thought I understood infinity, but I really hadn't.

Even if you think you've seen it all, you haven't. You *can't* possibly see it all, so you can't possibly know what's out there. Because nothing you can do, nothing you can imagine in your brain, can hold infinity. It's always bigger than anything you can think of. And then it's bigger than that.

And bigger than that.

What I had never thought of, in the large pond of infinity I had swum in, with all the realities around me, all the different universes I could reach in, is there might be a bigger fish in this pond. Not just a fish, but a shark. A world-eating monster of a shark, swimming its way closer and closer to why I hung suspended, in the ocean of my reality.

"Hey," Cass said. "Whatever you're doing, you need to hurry."

She broke my concentration, but the interruption was a good one. I was standing there. Motionless. Just holding the James Lee Burke book in my hand.

I could lose time going down the path I had been going. Forever has a way of drawing you that way, stealing minutes, hours, when you think about it. I needed to get back to what Blake had left for me.

"What?" I tried to sound thankful, but I know the tone was more frustrated.

"Boats," Cass said.

It was the Atlantic. Boats were likely to be on it. "It's the ocean, Cass."

"These are in a V-formation," she said. "Headed right for the middle of the beach."

Oh. Jeeves *was* bringing an army then.

"Want me to take them out?" she asked. Like it would be easy for her. The thought gave me pause. She thought she could hit the pilots of five boats, each bobbing up and down over the ocean as the crafted traveled fifty or so knots (sixty miles per hour, for the car folks) across the water...

That would be some good shooting.

"Can you?"

A millisecond of thought while she went to terminator mode. "Eh, probably not."

Well, it was good to hear Cass was human. Though it would have been nice if she wasn't, just this one time.

"Stay hidden then," I said. Cass was my ace in the hole. She was going to kill Jeeves, and that's what was important now.

"It's a lot of people."

"If we do anything today, we've got to kill Jeeves. You're our best shot there." Literally.

We both knew why we were here. Though I had just come to the realization that killing him was less about revenge, and more about world-saving. Now more than ever. "You see him, don't wait. Put him down."

"Clear," she said. "Still can't see you."

"I'm in a coffee shop," I told her, again. I couldn't remember the name. "I'll be back out in a second."

I went back to the factories. To the lines and lines of boxes of realities. To the storm, hovering nearby, eating those realities. Killing them all.

Killing our reality next.

I focused.

And looked. From this reality, where someone had bought a James Lee Burke book, brand new. And for some reason had left it here, in a coffee shop. And from this reality I searched for another, where that person might have picked up a slightly different story, and left it here instead.

The book in my hand shifted. Became a different paperback. From *Black Cherry Blues* to *The Concrete Blonde*, by Michael Connelly. This book was old, though, the cover dog-eared. I moved on, kept working the realities, and *The Concrete Blonde* became *Running Blind*. A Lee Child story.

I was still in the same area of the bookstore this person had bought the book in. The same mystery-detective-thriller section. Though that last title felt like the universe was mocking me a bit.

I opened another box in the universe. Flew through those realities. Tossed them left and right. *Polaris*, by Jack McDevitt. *The Real Story*, by Stephen R. Donaldson. Science Fiction. And then a left when I should have taken a right, when *Size 12 is not Fat* popped in, a Meg Cabot story.

That was a mighty big left. I went back right. Searched and searched until finally, the book I was looking for appeared in my hand.

Lost Horizon. James Hilton. A mountain on the front of the paperback, a plane flying across the range of peaks, a small illuminated monastery on the right side of the cover. The words *First Paperback in History* printed under the title. Maybe you have the book on your shelf.

I had read it, back when it was the new thing. So, I just remembered bits and pieces. Bunch of monks, a lama, that lived long lives. Saving what they could of the world, in preparation from some future disaster.

It had been awhile since I read it, but I knew what I wanted to check. I picked it up. Flipped to the back of the book. To the scene Conway was talking to the head monk of Shangri-La, the High Lama. (Page hundred and ninety-seven, for those of you with the same book.)

(Well, that's if you're in the same reality as me. Or something similar, maybe. Because there's a good chance this reality might not exist after today...)

Conway: The storm... this storm you talked of...

High Lama: It will be such a one, my son, as the world has not seen before. There will be no safety by arms, no help from authority, no answer in science. It will rage till every flower of culture is trampled, and all human things are leveled in a vast chaos.

Blake had asked me almost the same thing. Had told me, really, while she had been nuzzling my neck. Me holding her. Light. Warm. Electric. Her words had almost been word for word, as if it was something she had memorized. A storm that rages. A vast chaos. A storm the world has never seen before.

And she had kept pounding the thought in of Shangri-La into me. Asking me why I didn't want to know. Asking me if my purpose was *out there...*

I flipped on, because I remembered a certain part. It was the High Lama again, speaking. ... *I see, at a great distance, a new world stirring in the ruins... seeking its lost and legendary treasures. And they will all be here, my son... hidden.*

Preserved.

And that was what I needed.

I needed to know what Blake had been doing. And it made sense now, her being an archeologist. Her wanting to save things. Her research and trips.

It was a good feeling, understanding. But also a bad one. Because if she was here, and she had known about Jeeves, and was still trying to save things of *this* reality, then it meant that she hadn't figured a way to stop him. That—if she had been part of some group—those people hadn't figured it out either.

Instead, Blake had been taking the knowledge, the treasures of this reality, and saving them.

She had so wanted me to be a part of it.

What wouldn't I do? She had replied to me once, *If I could do what you could? All of this knowledge lost. Everything that could be saved...*

Blake had known of the storm. The universe-swallowing one. And —I was grasping here, filling in blanks—she had been rescuing parts of this world. Maybe the unique parts. Knowledge to be saved. To be hidden in a different place, maybe. A different reality. A place like Shangri-La. Hidden from the storm.

Her group maybe had done this in other realities. Other worlds. Maybe Blake had even been part of a group, a bunch of monastery-like lamas. People trying to save what they could while realities were eaten around them. While the universe grew smaller and smaller. While factories burned. While the infinitely paged book lost another page.

I saw all this too late. Too late to save Blake. Maybe even too late to save this world. But maybe, just maybe, not too late to save something of myself. The small part that had never died, that Blake had seen. The part of me she had tried to light a fire under, because she had known a moment like this would come around, someday.

Well, today was that day. Jeeves was here. He had brought his army. And a horizon swallowing blackness.

Heads or tails, I thought, if I could do all this. Any of this. It was late in the game, and I wasn't sure if I could be the person I needed to be. That the small part of me believed I could be. That Blake had believed I *was*.

I guessed it was time to find out.

Wish me luck. Because this is likely your reality too. I mean, you're reading the book.

CHAPTER FORTY-FOUR

I held *Lost Horizon* for a moment more. Felt the thinness of its paper. The slight bend in the cover, in my fingers. Looked at the words without reading them.

It tied me to Blake. I missed her. I missed my thoughts of her. I missed how she made me feel, and I didn't know if I could ever let that go.

Still, I closed the book. Tucked it inside a jacket pocket. It was pretty small, a light, tiny square of paper.

"Can I help you?" asked an old, wavering voice.

I looked to the door. The older man from one of the two tourist shops was peeking in. Wearing a plaid red and black shirt and suspenders. Not beach attire at all. He had glasses and a long patchy beard, more gray than black.

"Just needed a look at this," I said.

More people had gathered around behind him. The other older man from the other tourist shop (not wearing suspenders, but for some reason wearing a plaid shirt as well) and a small crowd. Some of them must have heard the glass breaking in the shop.

Thinking back, I should have just changed the realities to find one where the door was unlocked. It was something I did ninety-nine point nine percent of the time. Funny I chose not to do it then.

"Boats are maybe a mile out," Cass said, in my ear.

"Got it," I said.

"I think you're breaking and entering," the man said. The voice a little more firm. A little braver.

"You are correct," I said. "I one hundred percent am."

"Are you going to pay for the damages?"

I walked over, put a hand on the man. He pulled back a little and looked to the crowd for support. The crowd being the other old man and two or three others.

"You guys need to get home and lock the doors," I said.

"I knew it," said the other old man. "It's another storm."

He wasn't wrong.

"Not just a storm," I raised my voice higher, like I was broadcasting to a group... of three to four people. (I know, I rolled my eyes even as I was thinking it.)

I warned them all, not knowing if it was going to matter. "If you all can, get off the island. Find whoever you can and let them know too."

"Who's going to pay for the damage here?" the man asked again. "Shirley is going to be pissed."

Oh, everyone was going to pay if I couldn't stop the storm. Shirley might not even be around. She might have already left, disappeared, as I had searched for the book I needed.

Hell, she could even be one of the Remainers, coming in to kill me.

I didn't know. And the best I could do was clear the beach. There likely was going to be some shooting, soon.

"That will all get settled out, one way or the other," I said. "Best place for you all is back home." And I repeated my message. "Off the island, if you can. Inland."

Then I pushed past the group. Started running towards the beach.

Raising my hand to keep tapping the earpiece and making sure it stayed in. It was small and fancy, and somewhat embedded in my ear canal, but no matter how small, how fancy, or how embedded, those things always managed to find a way to fall out.

I guess so you could buy another when you lost one. But maybe that's the pessimist in me. Maybe they just fell out naturally, no matter how a company engineered them.

While I ran, I spoke to Cass.

"How far out there are the boats?"

"Eh," came the reply. "A mile out maybe. Just circled the top of the island."

I could hear them. Five big power boats, coming in as fast as they could. The ocean wasn't choppy today, so that was pretty fast. At least sixty miles an hour or so, in car speak.

I ran past the skimpy brush, the dying grass. Then hit the sand proper. The grains slid under my feet, so my run was more of a slogging motion. But I got there, in the middle of the beach. Facing north.

Watching the boats come in. They were inside a mile now. A pilot in each, a few other men (and/or women, it was hard to tell). They were all holding rifles. The boats weren't slowing down, not really. They were planning to hit the beach and jump out, like amphibious assaults in the movies.

"Sure you don't want me to shoot them?"

"Cass, I'm only going to say this once," I said. "You shoot when you see Jeeves. That's it."

"Even if you're in trouble?"

As much as it pained me to think it. "Yep. Even then."

Cass had one job. Maybe the most important job in the history of this world. Of this reality. And she had to focus on it.

"Your funeral."

She wasn't wrong there. It would be if this went sideways. They were already prepping the casket.

So, I needed to be fast. I needed to find what I was thinking of. And I needed to use my powers like I hadn't really used them in a while.

I had said adrenaline helped me find the reality I needed. Something about it focused me, accelerated my thoughts, almost like the world slowed down around me.

That was really going to be tested now.

I flipped through realities in the factory. Ignored the storm, munching on the box next to me. I flipped through box after box until I found one that I was looking for. Then I flipped through the universes like a person flipping through manilla envelopes until I pulled out the one I needed.

I stole some reality.

Well, maybe more than some.

A large ocean-sized chunk of it.

And froze the water around Tybee Island.

Not all of it. Certainly not the whole ocean. But enough of the Atlantic to get a mile out. I had found a reality with an ice age going on (the fools there must have not believed in global warming), and I stole a frozen chunk of the ocean there, replacing it with the watery wave part of the ocean here.

The waves, the shimmering watery crests, instantly replaced by thick, bright-white ice. Covered with a light shimmer of wetness, as if the sun had just melted a bit of the surface. The rapid exchange of a block of icy ocean for a block of wet ocean, the frigid temperatures of the ice age world with the temperate climate of this one, instantly caused a fog to burst up around all of us.

The theft had happened instantaneously. So, it wasn't good for any of the fish, or sharks, or turtles swimming those currents. It wasn't good for the natural currents, deep in the water, developed over hundreds or thousands or even hundreds of thousands of years.

And it certainly wasn't good for five boats traveling at sixty miles an hour or so.

The sound of a terrifying rending cut through the air, echoed by five high-pitched whines. Screaming, as metal was instantly sheared. Booms, as internal combustion engines were froze suddenly in place.

The wave of fog rolled over me. Burst over me. An explosion of mist. Inside of it came the tearing of plexiglass, plastic, wood. The tinkling of glass. The screams of people flung through the air and impaled.

And a car alarm, back along the beach, blaring insistently to anyone that would listen that it was sure it was getting broken into.

And then nothing. Nothing but the fog.

"Holy shit," Cass said in my ear.

Damn. The fog was going to affect our plan. The mist wasn't good for Cass. Or actually for me, with Cass being overwatch and Jeeves out here.

I hadn't thought this through. But it would still work.

I thought.

The fog kept washing over me in a roiling wave. A second before it had been me and the sunny sky, the next, a cold, icy mist enveloped the sandy beach. The mist was a weird mix of the southern heat and humidity known in the south, and the fanged, icy bite of a northern, wintery fog. Like someone had dropped an iceberg-sized piece of dry ice into the middle of the ocean at the equator.

It felt like a breezy mist. Or a chilly fog. A chilling mist. Something like that.

I took a step on the ocean. The ice was solid and thick, but I hadn't worn the best shoes for this. The surface was slick and wet, and I slid a bit. There was nothing around me to catch, nothing to hold up, nothing that I could see, just the shouts of people checking on one another. The shouts of people answering. And groans, where they couldn't shout.

I went after the groans. I had a picture of the V-shape of boats in my mind and could guess where they were in the mist. I'd come in from the side, from the left wing, and move left to right across them.

The fog hid everyone from me, but it also hid me from everyone. Which gave me the advantage. Anyone I saw I could feel free to kill, after all.

I was pretty sure the Remainers wouldn't feel the same way. They would hesitate, wondering if I was friend or foe. And that hesitation would lose them their life.

I was good at things like keeping my balance. Part of the benefits of a long lifetime of practice. I kept the center of my mass between each step, placed my feet carefully, and when I slid, went with the slide.

Some of the groans grew louder. The smell of burning oil mixed with the acrid smell of gasoline. A hulk thickened in the mist ahead. The hull of one of the powerboats. Or mostly the hull. Flames licked its stern, and black smoke swirled and mixed with the white mist.

I unsheathed the katana. Pulled the wakizashi from its scabbard. Got closer. A lump against the hull resolved itself as a man leaning back against it. Huddled over himself, his arm cradled in his stomach. Or his arm holding something in.

He went limp a moment later. The katana slid out of his chest as easy as it had gone in. He may have sighed, that sigh may have been a light, escaping groan.

Part of me wanted to look away. But I forced myself to get a good picture of the man. Older. Ragged hair and beard. Scrape along the side of this face. Crinkled lines around his eyes, tanned skin.

Killing unarmed people never felt good. But I had done it before, and they had come after me first. What was the saying, all's fair in love and war?

This wasn't love. And it certainly wasn't going to be fair. It was going to be dirty. And it was best to finish dirty work quickly. I flicked the blood off the blade and moved along, around to the rear of the boat.

A shape materialized in front of me. He grunted as the katana took him through the heart, and then dropped to the ground. I mean dropped to the ocean. Well, the frozen ocean. (You know what I mean.)

He had been holding a rifle. It clattered across the ice when he fell. A female voice called out a question. I hunted that voice and found the shape it belonged to. And then there were three Remainers dead.

I moved to the next boat. It was in much the same shape as the first. I did much the same thing there, except for the katana stuck a bit in the hull when I killed one person, so had to use the wakizashi for the second. He made a clinging sound when he fell, like a tinkling, ringing kind of sound, and I looked on the ice to find a belt of grenades in his hand.

What the hell had the Remainers needed those for? I was one guy, not a freaking army. Was it just a guy bringing something along for fun? Were they just going to lob grenades over Tybee Island and hope they got lucky?

Hell, I didn't know what their plan was, but I could use them. I tossed the belt over my shoulder. Tucked the wakizashi back into its scabbard, which itself was tucked into the strap holding the K-Bar to my leg. Pulled the pin on a grenade and tossed it back the way I had come, toward the first wreck. Tossed a second grenade in the boat in front of me.

Then slid quickly out of there. Towards the third boat, the middle of the V-formation. As fast as the ice would carry me.

The first explosion blew the mist from behind me. Pushed the fog away in front of me, everything empty and clear like the eye of a storm. For a moment I could see the third boat fifty yards ahead, bow down in the ice, like it was flipping head over heels. Or stern over bow, I guess. The big twin props of the engine poked high in the air, the metallic blades flashing briefly in the sudden light.

I could see the boat. The bad part about that was the Remainers there could see me. Two of them, to be exact, crawling out of the hatch. One with an assault rifle slung over his shoulder.

The second guy shouted as he saw me, and almost fell reaching back down into the hatch. The second guy was trying to find his balance on the back of a seat, swinging his assault rifle around. The two of them jostled each other, and then the last thing I saw of them was Assault Rifle's knee wobbling a bit on the back of the cushioned chair.

Then the mist waved back over us all, like curtains after a show.

Time to run. I slid my way out to sea. Taking the long way around to putting the rear of the boat between me and the assault rifle. One of the two men kept shouting, *"He's here!"* over and over. The words felt thin in the fog. Sharp. As if his scream could cut through it.

Then the assault rifle kicked in. Bullets ticked and tacked across the ice to my right. Wild shots, but close enough to worry me. I stepped and slid as fast as I could, until I took one long slide, and the hull of the third boat became a shadowy shape on my right.

Then I pulled a pin from a third grenade and tossed the grenade over the stern of the ship. Hopefully into the stern of the powerboat. I thought I heard it *tink* its way down into the hull of the boat.

And then thought that thought through.

I ran. Or ran-slid. Kind of like ice-skating, just in loafers. I had five seconds maybe, if I was lucky. When the third boat exploded, I was still close enough that the force picked me up, tossed me further back across the ocean, way out to sea, way behind the remaining two powerboats.

I rolled and bounced across the ice, the K-Bar dug into the outside of my thigh, and a sharp pain came from my ribs (from you know where) until I finally slid to a stop. Like a human snow plow. Or ice plow.

Ice was cold. Not a stunning realization, I guess. But definitely one that comes to mind when you're laying spread-eagled over a block of iceberg. I was soaking wet in places and frozen in others, and for a moment I wondered how something so flat and slick could hurt so much.

The belt of grenades was long gone. Somehow though, I still held the katana. The knuckles of my right hand were pretty raw and bleeding. My face rested against the cold ice, and it felt like my cheek was going to stick to it.

But I was alive.

And alive was a good thing.

Even if I had to suppress a violent, shaking shiver or two.

"Still there?" Cass asked. Sounding curious.

I grunted, quick and low. Not wanting any remaining Remainers to hear me. Which she understood. "Grunt twice if you're good."

I rolled my eyes and grunted twice.

"Better hurry," Cass said. Her tone said she knew I had rolled my eyes, though maybe that was just me reading something into the normal Cass tone. "Some vehicles coming in from the north. Grouped together."

Jesus, maybe Jeeves *was* bringing an army. Maybe I should have saved the grenades. Maybe I should let Cass get to work, and then we could figure out where Jeeves was, together. But I wasn't sure how many were coming, and who they all were.

I lay there, eyes closed, cheek sticky against the ice (but not stuck). I must be bleeding there, I thought. I was definitely cold and tired, and a little beat.

And the fight had really just started.

So, I pushed myself up. Found out I was in one piece, more or less. And risked a quick conversation. "Hold on."

Cass's voice was surprised. "Say again?"

I didn't. This was going to be quick and dirty. Which was the name of this fight. There were no real bridges leading into Tybee Island. Just a long stretch of road between Savannah and the beach, wandering sometimes through swamp-like land.

I went back to the tried-and-true. The same reality I had stolen from last night, saving Cass. (Was that really last night?) And pulled some more of the higher coastal shelf from that reality, swapping it with this one. Right along the north end of the island.

It took some effort. I couldn't see where I was stealing, which was usually something I needed. It was further away than I usually did my thing, and the further away, the harder the swap. At least it always felt that way.

I heaved a bit, and pulled another chunk of reality from that world. Hammered it in here. A large effing block of it.

And broke up the road heading into Tybee Island.

It wasn't like the night before, where I had stolen just enough of the coastal shelf to be able to stand on it. Where I had kind of stolen it in a stream, a little bit of it, and built up the land until my feet could touch the bottom. This was hard and brutal.

And a lot.

The ice shook underneath me. Big shaking heaves. Cracks and splits rent the air. Shouts came from where the boats had been frozen still. I slid and fell back to the ground. Well, the ice.

Cass swore over the earpiece. A quick exclamation.

And then it was over. Like the ringing toll of a bell, the waves of the ground moving faded into the distance. More alarms sounded from the beach, more car and truck and maybe even Jeep-truck alarms.

And Cass's voice again. More hushed this time. "Was that you?"

I grunted.

She echoed the grunt. As if seeing something that you didn't understand, and was taking a minute to get it. Then she finally said something. "You got some time now."

I got *back* up. Again. Still wanting to shiver. I headed back to where I thought the last two boats were. Turns out, my navigation was a little off. Something to do with the explosion and the tumble across the ice and the quick earthquake. I couldn't find either, and whether there were Remainers left or they were just being quiet now, I didn't know.

But I could smell the smoke still. Something was still burning, close by. Close enough the scents of burned plexiglass and oil and gas drifted by on an occasional breath. There was the crackling of small fires, I thought. Little pops and cracks that became larger pops and cracks.

And I realized it wasn't the crackling of fires I was hearing. It was the splitting of the ice. The warm temperatures here in this reality, the Atlantic Ocean to the east and the grenades had combined to weaken the flat piece of ice I had stolen and dropped here. And the quake here at the end, it had been the hammer to shatter what was left.

The large piece of ice I stood on shifted, quickly.

I caught myself and started running. Not the run slide I had been using before. Not the ice skater-like motion. But full on running to the west. Hoping I was close to the beach. Hoping that I could make it.

Shouts from the boats, a little north, a little behind me. There were some Remainers left. Then a large crack and a scream, and then the scream was gone.

The cracks multiplied. Not the cracks themselves, but the sound of them. Large and tiny splits, big crackings like the splitting of trees popping in half, small ones like the cracks you hear when you twist an ice cube tray.

I couldn't see anything but the mist and the whiteness of the ice I was running on. Each step was longer and faster. Each step I slid on somewhat before jumping to my left. Pumping my arms. The katana waving wildly in the air, as if it was trying to slice a way open in the fog.

One large boom behind me. A hollow ice-like boom. The large piece of ice I was on tilted up so that, in a moment, I would be sliding back towards the ocean.

I screamed and jumped and prayed.

And landed in a bit of wetness. A small puddle of ice-cold water. Salty in my mouth. But also sandy.

I was on the beach.

And I didn't think any of the Remainers from the boats had made it.

So, at the end of this fight I scored me a one, and Jeeves a big fat zero.

Too bad I felt like he was still out there. Waiting. That this was all just a prelude to him and me duking it out.

Well, I was waiting too. This was just the beginning of what I could do. If Jeeves wanted this to be the end. It would damn well be the end.

Time for round two.

CHAPTER FORTY-FIVE

I pushed myself off the sand. Cleaned the katana the best I could, wiping it on my pants and placing the blade back in its saya. Brushed the wet, cold grit off my face. Tugged my jacket so that it fit my shoulders better.

Ignored the ache in my side. The headache. The blood leaking down the cut in my cheek that smeared on my hand when I wiped it.

That would all be stuff for later.

The ground still shook. Little trembles, with an occasional big shudder. Behind me was the snapping of ice, and the watery bloops of broken pieces of iceberg sinking back beneath the ocean.

The fog had thinned out over the beach. It was more wisps here and there, thick arms of mist in some places. I found an open patch and looked north.

The lighthouse was still there.

My earpiece had fallen out of my ear. Somehow I found it on the sand, and after wiping it clean put it back in my ear. My phone had hung up on itself too. So, after making sure the earpiece had paired back, I redialed Cass's number.

She answered the phone with a question. "This all you?"

It was good to know she was alive. I didn't know what *all* meant, but it was probably a good assumption I did it. "I'd guess so. You good?"

"On the leaning lighthouse of Tybee?" she asked. "Yeah."

I checked. The lighthouse did seem to have a slight tilt to it now, leaning west. Greater than slight, actually. It definitely could have been related to its twin tower in Pisa.

"Have you seen him?" No need for me to specify who. We both knew who we wanted to kill.

Cass snorted, "In this fog?"

"Dammit."

"Yeah."

This whole plan had been luring Jeeves down here. Trapping him. Thinking he'd want to get in close and sneak a knife in me.

Jeeves had skipped the whole stabbing me part. Instead, he had brought a small army. Apparently wanting to wipe me off the face of the Earth, with whatever piece of land I was standing on.

Well, two could play at that game.

Like I said, people really hadn't seen what I could do.

I warned Cass, "Grab a hold of something."

She sighed. Or groaned. It was kind of the same thing with her.

I dove back into the reality multiverse. The one with all the factories and all the conveyor belts and boxes. And one angry storm. Flipped through the boxes until I found what I needed. All of it.

The earth rumbled around me. Then bounced as I pushed more land under the road north, making sure to break all of that up. Making sure to have the Atlantic push in and over the road, flood the swamps there so that Tybee Island was really an island.

More car alarms beeped and booped around me. Loud blaring calls for help. And some kind of blippedy-bloop alarm. Lights flashed all around us, headlights, taillights, hazard lights, lights that vibrated and shook as the ground trembled underneath us.

The lighthouse bounced a bit too. Or maybe that was just where I was standing, with the ground shaking underneath me. But the brick tower tilted more and more inland. Cass swore and maybe, maybe screamed, biting it back some. But I wouldn't bring that up to her (you know why).

I pulled from another reality. Pulled a nice stationary lighthouse and replaced the leaning one. Held it there, kind of in situ, pausing until the earth stopped shaking so much, and then hammered that reality in.

The tower stabilized. Straight as an arrow now. Pointing up to the sun.

Finally, I brought in a heavy wind. Something brisk and fluttery from the ocean. It was heavy with the scent of salt, so heavy I could taste it. And it carried the mist away in big, sweeping gusts.

Like smoke on a battlefield, the fog broke apart. First in thick, curvy arms that waved a bit as sunlight cut through the openings in the mist. Then in small, smoky tendrils that wisped up from the icy patches on the ocean. And finally, just the bright light of the sun, hanging high overhead in the blue sky.

"Damn," Cass said, in a quiet voice.

Around me was the beach. What was left of it. A lot of houses had fallen down. Restaurants, diner shacks, little stores on the corner. I felt a little regret, thinking about some of the people who lived there. Who may not live there anymore, being dead and all, and I pushed that regret down.

Vengeance is a hard mistress. It allows for nothing like regret. There's just a world-swallowing anger, and you have to ride that horse until the race is over, or it collapses to the track.

The ocean shimmered behind me. Almost blue, with white frozen patches of ice bobbing in the water. Sunlit crests of waves, pushing the blocks of ice around. The boats were all gone, all five, though I thought I could see the hull of the middle one poking up from the water.

I wiped my face with the back of my arm. Where my cheek was

bleeding. My jacket left more grit on my face than it took off. There was a towel on the beach in front of me, a red and white thing, and I picked it up before sighing in disgust as sand poured off of it.

Well, in for a penny...

My jacket disappeared. I'd miss it. The towel. My pants and shirt too. In its place was a lot of SWAT-like gear. All black with white letters. A bulletproof vest. A belt with a Glock tucked into a holster.

I shrugged again, making sure the katana still hung on my back. I checked the K-Bar on my leg, a little muscle memory motion of my hand. The hilt was cool to the touch, a nice hard metal.

In my hand was a towel. White with those effing seahorsey monsters dotted across it. Karma was a bitch, it seemed. If there was *one* universe I wished that black storm would go ahead and eat...

Well, maybe I could talk Jeeves into sending it there instead.

I'm just kidding.

Maybe. These seahorseys are pretty ugly.

I reached for one more thing. A nice little beret. It was the only hat I could find that I liked. Black. I turned it backwards on my head and felt like I was ready. Black tactical suit, bulletproof vest, beret.

Clothes make the man, after all.

Cass spoke then. In kind of a hushed tone, for her. "Gavin?"

"Yeah."

"This whole thing has been about killing Jeeves, right?"

"Yeah."

"So, what's that on the horizon?"

It wasn't really a lost horizon. Or maybe it was, maybe that's where everything just... disappeared. The entire eastern curve of the Earth was black now. Larger. Now the eastern side of the world held a thick horizontal bar of clouds, so thick the blackness emitted no light. No sound. Like a black hole, the storm seemed to be absorbing everything around it. The blue sky, the bright yellow sunlight, and even as I watched, a puffy white cloud just kind of was... slurped up by the blackness.

As if the storm was alive, and aware. As if it had sensed what I had done, and was eager to swallow all of it. As if the more I brought in, the more realities I stole, the hungrier the storm got. Like a black hole, the more it ate, the stronger it became.

Not a black hole then.

A black horizon.

I couldn't explain any of that to Cass, though. Not now. I wasn't sure it was something she would believe. I wasn't sure it was something I believed, even though it sat there in front of me, growing larger by the moment.

However big you think it is, it's bigger than that. A pit with no bottom. A stomach that could never be full. Though I wish it would swallow a car alarm or a hundred now.

"It's bad news," I said.

"No shit." A standard Cass comeback. "What aren't you telling me?"

I took a breath. Then another. Thinking, well, Cass, I'm not telling you a fuck ton of stuff. More than that, probably. I could start with Blake's probably not your real sister. Or Jeeves is from another world. And this world is likely being killed, right now, in front of our eyes, by some reality-murdering black hole of a storm.

How do you say all that in a quick sentence, so that the person you're talking to believes it, and doesn't have any follow-up questions? Because time was critical. I could feel it.

And Jeeves was still out there. I was sure of that. And whoever else he had had more of his army too. Field Marshal and all.

We just didn't have the time for me to say much.

"You trust me?"

Cass's answer was quick and to the point. "No."

Well, I could understand that.

"How about this? We find Jeeves. Ask him a question. Then kill him."

Even if I wasn't sure we had even that time.

Cass grunted. I knew her well enough now to know she was thinking. Tossing the idea around a bit.

"About the storm?"

I let out a breath. Cass was putting a few things together. "Yes."

Another long moment.

"Fine."

"So just wound him," I said. It was funny to me I thought it was possible, and maybe even an indication of how much I thought of Cass's ability, that she could shoot to just wound from a half-mile away.

I hoped that was possible. I didn't care if Cass blew off his leg, as long as I had time to ask him about the storm. I was sure he had brought it here. To this reality. This world. And I didn't care so much for the why of it. I just wanted to see if he could turn it off, before I killed him.

"I don't like it," Cass said.

"I know," I said. "Me neither."

"You going to explain this? After?"

I rolled my eyes. I'd tell her what I could, but I wasn't sure about Blake. I didn't know enough, and what I knew was guesswork and hints. I wasn't sure how she would take any of it. "I told you I would."

"Okay."

"Let's find Jeeves then." Which would be hard to do with all this noise. I made my finger wagging motion. Like changing a channel. And switched out all the cars blaring their alarms with nice, quiet, no-alarm vehicles.

It was amazing what adrenaline could do. Give the power to a parent to lift a car off a kid. Give a soldier the ability to jump out of a trench and rush into incoming fire. Give me clear, easy access to the realities I most needed.

The world went quiet around me. A nice, peaceful quiet. The quiet from the center of a storm. I took a deep breath of it, my chest expanding, the salty air filling my lungs.

Then I frowned. An alarm was still going off, down the street. A blippedy-bloop kind of alarm. It was a little muted with the distance, but still kind of annoying.

I headed off the beach. Into the mess of crumbled houses and broken pavement of Butler Avenue. Of people pulling themselves out of the rubble of collapsed stores, some of them looking around, some of them staring at the black horizon. One of them, the older man from the tourist shout, giving me a quick shout.

I ignored him, like he had ignored me earlier. I had warned him. Instead I headed north, walking down the center of Butler Avenue, looking for Jeeves. I had a question for him.

I hoped his answer would be what I needed. Well, what we needed. It's all our world, after all.

CHAPTER FORTY-SIX

BUTLER AVENUE HAD BEEN BROKEN UP BY THE QUAKE. THE blacktop was cracked and bits of pebbled black tar lay everywhere. Large chunks of the road tilted here and there, where the ground had opened up underneath it. And the ground shivered underneath my feet, enough that I placed each foot carefully as I walked. It was like the Earth itself was scared of the storm blowing in from the east.

I guessed it should be.

The blippedy-bloop alarm got louder. I headed towards the car, a bit north of me on the street. It looked like one of the electric hybrid cars, a silver hatchback one. It was small, but the lights flickered wildly, and its alarm made a shrill sound, as if making up for its size with volume.

I covered my earpiece with my hand. "What's the rundown?"

"Well," Cass said. "Pretty much everything is destroyed."

"I mean with the Remainers."

A pause. Like she was looking through her scope. "There are some people pulling people out of the ocean up north. Some of the trucks there. More people on the other side of the water. A lot of them have guns."

It wouldn't take long for them to find a boat and get across. If they couldn't just swim whatever distance they needed. I wondered how many I would have to kill. Or even how many were there.

"They see you?" I was worried about fixing the lighthouse, but I thought I could get away with it, with the whole world shaking. Not likely someone would have taken a moment to look and watch the lighthouse kind of straighten back up.

"Trust me, no one is looking up here right now."

I guessed that would be good enough. Time to find Jeeves.

Of course, the whole plan had originally been for him to find me. And I had forgotten about that part. So, when Jeeves did find me, it was a hell of a surprise. Life-takingly so.

I was nearing the car when it went down. The blippedy-bloop alarm was really shrill. An ear-piercing thing, like the hybrid could make up for its small size with pure volume. I thought about poking my head into the driver's side to see if I could shut it off. Maybe "find" a set of keys.

Kind of a silly thing to do, while I was trying to save the world. But a guy's got to be able to think. I mean, we've all been next to a car alarm that loud, that annoying, right? Wanting to scream at someone to click the fob and turn that thing off?

So, I got to the side of the silver hatchback. Its hazard lights flashing, like a scream for a help. Or maybe it was a warning. I definitely should have taken it that way, sticking my head into the driver's side door looking for a key fob somewhere.

Then I felt something in my side. I little pressure. A lot of pain.

At the same time there was a single gunshot.

I grunted and fell backwards. Onto my ass, on the broken blacktop. One of my hands was pressed to my side again. The right side this time. A matching stabbing. There was a knife there, buried to the hilt.

And then the pain kicked in. A hot, wet, sharp pain. It burned and stung in equal measures.

Dammit.

Then hearing the gunshot caught up to me. My brain was behind the time, and I moved sluggishly. I slid around on my ass, pushing my back against the front side fender of the hatchback. Felt the saya catch against the side mirror of the car, and tried to tug it off my shoulder, which caused another wave of pain in my side.

My eyes caught a body lying in front of me, on his back. As if a bullet had caught him and spun him around. The man wore a gray suit. There was a splash of yellow over his breast pocket, a daffodil. His chest wasn't moving, and it looked like his eyes were open.

"You good?" Cass asked.

I closed my eyes. Grabbed the hilt of the knife and pulled it out in a yank. Bit back a scream. Which was a good thing, because I felt my breathing gurgle a bit. I coughed up a bit of phlegm, spat it out. It was more red than green.

Blood leaked like crazy from the wound. Fast, too fast. Not having anything handy, I grabbed my beret and stuffed it into my side. Holding it tight with my hand.

And swore. It was an odd thing, but a bulletproof vest didn't really protect you from a good stabbing. Which I should have maybe thought of when I was putting my outfit together, but honestly what was I going to wear? Chain mail?

"Gavin?"

Dammit, I had finally worn something not stained with blood or seahorses for all of five minutes. The whole clothes makes the man thing had been nice, for a moment. Maybe it just wasn't my thing anymore.

"Gavin," Cass sounded concerned. "You okay?"

I kept the beret against my side. Felt it warm up with a wetness. All I could do was hold it tight and pray. Hope that whatever kept my body going could actually keep it going.

"Maybe," I finally said.

I stood, carefully pulling myself up with a hand on the hatchback's mirror. Ducked my head back into the car, hoping to find a cigarette lighter, like you see in the movies. Maybe I could use it to sear my wound shut.

But all the hatchback had was a charger in the lighter socket. With a white cord plugged into it. With no phone at the other end, just a little plug for a phone.

I swore again. But not aloud. That took breath better used for breathing.

I twisted back out of the car. Carefully. One hand holding the beret to my side. Went over to look at Jeeves with his eyes open. Drops of blood spattering to the blacktop next to me.

"He dead?"

"I think so." I stood over the man, with a sinking feeling, because past him, past the beach and the ocean, was the growing storm. The swelling blackness.

Then it hit me.

Like I said, my brain was sluggish right at the moment. With the whole wanting to survive thing.

I looked back at Jeeves. His open eyes. Green eyes. Not blue. His face had a reddish stubble to it. And his hair, although gray, had the same tint. Like someone had dusted red hair with a healthy amount of talcum powder.

It wasn't Jeeves.

This wasn't the man who needed to die.

It was a different man.

I swore again. Aloud this time. And winced.

Jeeves had come prepared with his own trick as well. I had so thought he'd want to be the one to push the blade in at the end. I hadn't realized he might be smarter than that.

I let out a breath. Carefully. "It's not him."

"What?" Cass sounded surprised, and I could almost feel her looking through her scope at me. At the body.

Then there was a whooshing sound. Not from the phone. But from behind me. West, inland from the beach. I barely hear it over this fucking car alarm.

But I knew the sound.

You probably know it too. Maybe from a movie. The sound a rocket launcher makes, after the guy holding it locks onto his target and pulls the trigger.

A plume of smoke erupted from in front of one of the restaurants. The rocket shot north, leaving a white cloud trailing behind it. A nice line across the sky, as the missile wound its way to the lighthouse.

I didn't even have time to shout a warning.

The top of the lighthouse shattered in an explosion of fire and heat. Bricks and glass and steel tumbled out over the air, landing in plops in the sand around the building, leaving a jagged hole in the top of the building.

I hadn't seen anyone jump out of it.

There had been the whoosh. The explosion. And still, this fucking car alarm not shutting up next to me.

A whisper broke out of me, "Cass..."

Then something connected with the side of my head. The blow spun me around over the hood of the hatchback, and I slid down that to land in front of the car. Too stunned to scream, although my side did that part for me. Scream, that is. In crazy pain.

"Cass..." I said again. Speaking into the earpiece. I shouted her name again, before realizing the earpiece had flown out of my ear.

Then a person walked into my vision. A man in a gray suit, with gray hair, gray eyes, flashing with an intense, focused look. A yellow splash of a flower over his breast pocket. A gun in his hand.

And a big, fat smile.

Jeeves.

He looked at me. Then frowned and looked at the car. Fired his gun a few times into the hood of the car, pulling the trigger until the blippedy-bloop alarm became the wail of something dying, until, finally, it was peacefully quiet. Nothing but the washing of the waves on the beach and the incoming breeze, fleeing before the black tempest on the horizon.

"There," Jeeves said, in what I had thought of as his clipped British accent. If he was even British at all. "Now we can talk."

CHAPTER FORTY-SEVEN

I dragged myself back to a seated position, pushing my back against the front bumper of the hatchback. Feeling lightheaded as I dead so. *Hah!* Dead so. I must be losing a lot of blood, which honestly, I should be used to by now.

I was pretty sure I meant *did so.*

I am not snicker-giggling.

But Jeeves was looking at me kind of funny. The beach and ocean behind him, and the storm swelling over the horizon behind that.

"Talk?" I asked, hoping my voice came out nonchalantly. Like I had Jeeves right where I wanted him.

"Sure," he said. Keeping his gun pointed at me. I thought it was even *my* Glock, and sure enough, my holster rig was empty. "We've got time now, sport."

We certainly did. I didn't have anything or anyone left.

Blake dead. Now Cass. No one else on my side.

I knew I was angry. But it was a faded kind of anger. Like the emotion hid behind a thick, lead-lined curtain. Or maybe it hovered, far in the distance.

A second guy came up and stood behind Jeeves. A younger guy, one of his crew. Maybe someone from the British military. Maybe a guy who had traveled realities with Jeeves.

He stood a little back and to the right of Jeeves. Well, a bit back and to my right. I think. I did a little thing in my head, holding my left hand up to Jeeves, looking at the L-shape my finger and thumb made on here.

Yeah, I was right. He was right. The guy that is, was on my right, but still behind Jeeves.

Stupid blood loss.

The second guy had lost his rocket launcher. He had a rifle now instead, it looked like an AK-47, but you're hearing this from a guy who just had to check his left from his right, so take what I'm telling you with a grain of salt.

Anyway, the second man also had his AK pointed at me.

Jeeves frowned again. Looked at my beret, and my side. Stained red.

"Carl got you good, didn't he?"

I took a breath. It was hard to do. "Feels like it."

Jeeves looked at the second guy, nodded to me. The second guy stayed alert, and if possible, held the gun *more* at me. Not that I could do anything. I had no gun. I couldn't feel the saya on my back. The way I had landed had twisted the K-Bar underneath my leg.

I could try stealing reality. If I could focus and find something that would help. But Jeeves and this guy would probably remain. And they were close. Too close.

My chances didn't look good.

What did I tell you, earlier on? How some people always seemed to find a winning lottery ticket? And some people always seemed to pick the losing numbers?

Jeeves popped the trunk of the hybrid, then went to the rear of the car, lifting up the hatch. I could hear him search around for something, then grunt. When he came back, it was with a road flare in one hand. And he was still grinning.

"Well, my friend, there's no first aid kit."

Oh. *Shit*. I closed my eyes. This was going to hurt.

Jeeves pulled my hand with the beret off my stabbed area. Then he yanked my shirt up. My eyes closed, and I went ahead and screamed then, knowing that I would still be screaming for a while.

A popping sound. Then a fizzling sound, like the sparklers you light off at the Fourth of July. Hot little bits dribbled over me, as I felt Jeeves lean over me and stick the flare over my side.

I'm not sure how long I screamed. I don't really remember anything but the burning. Anything but coming to, opening my eyes, the world blurry around me. My jaw was clenched, my teeth had a grit between them, my lips were pulled back in a feral snarl.

I held that face, I wasn't sure I could really move, blinking my eyes over and over until the world cleared up in front of me. Feeling a burning along my side. A hot wetness inside me. Smelling burnt hair and melty skin. The sizzling of the road flare, off to the side of me.

Jeeves squatted in front of me. Close, so that he hovered over me. One foot on either side of my legs.

"There we go," he said.

I unclenched my teeth. Tried to let my lips go back to where lips normally rest. Felt something salty in my mouth, and spat out a little blood. At least the searing pain had brought me back from the edge of snicker-giggling myself to death. So I could choke out the next words. "Yeah. There we go."

"So, let's talk," he said.

I wanted to laugh and couldn't. All I could do was focus on breathing. The gurgling feeling, as I drew in light breaths. And stare at the black horizon. "I thought you didn't want to talk."

His grin got wider. "To be honest, I was surprised too." Then Jeeves nodded behind him. To the storm.

"Do I need to catch you up with that?"

The world-eating tempest? No, I got that part. This time, the weather reports would be accurate. Though they wouldn't know it until it was too late.

"No," I said. "I finally got it."

"Good," Jeeves said. "It lets us get to the important part, quickly."

"Yeah?"

"You bet." He seemed to lean into me. Put the barrel of my Glock in the center of my chest. "I want you to do it."

"Do what?"

"Make something appear," he said. "Something disappear."

Here's the part where I turned the tables on Jeeves. Where I saved the day. I mean, he was *asking* me to. But whatever I could steal, whatever I could find, I didn't think I could find it in time, and steal it in time, to save myself.

Jeeves was prepared, too. He was right up on me. I don't know if it was the blood loss or just the pain, but I couldn't think of anything right then to steal. Nothing that could help me. Not in time.

"I knew it," Jeeves said. His eyes didn't seem connected to his words. They didn't smile when he grinned, they didn't open or shut as thoughts passed through his mind. To me, they looked dead, with a kernel of pain in their center. "You're a liar. She lied, as well."

She? Blake?

The lead-lined curtain pulled aside a little bit.

The road flare spat out some sparks to the side of us. Red dots scattered between us. I held my left hand, the hand not covered in blood, in front of Jeeves face and did my finger-wiggling thing.

The road flare stopped sizzling. Stopped spitting red sparks. Because it was capped again.

I know, not the greatest of tricks, but easy to do. Finding a new road flare in some other reality, and swapping it out for this one.

I was in bad shape.

The sound of the sizzling stopped. Jeeves looked to his… left. Definitely his left. Went to look back at me before looking again.

And let out a long, long breath. A breath that sounded like he had been holding it forever.

"You *can* do it," he said.

A corner of my lip turned up.

Jeeves laughed and whooped. Punched his hand in the air. Actually jumped up and down in a circle over me.

The second guy moved a little aside, keeping his AK on me.

When Jeeves returned to the world, he was squatting over me again. The Glock a little more careless in his hand. Tears streamed from both eyes, tears of happiness, I thought. They ran freely down both cheeks. Forced something down in his throat, like he was having trouble swallowing.

"I've been to a hundred worlds," he said. "Maybe a thousand."

"Looking for her."

And just like that, his smile was back.

"Exactly."

"And, not finding her, you destroyed every one."

He nodded. "It's the only way."

What did he mean, it's the only way?

"You don't understand," Jeeves said. "But you will."

"Well, we're talking," I said. "Illuminate me. I thought this whole thing was about your daughter."

"For me?" he asked. "Absolutely. There's a world that exists where Joan lives, and laughs, and waits for me."

Dead is dead. I didn't know how to explain that to Jeeves. I mean, there is infinity, and sure infinity didn't mean what I had thought it meant, but there was also *unique.* From the Latin *unos.* As in singular. One.

One Blake.

One Joan.

One Gavin.

I wanted to explain it to him. Go down the rules. But some of them had gotten fuzzy. And, to be honest, from the look in his eyes, Jeeves just wasn't going to get them.

Though he also saw something in mind.

"You don't understand yet," he said again. "She died because of the machine."

I thought I could put that together. Though, I want to remind you, there was the whole left and right thing still.

"The machine that switched realities?"

"*Yes,*" Jeeves said. "It's out there. It steals and switches things. And it killed my daughter." He looked at the man with the AK. "Joseph's wife. Carl's mom."

Oh shit. I was right. There was a whole group of crazy people out there, destroying worlds.

"And you guys destroy every one you find," I said, "when you don't find them."

"You *get* it," he said. Maybe surprised.

But I didn't. Not by a long shot.

"Yeah," I said. "I kind of don't."

Jeeves sat right in front of me then. Cross-legged. Maybe his legs were getting tired. Doing so he got in the way of the guy with the AK. That guy stepped a little more to his right. (I was a little proud here, I didn't have to look at my hand to tell that).

But I still didn't get Jeeves. He was going to every world, looking for his daughter. But she was going to be dead in every world he found. Or, if he found a world where Joan existed, she was going to be so different he wouldn't be able to see her as *his.*

So, he would go to a world. Look for his daughter and not find her. And then basically burn that world down. Move on to the next.

Not understanding what I knew. Infinity was infinity. But unique was unique.

"You can help us," he said. "You can find my Joan. Joseph's Grace. You can look and find them, and then we can all just go there."

He would never understand. I could find someone close maybe. But never his Joan. She was dead. Gone. Just like Blake.

There would be someone close, sure. But at some point Jeeves would become aware that the Joan I had found, she wasn't really his Joan. It might be the way she sneezed. Maybe her favorite flower was something blue. Maybe she preferred wheat toast instead of white. But there would *always* be a difference.

And when Jeeves saw it, no matter how slight the difference, he would know. Know that Joan wasn't his. And that knowing would lead to anger. It would lead him to burning that world down. And moving on to another.

It was kind of what crazy did.

"So, how about this?" he asked. "I keep you alive. I take you out of this world. All you have to do is find the one where Joan waits for me."

Trust me, I knew what he wanted. I wanted it to. Because losing someone that meant that much to you, there was no coming back from it. It was a pain that never went away. All Jeeves wanted was to push the pain away a bit. Find someone close. Feel happy again, for a brief moment.

But that crazy would come back. It was a road I refused to travel. Because I knew where it led.

"Why?" I wondered.

Jeeves cocked his head. "Your woman didn't tell you? What was her name, Blake?"

My woman. The curtain slid more and more to the side, revealing an anger almost sun-like in its fury.

Blake, I wish you had. Maybe you would be alive. Maybe this world wouldn't be ending.

But she hadn't trusted me enough to tell me. I didn't know why. I guessed it was because she was here on a mission. To save what could be saved. And she believed I could be a part of that, but only enough to leave hints to me. To see where I would take it.

And I had ignored all of those. Laughed at them, even.

I'm king of the world...

Damn me.

"She's one of those that run the machine," Jeeves said. "I thought she had been lying to me, when she came and told me about you. I thought she was just trying to save this world."

Blake would have tried that, I thought. She would have wanted to save Jeeves, like she had wanted to save me. But even more, she would have wanted to stop the storm from coming. From eating reality after reality.

I had thought my problems great. Turns out, Blake had been working for something greater. Some group that had a machine that did what I did. I had thought she didn't understand me, but it was me, that hadn't really understood her.

So, I shook my head. Spat out another bit of blood.

Maybe I still could. I pulled myself up a bit. Slid up a bit on the front bumper of the hybrid.

"Can we?" I asked. My voice quiet. Because I thought I knew the answer. "Save this world?"

My world. Cass's. Even Blake's, to some degree. A unique world for us, being currently eaten by a blackness on the horizon.

His eyes shifted. Dried up a bit. The tears rolled down slower, and less. As if Jeeves could follow my train of thought. Where I was going. And he didn't like it.

I spat more blood out to the side. My mouth was full of it, so it was easy to do. Shifted more, motions to distract Jeeves and the man holding the gun, because my right hand was sneaking down the side of my leg to get the K-Bar.

With just a little luck, I could get the blade into Jeeves before either of them shot me. Hell, even if they shot me. Jeeves was close enough I thought I could make it. With a little bit of luck.

The moment became very quiet. Nothing but the waves crashing on the beach. The slow-pitched fluttering of the breeze.

His answer was simple. A slow shake of the head. A realization of where he and I were headed.

My hand closed over the hilt of the knife.

Jeeves looked at me expectantly. Then oddly. And I think he realized what was going to happen, and my Glock, off to the side in his hand, started tracking to my center.

I ripped the curtain down and screamed.

At the same time I pulled the knife from my leg.

His eyes flickered with madness, and Jeeves moved fast. Much too fast for me.

I still tried to thrust, leaning forward with the motion, not feeling the pain in my side scream in pain.

It was going to be close. But I was going to lose. Not only me, but everyone in this world. Everything Blake had tried to save.

Even some poor sap who happened to be able to steal a bit of reality.

CHAPTER FORTY-EIGHT

A GUNSHOT RANG OUT. A PUFF OF AIR ZIPPED ALONG THE top of my head. It fluffed the hair there. But there was no sudden blackness. No ending of *me*.

I let out a breath I hadn't known I was holding.

Then another. Gunshot, that is. Not a breath. Followed by a rattling of something heavy and maybe plastic against the road.

Another moment passed. Finally, I opened my eyes. Dropped my knife.

Jeeves lay before me, sprawled on the broken blacktop. More like writhing. His legs moved loosely, like a baby's legs moved, laying in a crib. He had a hand pressed to his shoulder and even from here I could see the blood pouring through his fingers.

My Glock lay between us.

I grabbed it. I did feel my side this time. Still, I pushed myself up along the front of the car, my hand kind of pulling on the bumper a bit, until I got halfway up. I took a second there, keeping an eye on Jeeves. My side screamed in a burning pain, and it felt like something sharp stabbed me as I pushed. I took a deep breath and pushed myself to a standing position.

The second guy was lying spread-eagled off to the side. His rifle a few feet away. He wasn't moving at all. There was a mess of bone and blood and pink-like stuff behind his head, kind of in a spray along the road.

Definitely dead.

I looked back to the lighthouse. Twists of black smoke wound their way from the jagged top. But there was no movement there.

I shouted for Cass. My side didn't like that so much. I tried shouting again, but it was more of a whisper and some spitting of blood.

Jeeves let out a groan. He was pulling himself back along the road. I kicked his leg, watched him look at me, and then I waved the gun.

And, finally, I smiled.

He stopped moving. I pulled the phone out of my pocket and saw the call had ended a few minutes before. I redialed the number, and it rang and rang and rang. Like the tolling of some final bell.

Jeeves laughed. More of a chuckle, I guess. Something low and guttural that caused my spine to shiver in anger. That caused the fury I held inside to spit and flare.

I forced myself over to the second guy. Picked up his AK. It had a little scope on it, nothing fancy, nothing like a sniper's scope. Just something to get a little distance to the shot. I looked through it at the light-house. Paying attention to Jeeves, out of the side of my eyes.

Tiny flames licked the top of the building. There was a gap on one side, a break in the wall at the top, and the smoke was strongest there. I thought, looking at it, that the barrel of Cass's gun, the Browning, poked out along the gap. Resting there alone.

The phone rang and rang, tolling on.

I tried shouting again. Not caring about my side or the stabs pain. I just took the biggest breath I could and screamed her name.

There was no wave. No answering of the phone.

Jeeves' laugh grew louder.

My anger swelled with it. I dropped the AK, letting it clatter back to the road again. Went back to Jeeves. Not really feeling pain anymore.

"Something funny to you?"

His face held pain. The yellow flower over his breast pocket was gone. The shoulder there was a mess. There was an exit wound in the back of it and I was sure there were bits of bone and muscle broken and torn. Not that I really looked.

His eyes were dead again. And he had on the grin. The manic one. His teeth red with blood. "What do you think?"

I squatted next to the man. Like he had with me. Holding the Glock dead center of his chest. I wasn't Cass, but I wouldn't miss from there.

What did I think?

I thought Blake was dead. Cass too. And all the power I had, everything I could do, and I couldn't bring any of them back.

Why the fuck did I have this, if good people kept dying on me? If someone like Jeeves could come along and kill them? If any crazy person, at any time, could just take the life of someone for some crazy reason like finding his daughter?

It all made me angry. Furiously so. The angry sun inside me went supernova.

It was an emotion I thought I had buried in the thousands of years of living. Tucking little bits of pain inside.

The pain of no purpose. Of watching people die. Of more and more loss, with no real understanding of *why*. The drudgery and the senselessness, I had lived that for thousands of years, pushed that over my anger until I was some apathetic being that didn't care about the world. About anything in its past. About anything in my future. Until I was someone who Blake hadn't trusted enough to tell me *anything*.

What would you do?

God, Blake, what wouldn't I do?

The supernova of anger grew a thousandfold. A million. Became a bright fury that illuminated all the darkness, revealed anything and everything to me.

In my mind, all of the factories opened. All the boxes too. All the realities in all the universes immediately where I needed them. Whatever I thought, whoever I thought of, anything and everything was *right there*.

I felt like an angel. I floated above the Earth, above Tybee Island, and it all spread out underneath me. All the lines of all the realities merged here, in this world, everything I had switched before and an infinite number of *more*. All of it tied together in a cat's cradle threaded through millions and millions of fingers.

I could see it all.

I pulled a thread.

Virus, what virus?

The World Trade Center came back. Replaced Ground Zero.

The Challenger made it to orbit.

The Titanic continued its cruise.

Nagasaki. Hiroshima. Both cities with all its people returned from the dead.

I stopped the earthquakes around Tybee Island. Switched the iceberg back to the frozen planet I had pulled it from, let the water level in this water flow back to normal. I fixed the lighthouse so it hadn't been hit with a rocket, then straightened it again. The lighthouse with a Schrodinger's Cass in it.

Oh, I snicker-giggled there. I was the storm. I was the tempest. All these threads. All this I could do. Should do. Shouldn't do. I could do it all, there was nothing I couldn't find, couldn't switch, couldn't steal. I was really, truly, king of the world.

Not just king of the world. King of the universe. King of *all* the universes. No matter that the one I currently lived in started to blur underneath me with all the changes.

So, what if Cass was dead? If Blake was dead? I could find another. I *knew* I could.

I started my search. Reality after reality. All were open to me, and I flipped through one universe after another. Found a Blake with short hair. With pink hair and a tie-dye t-shirt. With black hair and dreads.

I kept flipping. Each Blake I found, I discarded. There were millions of strings. I just had to find the right thread, that led me to the right Blake. And I could do it, I knew it.

Below me, the Two Towers flickered away. Ground Zero returned. This time a pile of dead people in the center. The Titanic had sunk again. Hiroshima was town of ghosts, but Nagasaki still stood. Then the cities flipped, ghosts and real people walking side by side.

The crazy kid with a gun flickered back and forth between realities until his eyes grew wide and crazy. Shooting everyone and everyone he saw until his gun was empty. Then still pulling the trigger and screaming.

The Fountain of Youth—I found that world again. The empty one with nothing in it. With all the people somehow dead or gone. I pulled the fountain back here. Placed it in the middle of Butler Avenue, among the broken blacktop and the non-alarming cars. Let everyone take a swim in that. See how they like living forever.

And still kept up my search. Kept throwing Blake's away. Because if infinity means anything, it meant there was another one of her out there. Infinity means that where there was one Blake, there could surely be another.

Here a Blake. There a Blake. I found one with black hair and a horse-like laugh. Grew angrier and angrier. The galaxy-spanning supernova became universe-spanning.

Blake was dead. Cass was dead. Dead is dead. A million people I had known in my life. All dead.

I could find them all. I could *steal* them all. Bring them all back to this world. *This* reality.

Which shimmered underneath me, in some blurry world *between* realities.

I discarded another Blake. This one was shorter. Lips thinner. Hazel eyes. One with a mole above the corner of her lips. One with a tiny white lily tucked behind her ear.

At the same time I floated above it all, screaming *dead is dead*. Still looking, but screaming, looking for Blake, my Blake, *dead is dead* but still looking, because I could do anything, dammit, and if I could do anything, I could do *this*.

Someday, you're going to need to know...

There was no string, no thread for the storm. As if it had swallowed it. So, I pushed at the storm. I hammered at it. I screamed.

Nothing seemed to face it, not all the power I had, not everything I could do, it was all useless in the face of the world-eating tempest.

Jeeves here laughing, looking for a daughter that would never be found. And not finding her, had destroyed this world. I found him, though, in other places, other men. With a family, with daughters and sons and friends. None of them knowing the Jeeves here, the one in my world, had destroyed reality after reality looking for *his* daughter.

Another Blake. Closer to mine. Tall and thin and elegant. But her eyes were different, I could *see* it. They looked at me and didn't recognize me. Didn't want me. Didn't have the understanding I *needed*.

She was out there. I could *feel* it. I stole more and more. Switched more and more. Tossed away Blake after Blake. Tangled threads more and more until finally I saw her again.

Really saw her. Not a Blake in another world. But the Blake in my world. The Blake from the blurred, smudged, sea-water stained photo.

And, I swear, a whisper...

Miss me yet?

And just like that, sanity returned.

Oh god Blake. *Yes.*

I let out a large breath. A breath I had been unknowingly holding.

And all the anger just ... went away. Leaving the pain. Fresh and bright, piercingly achingly empty pain.

But pain I needed. Pain was life. It could steer us the wrong way, but it could also strengthen our resolve. Help us see and do the things we needed.

You are *different...*

The world here seemed peaceful again, now that I was no longer screaming. No longer shouting *dead is dead*. No longer a universe-spanning supernova of crazy. And all the realities I had been looking at, the thousands and thousands of boxes, the millions and millions of other universes, *different* universes, fell away.

Faded away.

Then were gone.

There was a moment of silence. Where the idea of me floating above everything slowly drifted away, where my consciousness sank back down to Tybee Island, to the me standing next to Jeeves, and slipped back inside the person I was.

The person I was.

The guy with the rules.

There was a reason I had made them. A reason I didn't press past certain limits. Because doing that led to madness. A man who could do anything, everything, well that person wouldn't mean *anything*.

Not this Blake, I promised her. *Not ever this.*

Dead is dead, after all.

I let her go. As much as I could. I let it all go and stood there looking at Jeeves. Who looked back up at me with a mixture of fear and... laughter? Enjoyment? I couldn't understand his expression, I could only tell you it felt weird, looking down at the man.

"You can do it," he said. Relieved.

I shook my head. My voice, when I spoke, was hoarse. "No. I can't."

"You *can*," Jeeves said. His voice strong, maniacally so. The strength of a fervor of religion. Of *belief*. Maybe, like Cass, he had been able to see what I had done. What he thought I could do.

He just couldn't see what I wouldn't do.

"I can see it," he said. His voice full of a happiness that wasn't really real.

For good or ill, loss makes us who we are. From there, it's to us to determine what it makes us. And I finally understood what it made me.

I squatted back down. The Glock light in my hand. I kept the barrel pointed at his chest. Jeeves didn't look scared. He looked thrilled. As if he had actually seen his Joan, and waited for me to take him there.

Fervor is a funny thing.

"You know what your problem is Jeeves?"

His eyes lost their crazy for a moment. Just a little. His head tilted, like he was puzzled. "No."

He would never understand. Some people never would. "You can't let shit go."

And his smile was back. The bloodstained one. Accompanied by the dead eyes. "I don't understand."

I knew it, and still for some reason tried to explain. "Pain is there for a reason. You can't bury it. You can't make it go away, or find something to replace the loss, make you feel better. You've got to find a way to live with the pain, get past the loss.

"If you let it, pain can make you a better person. It can help you make the world better around you. And, at the very least, if you can't do that, if you can't make the world a better place, pain should keep you from fucking destroying it."

I let out a breath. A deep sigh that seemed to go on forever. "Because the pain is always going to be there, and you still have to live on."

His head stayed tilted. I thought I saw that kernel of pain, or maybe it was hope, crazy hope, tucked up behind the deadness in his eyes. "So... you're going to help me?"

"Nope." I shot him in the face. Wiped my cheek with the palm of my hand holding the gun. "That's my problem too."

I dropped the Glock on the man's chest. A man who had ended who knows how many worlds. Who knew how many billions of lives.

Including mine.

Then I started my way to the lighthouse. The world would give you moments of joy, but also moments of pain. And I had my fill of the latter. I was hoping, but not really. Because the world wasn't a kind place, not to anyone, but especially to a man who could live forever.

I knew where hope could lead me. I had seen the depths to which it could take a man. How close to the edge it could bring you. And I wasn't going to fall into that well.

CHAPTER FORTY-NINE

———

BUTLER AVENUE WAS SMOOTH AGAIN, ALTHOUGH CRACKS existed in it, and there were edges of blacktop protruding everywhere. Like the earth had settled, but the quakes in some way remained. At least, evidence of them.

It was peacefully quiet. There was no one else around. I wasn't sure if I had killed them all, with the rapid thefts of other realities, or if they had just fled. Either way, I wasn't proud of myself.

The storm sat off to the east. Larger now. Fully a third of the horizon. Like someone had peeled back the sky, revealing the night behind it.

Maybe peeling was a bad word. More like tearing back the sky. The horizontal black bar spreading across the sky was swollen in places, as if the storm was eager to swallow everything. A black hole that let nothing escape. A dark, hungry, black horizon, indeed.

I moved through some dry grass. My pants brushed through the blades. A bird tweeted, there was a flutter of wings, and then it was gone.

My side hurt. Burns are nasty things. Getting stabbed and burned was nastier. I know I walked funny, with my arm holding my side, my breathing ragged.

Still, the lighthouse was the goal. And I made it. Standing straight in the air, completely whole, as if it hadn't been hit with a rocket launcher. As if there had been no earthquake(s).

The door swung open with a light touch.

Inside was a little tourist's shop. Little pictures and frames of the island. Little carvings of dolphins and whales and miniature lighthouses. Toys, little boats, and ducks that would float on the water. And for some reason, squirt guns.

There was a counter in the back. And a door there. The door led to a set of stairs, something that circled up and up to the top of the tower. Maybe not the original stairs, I had switched so many of them that who knew where this lighthouse had originally come from.

They led up, just the same.

It was a tough climb. I couldn't tell you how long it took. I could just tell you each step hurt, and as I climbed more and more it was less of me taking steps, then me pulling myself along with the side rail.

But I got to the top. There was another door there. A brown wooden thing with a polished brass knob.

It swung open just as easily as the one downstairs. A soundless swing.

The first thing I saw was a ladder, leading up to the top of the light-house. Where the beacon would be, and the little platform circling it. A hatch lay at the top of the ladder, and it was open.

There was a desk here. Some chairs. A monitor and a computer on the desk. A plush blue couch that may or may not open up into a bed.

I didn't want to climb it. And turns out, I didn't need to. Because Cass lay in the corner of the room. The corner that may have been the jagged opening I had seen, with all the smoke billowing out of it. Where she might have taken a few shots that had saved my life.

She lay there. Eyes closed. Not moving.

But alive.

I knelt next to her. Her face was covered with burns and black soot. The bandage on her temple was gone, the wound there had broken open and was leaking blood again. The eyebrow under the wound was burned off, a mess of angry red skin, and her eye was swollen shut.

One leg looked broken, like she had landed on it funny. Maybe jumping down the ladder as an incoming rocket tracked its way across the sky towards the top of the lighthouse. Her chest moved up and down in shuddering breaths. Uneasy, panicked breaths. The kind of breaths that might stop at any moment.

She wouldn't wake. But I barely touched her. I didn't want to move her. I didn't know what to do from here.

Could I save her?

Should I?

You going to explain this? After?

I had told her I would. In the end the decision hinged on those simple words. On Blake, maybe being the reason. She had been important to both of us, and maybe her memory deserved everything we could give it.

Cass might not want me to save her. She might not appreciate the cost. But she would, I thought, understand the reason.

I'll admit it, the snicker-giggle helped me to feel better.

Still, I had to get her there.

So, I picked Cass up. She was so much smaller than Blake. And light. Lighter than I would have imagined. Lighter than I *knew*.

She groaned, briefly, as I cradled her in my arms. Her broken leg dangled funny. But her chest kept up the panicky breathing, and that was the only thing I could hope for.

I'll spare you the details. It was a long, agonizing thing. I almost passed out any number of times. I stopped and waited, when Cass stopped breathing, until she started up again.

Anyway, it took forever, but I got her to the fountain.

Yeah, you know the one. The Fountain of Youth.

It was the same as I had remembered. A circular pool of crystal-blue water, surrounded by white, dappled stone, lined almost with pulsing, bluish veins. It wasn't quite a wall, more of a marbled lip rising around the fountain.

The water rippled and bubbled in the center of the pool. A gurgling type sound emanated from it. And the ripples pushed outwards until the tiny, baby-like waves bumped up against the speckled white rock.

I lay Cass in the water. I knew from experience it was shallow, like a half-poured bath. She shuddered once and went still.

So still.

I cupped some of the fountain's water and poured it into her mouth. Then some more. The water, where it touched my hands, healed the rash of skin there. From where I had slid across the ice.

Cass choked. Once, twice. Her head jerked with the motion, splashed back into the fountain. Her tangled hair lay in wet curls here and there and bobbed and weaved in the ripples.

But her breathing grew stronger. Steadied. It did take some time. I sat on the lip of the pool and dribbled the water over her face, washed it until the burn healed. Until her eyebrow grew back. Until the split across her temple closed up.

Her broken leg even straightened up. In little pops and snicks. Which I have to tell you was really eerie, almost spine-tingling so, to watch.

Once she opened her eyes. They looked unfocused when she did. I told her to relax in those times. I wasn't sure if she recognized my voice, but her eyes did close back up, and she feel into a deep sleep.

I took a sip or two of the fountain water myself. Just to get a little strength. I could feel my insides heal, a peppermint patty type of feeling, like a cool prickling sensation rippling along my ribs. It kind of burned, and it kind of tickled, and it made me sneeze once.

Which was painful. So, I drank a little more.

After all that, I carried Cass to a nice truck. Not a Jeep-truck, but a nice four-door thing with big tires and an eight-cylinder engine. I put her in the back, laying her on the rear bench seat and kind of strapping her in with both seatbelts. It looked funny, but I thought she'd stay.

I also found a blanket in the back. Which I tucked her in with. Because that's what you do.

Then I got in and drove off of the island. Heading west. Away from Tybee Island and the hovering tempest off the coast.

The truck had a lot of gas, and I planned to use it.

Finally—I did splash a little water on the outside of my ribs. Just to keep the wounds there from getting infected. But I didn't get into the pool. I didn't heal the nasty twisted smile of a scar on the left side of my ribcage, or the melty, blackened, smeared patch of skin on the other side. I didn't take a quick dive in the pool and wash the healed scars of old pains away.

I had a feeling those would be important to me. Reminders of the many mistakes I had made. Especially with the black horizon waiting in the east, swelling larger and larger, the storm that ate everything and anything.

A man has to know his limits, after all.

CHAPTER FIFTY

WHAT TO SAY, NOW?

Not much I could say, really. Not with the world currently getting eaten. With this storm gobbling everything up. With threads snapping between this reality and an infinite number of others, all these loose threads dangling in the metaverse factory thing in my brain.

But I can give you the highlights.

Cass finally woke on the trip. I think we were in North Carolina. She climbed up into the front of the truck and buckled her seatbelt, keeping the blanket tucked around her.

She wasn't happy or unhappy about what happened with the fountain. I gave her a quick rundown of the rules. Especially the *we can live forever but also definitely die* part. She took it like she took anything I told her, with a slight frown on her face and an occasional grunt.

She was more upset when I told her about Blake. That I believed she wasn't really her sister. That she had come in from another reality, and that she belonged to a group of people looking to save what they could from this world. That they had *exchanged* Blakes somehow, maybe using their machine.

Being Cass, other than maybe having a larger frown, she took it all in. Hid whatever emotion she might or might not be feeling. Which made me feel a little sad, now that I knew her better.

I shared all my guesses. That Blake had known a storm was coming. That she thought I might be able to help, and that she had tried to get me to see it. Understand it. That the group of people who had sent Blake had maybe sent her to save what she could.

And that there was another group. The Remainers, doing all the destroying. The group of people who had lost loved ones in thefts of reality in their own worlds, and now were searching for them, and destroying every world where they struck out.

"Funny," Cass murmured, looking out the side window. "What love does."

That thought paralleled what I had been thinking along the drive. Had Jeeves loved his daughter? Real love? Was what he felt for Joan like what Blake had meant to me?

I wasn't sure. But I didn't think love led to destruction. It can be painful, trust me, I know. Losing someone you loved could hurt for years, the rest of your life.

It could lead to vengeance. I knew that, as well. But after that, when you killed innocents, burned up worlds in some all-encompassing storm? I thought that was just madness. Madness fueled by what had once been love, but now was something more twisted. More insane. Something that when you looked at yourself in the mirror and saw passion, love, what the mirror saw was something much darker, a shadowed, monstrous abyss.

The two groups were in a fight for this world. Maybe other worlds. I had seen the other factories, the other realities that this storm had eaten. There was some war going on in the metaverse (I've started using this word now, because I'm not sure what else describes an infinite number of realities for an infinite number of worlds in an infinite number of universes—well, you get the idea).

It felt like the war was being lost by Blake's side. Looking at it, there had been one Blake here. And Jeeves had brought a bunch of people with him. Not to mention the factories in the metaverse burning. It seemed like the Remainers were going all General Sherman on every world, every reality, in their insane quest.

I wondered why Blake had tried. She had gone to see Jeeves in Chicago. I didn't think I would ever know. All I could feel was the pain of not being with her. Of not being the person she had wanted me to be.

I could only guess that she had been being Blake. Trying to save everything. Everyone. No matter how lost the cause.

Cass wasn't happy with my part in that. Maybe she understood me a bit better and didn't quite *hate* me, but she definitely didn't like me much for it. And, you'll know I'm being honest here, when I say I didn't like me much either.

There was a lot of quiet then. For a long stretch of road. We still headed west, away from the storm. We listened to the radio as we drove. The world was in a state of shock. And a state of panic. The storm was only growing larger. Nothing sent in came back out. Not jets. Planes. Boats. Aircraft carriers.

Everything got eaten.

No one understood it.

And the storm kept getting larger. It swelled until it covered most of the mid-Atlantic. It had creeped closer until it was a mile or so off of the entire eastern coast. It had swollen on the other side of the ocean as well, so that the darkness was reaching out to the western part of Africa. Spain. Europe.

The only thing that stopped the storm was the coast. Not quite stopped it. But slowed the darkness down. As if land was a bigger morsel to eat, all the people and vehicles and buildings and animals and trees took longer to snack through, so the storm paused a bit, as if to make more room in its dark belly to swallow it all.

There was a lot of silence from Cass. I guessed it was a lot to take in. And when she spoke, it wasn't about Blake or the Fountain of Youth or the storm, it was something more practical. Which was Cass. Her mind already digging for information. Things she could use. "You find the thing Jeeves was using?

"The what?"

"Whatever it is he tracked you with." she said. "Be nice to know how they do it."

Dammit. I swerved off the road a bit, recovered. Looked at Cass with something like chagrin.

I just flat out hadn't thought about it. I had been tired and hurt and just wanting to see if Cass was alive. I had been left with an empty feeling, killing Jeeves. Like an emotion leaking away from you, leaving you exhausted. Like shattering a mirror and feeling the pain and rage and anger just... go away.

Whatever the thing was, it was gone now. I definitely wasn't turning around and driving back to look for it. Even if Tybee Island wasn't in mid-gulp.

Cass saw the answer in my face. Shrugged again, a little motion under the blanket. And gave a little smile, a tiny curve of her lips, which lit up a different side of Cass. A self-deprecating side I didn't know she had. "I guess this means we're not through."

"What do you mean?"

She shrugged. "These two groups. The one Blake is from. And the Remainers. She would have wanted them stopped, right?"

She would have. I guessed I was thinking along those same lines. I just hadn't gotten that far yet.

"So, we find the one group, see if we can help," Cass said. "And we find the other group and kill them all."

That was Cass and her terminator logic. Her deadly binary ones and zeros. Help, or kill.

Which, honestly, I couldn't argue with in the moment. Not with the black horizon darkening the rearview mirror.

"Deal," I said. Soldiers in a trench.

And that was that.

A day of driving went that way. Mostly quiet. Some little conversation. We stopped at a fast-food place and fueled up at a gas station. Cass bought a scratch-off that won her a thousand dollars. Then looked at me funny.

I didn't say anything. Or do anything. No fingers crossed, promise. I told you earlier, some people just make their own luck.

It was when we reached Illinois that we started seeing traffic come with us. More people fleeing the coast. It felt like we had been one or two fish swimming on the interstate river, and then all of a sudden schools of fish joined. Little hybrids, sedans, trucks and sports utility vehicles and big rigs, some without their trailers.

The interstate became flooded. It pooled in places, and all the fish swam in circles. Trying to make their way west. The interstates became logjams, and the back roads followed suit as we all tried to find different routes west.

I swore a lot. And drove a little more reckless. Wrecked the truck trying to drive across the median, ran into a grass-covered concrete divider that tore out the left front wheel. Cass just rolled her eyes, but it allowed me to steal reality for another Jeep-truck instead.

I did like those. Even if I hated the push-button start. I had looked for one with keys, maybe they were hard to find.

We did stop in Chicago, at my condo there. Where Blake and I had spent a lot of time. The roads heading into the city were far less busy than the roads heading out. It was easy to pull right up to my building.

I paused there for a moment. Cass tugged me through the doors. The bloodstain Blake had left on the sidewalk was long gone. Not a lot of people walked around, and those that did either hurried in a panic or stood in small groups speaking in soft, hushed tones.

We both went up to my place. Cass had been there once or twice before. I grabbed some clothes, a bag, and some things of Blake's. Mostly though, I had come for her books. And I grabbed them all.

I was pretty sure Blake had left more hints there. I had missed them once. I would not miss them again.

Cass and I got back in the Jeep-truck. Headed west. The interstates opened back up again, as if people feared the west coast too and wanted to stay in the center of the United States.

I had a place in Colorado, in the Rockies. I thought we'd have a little time there. A few days, maybe a week, at the rate of the swelling storm. Enough, hopefully, to figure out our next steps.

I hoped.

Yeah, I know what I had said about hope. I felt the eye-roll. The funny thing is, I keep coming back to it.

So, back to the highlights. The long drive to the Rockies. The cabin I had there. A nice thing, one of those you see on HGTV that million-aires might buy. A couple of levels, a big hot tub, a sauna. A well-stocked pantry and bar. And a big wooden deck, facing what would normally be the sunrise, but now was just a widening black line, like a permanent fat sharpie had lined out the entire eastern horizon.

The cabin was a little dusty but cleaned up quick. There were extra clothes. And hot showers. And bandages. I was still healing.

God the shower felt good.

We both settled in quickly, but maybe still needed some space. Cass took a few books and went out to the deck, taking a light coat with her. It was late summer, but the breeze coming in off the mountains was still brisk. She found a lounge chair and started reading.

I did the same. To the crackling fire on the inside. I had seen enough of black horizons. I could feel it, the darkness in the east. Eating every-thing. I set a glass of juice on the coffee table, ruby red grapefruit juice with ice, and kicked my legs up. Sipped the drink, felt the citrus tang on the back of my tongue, and read.

That was our job now. We would flip through every page of every book, leave no page unturned (as they say) until we figured this out. Where to go. *How* to go. And what to save, as we traveled.

Jeeves had destroyed other realities, billions of lives, searching for his daughter. Who knew how many other versions of him were out there, doing the same thing. Maybe not Jeeves, per se, but other men and women who had stared into the abyss and became the monster.

Like Cass said, it was funny what love could do.

The two of us would find this other group too. The ones losing the fight against the Remainers. And see if they needed a hand.

We'd have questions for both sides. And if we didn't like the answers, well, I had a walking terminator with me. They'd get to know Cass real well. We'd get medieval on the motherfuckers.

The cost of our world surely deserved that, at least. I'd make sure that bill got paid. That the passing of another world into the storm would be worth *something*. Whatever I did, I would make sure of that.

Make sure it meant more than something. Make sure it would be worth everything.

At the very least, make sure it was worth Blake.

And then, maybe, I could let her go.

―――

Enjoy *The Black Horizon*?

Help get the word out about The Reality Thief by leaving a review for *The Black Horizon* at your bookseller of choice. These reviews help drive other readers to find this story, so even a few words would be greatly appreciated.

Also - take a moment and visit chrisjcranford.com, be a part of the this universe and others. Steal some of your own reality with another story. Discover all the other worlds I'm building. Or just reach out and say hello.

There will be more of Gavin and Cass. Worlds yet to exist. Worlds that do exist, somewhere. Can't wait to bring those to you.

ABOUT THE AUTHOR

When Chris isn't trying to figure out how to write a bio, he spends time contemplating the fate of the universe. Probably while walking into a door jamb. He's accepted that the two go hand-in-hand.

He currently resides in Florida, though he has some Magellan in him, and loves to wander. He's always wanted to see the Pyramids, so Egypt may be next on his list.

It is his dream to write stories that —through their telling—influence others to live a little better. Stand a little taller. Smile a little wider. Hold someone a little longer. Fiction should be the dream real life aspires to be.

Dogs are his buddies. Football is his hobby. Books are his passion.

Find out more about Chris, his origin story, upcoming books and events at:

www.chrisjcranford.com

facebook.com/chrisjcranford

x.com/chrisjcranford

instagram.com/chrisjcranford